LITTLE DEE AND THE PENGUIN

LITTLE DEE AND THE PENGUIN

by Christopher Baldwin

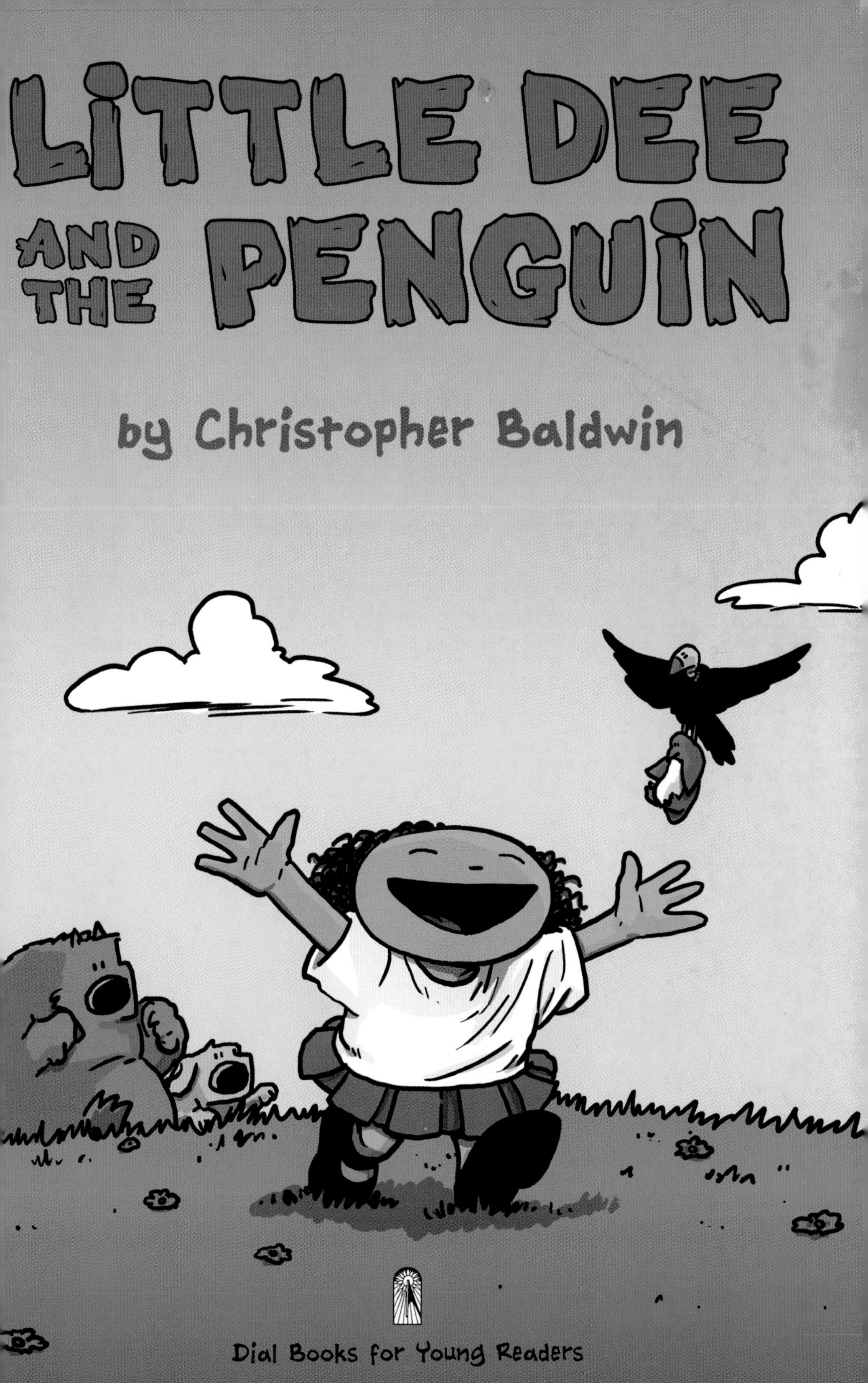

Dial Books for Young Readers

For Miles and Arlo

DIAL BOOKS FOR YOUNG READERS
PENGUIN YOUNG READERS GROUP
An imprint of Penguin Random House, LLC
375 Hudson Street
New York, NY 10014

Copyright © 2016 by Christopher John Baldwin.

Library of Congress Cataloging-in-Publication Data

Baldwin, Christopher, date.
Little Dee and the penguin / by Christopher Baldwin.
pages   cm
Summary: After her park ranger father dies, Little Dee is swept off on an adventure with a group of animals as they try to protect their penguin friend from being eaten by a pair of hungry polar bears.
1. Graphic novels. [1. Graphic novels. 2. Human-animal relationships—Fiction.
3. Animals—Fiction. 4. Humorous stories.] I. Title.
PZ7.7.B28Li 2016   741.5'973—dc23   2015010378

Printed in China
PB ISBN 978-0-8037-4108-9
Library Binding ISBN 978-1-101-99429-0

1 3 5 7 9 10 8 6 4 2

Book design by Jasmin Rubero
Text hand-lettered by Christopher Baldwin

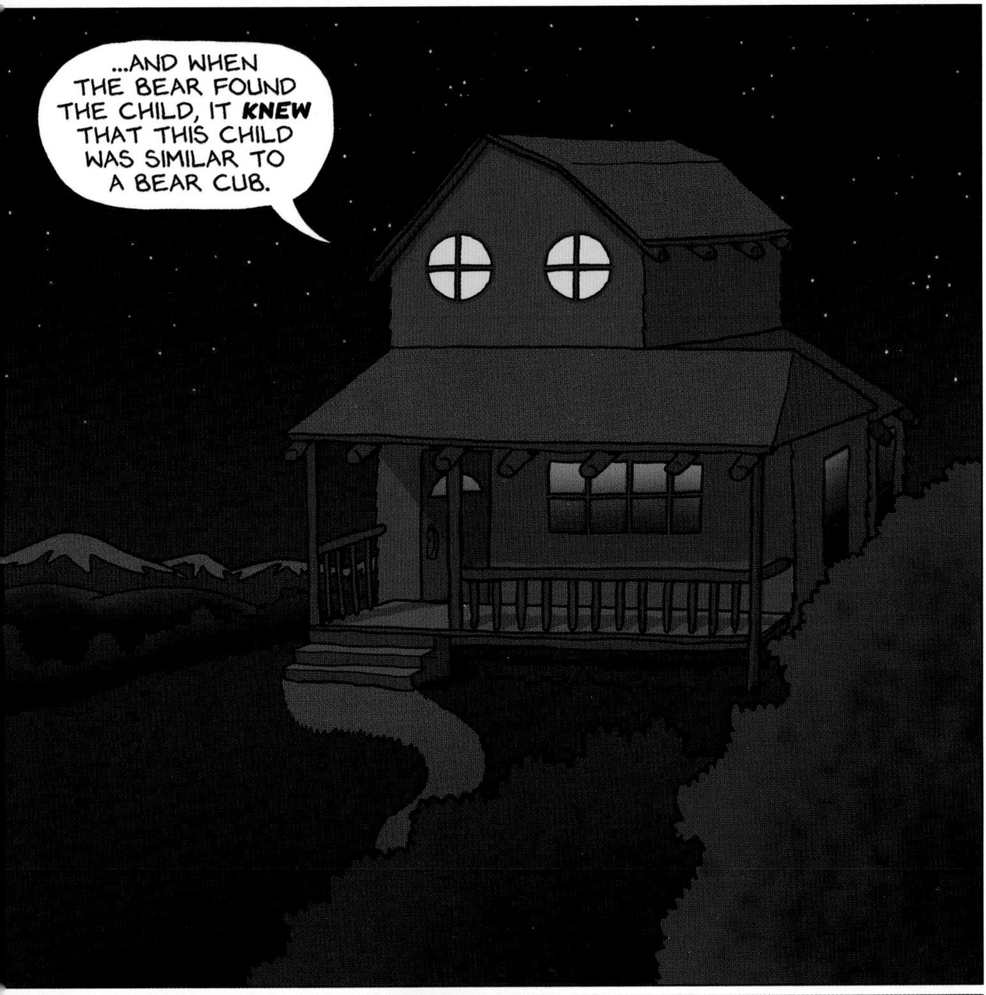
...AND WHEN THE BEAR FOUND THE CHILD, IT **KNEW** THAT THIS CHILD WAS SIMILAR TO A BEAR CUB.

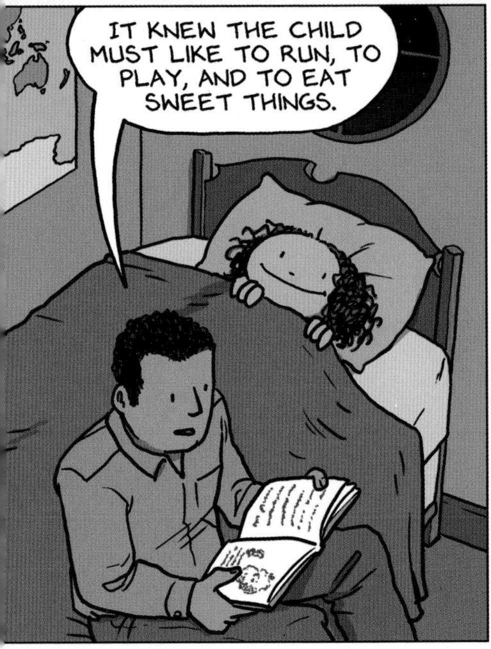
IT KNEW THE CHILD MUST LIKE TO RUN, TO PLAY, AND TO EAT SWEET THINGS.

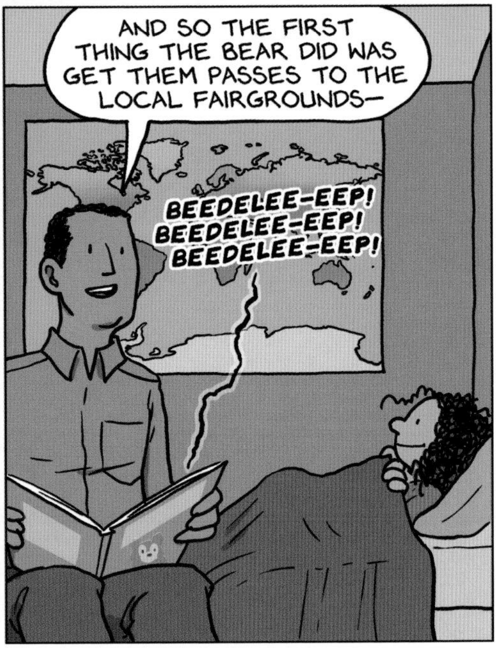
AND SO THE FIRST THING THE BEAR DID WAS GET THEM PASSES TO THE LOCAL FAIRGROUNDS—
BEEDELEE-EEP!
BEEDELEE-EEP!
BEEDELEE-EEP!

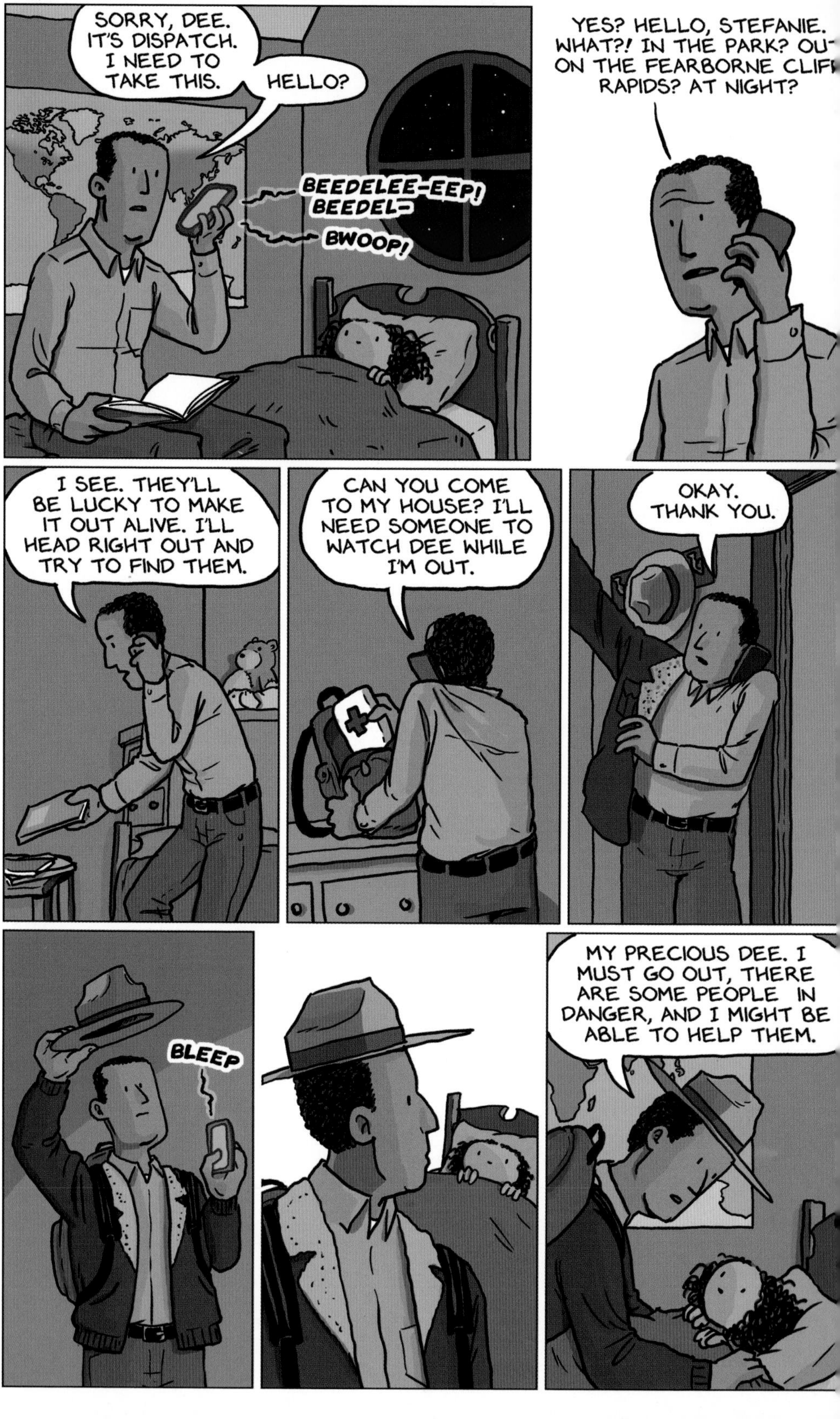

SORRY, DEE. IT'S DISPATCH. I NEED TO TAKE THIS.
HELLO?
BEEDELEE-EEP! BEEDEL–
BWOOP!
YES? HELLO, STEFANIE. WHAT?! IN THE PARK? OU- ON THE FEARBORNE CLIF RAPIDS? AT NIGHT?
I SEE. THEY'LL BE LUCKY TO MAKE IT OUT ALIVE. I'LL HEAD RIGHT OUT AND TRY TO FIND THEM.
CAN YOU COME TO MY HOUSE? I'LL NEED SOMEONE TO WATCH DEE WHILE I'M OUT.
OKAY. THANK YOU.
BLEEP
MY PRECIOUS DEE. I MUST GO OUT, THERE ARE SOME PEOPLE IN DANGER, AND I MIGHT BE ABLE TO HELP THEM.

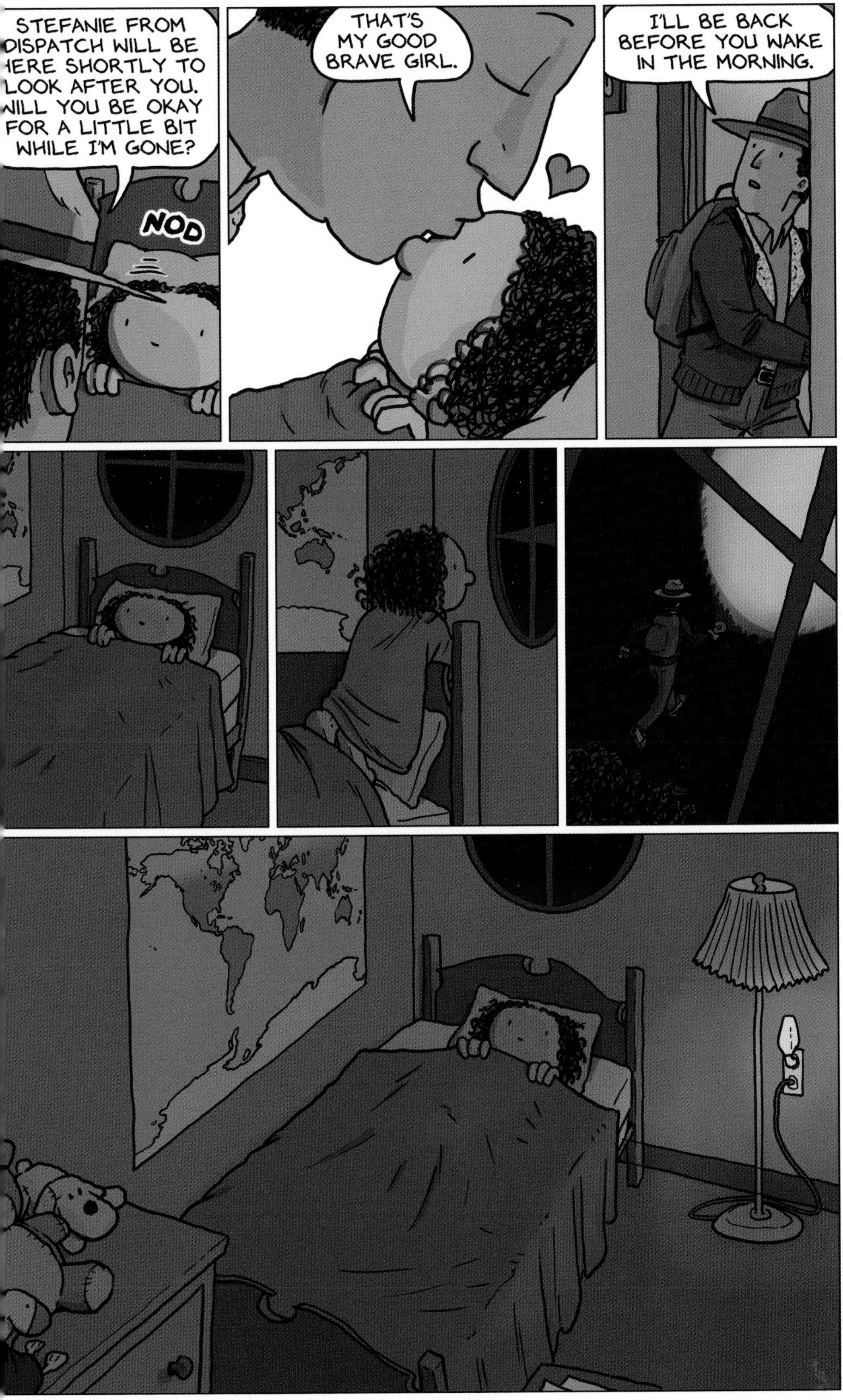
STEFANIE FROM DISPATCH WILL BE HERE SHORTLY TO LOOK AFTER YOU. WILL YOU BE OKAY FOR A LITTLE BIT WHILE I'M GONE?
NOD
THAT'S MY GOOD BRAVE GIRL.
I'LL BE BACK BEFORE YOU WAKE IN THE MORNING.

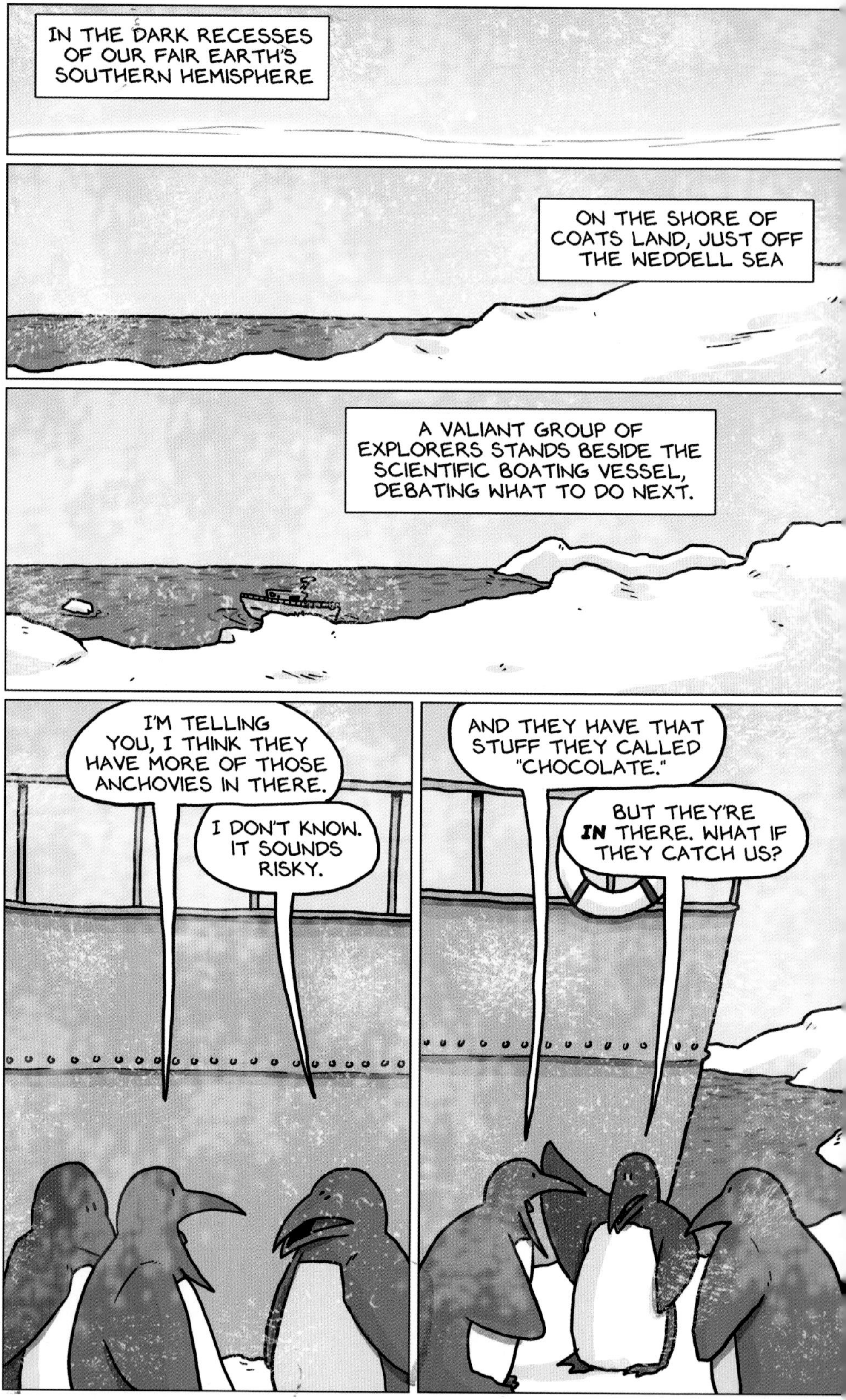
IN THE DARK RECESSES OF OUR FAIR EARTH'S SOUTHERN HEMISPHERE
ON THE SHORE OF COATS LAND, JUST OFF THE WEDDELL SEA
A VALIANT GROUP OF EXPLORERS STANDS BESIDE THE SCIENTIFIC BOATING VESSEL, DEBATING WHAT TO DO NEXT.
I'M TELLING YOU, I THINK THEY HAVE MORE OF THOSE ANCHOVIES IN THERE.
I DON'T KNOW. IT SOUNDS RISKY.
AND THEY HAVE THAT STUFF THEY CALLED "CHOCOLATE."
BUT THEY'RE **IN** THERE. WHAT IF THEY CATCH US?

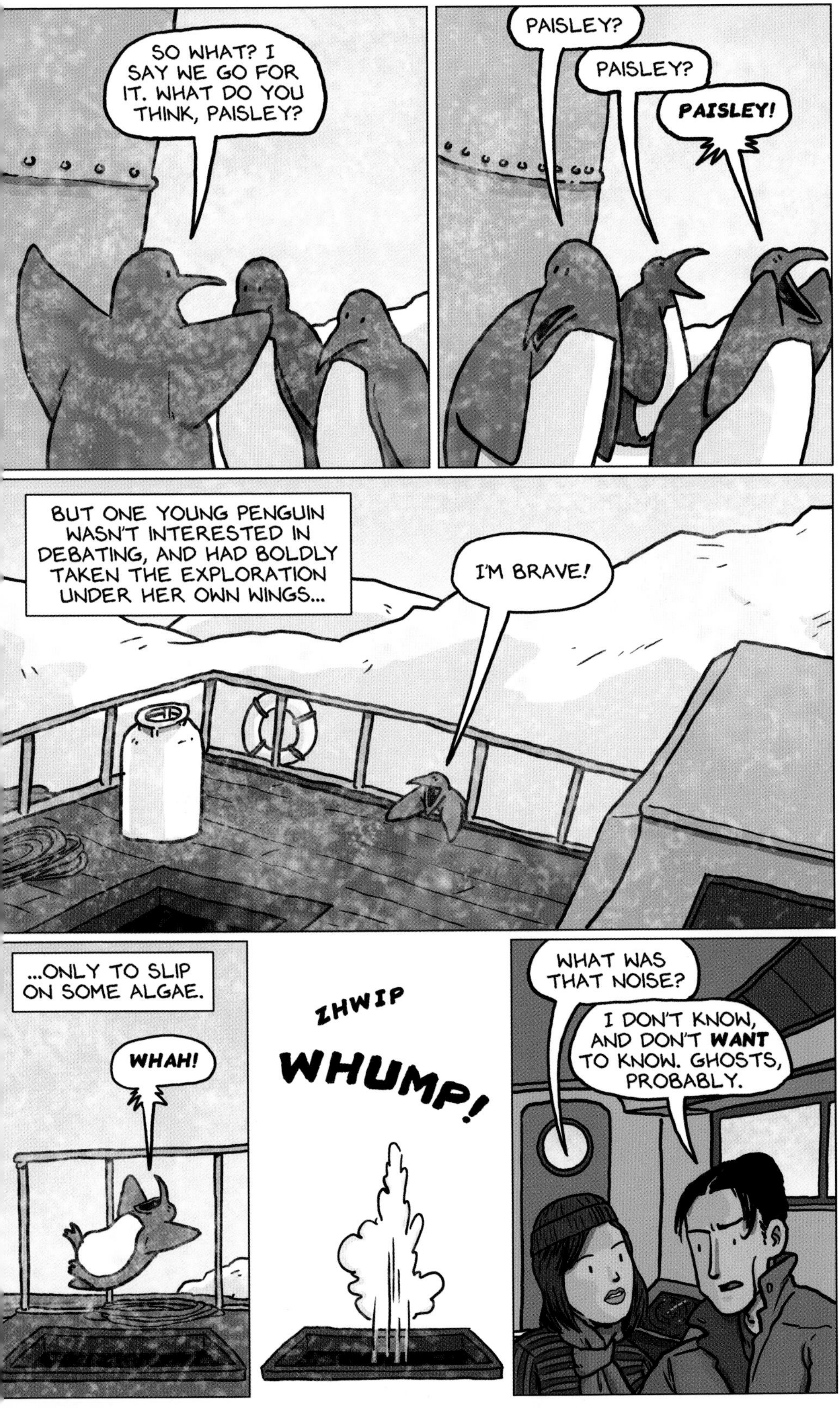
SO WHAT? I SAY WE GO FOR IT. WHAT DO YOU THINK, PAISLEY?
PAISLEY?
PAISLEY?
PAISLEY!
BUT ONE YOUNG PENGUIN WASN'T INTERESTED IN DEBATING, AND HAD BOLDLY TAKEN THE EXPLORATION UNDER HER OWN WINGS...
I'M BRAVE!
...ONLY TO SLIP ON SOME ALGAE.
WHAH!
ZHWIP
WHUMP!
WHAT WAS THAT NOISE?
I DON'T KNOW, AND DON'T WANT TO KNOW. GHOSTS, PROBABLY.

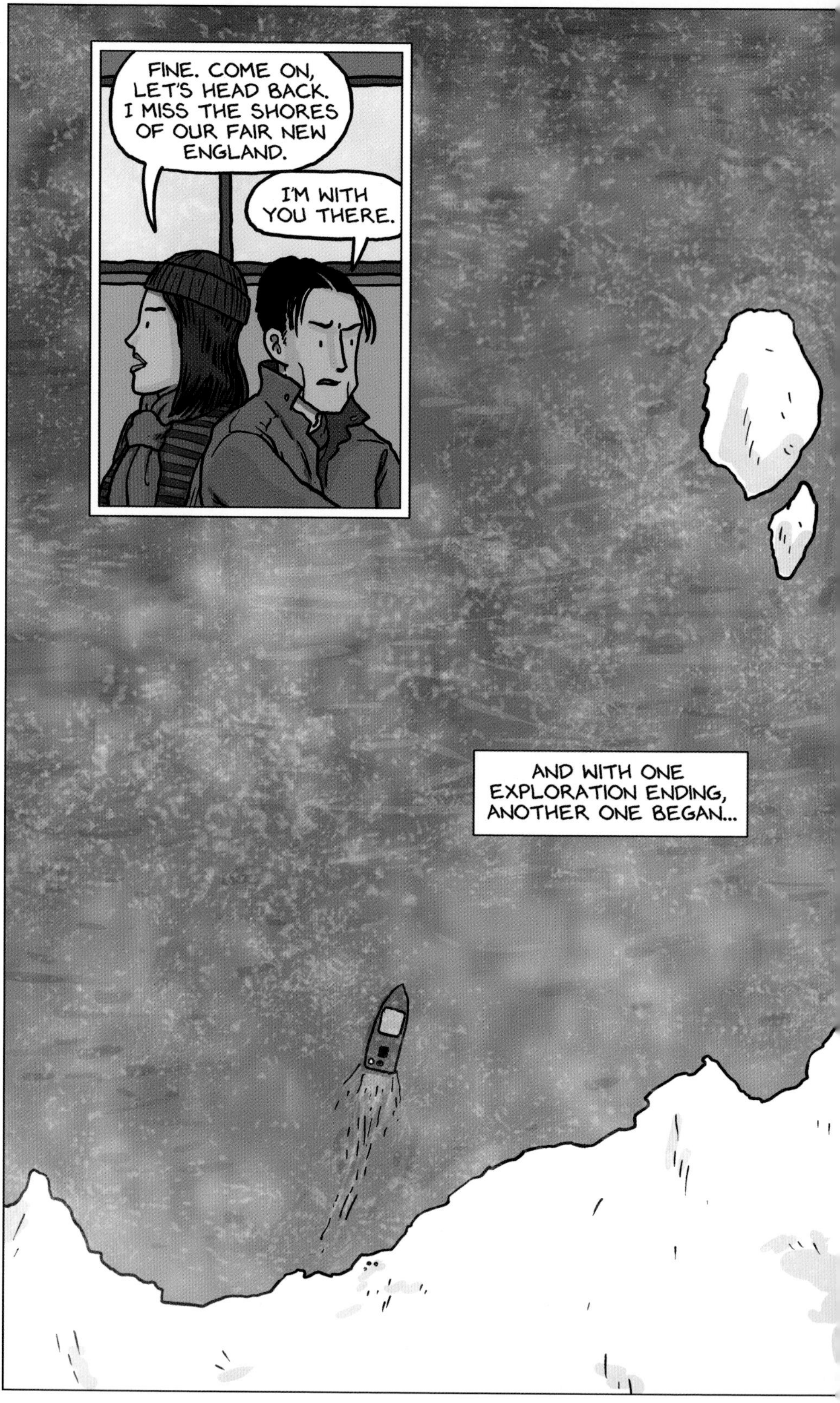
FINE. COME ON, LET'S HEAD BACK. I MISS THE SHORES OF OUR FAIR NEW ENGLAND.
I'M WITH YOU THERE.
AND WITH ONE EXPLORATION ENDING, ANOTHER ONE BEGAN...

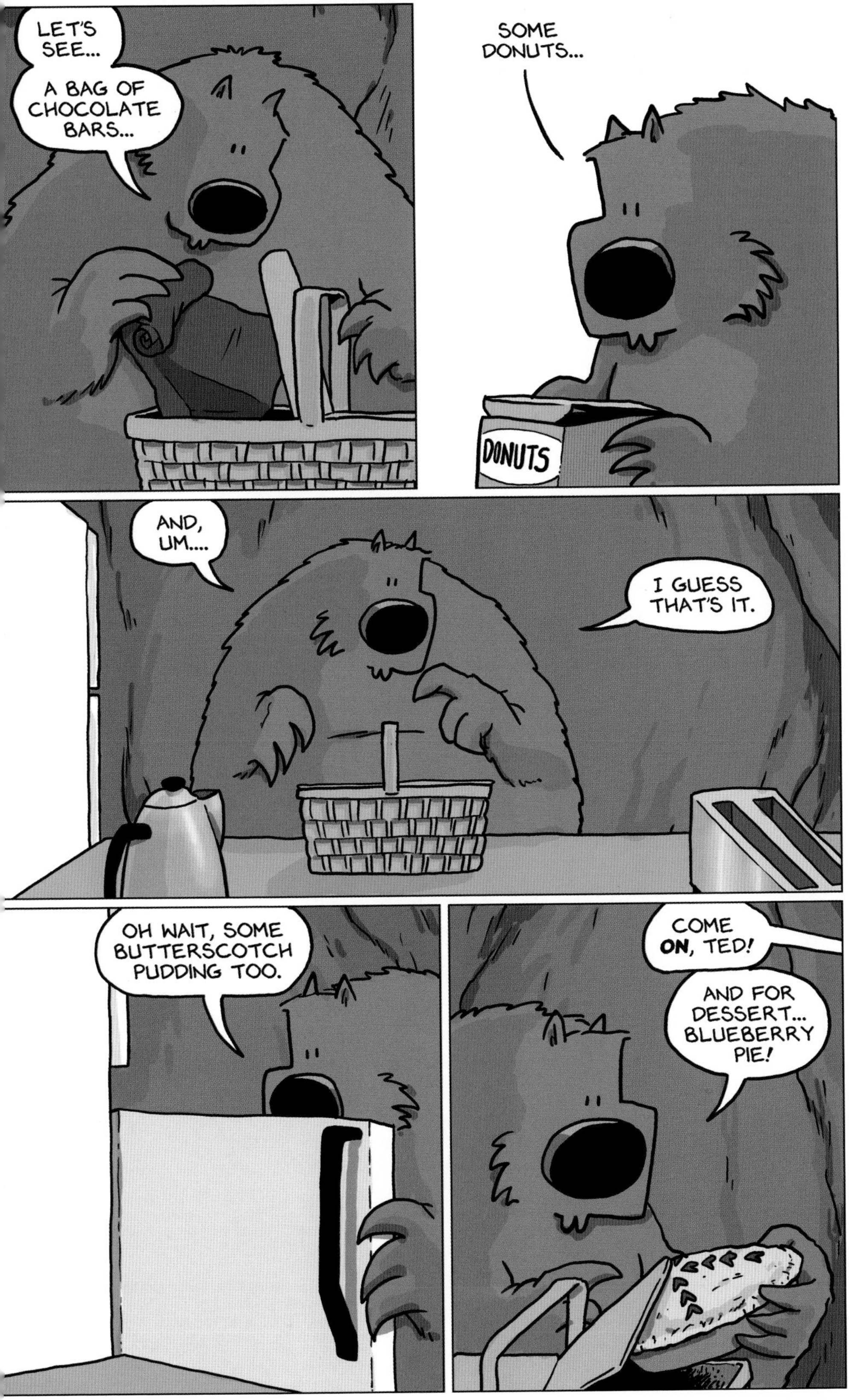
LET'S SEE...
A BAG OF CHOCOLATE BARS...
SOME DONUTS...
DONUTS
AND, UM....
I GUESS THAT'S IT.
OH WAIT, SOME BUTTERSCOTCH PUDDING TOO.
COME **ON**, TED!
AND FOR DESSERT... BLUEBERRY PIE!

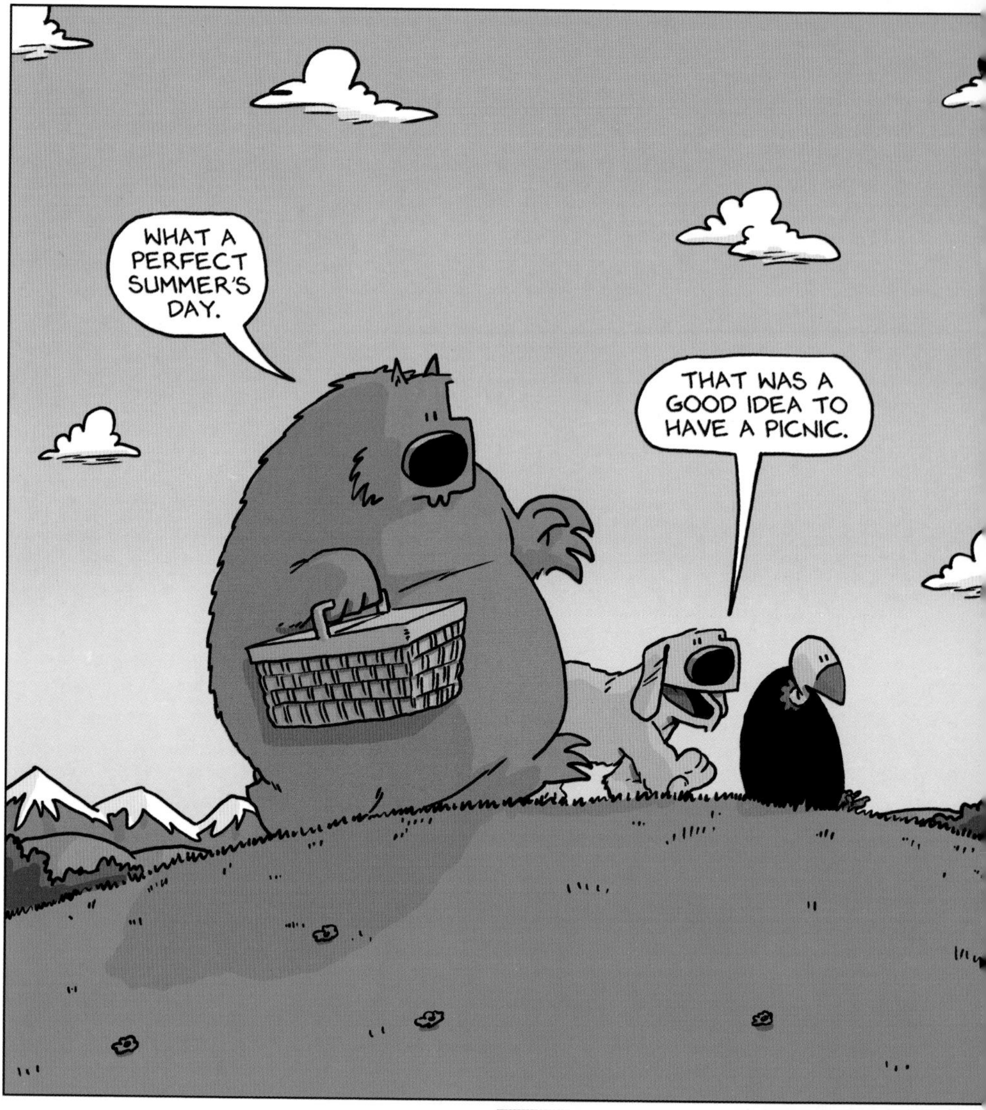
WHAT A PERFECT SUMMER'S DAY.
THAT WAS A GOOD IDEA TO HAVE A PICNIC.

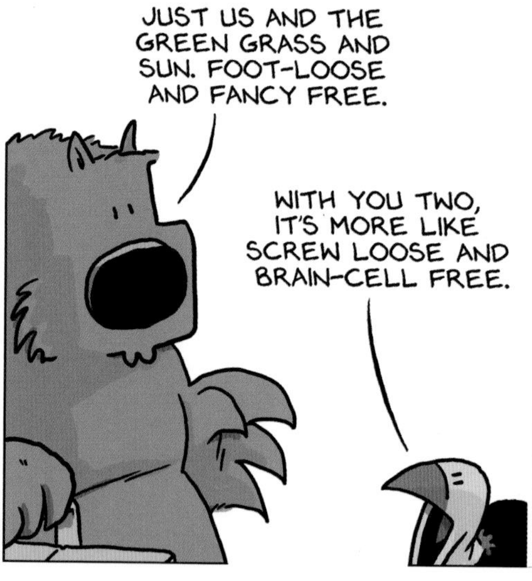
JUST US AND THE GREEN GRASS AND SUN. FOOT-LOOSE AND FANCY FREE.
WITH YOU TWO, IT'S MORE LIKE SCREW LOOSE AND BRAIN-CELL FREE.

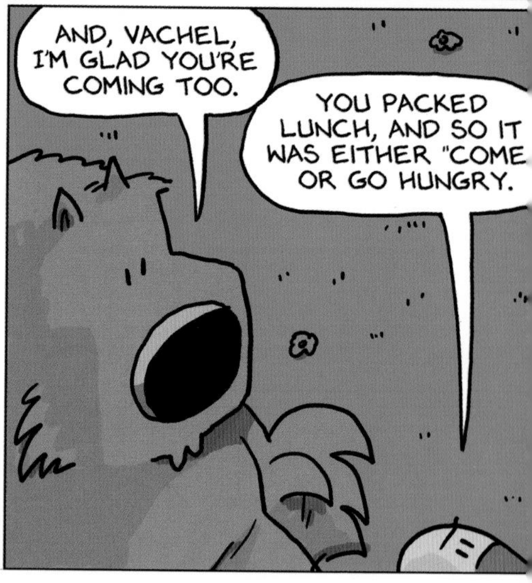
AND, VACHEL, I'M GLAD YOU'RE COMING TOO.
YOU PACKED LUNCH, AND SO IT WAS EITHER "COME OR GO HUNGRY.

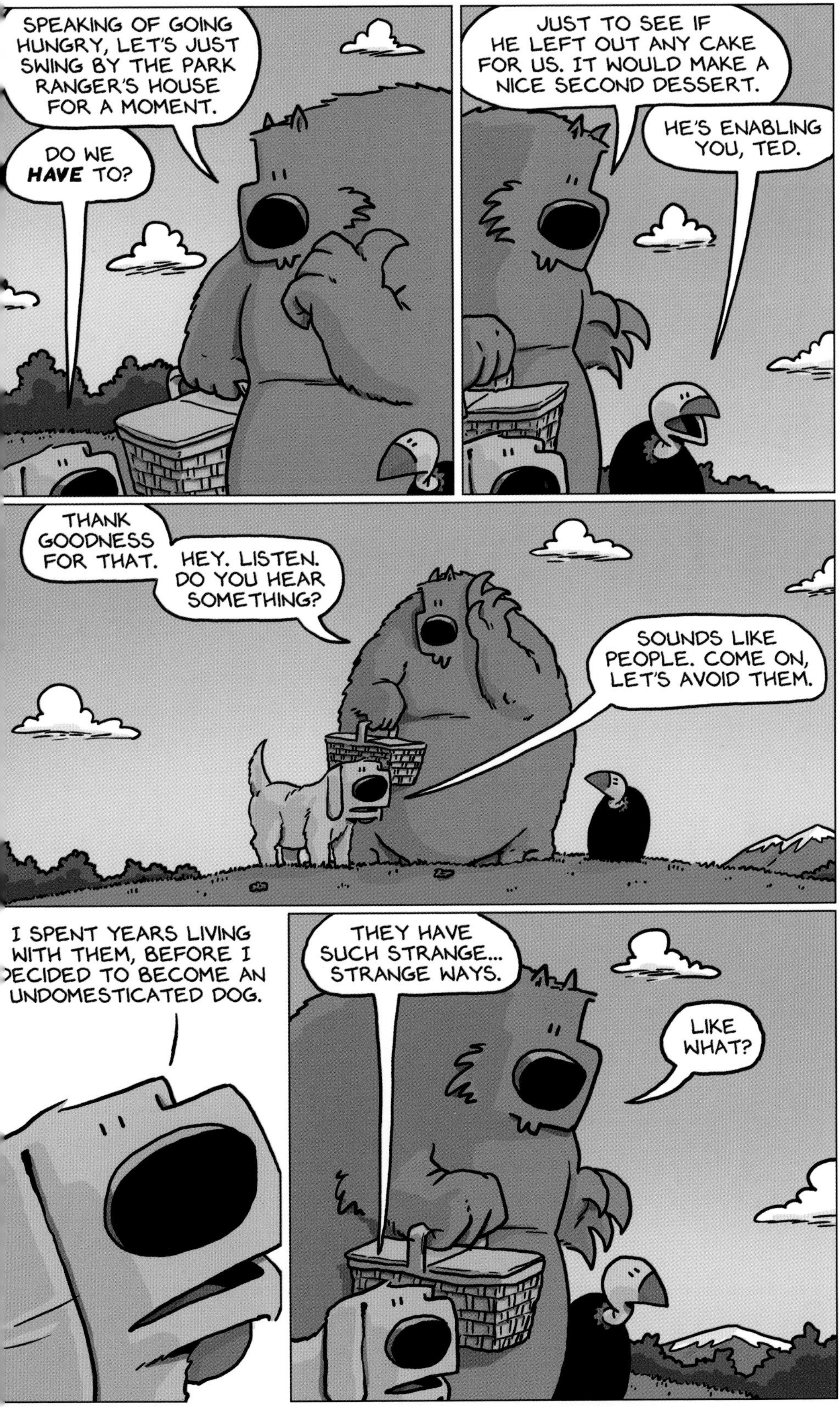

SPEAKING OF GOING HUNGRY, LET'S JUST SWING BY THE PARK RANGER'S HOUSE FOR A MOMENT.
DO WE **HAVE** TO?
JUST TO SEE IF HE LEFT OUT ANY CAKE FOR US. IT WOULD MAKE A NICE SECOND DESSERT.
HE'S ENABLING YOU, TED.
THANK GOODNESS FOR THAT.
HEY. LISTEN. DO YOU HEAR SOMETHING?
SOUNDS LIKE PEOPLE. COME ON, LET'S AVOID THEM.
I SPENT YEARS LIVING WITH THEM, BEFORE I DECIDED TO BECOME AN UNDOMESTICATED DOG.
THEY HAVE SUCH STRANGE... STRANGE WAYS.
LIKE WHAT?

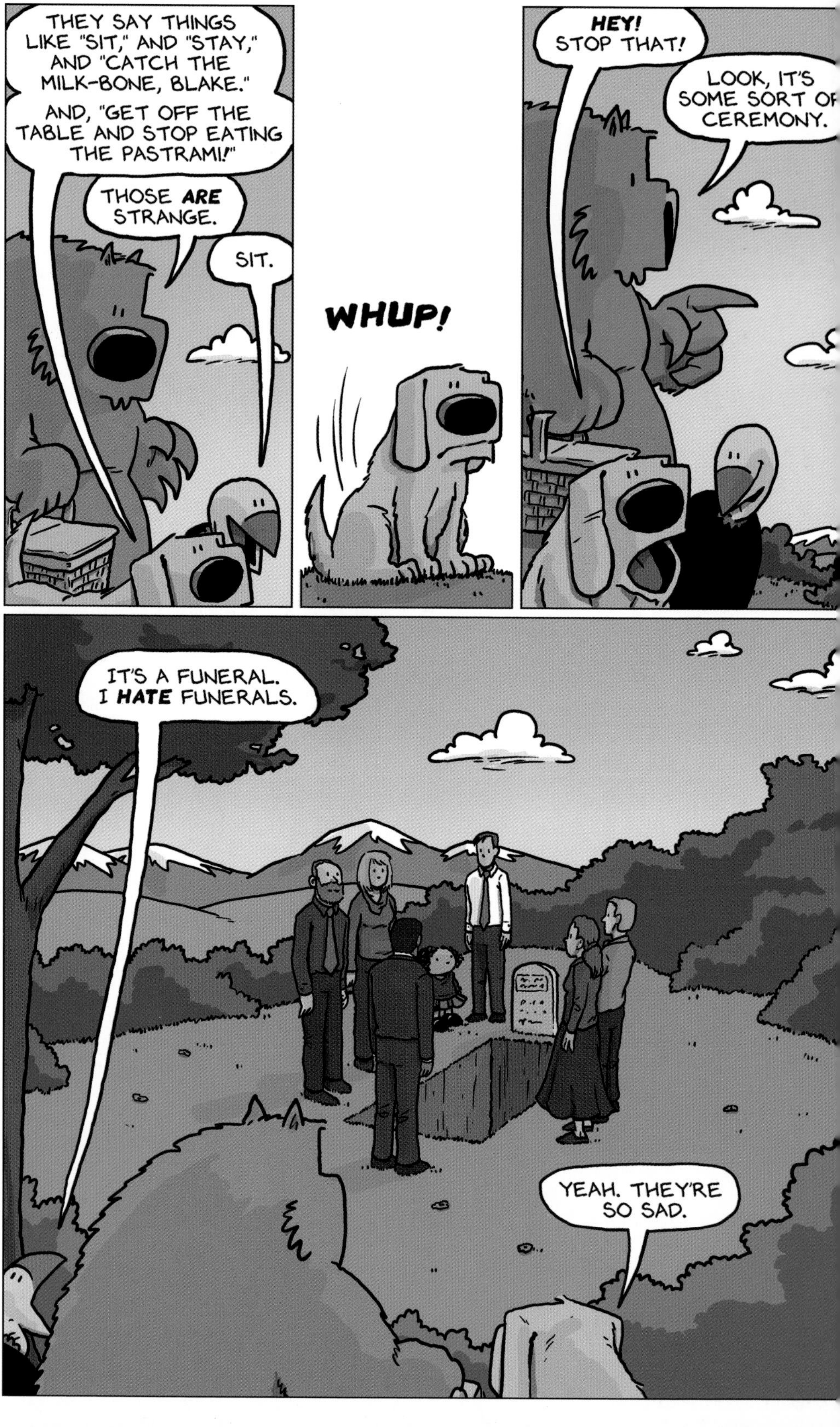

THEY SAY THINGS LIKE "SIT," AND "STAY," AND "CATCH THE MILK-BONE, BLAKE."
AND, "GET OFF THE TABLE AND STOP EATING THE PASTRAMI!"
THOSE **ARE** STRANGE.
SIT.
WHUP!
HEY! STOP THAT!
LOOK, IT'S SOME SORT OF CEREMONY.
IT'S A FUNERAL. I **HATE** FUNERALS.
YEAH. THEY'RE SO SAD.

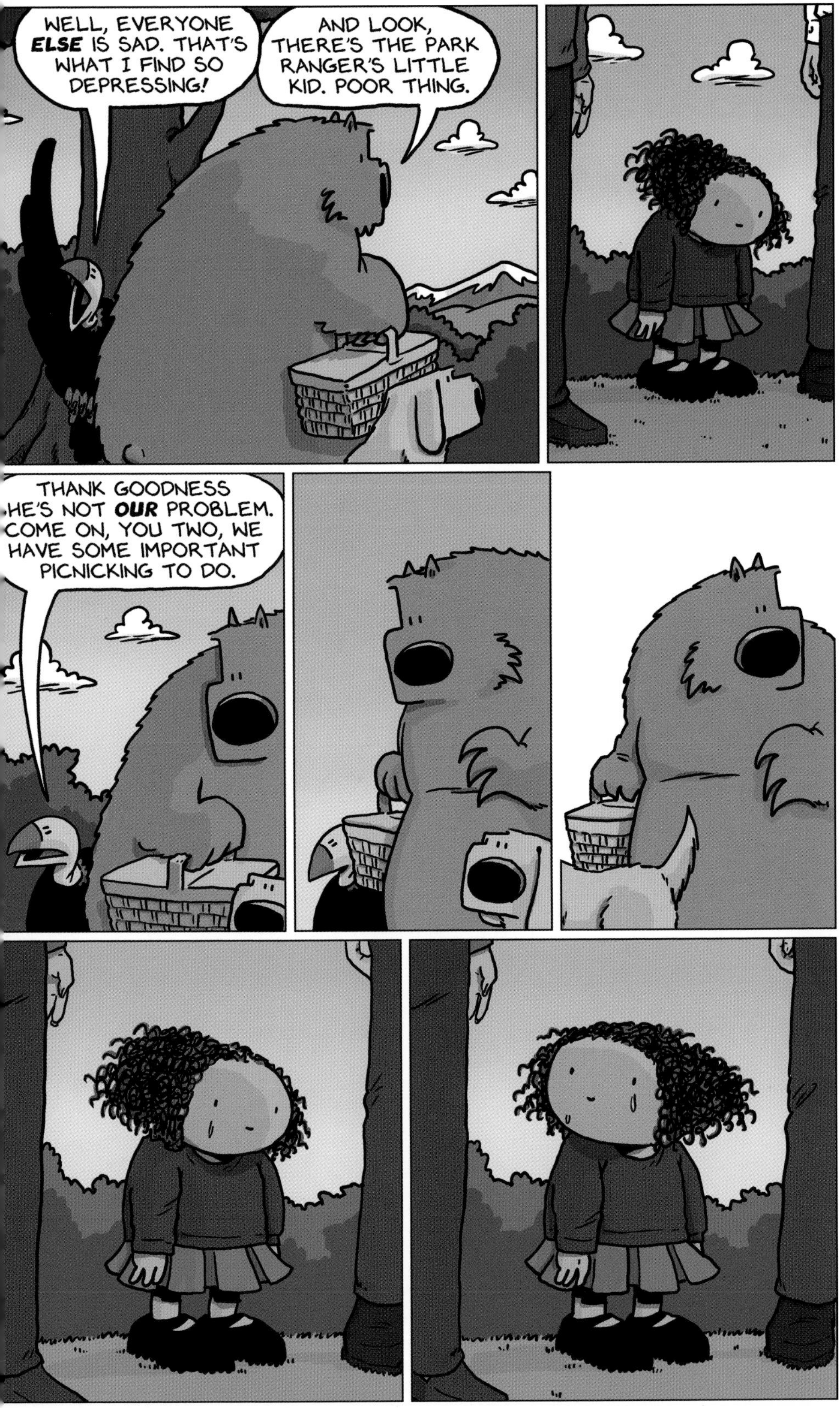
WELL, EVERYONE ELSE IS SAD. THAT'S WHAT I FIND SO DEPRESSING!
AND LOOK, THERE'S THE PARK RANGER'S LITTLE KID. POOR THING.
THANK GOODNESS HE'S NOT OUR PROBLEM. COME ON, YOU TWO, WE HAVE SOME IMPORTANT PICNICKING TO DO.

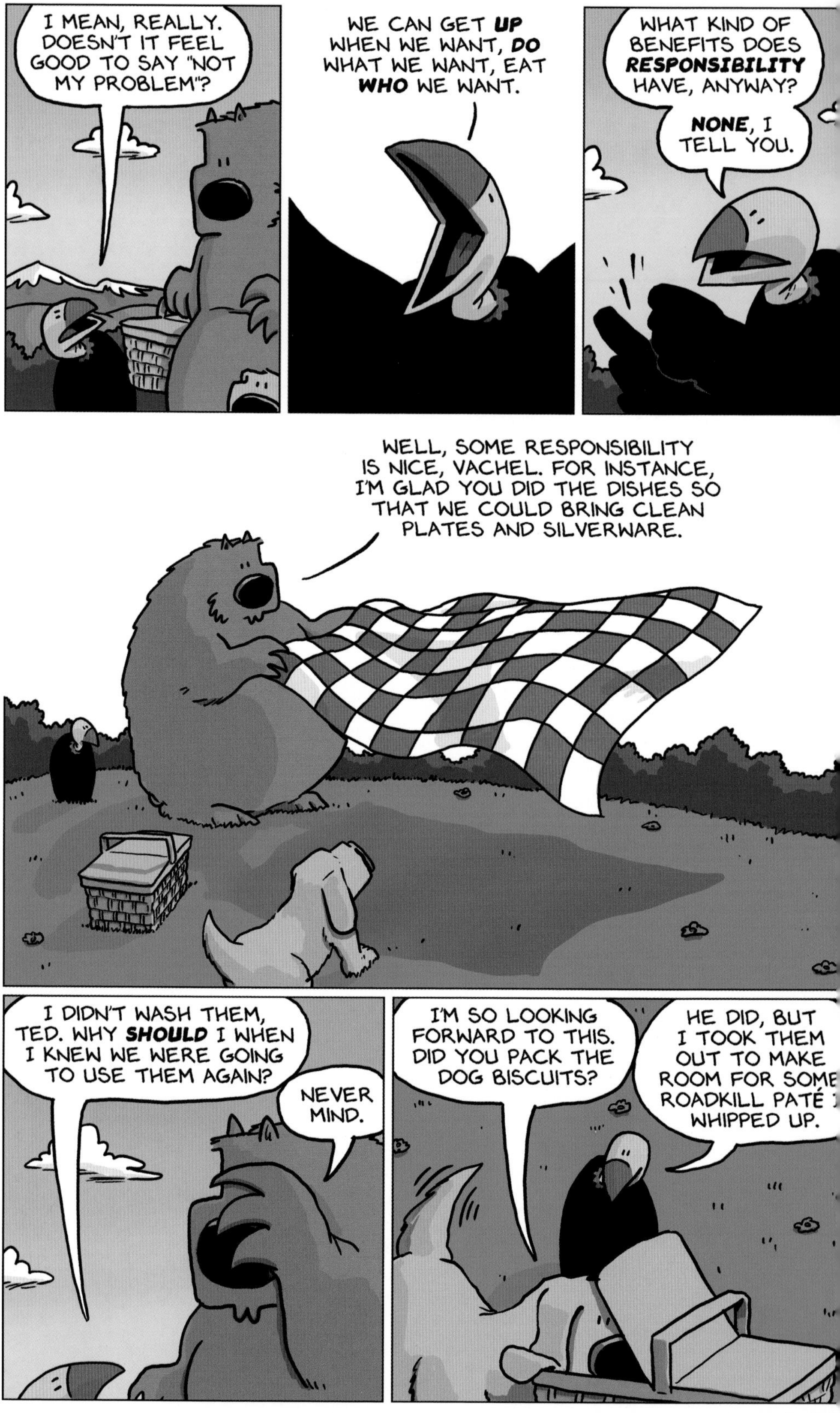
I MEAN, REALLY. DOESN'T IT FEEL GOOD TO SAY "NOT MY PROBLEM"?
WE CAN GET **UP** WHEN WE WANT, **DO** WHAT WE WANT, EAT **WHO** WE WANT.
WHAT KIND OF BENEFITS DOES **RESPONSIBILITY** HAVE, ANYWAY?
NONE, I TELL YOU.
WELL, SOME RESPONSIBILITY IS NICE, VACHEL. FOR INSTANCE, I'M GLAD YOU DID THE DISHES SO THAT WE COULD BRING CLEAN PLATES AND SILVERWARE.
I DIDN'T WASH THEM, TED. WHY **SHOULD** I WHEN I KNEW WE WERE GOING TO USE THEM AGAIN?
NEVER MIND.
I'M SO LOOKING FORWARD TO THIS. DID YOU PACK THE DOG BISCUITS?
HE DID, BUT I TOOK THEM OUT TO MAKE ROOM FOR SOME ROADKILL PATÉ I WHIPPED UP.

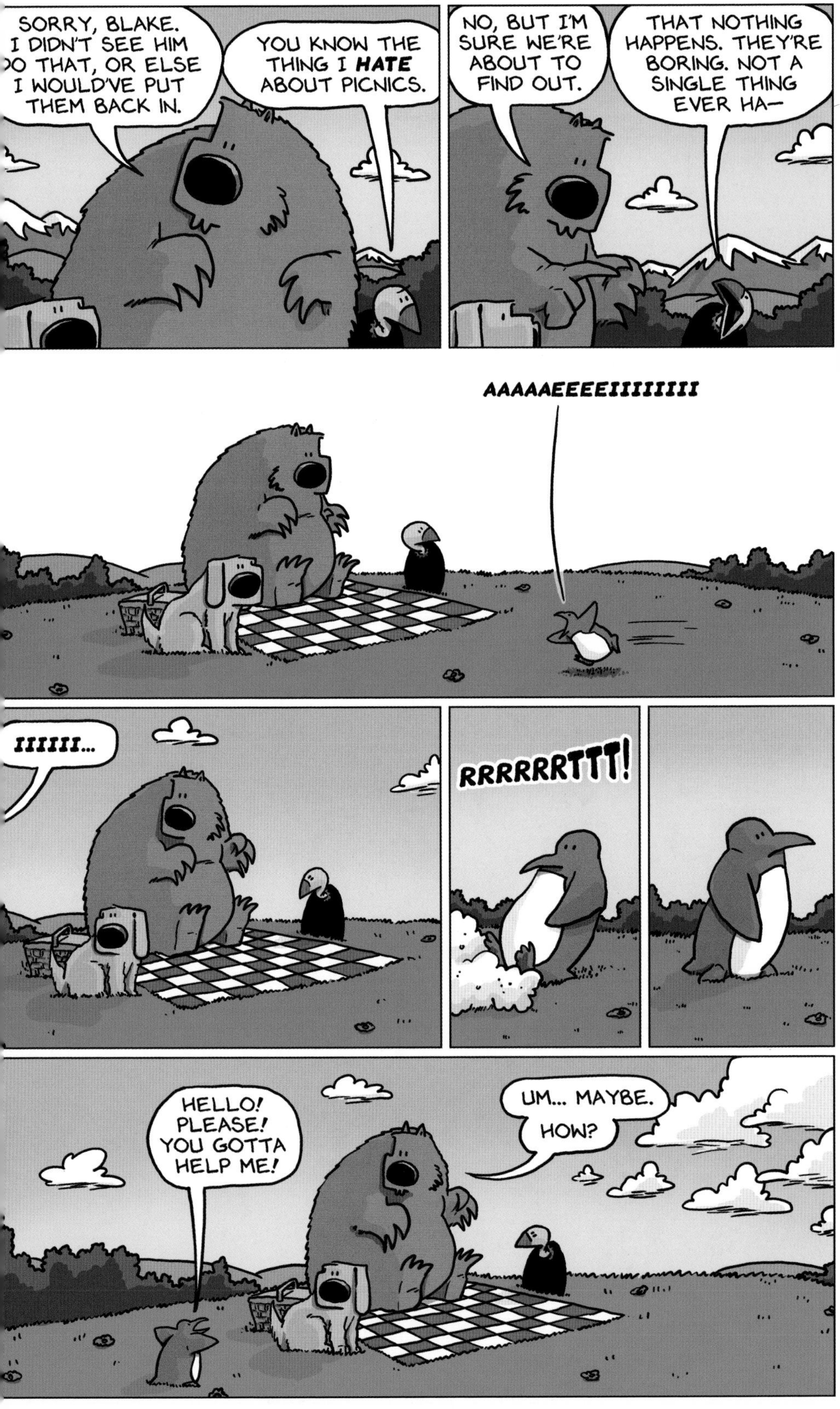
SORRY, BLAKE. I DIDN'T SEE HIM DO THAT, OR ELSE I WOULD'VE PUT THEM BACK IN.
YOU KNOW THE THING I **HATE** ABOUT PICNICS.
NO, BUT I'M SURE WE'RE ABOUT TO FIND OUT.
THAT NOTHING HAPPENS. THEY'RE BORING. NOT A SINGLE THING EVER HA—
AAAAAEEEEIIIIIIII
IIIIII...
RRRRRRTTT!
HELLO! PLEASE! YOU GOTTA HELP ME!
UM... MAYBE. HOW?

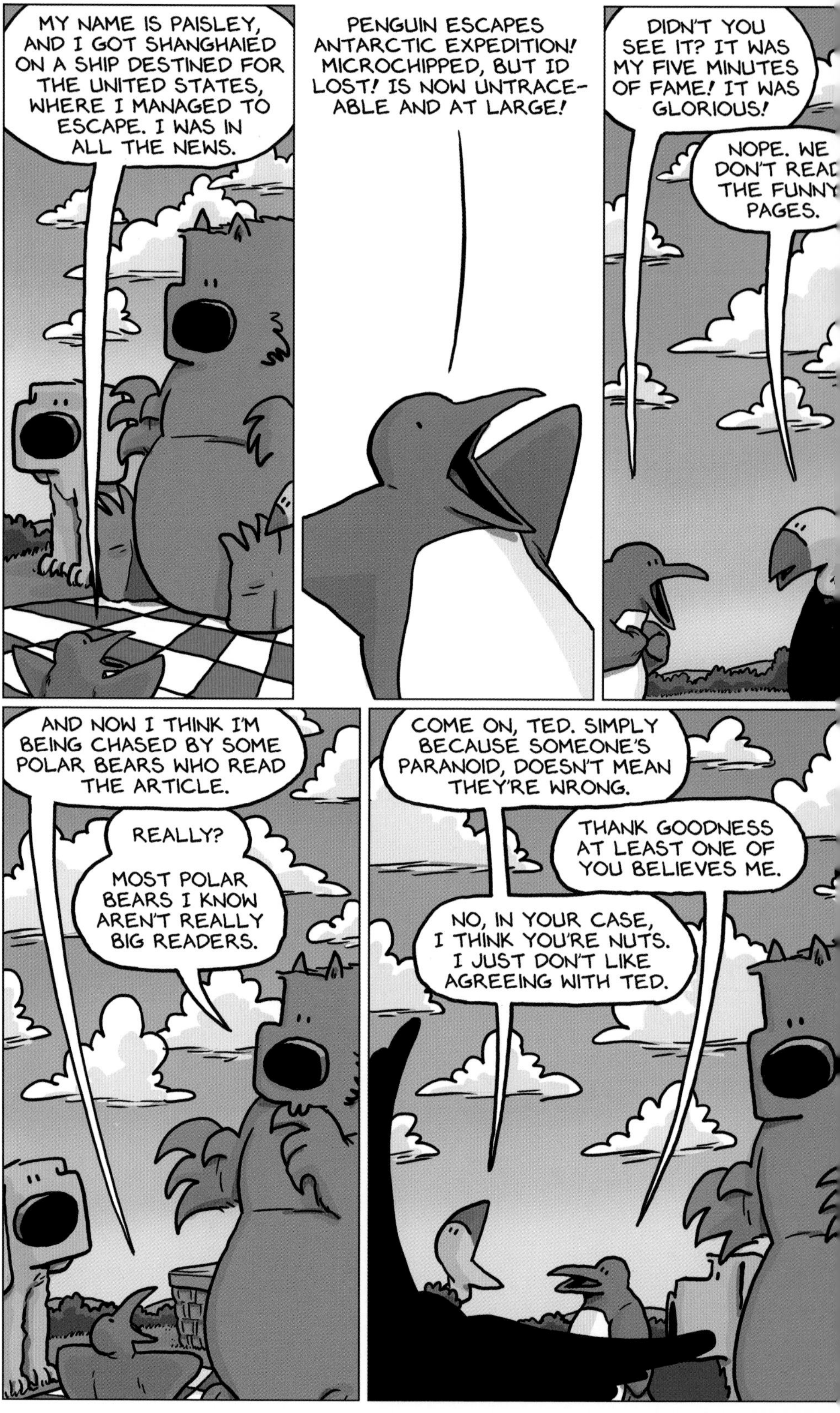
MY NAME IS PAISLEY, AND I GOT SHANGHAIED ON A SHIP DESTINED FOR THE UNITED STATES, WHERE I MANAGED TO ESCAPE. I WAS IN ALL THE NEWS.
PENGUIN ESCAPES ANTARCTIC EXPEDITION! MICROCHIPPED, BUT ID LOST! IS NOW UNTRACE-ABLE AND AT LARGE!
DIDN'T YOU SEE IT? IT WAS MY FIVE MINUTES OF FAME! IT WAS GLORIOUS!
NOPE. WE DON'T READ THE FUNNY PAGES.
AND NOW I THINK I'M BEING CHASED BY SOME POLAR BEARS WHO READ THE ARTICLE.
REALLY?
MOST POLAR BEARS I KNOW AREN'T REALLY BIG READERS.
COME ON, TED. SIMPLY BECAUSE SOMEONE'S PARANOID, DOESN'T MEAN THEY'RE WRONG.
THANK GOODNESS AT LEAST ONE OF YOU BELIEVES ME.
NO, IN YOUR CASE, I THINK YOU'RE NUTS. I JUST DON'T LIKE AGREEING WITH TED.

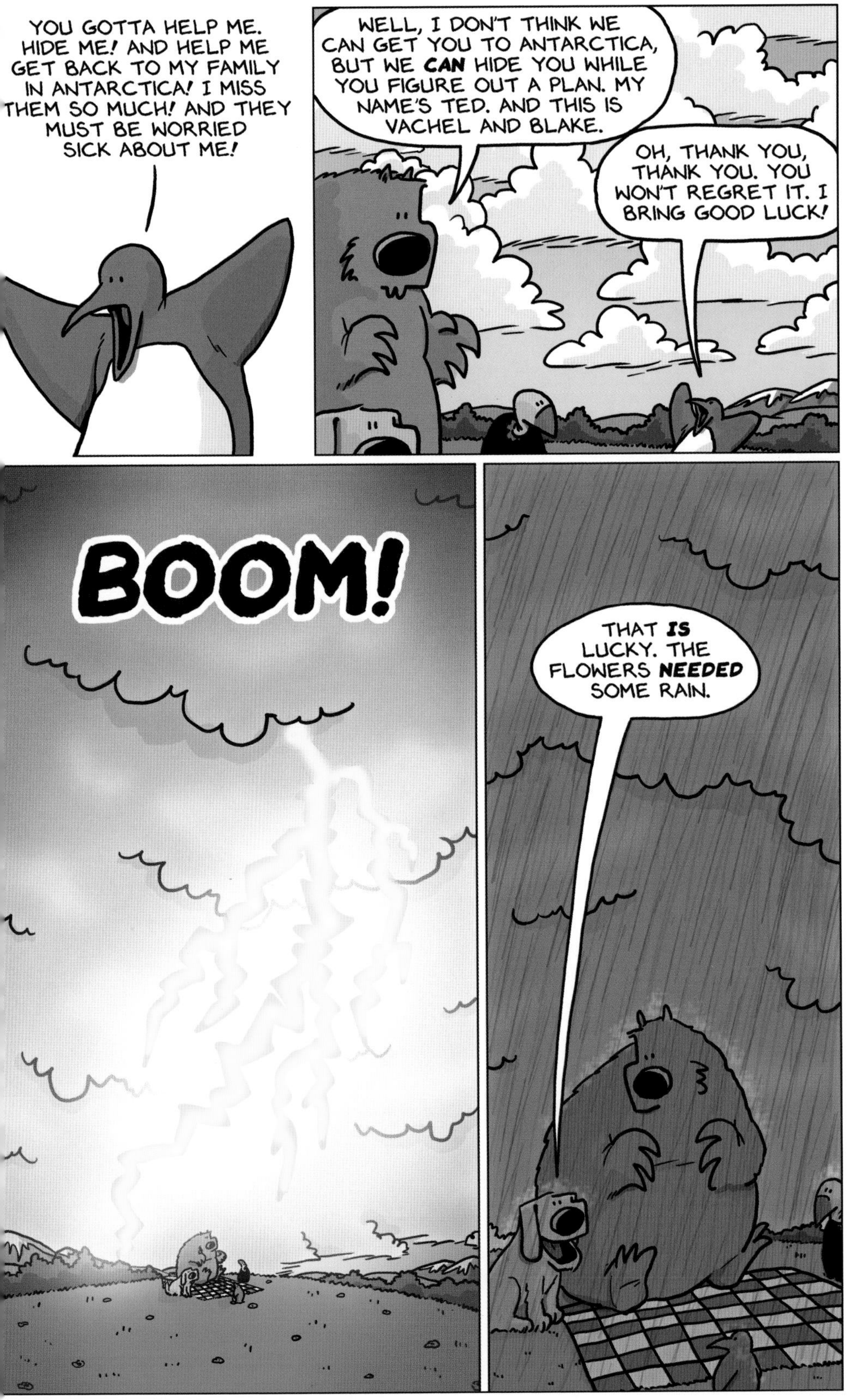
YOU GOTTA HELP ME. HIDE ME! AND HELP ME GET BACK TO MY FAMILY IN ANTARCTICA! I MISS THEM SO MUCH! AND THEY MUST BE WORRIED SICK ABOUT ME!
WELL, I DON'T THINK WE CAN GET YOU TO ANTARCTICA, BUT WE **CAN** HIDE YOU WHILE YOU FIGURE OUT A PLAN. MY NAME'S TED. AND THIS IS VACHEL AND BLAKE.
OH, THANK YOU, THANK YOU. YOU WON'T REGRET IT. I BRING GOOD LUCK!
BOOM!
THAT **IS** LUCKY. THE FLOWERS **NEEDED** SOME RAIN.

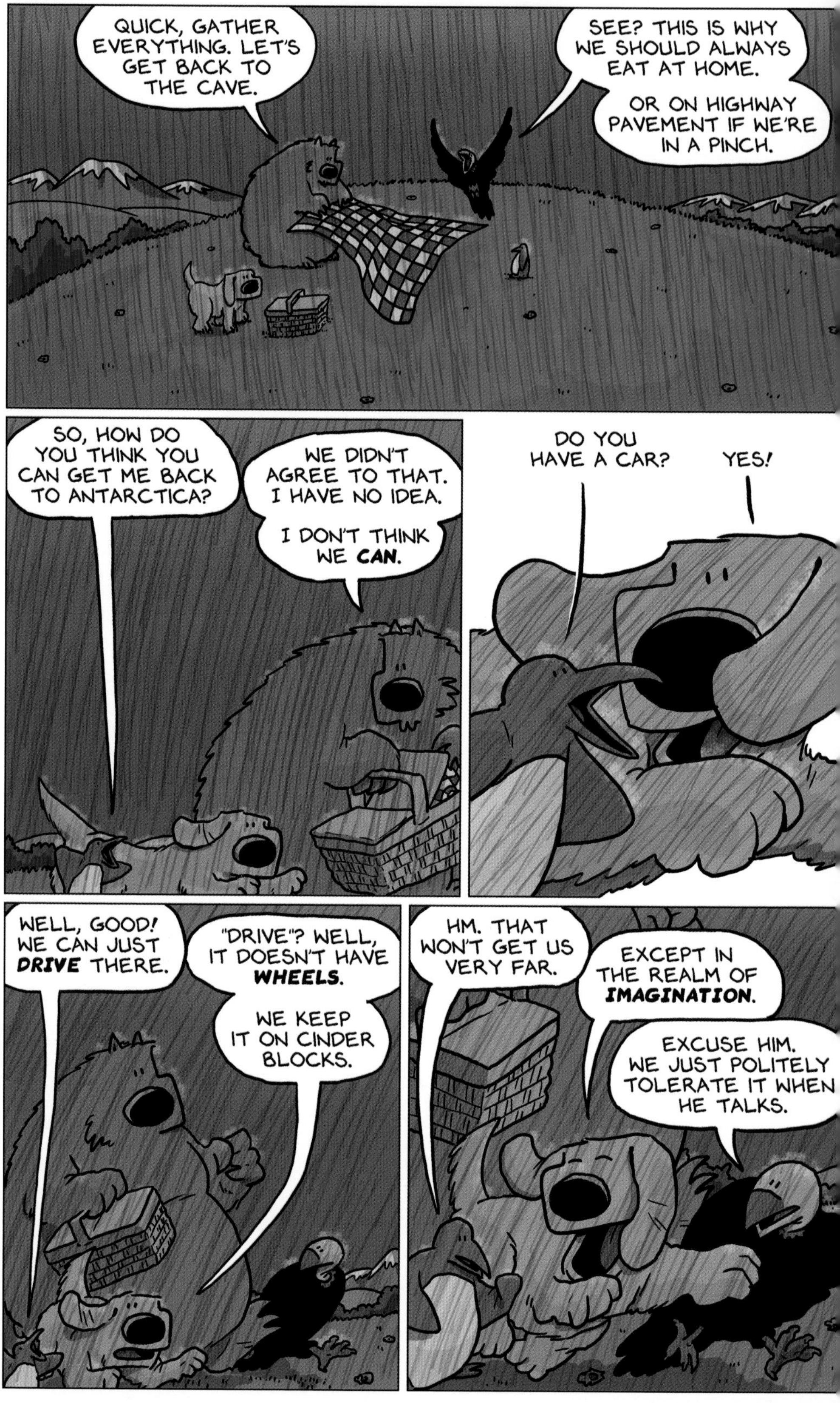
QUICK, GATHER EVERYTHING. LET'S GET BACK TO THE CAVE.
SEE? THIS IS WHY WE SHOULD ALWAYS EAT AT HOME.
OR ON HIGHWAY PAVEMENT IF WE'RE IN A PINCH.
SO, HOW DO YOU THINK YOU CAN GET ME BACK TO ANTARCTICA?
WE DIDN'T AGREE TO THAT. I HAVE NO IDEA.
I DON'T THINK WE **CAN**.
DO YOU HAVE A CAR?
YES!
WELL, GOOD! WE CAN JUST **DRIVE** THERE.
"DRIVE"? WELL, IT DOESN'T HAVE **WHEELS**.
WE KEEP IT ON CINDER BLOCKS.
HM. THAT WON'T GET US VERY FAR.
EXCEPT IN THE REALM OF **IMAGINATION**.
EXCUSE HIM. WE JUST POLITELY TOLERATE IT WHEN HE TALKS.

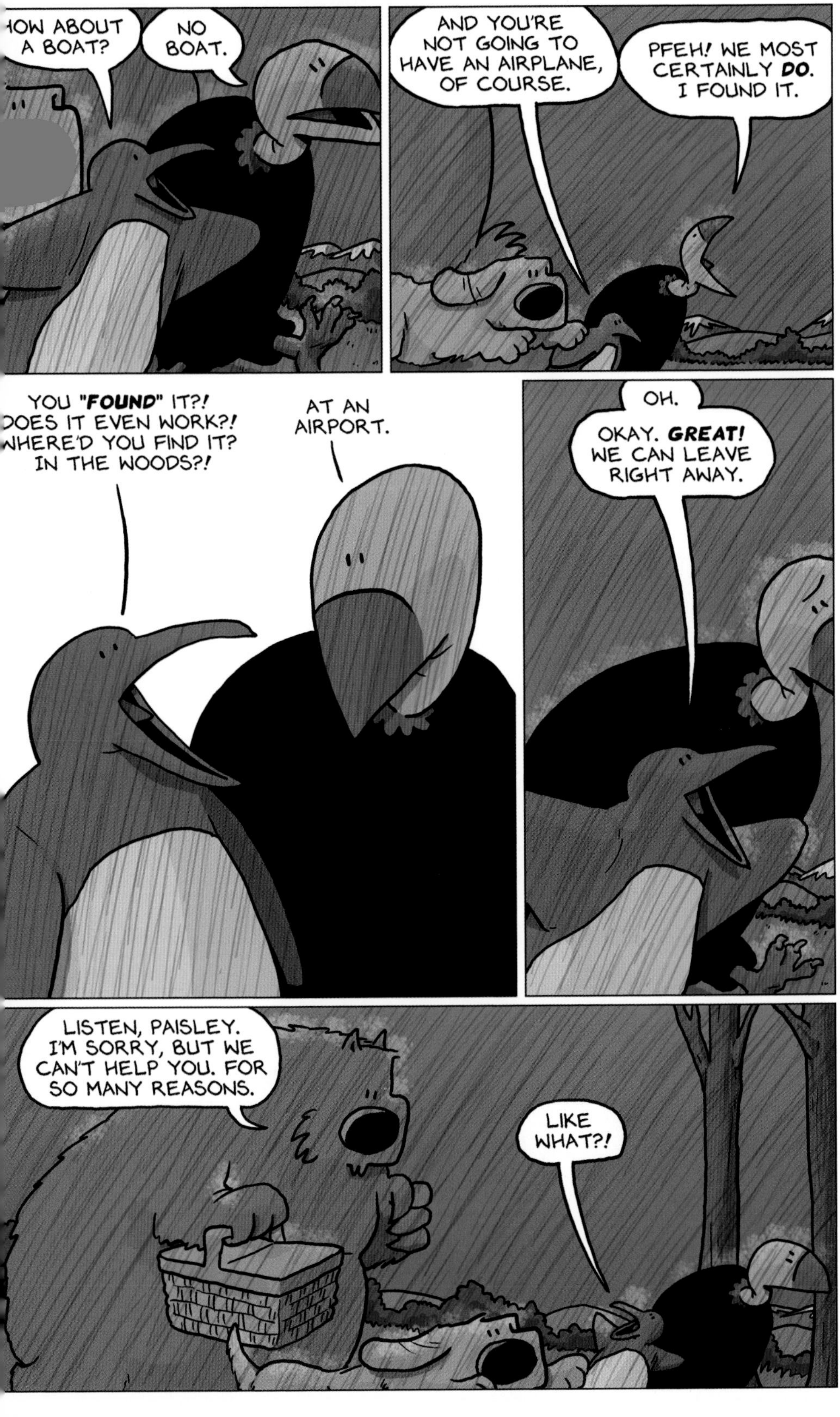

HOW ABOUT A BOAT?
NO BOAT.
AND YOU'RE NOT GOING TO HAVE AN AIRPLANE, OF COURSE.
PFEH! WE MOST CERTAINLY **DO**. I FOUND IT.
YOU "**FOUND**" IT?! DOES IT EVEN WORK?! WHERE'D YOU FIND IT? IN THE WOODS?!
AT AN AIRPORT.
OH.
OKAY. **GREAT!** WE CAN LEAVE RIGHT AWAY.
LISTEN, PAISLEY. I'M SORRY, BUT WE CAN'T HELP YOU. FOR SO MANY REASONS.
LIKE WHAT?!

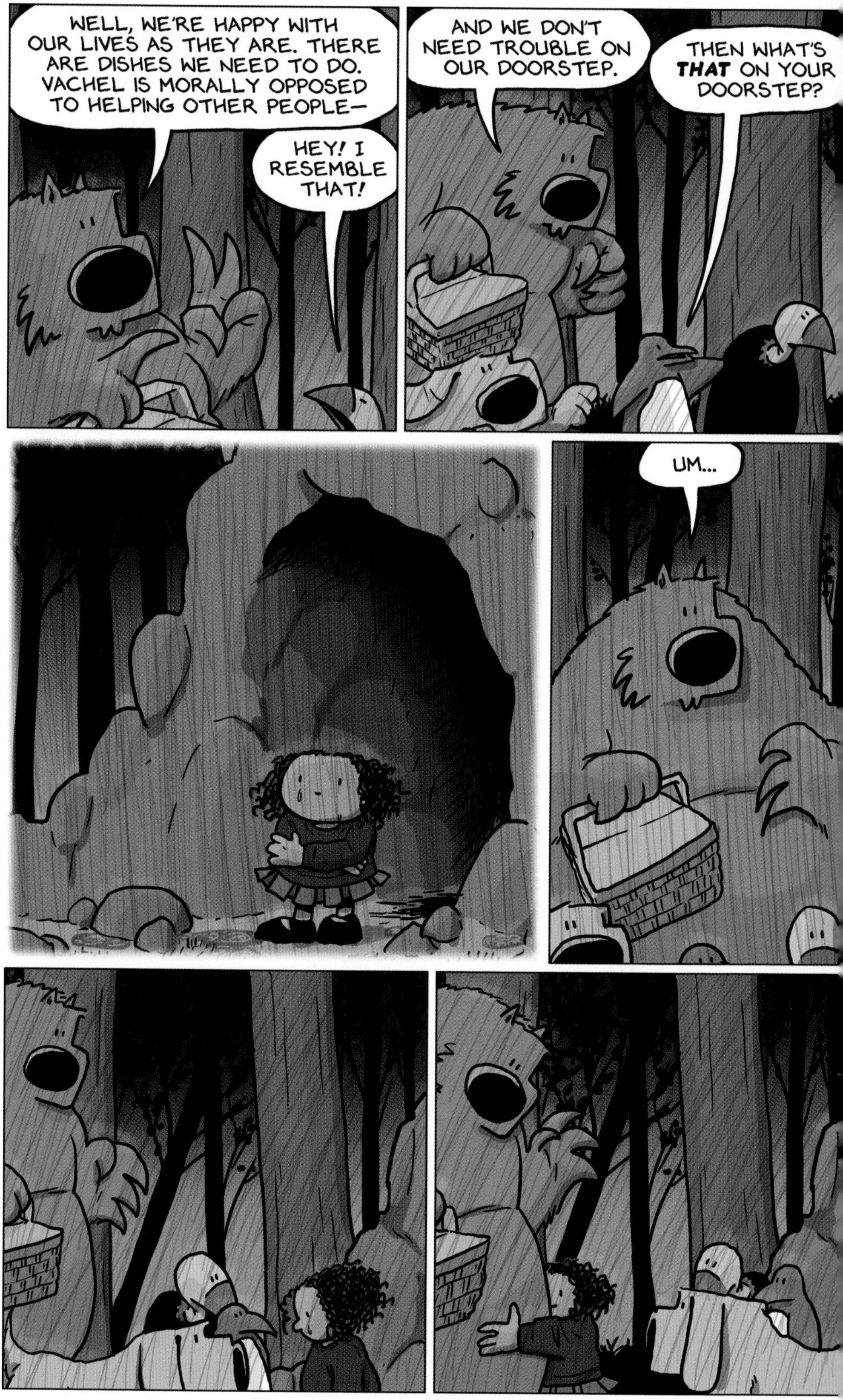
WELL, WE'RE HAPPY WITH OUR LIVES AS THEY ARE. THERE ARE DISHES WE NEED TO DO. VACHEL IS MORALLY OPPOSED TO HELPING OTHER PEOPLE—
HEY! I RESEMBLE THAT!
AND WE DON'T NEED TROUBLE ON OUR DOORSTEP.
THEN WHAT'S **THAT** ON YOUR DOORSTEP?
UM...

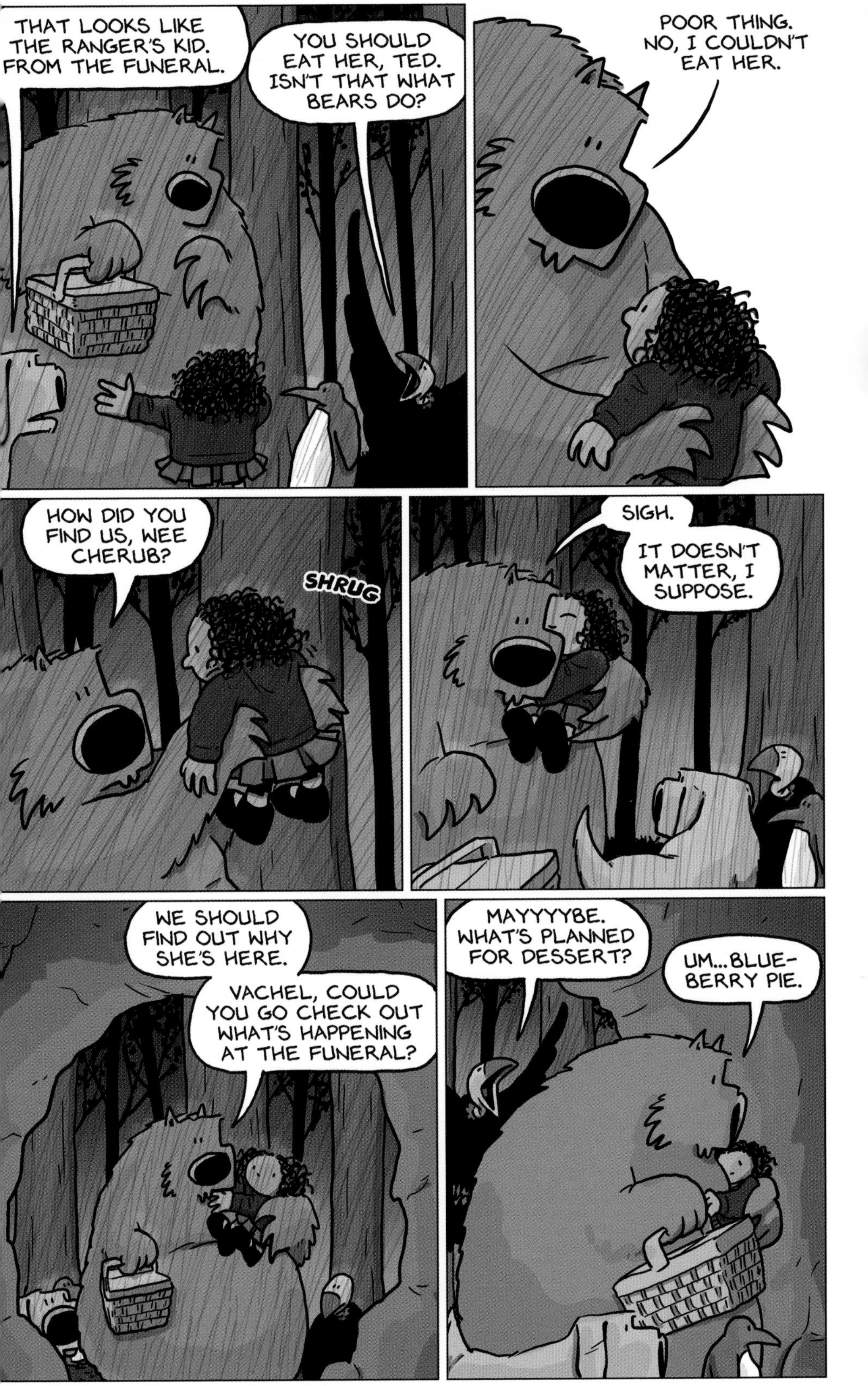
THAT LOOKS LIKE THE RANGER'S KID. FROM THE FUNERAL.
YOU SHOULD EAT HER, TED. ISN'T THAT WHAT BEARS DO?
POOR THING. NO, I COULDN'T EAT HER.
HOW DID YOU FIND US, WEE CHERUB?
SHRUG
SIGH.
IT DOESN'T MATTER, I SUPPOSE.
WE SHOULD FIND OUT WHY SHE'S HERE.
VACHEL, COULD YOU GO CHECK OUT WHAT'S HAPPENING AT THE FUNERAL?
MAYYYYBE. WHAT'S PLANNED FOR DESSERT?
UM...BLUE-BERRY PIE.

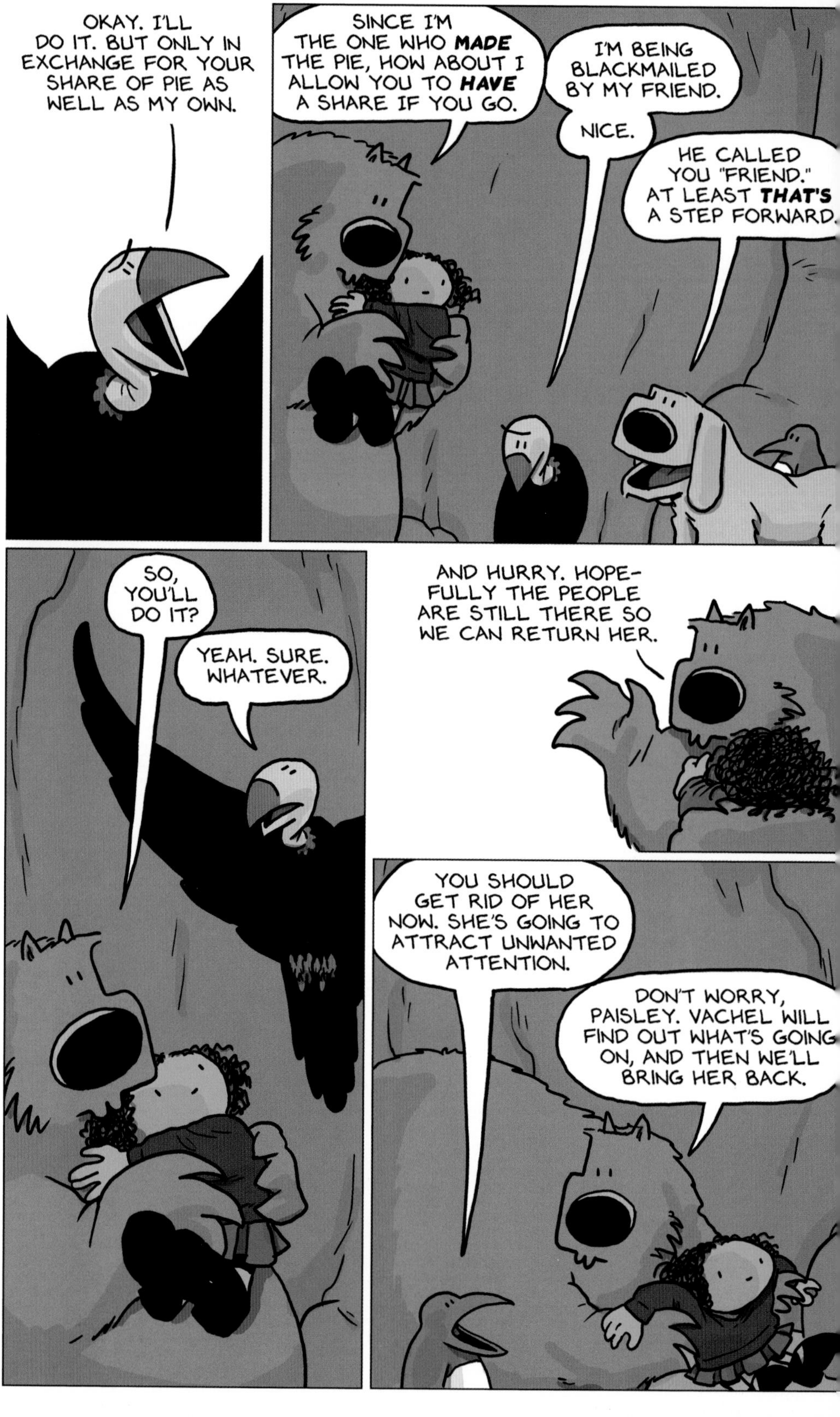

OKAY. I'LL DO IT. BUT ONLY IN EXCHANGE FOR YOUR SHARE OF PIE AS WELL AS MY OWN.
SINCE I'M THE ONE WHO **MADE** THE PIE, HOW ABOUT I ALLOW YOU TO **HAVE** A SHARE IF YOU GO.
I'M BEING BLACKMAILED BY MY FRIEND.
NICE.
HE CALLED YOU "FRIEND." AT LEAST **THAT'S** A STEP FORWARD.
SO, YOU'LL DO IT?
YEAH. SURE. WHATEVER.
AND HURRY. HOPE-FULLY THE PEOPLE ARE STILL THERE SO WE CAN RETURN HER.
YOU SHOULD GET RID OF HER NOW. SHE'S GOING TO ATTRACT UNWANTED ATTENTION.
DON'T WORRY, PAISLEY. VACHEL WILL FIND OUT WHAT'S GOING ON, AND THEN WE'LL BRING HER BACK.

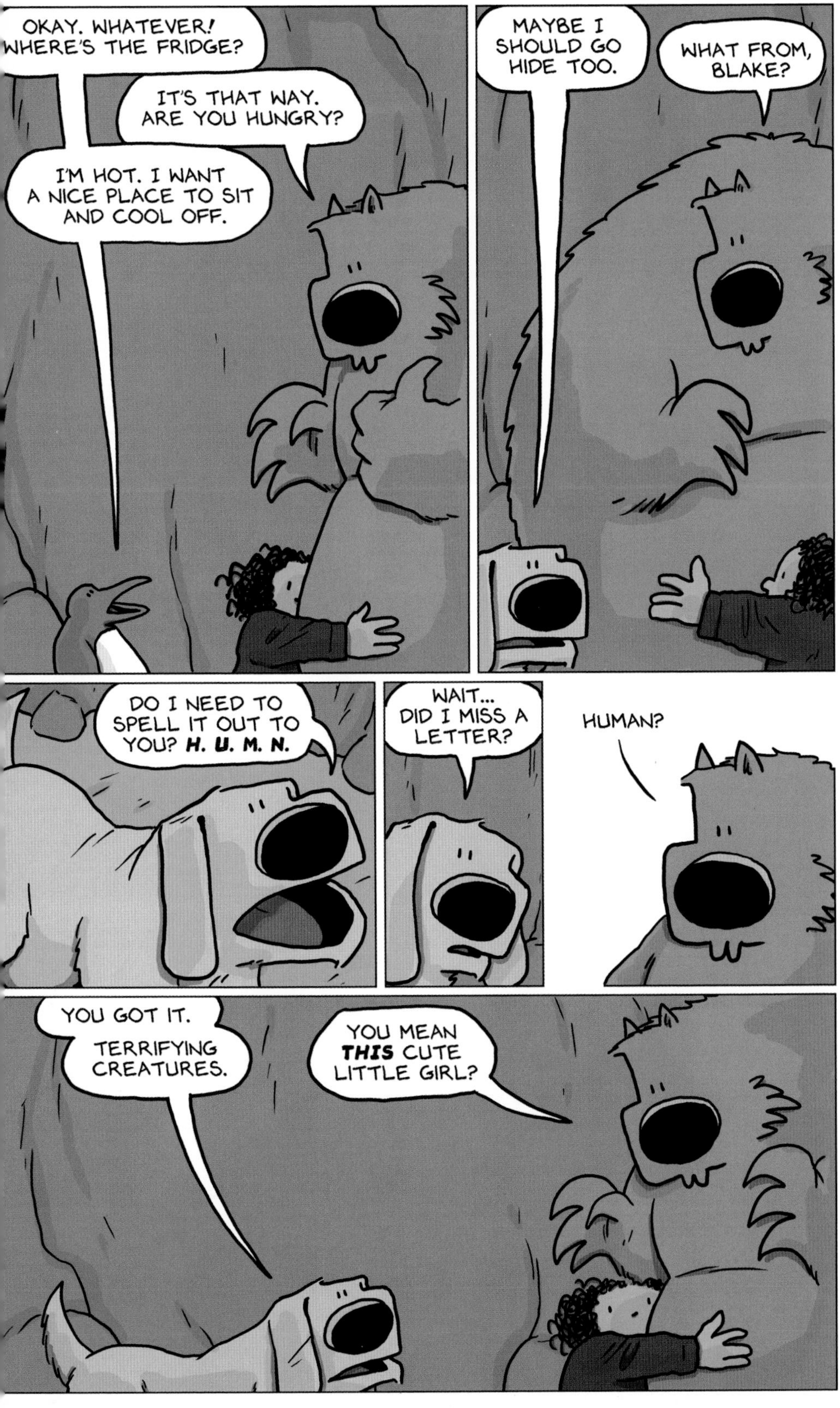
OKAY. WHATEVER! WHERE'S THE FRIDGE?
IT'S THAT WAY. ARE YOU HUNGRY?
I'M HOT. I WANT A NICE PLACE TO SIT AND COOL OFF.
MAYBE I SHOULD GO HIDE TOO.
WHAT FROM, BLAKE?
DO I NEED TO SPELL IT OUT TO YOU? **H. U. M. N.**
WAIT... DID I MISS A LETTER?
HUMAN?
YOU GOT IT.
TERRIFYING CREATURES.
YOU MEAN **THIS** CUTE LITTLE GIRL?

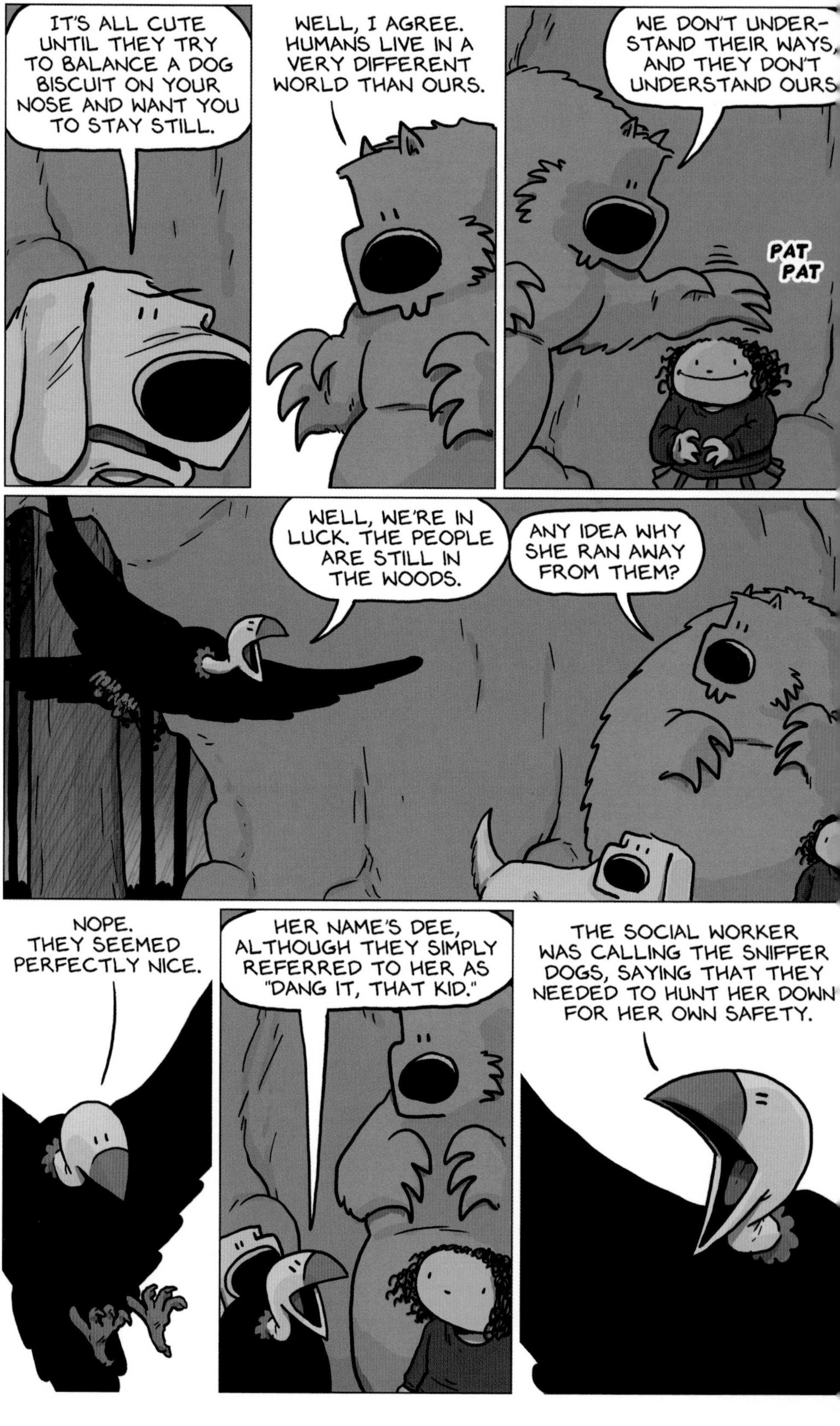
IT'S ALL CUTE UNTIL THEY TRY TO BALANCE A DOG BISCUIT ON YOUR NOSE AND WANT YOU TO STAY STILL.
WELL, I AGREE. HUMANS LIVE IN A VERY DIFFERENT WORLD THAN OURS.
WE DON'T UNDER-STAND THEIR WAYS, AND THEY DON'T UNDERSTAND OURS.
PAT PAT
WELL, WE'RE IN LUCK. THE PEOPLE ARE STILL IN THE WOODS.
ANY IDEA WHY SHE RAN AWAY FROM THEM?
NOPE. THEY SEEMED PERFECTLY NICE.
HER NAME'S DEE, ALTHOUGH THEY SIMPLY REFERRED TO HER AS "DANG IT, THAT KID."
THE SOCIAL WORKER WAS CALLING THE SNIFFER DOGS, SAYING THAT THEY NEEDED TO HUNT HER DOWN FOR HER OWN SAFETY.

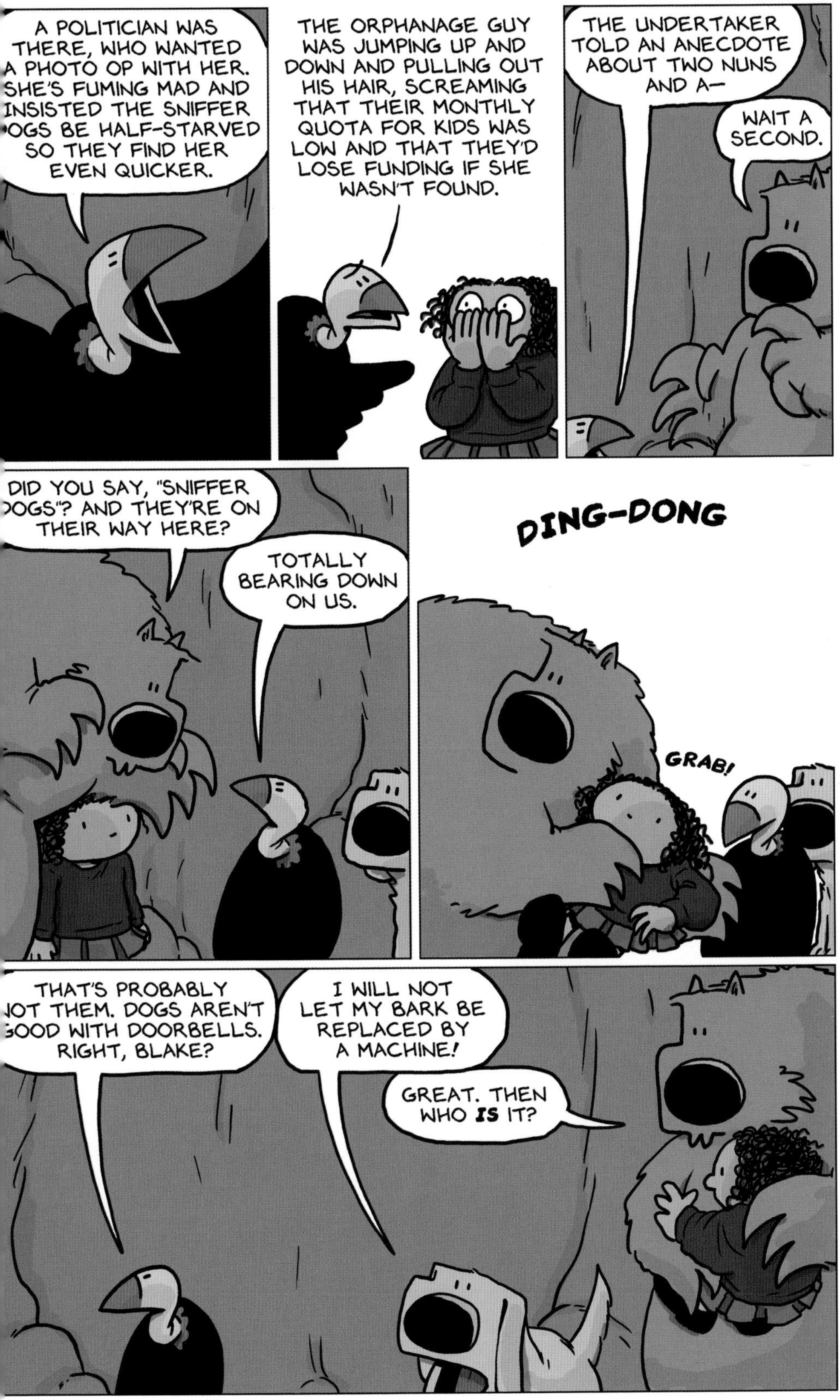
A POLITICIAN WAS THERE, WHO WANTED A PHOTO OP WITH HER. SHE'S FUMING MAD AND INSISTED THE SNIFFER DOGS BE HALF-STARVED SO THEY FIND HER EVEN QUICKER.
THE ORPHANAGE GUY WAS JUMPING UP AND DOWN AND PULLING OUT HIS HAIR, SCREAMING THAT THEIR MONTHLY QUOTA FOR KIDS WAS LOW AND THAT THEY'D LOSE FUNDING IF SHE WASN'T FOUND.
THE UNDERTAKER TOLD AN ANECDOTE ABOUT TWO NUNS AND A—
WAIT A SECOND.
DID YOU SAY, "SNIFFER DOGS"? AND THEY'RE ON THEIR WAY HERE?
TOTALLY BEARING DOWN ON US.
DING-DONG
GRAB!
THAT'S PROBABLY NOT THEM. DOGS AREN'T GOOD WITH DOORBELLS. RIGHT, BLAKE?
I WILL NOT LET MY BARK BE REPLACED BY A MACHINE!
GREAT. THEN WHO **IS** IT?

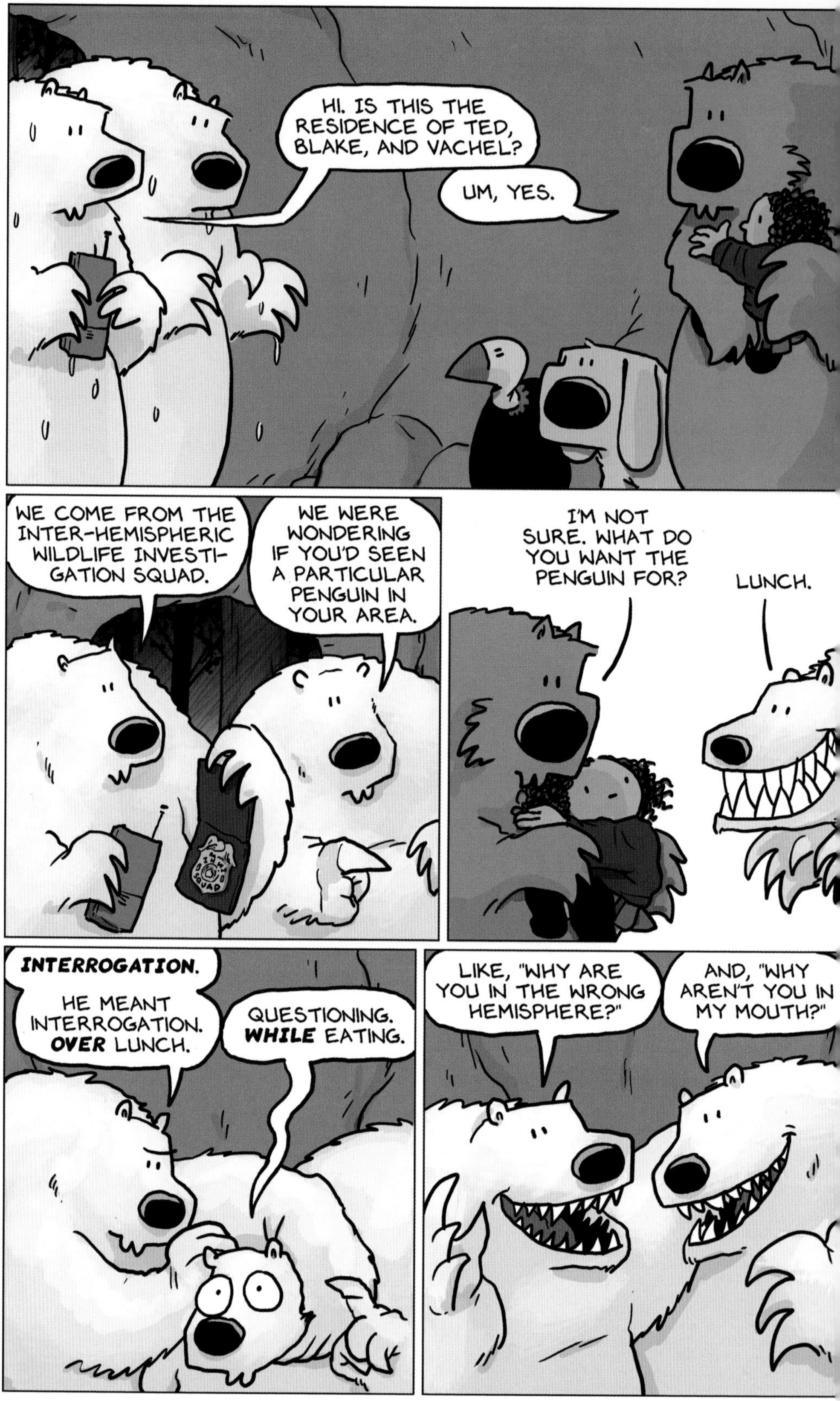
HI. IS THIS THE RESIDENCE OF TED, BLAKE, AND VACHEL?
UM, YES.
WE COME FROM THE INTER-HEMISPHERIC WILDLIFE INVESTI-GATION SQUAD.
WE WERE WONDERING IF YOU'D SEEN A PARTICULAR PENGUIN IN YOUR AREA.
I'M NOT SURE. WHAT DO YOU WANT THE PENGUIN FOR?
LUNCH.
INTERROGATION.
HE MEANT INTERROGATION. **OVER** LUNCH.
QUESTIONING. **WHILE** EATING.
LIKE, "WHY ARE YOU IN THE WRONG HEMISPHERE?"
AND, "WHY AREN'T YOU IN MY MOUTH?"

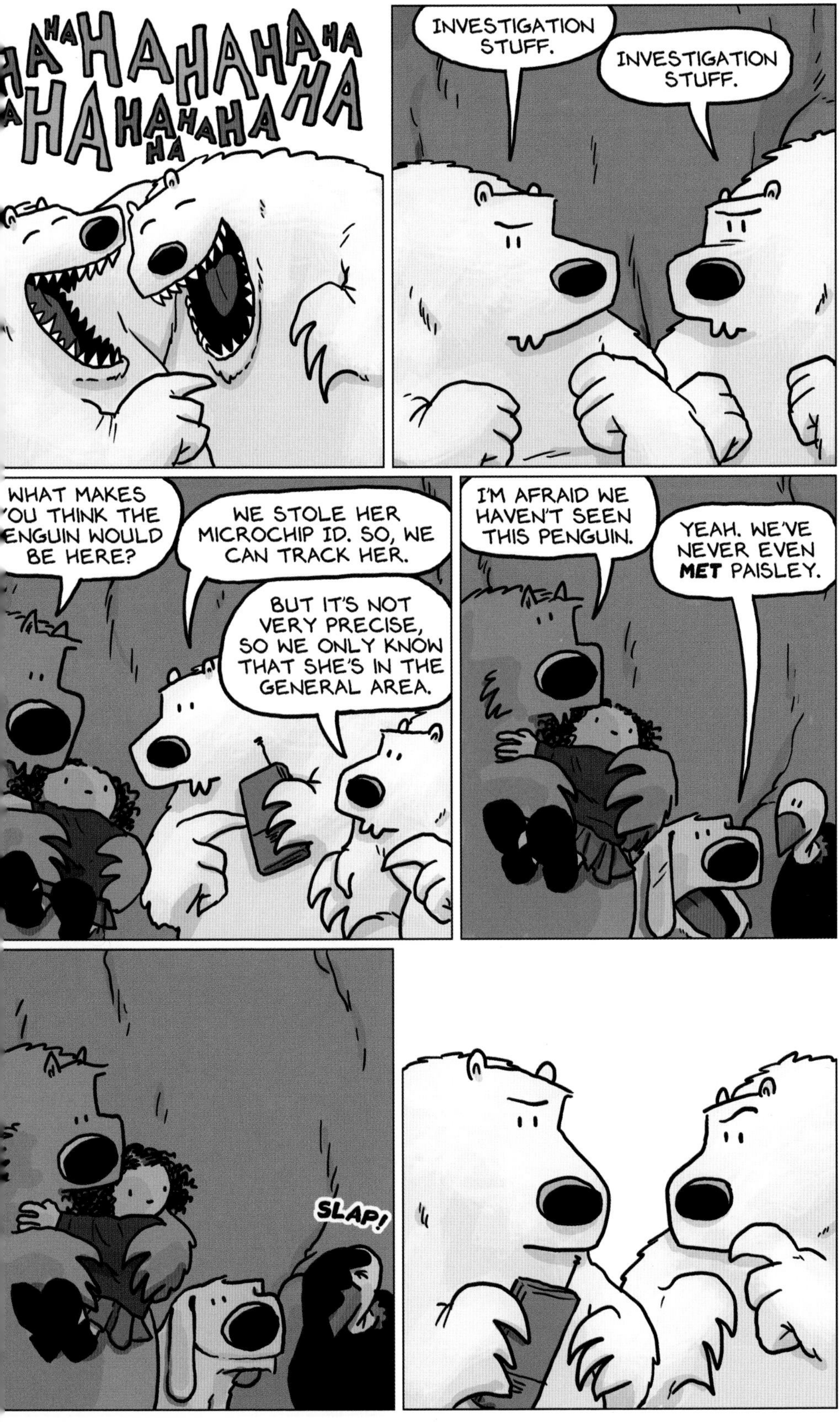

HAHAHAHAHAHAHA HAHAHAHAHAHAHA
INVESTIGATION STUFF.
INVESTIGATION STUFF.
WHAT MAKES YOU THINK THE PENGUIN WOULD BE HERE?
WE STOLE HER MICROCHIP ID. SO, WE CAN TRACK HER.
BUT IT'S NOT VERY PRECISE, SO WE ONLY KNOW THAT SHE'S IN THE GENERAL AREA.
I'M AFRAID WE HAVEN'T SEEN THIS PENGUIN.
YEAH. WE'VE NEVER EVEN **MET** PAISLEY.
SLAP!

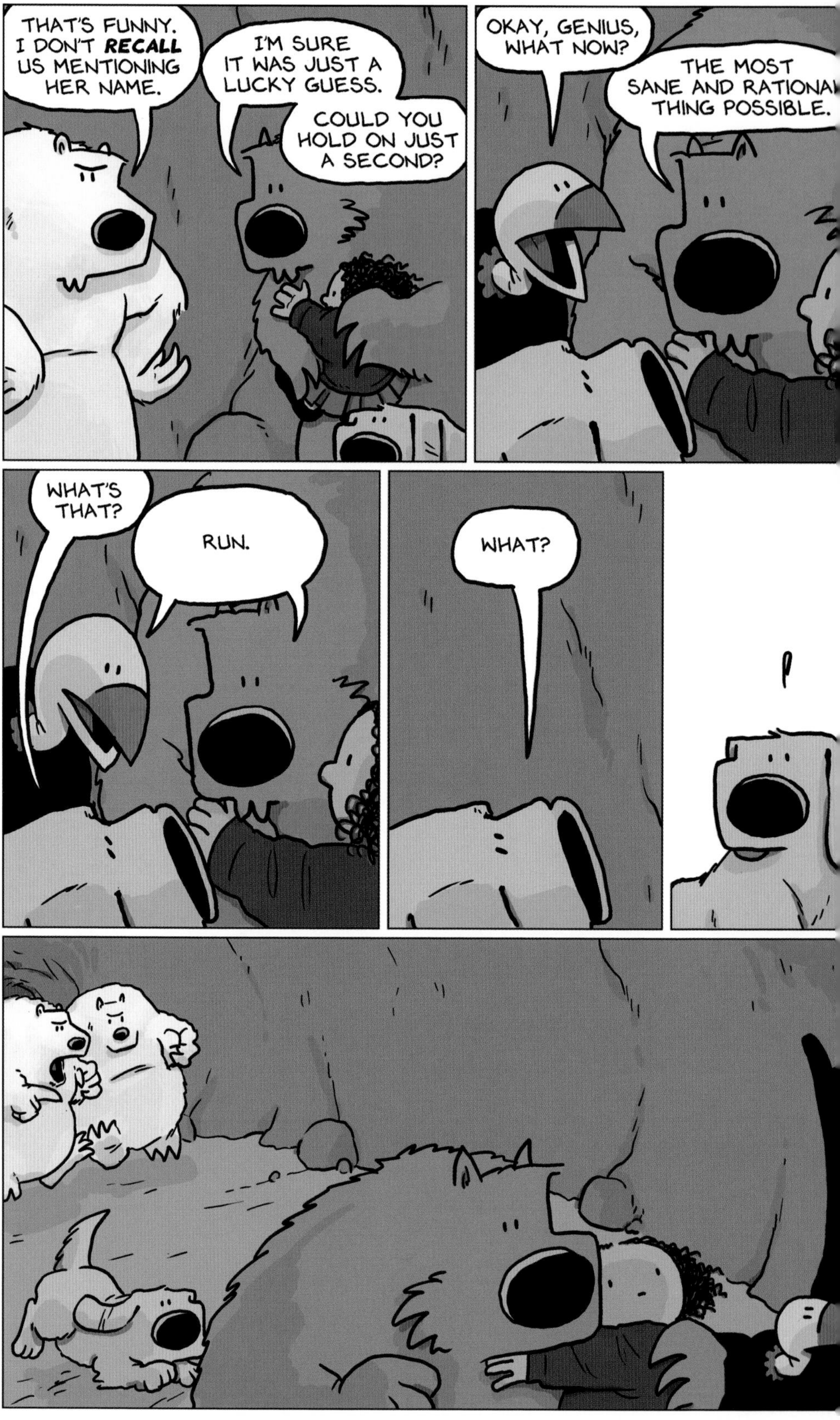
THAT'S FUNNY. I DON'T **RECALL** US MENTIONING HER NAME.
I'M SURE IT WAS JUST A LUCKY GUESS.
COULD YOU HOLD ON JUST A SECOND?
OKAY, GENIUS, WHAT NOW?
THE MOST SANE AND RATIONAL THING POSSIBLE.
WHAT'S THAT?
RUN.
WHAT?

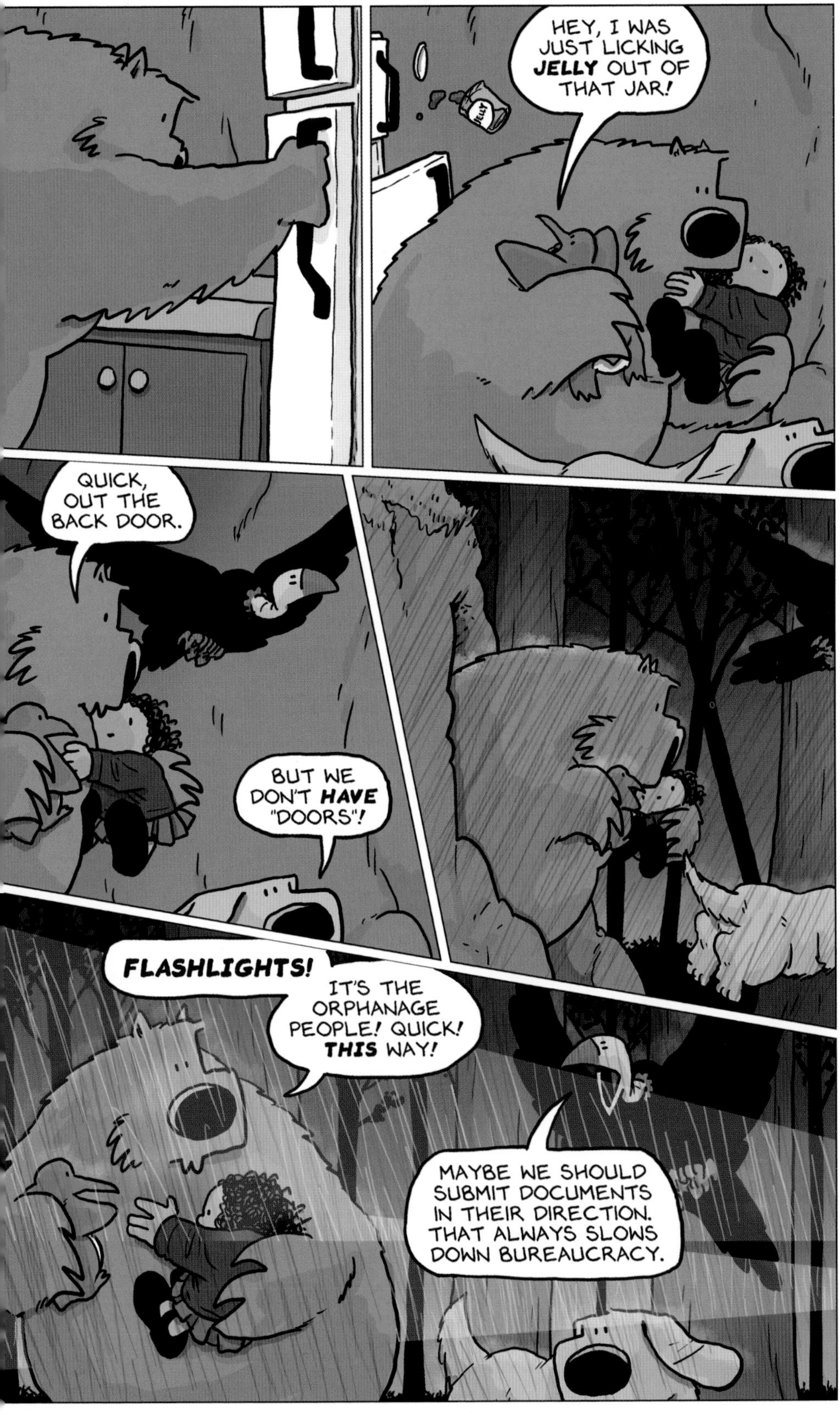
HEY, I WAS JUST LICKING **JELLY** OUT OF THAT JAR!
JELLY
QUICK, OUT THE BACK DOOR.
BUT WE DON'T **HAVE** "DOORS"!
FLASHLIGHTS!
IT'S THE ORPHANAGE PEOPLE! QUICK! **THIS** WAY!
MAYBE WE SHOULD SUBMIT DOCUMENTS IN THEIR DIRECTION. THAT ALWAYS SLOWS DOWN BUREAUCRACY.

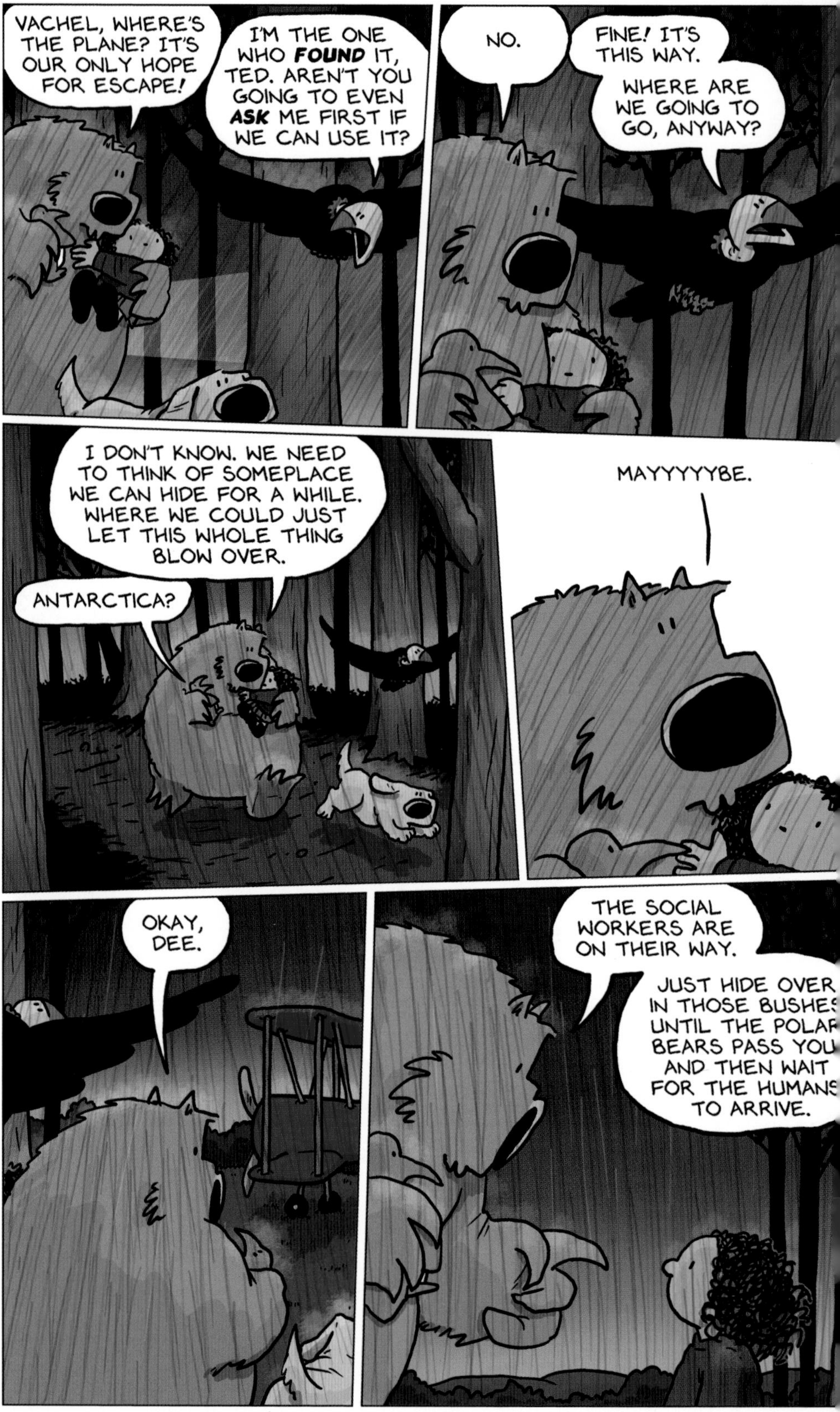

VACHEL, WHERE'S THE PLANE? IT'S OUR ONLY HOPE FOR ESCAPE!
I'M THE ONE WHO **FOUND** IT, TED. AREN'T YOU GOING TO EVEN **ASK** ME FIRST IF WE CAN USE IT?
NO.
FINE! IT'S THIS WAY.
WHERE ARE WE GOING TO GO, ANYWAY?
I DON'T KNOW. WE NEED TO THINK OF SOMEPLACE WE CAN HIDE FOR A WHILE. WHERE WE COULD JUST LET THIS WHOLE THING BLOW OVER.
ANTARCTICA?
MAYYYYYBE.
OKAY, DEE.
THE SOCIAL WORKERS ARE ON THEIR WAY.
JUST HIDE OVER IN THOSE BUSHE UNTIL THE POLA BEARS PASS YOU AND THEN WAIT FOR THE HUMAN TO ARRIVE.

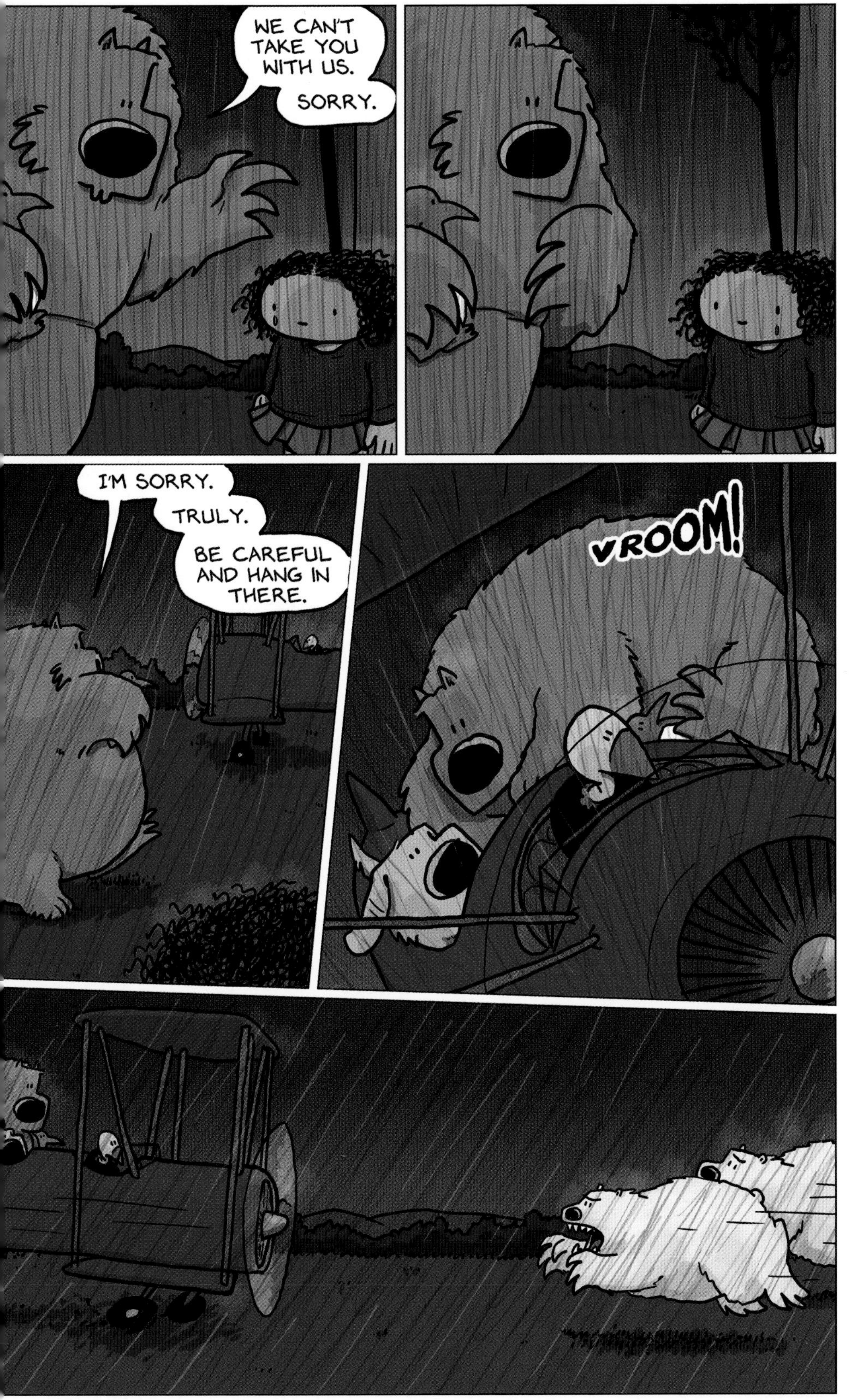
WE CAN'T TAKE YOU WITH US.
SORRY.
I'M SORRY.
TRULY.
BE CAREFUL AND HANG IN THERE.
VROOM!

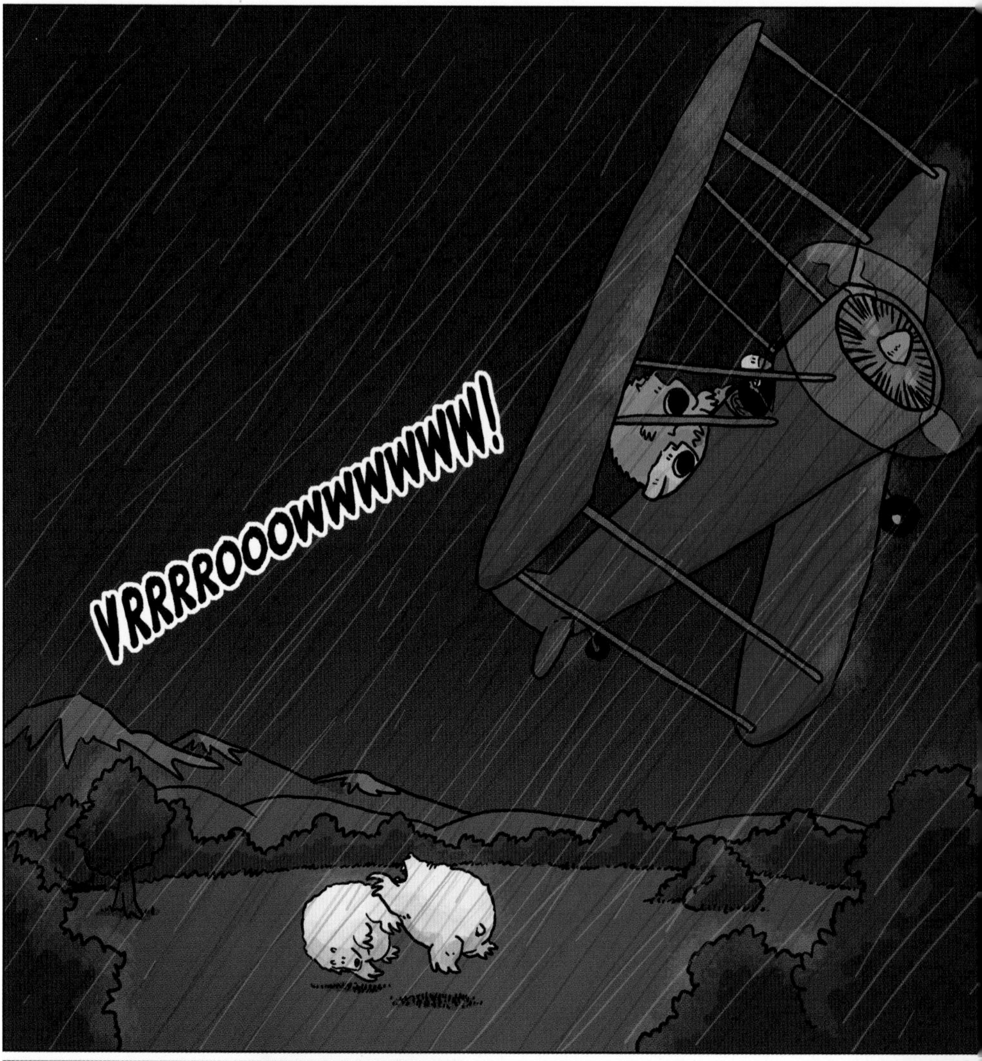
VRRRROOOWWWWWW!

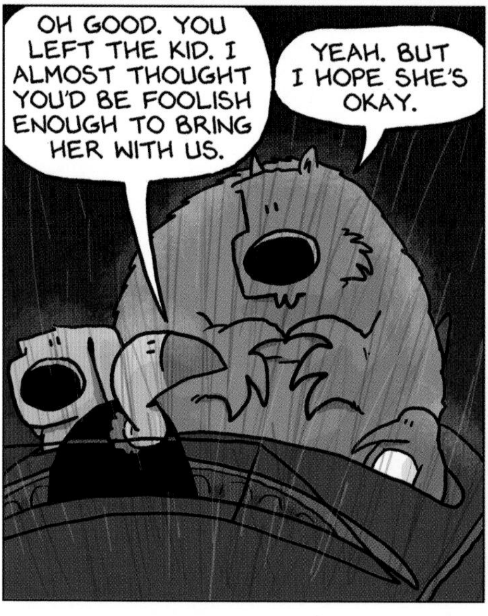
OH GOOD. YOU LEFT THE KID. I ALMOST THOUGHT YOU'D BE FOOLISH ENOUGH TO BRING HER WITH US.
YEAH. BUT I HOPE SHE'S OKAY.

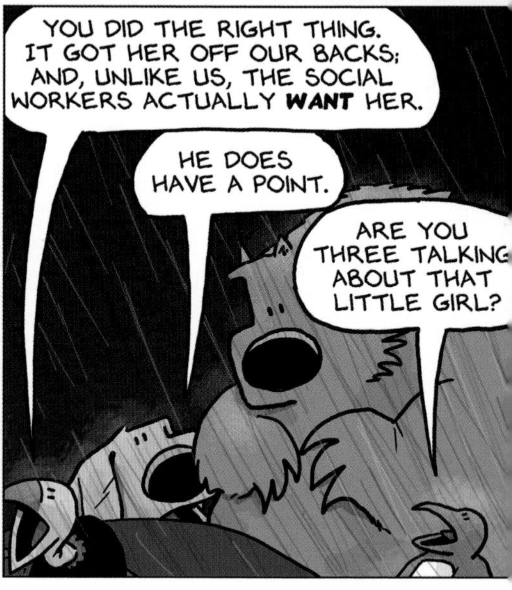
YOU DID THE RIGHT THING. IT GOT HER OFF OUR BACKS; AND, UNLIKE US, THE SOCIAL WORKERS ACTUALLY **WANT** HER.
HE DOES HAVE A POINT.
ARE YOU THREE TALKING ABOUT THAT LITTLE GIRL?

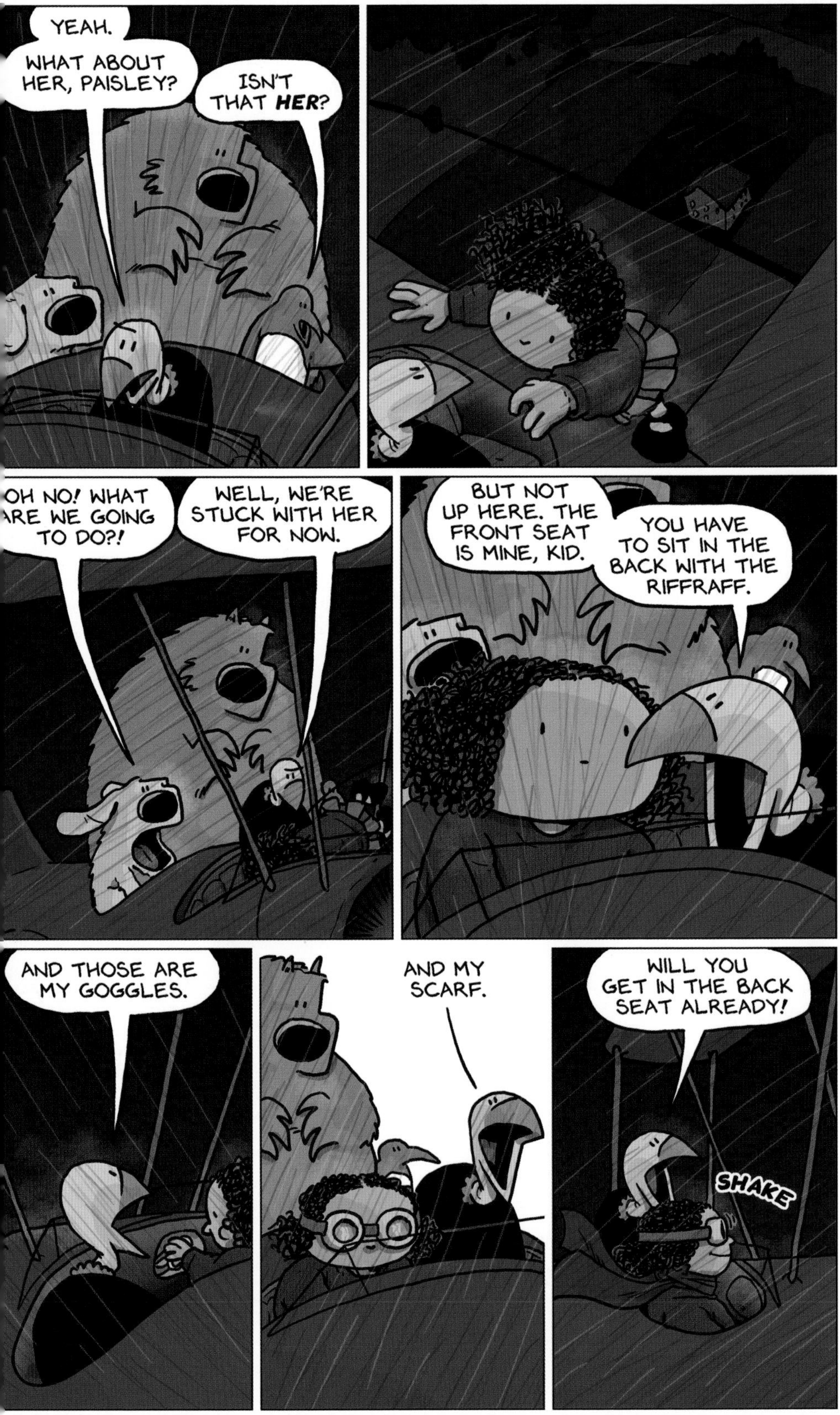
YEAH.
WHAT ABOUT HER, PAISLEY?
ISN'T THAT **HER**?
OH NO! WHAT ARE WE GOING TO DO?!
WELL, WE'RE STUCK WITH HER FOR NOW.
BUT NOT UP HERE. THE FRONT SEAT IS MINE, KID.
YOU HAVE TO SIT IN THE BACK WITH THE RIFFRAFF.
AND THOSE ARE MY GOGGLES.
AND MY SCARF.
WILL YOU GET IN THE BACK SEAT ALREADY!
SHAKE

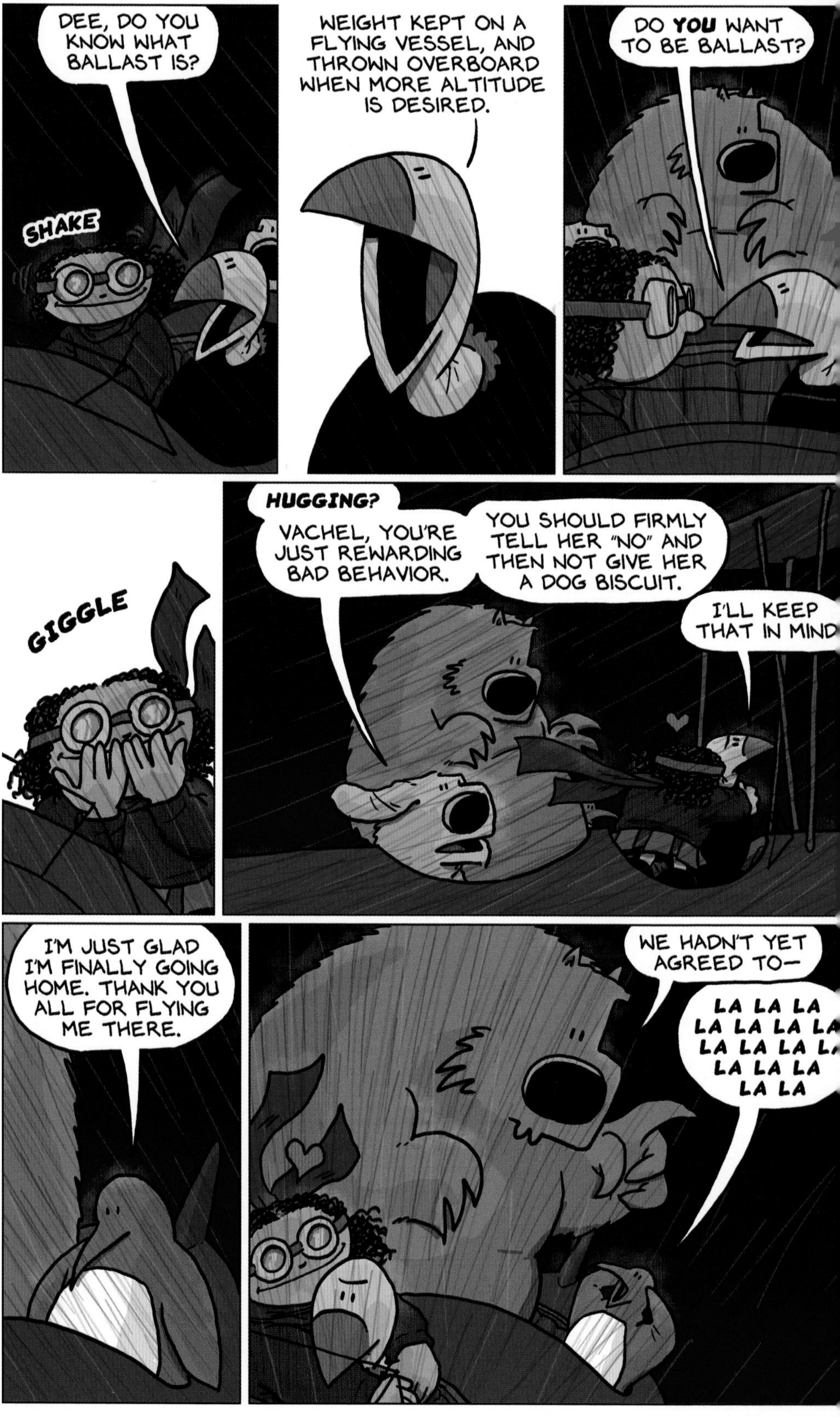
DEE, DO YOU KNOW WHAT BALLAST IS?
SHAKE
WEIGHT KEPT ON A FLYING VESSEL, AND THROWN OVERBOARD WHEN MORE ALTITUDE IS DESIRED.
DO **YOU** WANT TO BE BALLAST?
GIGGLE
HUGGING?
VACHEL, YOU'RE JUST REWARDING BAD BEHAVIOR.
YOU SHOULD FIRMLY TELL HER "NO" AND THEN NOT GIVE HER A DOG BISCUIT.
I'LL KEEP THAT IN MIND
I'M JUST GLAD I'M FINALLY GOING HOME. THANK YOU ALL FOR FLYING ME THERE.
WE HADN'T YET AGREED TO—
LA LA LA LA LA LA LA LA LA LA LA LA LA LA LA LA

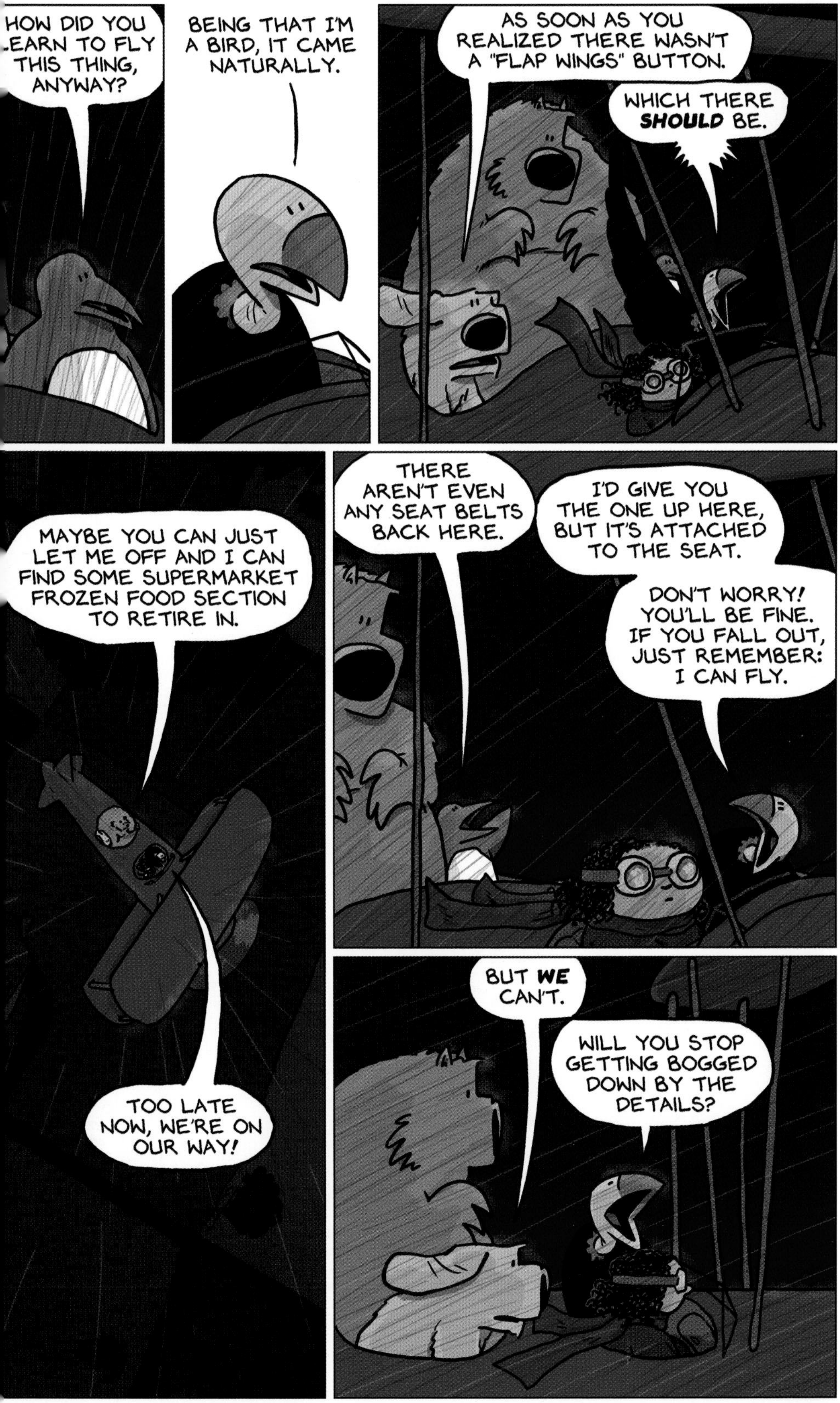
HOW DID YOU LEARN TO FLY THIS THING, ANYWAY?
BEING THAT I'M A BIRD, IT CAME NATURALLY.
AS SOON AS YOU REALIZED THERE WASN'T A "FLAP WINGS" BUTTON.
WHICH THERE **SHOULD** BE.
MAYBE YOU CAN JUST LET ME OFF AND I CAN FIND SOME SUPERMARKET FROZEN FOOD SECTION TO RETIRE IN.
TOO LATE NOW, WE'RE ON OUR WAY!
THERE AREN'T EVEN ANY SEAT BELTS BACK HERE.
I'D GIVE YOU THE ONE UP HERE, BUT IT'S ATTACHED TO THE SEAT.
DON'T WORRY! YOU'LL BE FINE. IF YOU FALL OUT, JUST REMEMBER: I CAN FLY.
BUT **WE** CAN'T.
WILL YOU STOP GETTING BOGGED DOWN BY THE DETAILS?

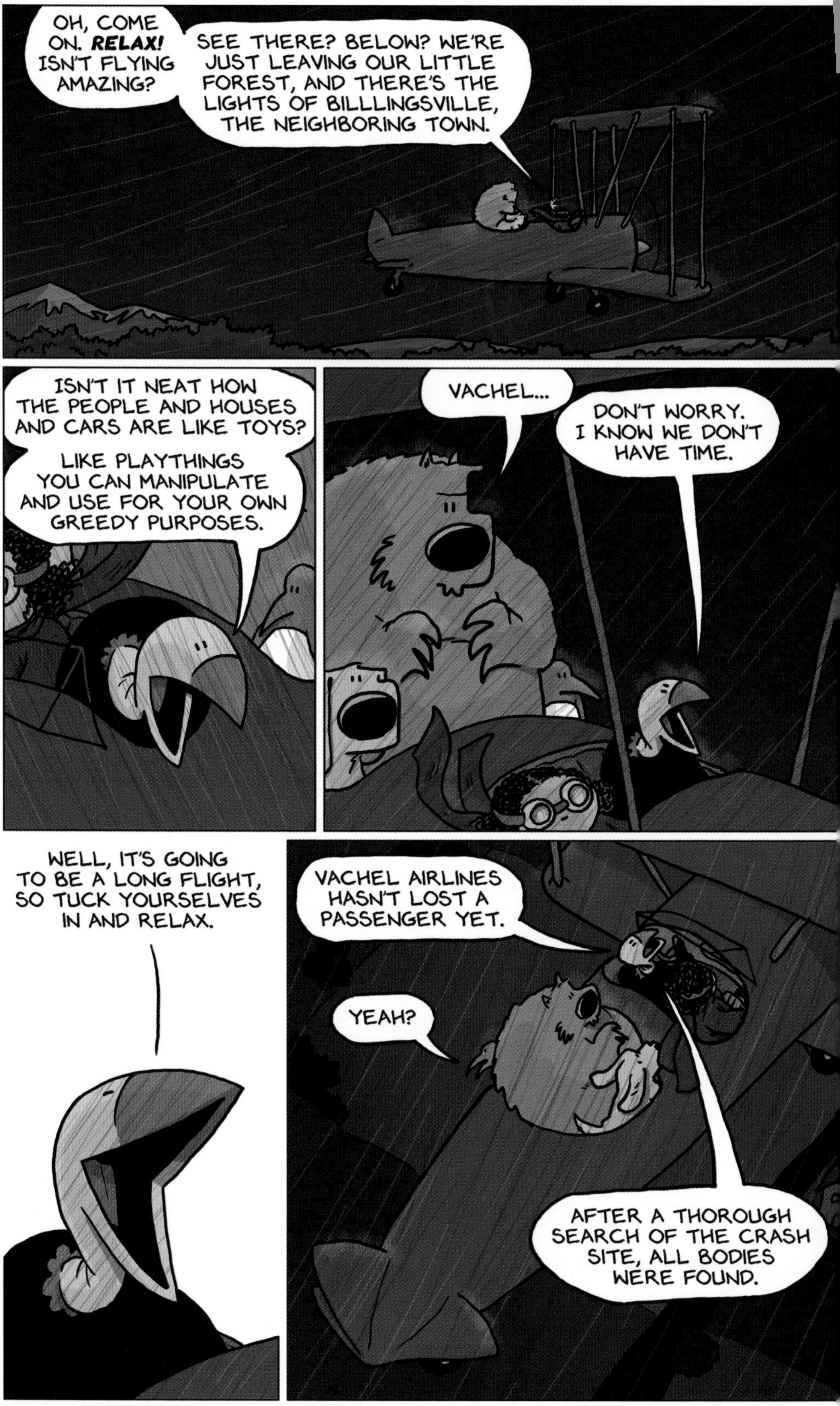

OH, COME ON. ***RELAX!*** ISN'T FLYING AMAZING?
SEE THERE? BELOW? WE'RE JUST LEAVING OUR LITTLE FOREST, AND THERE'S THE LIGHTS OF BILLLINGSVILLE, THE NEIGHBORING TOWN.
ISN'T IT NEAT HOW THE PEOPLE AND HOUSES AND CARS ARE LIKE TOYS?
LIKE PLAYTHINGS YOU CAN MANIPULATE AND USE FOR YOUR OWN GREEDY PURPOSES.
VACHEL...
DON'T WORRY. I KNOW WE DON'T HAVE TIME.
WELL, IT'S GOING TO BE A LONG FLIGHT, SO TUCK YOURSELVES IN AND RELAX.
VACHEL AIRLINES HASN'T LOST A PASSENGER YET.
YEAH?
AFTER A THOROUGH SEARCH OF THE CRASH SITE, ALL BODIES WERE FOUND.

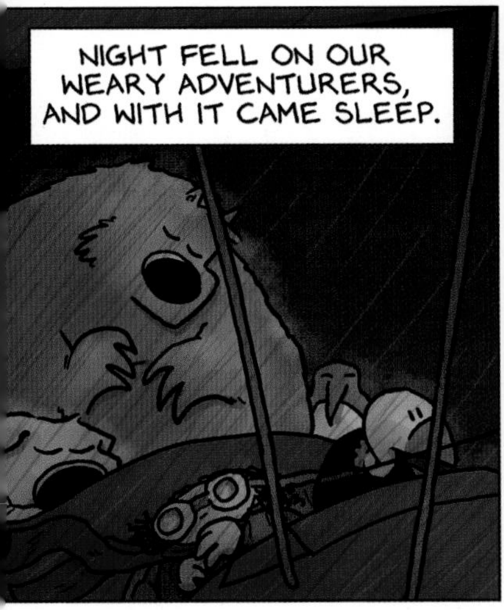
NIGHT FELL ON OUR WEARY ADVENTURERS, AND WITH IT CAME SLEEP.

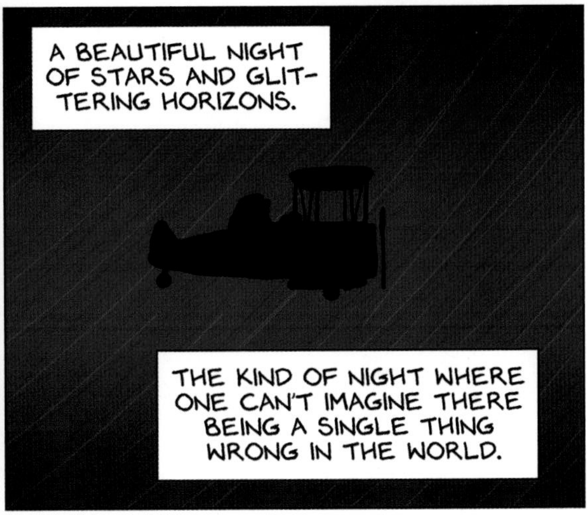
A BEAUTIFUL NIGHT OF STARS AND GLIT-TERING HORIZONS.
THE KIND OF NIGHT WHERE ONE CAN'T IMAGINE THERE BEING A SINGLE THING WRONG IN THE WORLD.

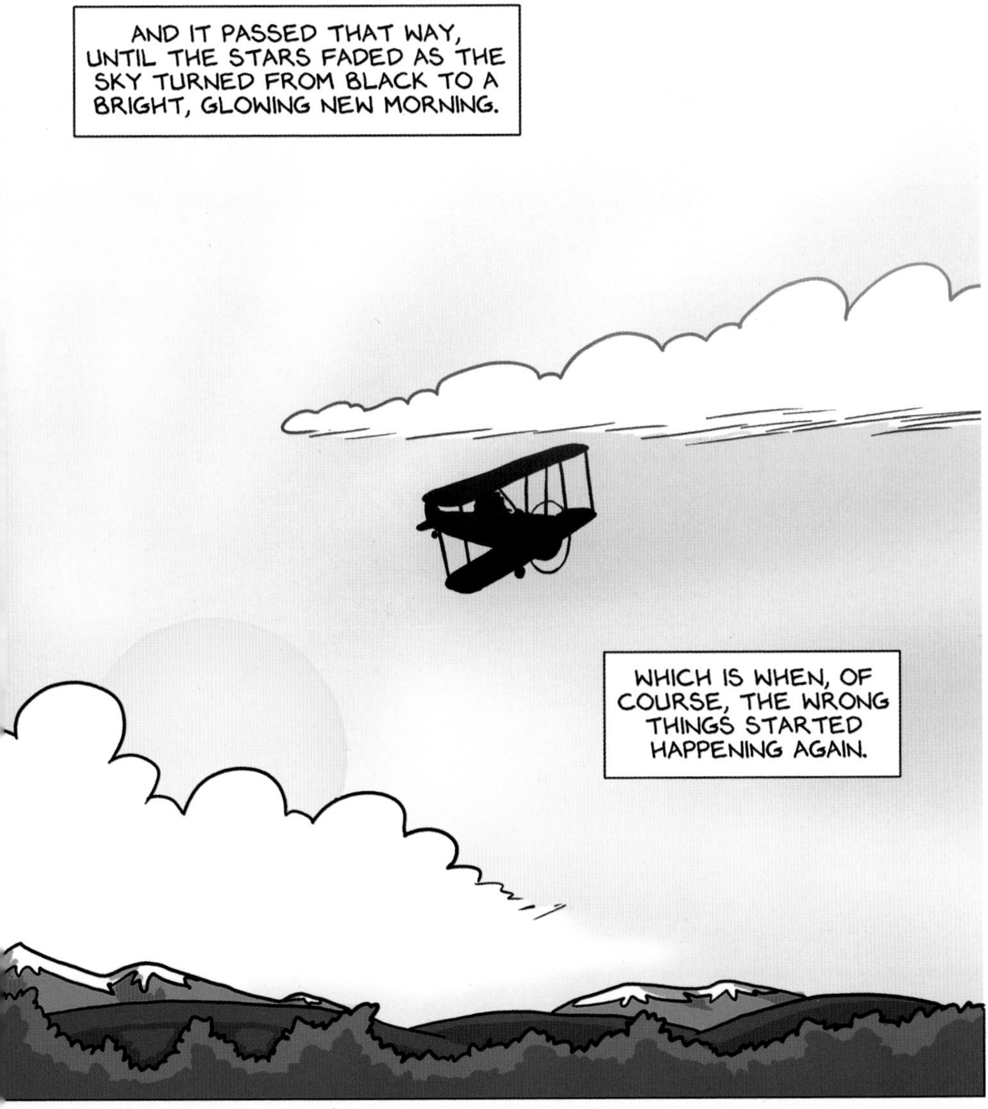
AND IT PASSED THAT WAY, UNTIL THE STARS FADED AS THE SKY TURNED FROM BLACK TO A BRIGHT, GLOWING NEW MORNING.
WHICH IS WHEN, OF COURSE, THE WRONG THINGS STARTED HAPPENING AGAIN.

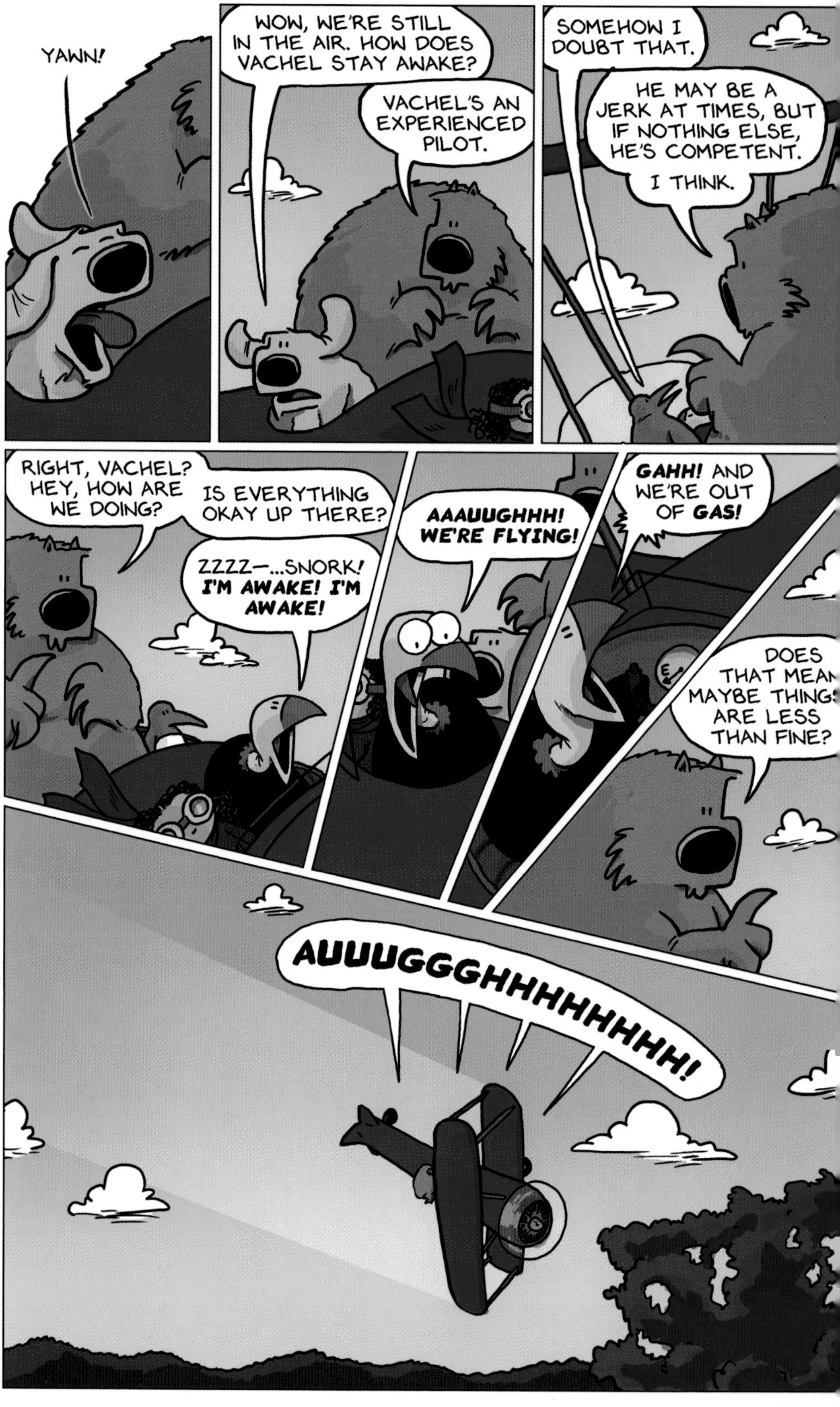
YAWN!
WOW, WE'RE STILL IN THE AIR. HOW DOES VACHEL STAY AWAKE?
VACHEL'S AN EXPERIENCED PILOT.
SOMEHOW I DOUBT THAT.
HE MAY BE A JERK AT TIMES, BUT IF NOTHING ELSE, HE'S COMPETENT.
I THINK.
RIGHT, VACHEL? HEY, HOW ARE WE DOING?
IS EVERYTHING OKAY UP THERE?
ZZZZ—...SNORK! I'M AWAKE! I'M AWAKE!
AAAUUGHHH! WE'RE FLYING!
GAHH! AND WE'RE OUT OF GAS!
DOES THAT MEAN MAYBE THINGS ARE LESS THAN FINE?
AUUUGGGHHHHHHHH!

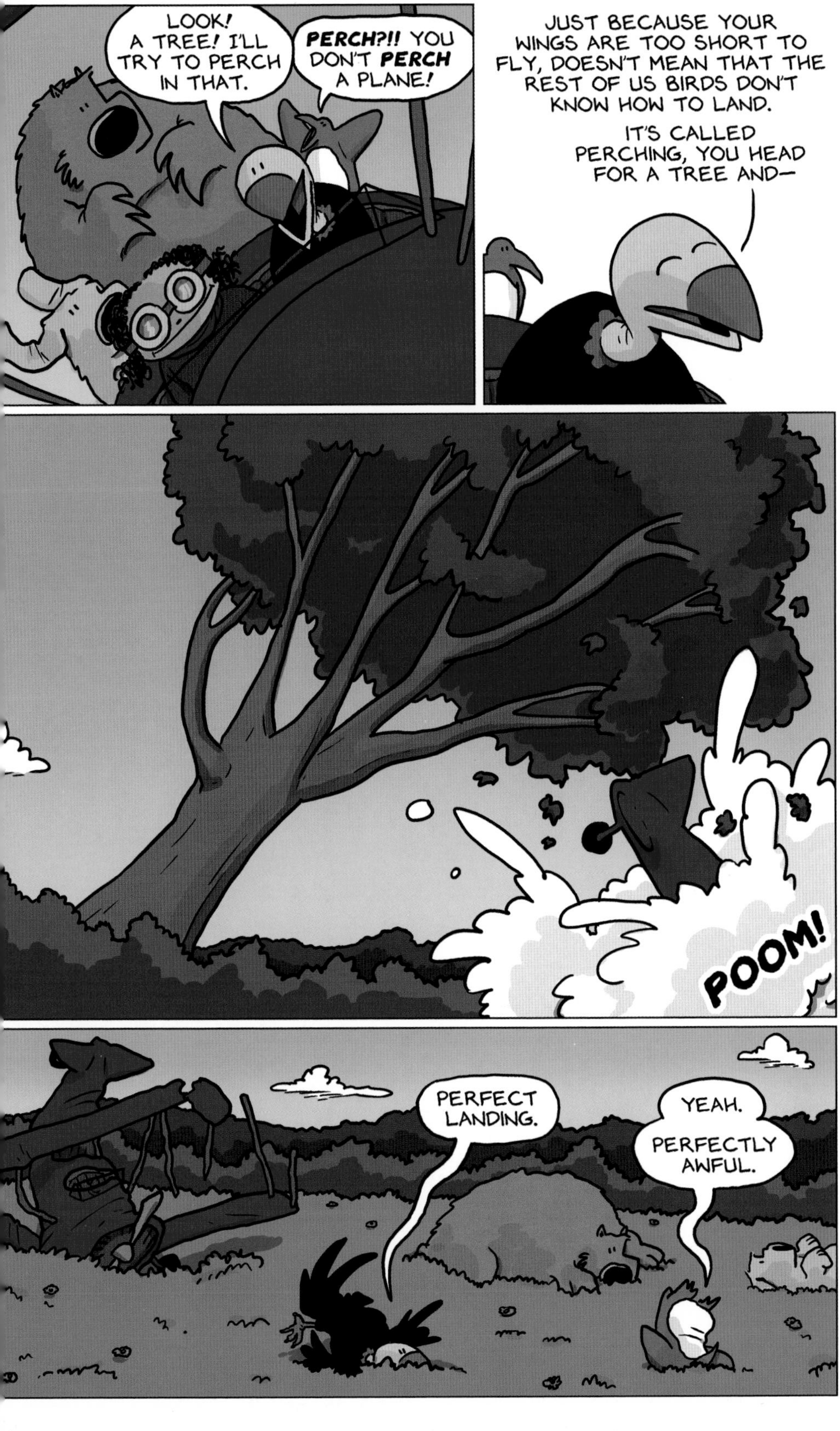

LOOK! A TREE! I'LL TRY TO PERCH IN THAT.
PERCH?!! YOU DON'T PERCH A PLANE!
JUST BECAUSE YOUR WINGS ARE TOO SHORT TO FLY, DOESN'T MEAN THAT THE REST OF US BIRDS DON'T KNOW HOW TO LAND.
IT'S CALLED PERCHING, YOU HEAD FOR A TREE AND—
POOM!
PERFECT LANDING.
YEAH. PERFECTLY AWFUL.

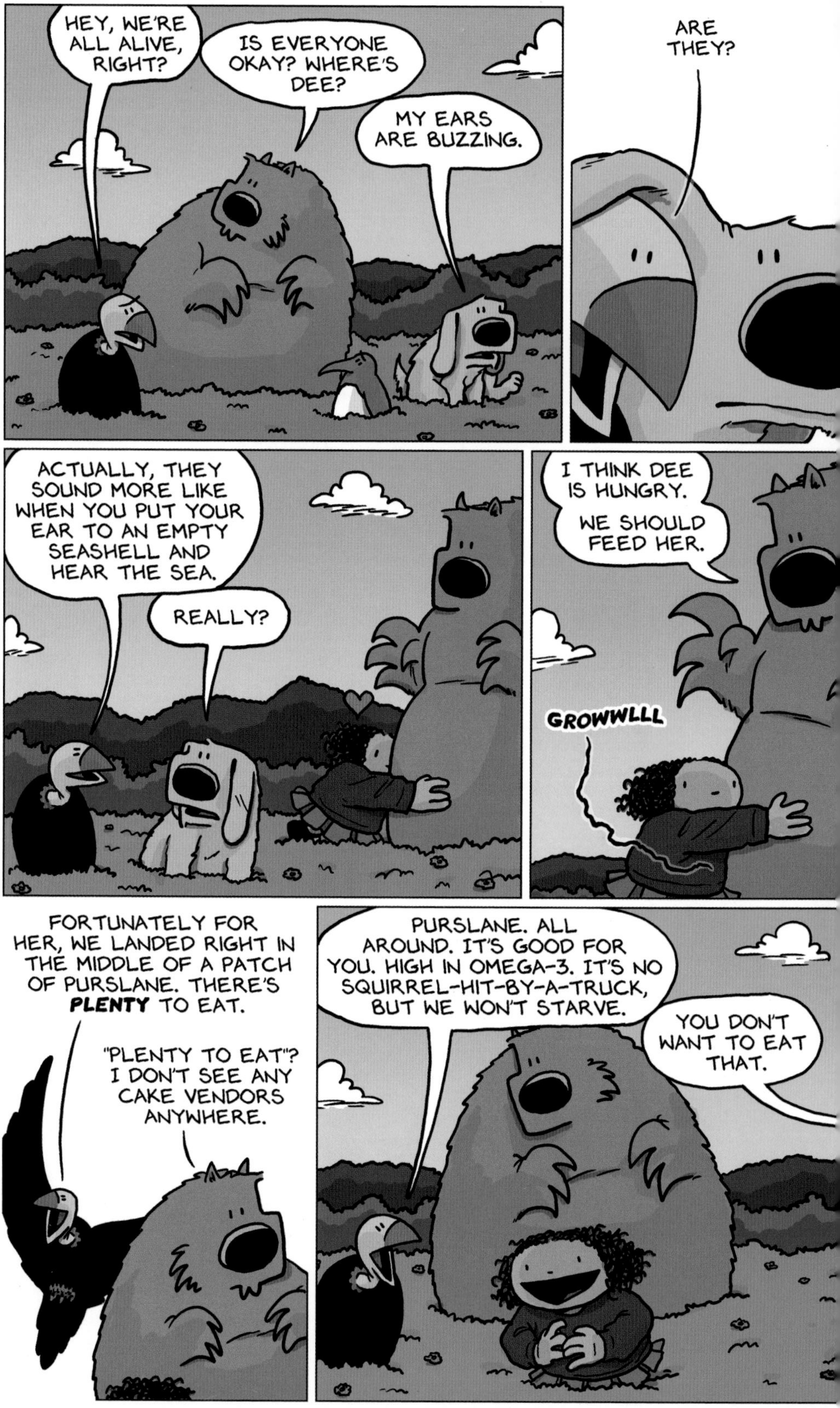
HEY, WE'RE ALL ALIVE, RIGHT?
IS EVERYONE OKAY? WHERE'S DEE?
MY EARS ARE BUZZING.
ARE THEY?
ACTUALLY, THEY SOUND MORE LIKE WHEN YOU PUT YOUR EAR TO AN EMPTY SEASHELL AND HEAR THE SEA.
REALLY?
I THINK DEE IS HUNGRY.
WE SHOULD FEED HER.
GROWWLLL
FORTUNATELY FOR HER, WE LANDED RIGHT IN THE MIDDLE OF A PATCH OF PURSLANE. THERE'S **PLENTY** TO EAT.
"PLENTY TO EAT"? I DON'T SEE ANY CAKE VENDORS ANYWHERE.
PURSLANE. ALL AROUND. IT'S GOOD FOR YOU. HIGH IN OMEGA-3. IT'S NO SQUIRREL-HIT-BY-A-TRUCK, BUT WE WON'T STARVE.
YOU DON'T WANT TO EAT THAT.

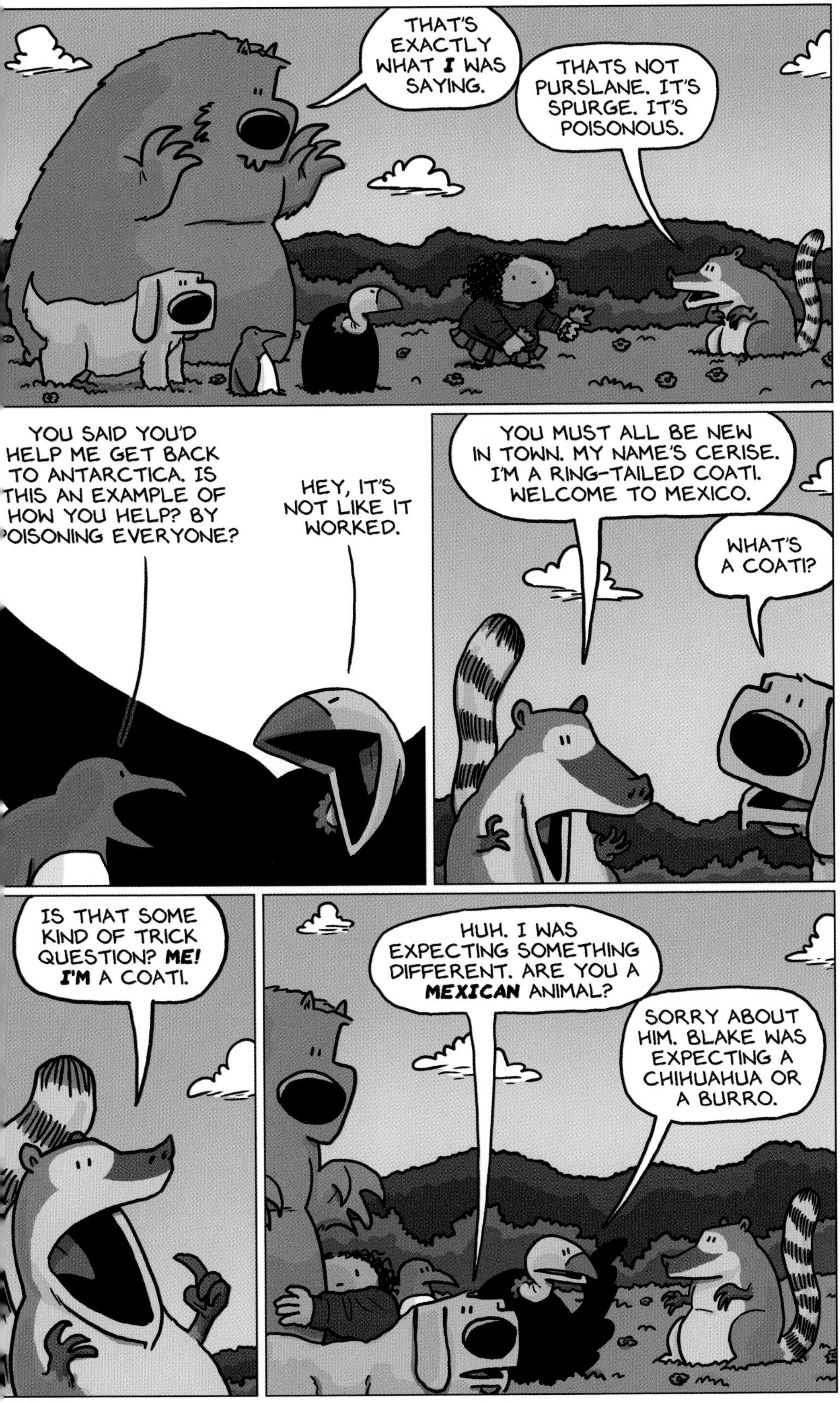
THAT'S EXACTLY WHAT I WAS SAYING.
THATS NOT PURSLANE. IT'S SPURGE. IT'S POISONOUS.
YOU SAID YOU'D HELP ME GET BACK TO ANTARCTICA. IS THIS AN EXAMPLE OF HOW YOU HELP? BY POISONING EVERYONE?
HEY, IT'S NOT LIKE IT WORKED.
YOU MUST ALL BE NEW IN TOWN. MY NAME'S CERISE. I'M A RING-TAILED COATI. WELCOME TO MEXICO.
WHAT'S A COATI?
IS THAT SOME KIND OF TRICK QUESTION? ME! I'M A COATI.
HUH. I WAS EXPECTING SOMETHING DIFFERENT. ARE YOU A MEXICAN ANIMAL?
SORRY ABOUT HIM. BLAKE WAS EXPECTING A CHIHUAHUA OR A BURRO.

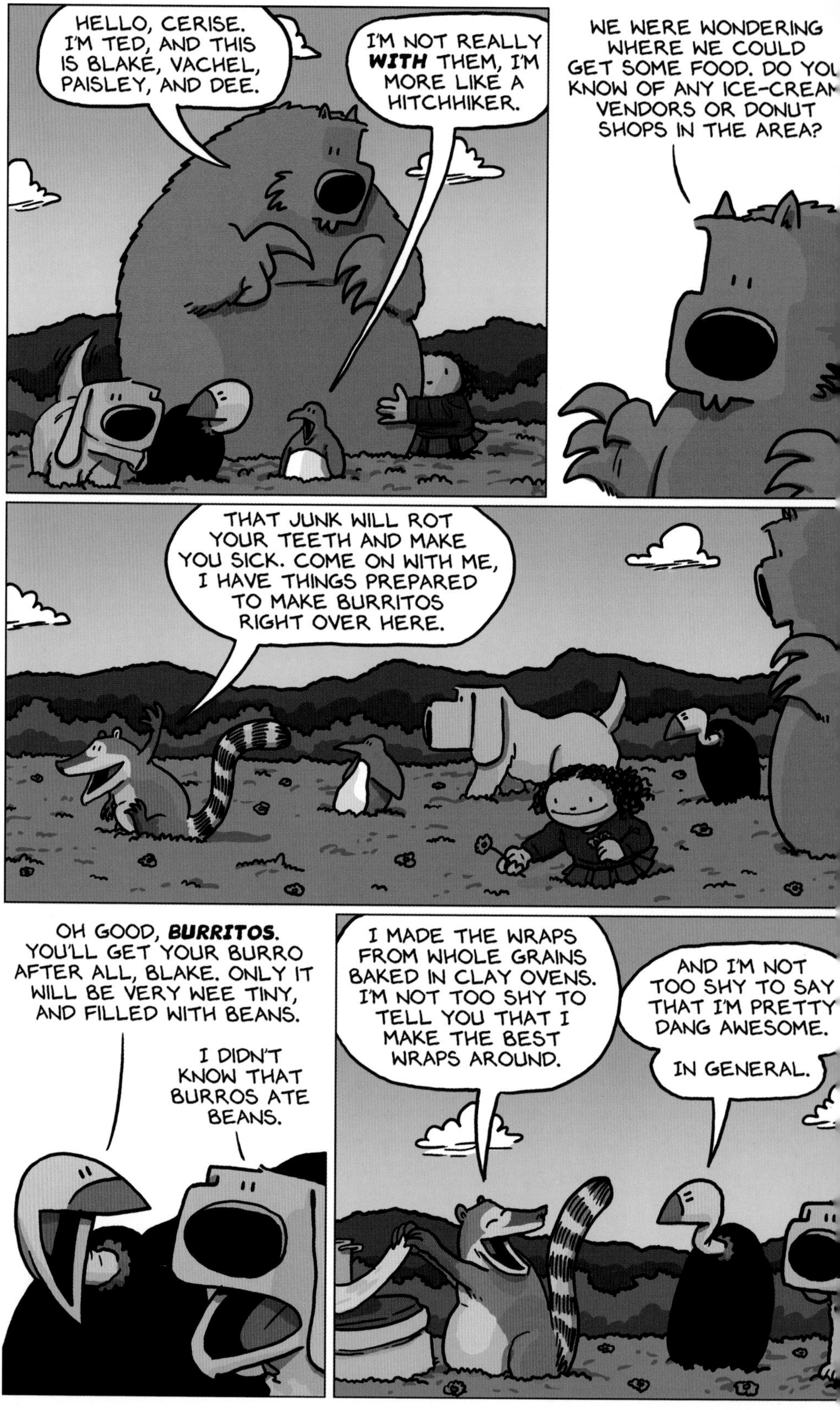
HELLO, CERISE. I'M TED, AND THIS IS BLAKE, VACHEL, PAISLEY, AND DEE.
I'M NOT REALLY **WITH** THEM, I'M MORE LIKE A HITCHHIKER.
WE WERE WONDERING WHERE WE COULD GET SOME FOOD. DO YOU KNOW OF ANY ICE-CREAM VENDORS OR DONUT SHOPS IN THE AREA?
THAT JUNK WILL ROT YOUR TEETH AND MAKE YOU SICK. COME ON WITH ME, I HAVE THINGS PREPARED TO MAKE BURRITOS RIGHT OVER HERE.
OH GOOD, **BURRITOS**. YOU'LL GET YOUR BURRO AFTER ALL, BLAKE. ONLY IT WILL BE VERY WEE TINY, AND FILLED WITH BEANS.
I DIDN'T KNOW THAT BURROS ATE BEANS.
I MADE THE WRAPS FROM WHOLE GRAINS BAKED IN CLAY OVENS. I'M NOT TOO SHY TO TELL YOU THAT I MAKE THE BEST WRAPS AROUND.
AND I'M NOT TOO SHY TO SAY THAT I'M PRETTY DANG AWESOME.
IN GENERAL.

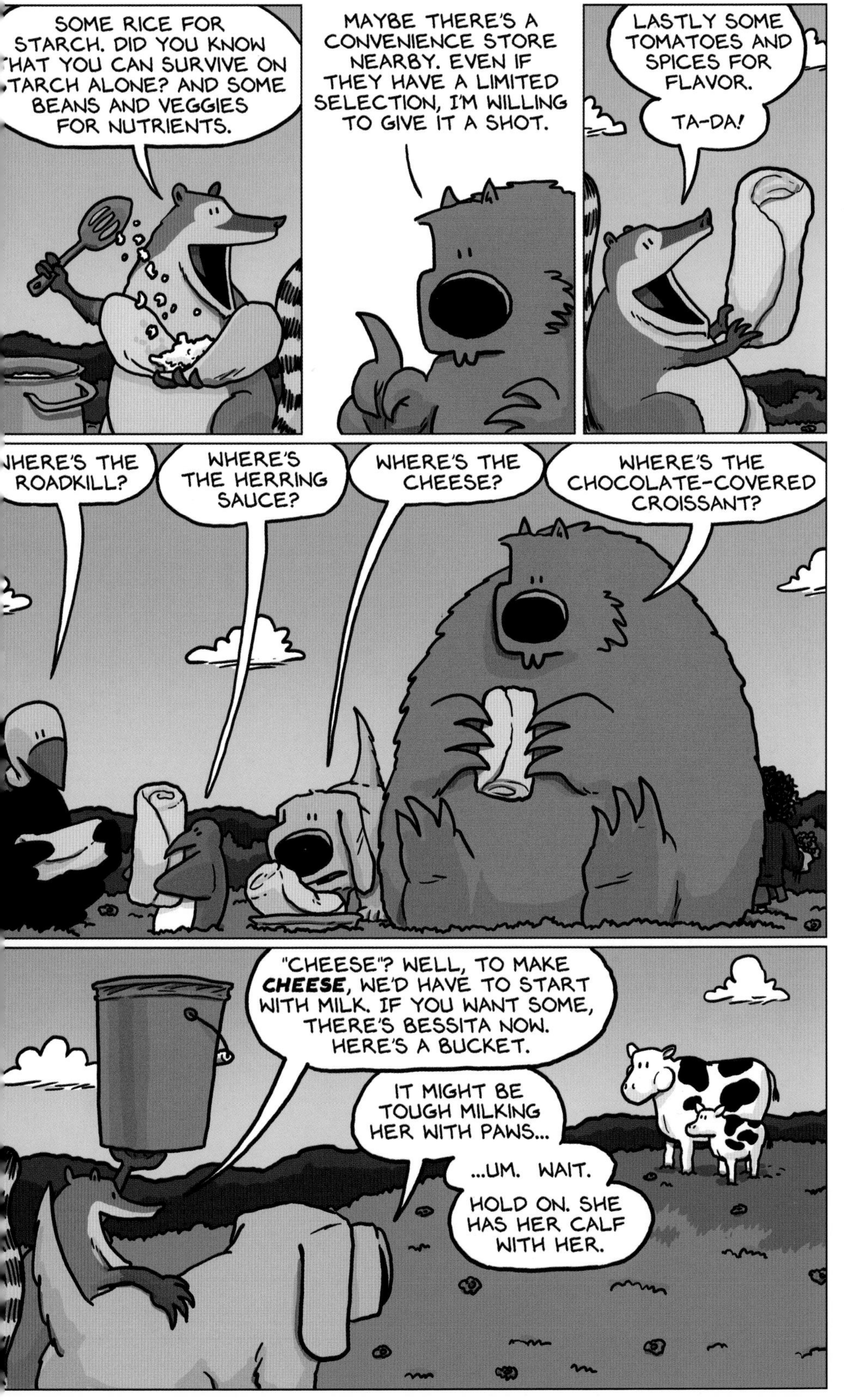

SOME RICE FOR STARCH. DID YOU KNOW THAT YOU CAN SURVIVE ON STARCH ALONE? AND SOME BEANS AND VEGGIES FOR NUTRIENTS.
MAYBE THERE'S A CONVENIENCE STORE NEARBY. EVEN IF THEY HAVE A LIMITED SELECTION, I'M WILLING TO GIVE IT A SHOT.
LASTLY SOME TOMATOES AND SPICES FOR FLAVOR.
TA-DA!
WHERE'S THE ROADKILL?
WHERE'S THE HERRING SAUCE?
WHERE'S THE CHEESE?
WHERE'S THE CHOCOLATE-COVERED CROISSANT?
"CHEESE"? WELL, TO MAKE **CHEESE**, WE'D HAVE TO START WITH MILK. IF YOU WANT SOME, THERE'S BESSITA NOW. HERE'S A BUCKET.
IT MIGHT BE TOUGH MILKING HER WITH PAWS...
...UM. WAIT.
HOLD ON. SHE HAS HER CALF WITH HER.

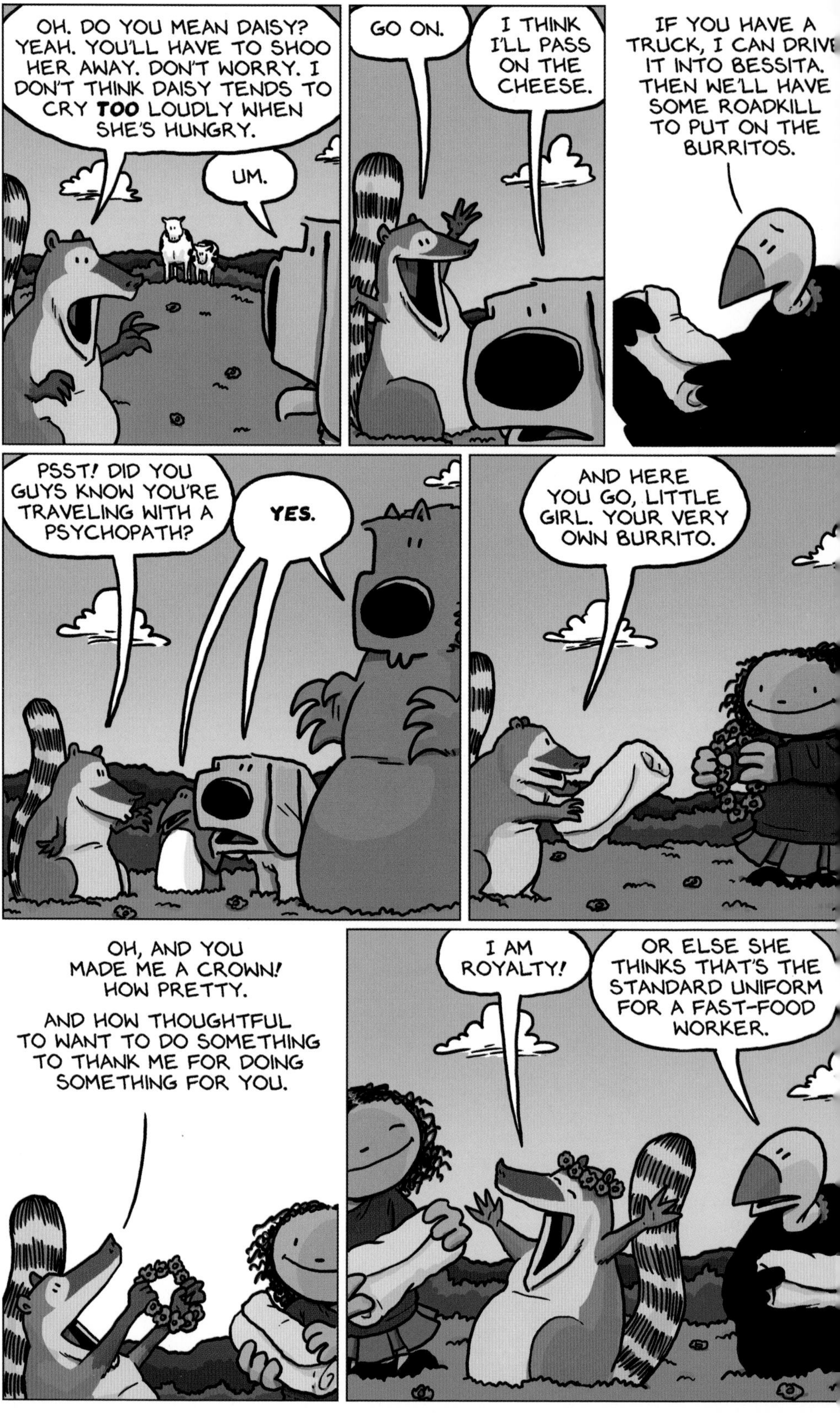
OH. DO YOU MEAN DAISY? YEAH. YOU'LL HAVE TO SHOO HER AWAY. DON'T WORRY. I DON'T THINK DAISY TENDS TO CRY **TOO** LOUDLY WHEN SHE'S HUNGRY.
UM.
GO ON.
I THINK I'LL PASS ON THE CHEESE.
IF YOU HAVE A TRUCK, I CAN DRIVE IT INTO BESSITA. THEN WE'LL HAVE SOME ROADKILL TO PUT ON THE BURRITOS.
PSST! DID YOU GUYS KNOW YOU'RE TRAVELING WITH A PSYCHOPATH?
YES.
AND HERE YOU GO, LITTLE GIRL. YOUR VERY OWN BURRITO.
OH, AND YOU MADE ME A CROWN! HOW PRETTY.
AND HOW THOUGHTFUL TO WANT TO DO SOMETHING TO THANK ME FOR DOING SOMETHING FOR YOU.
I AM ROYALTY!
OR ELSE SHE THINKS THAT'S THE STANDARD UNIFORM FOR A FAST-FOOD WORKER.

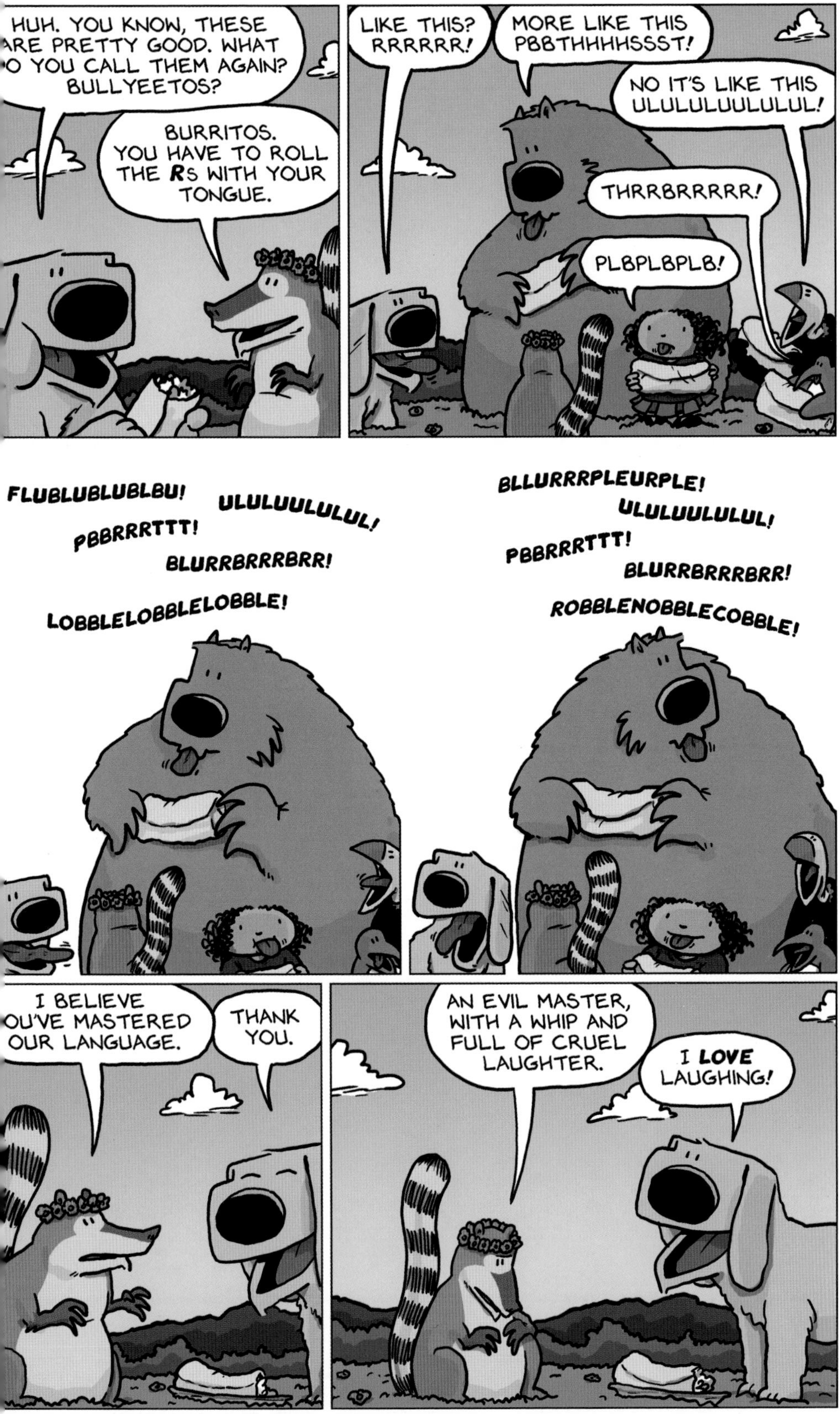
HUH. YOU KNOW, THESE ARE PRETTY GOOD. WHAT DO YOU CALL THEM AGAIN? BULLYEETOS?
BURRITOS. YOU HAVE TO ROLL THE RS WITH YOUR TONGUE.
LIKE THIS? RRRRRR!
MORE LIKE THIS PBBTHHHHSSST!
NO IT'S LIKE THIS ULULULUULULUL!
THRRBRRRRR!
PLBPLBPLB!
FLUBLUBLUBLBU!
ULULUULULUL!
PBBRRRTTT!
BLURRBRRRBRR!
LOBBLELOBBLELOBBLE!
BLLURRRPLEURPLE!
ULULUULULUL!
PBBRRRTTT!
BLURRBRRRBRR!
ROBBLENOBBLECOBBLE!
I BELIEVE YOU'VE MASTERED OUR LANGUAGE.
THANK YOU.
AN EVIL MASTER, WITH A WHIP AND FULL OF CRUEL LAUGHTER.
I LOVE LAUGHING!

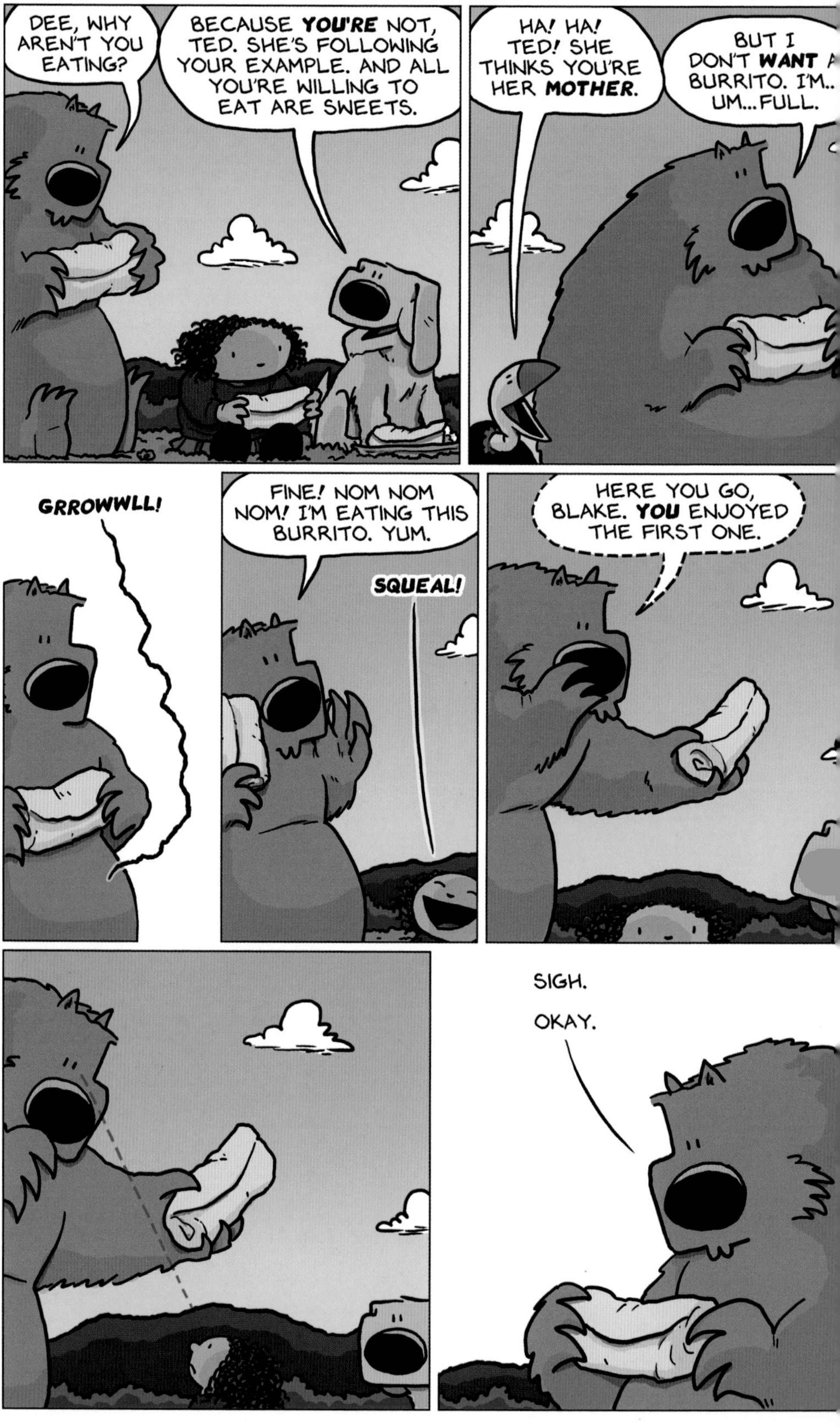
DEE, WHY AREN'T YOU EATING?
BECAUSE **YOU'RE** NOT, TED. SHE'S FOLLOWING YOUR EXAMPLE. AND ALL YOU'RE WILLING TO EAT ARE SWEETS.
HA! HA! TED! SHE THINKS YOU'RE HER **MOTHER**.
BUT I DON'T **WANT** A BURRITO. I'M.. UM...FULL.
GRROWWLL!
FINE! NOM NOM NOM! I'M EATING THIS BURRITO. YUM.
SQUEAL!
HERE YOU GO, BLAKE. **YOU** ENJOYED THE FIRST ONE.
SIGH.
OKAY.

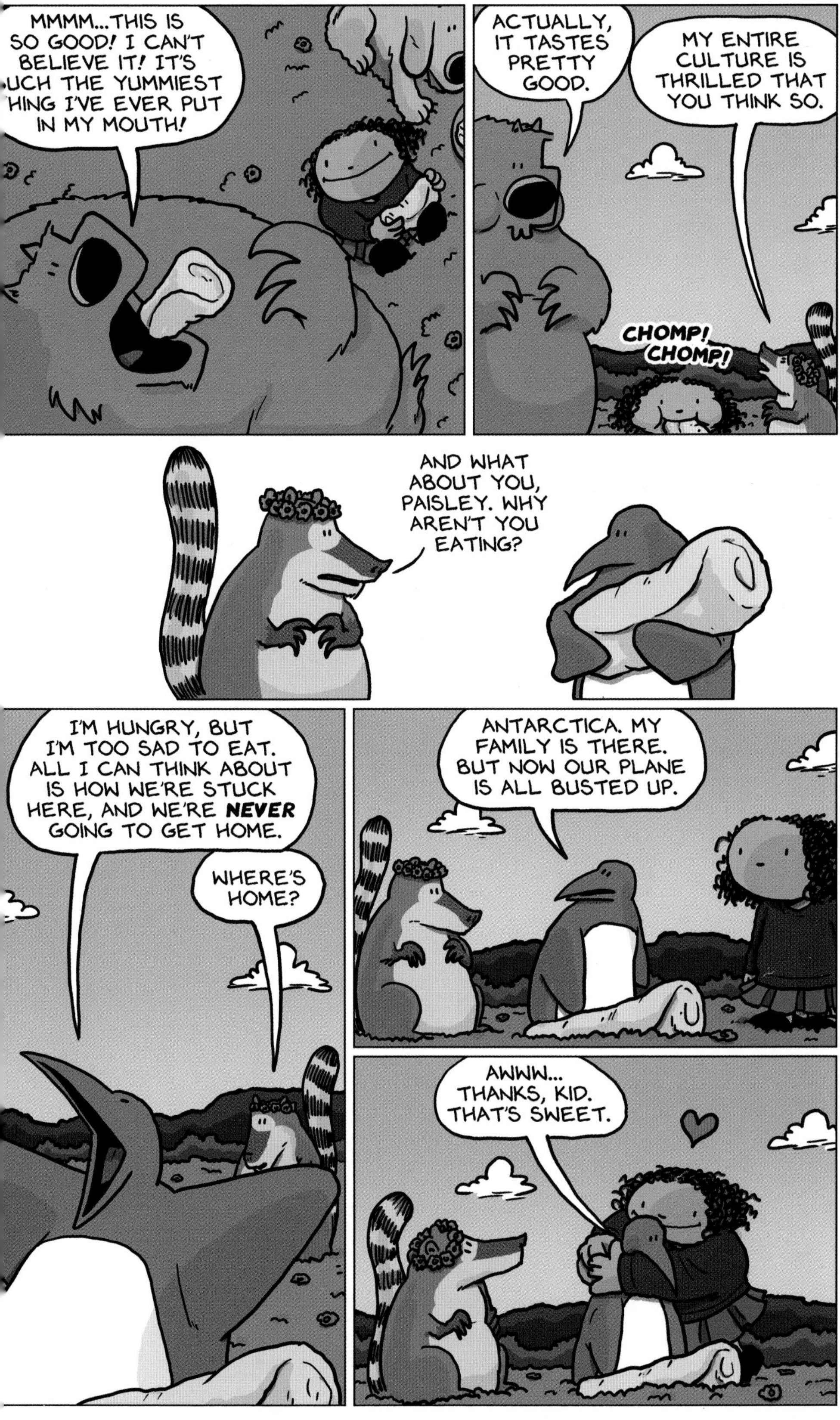

MMMM...THIS IS SO GOOD! I CAN'T BELIEVE IT! IT'S UCH THE YUMMIEST HING I'VE EVER PUT IN MY MOUTH!
ACTUALLY, IT TASTES PRETTY GOOD.
MY ENTIRE CULTURE IS THRILLED THAT YOU THINK SO.
CHOMP! CHOMP!
AND WHAT ABOUT YOU, PAISLEY. WHY AREN'T YOU EATING?
I'M HUNGRY, BUT I'M TOO SAD TO EAT. ALL I CAN THINK ABOUT IS HOW WE'RE STUCK HERE, AND WE'RE **NEVER** GOING TO GET HOME.
WHERE'S HOME?
ANTARCTICA. MY FAMILY IS THERE. BUT NOW OUR PLANE IS ALL BUSTED UP.
AWWW... THANKS, KID. THAT'S SWEET.

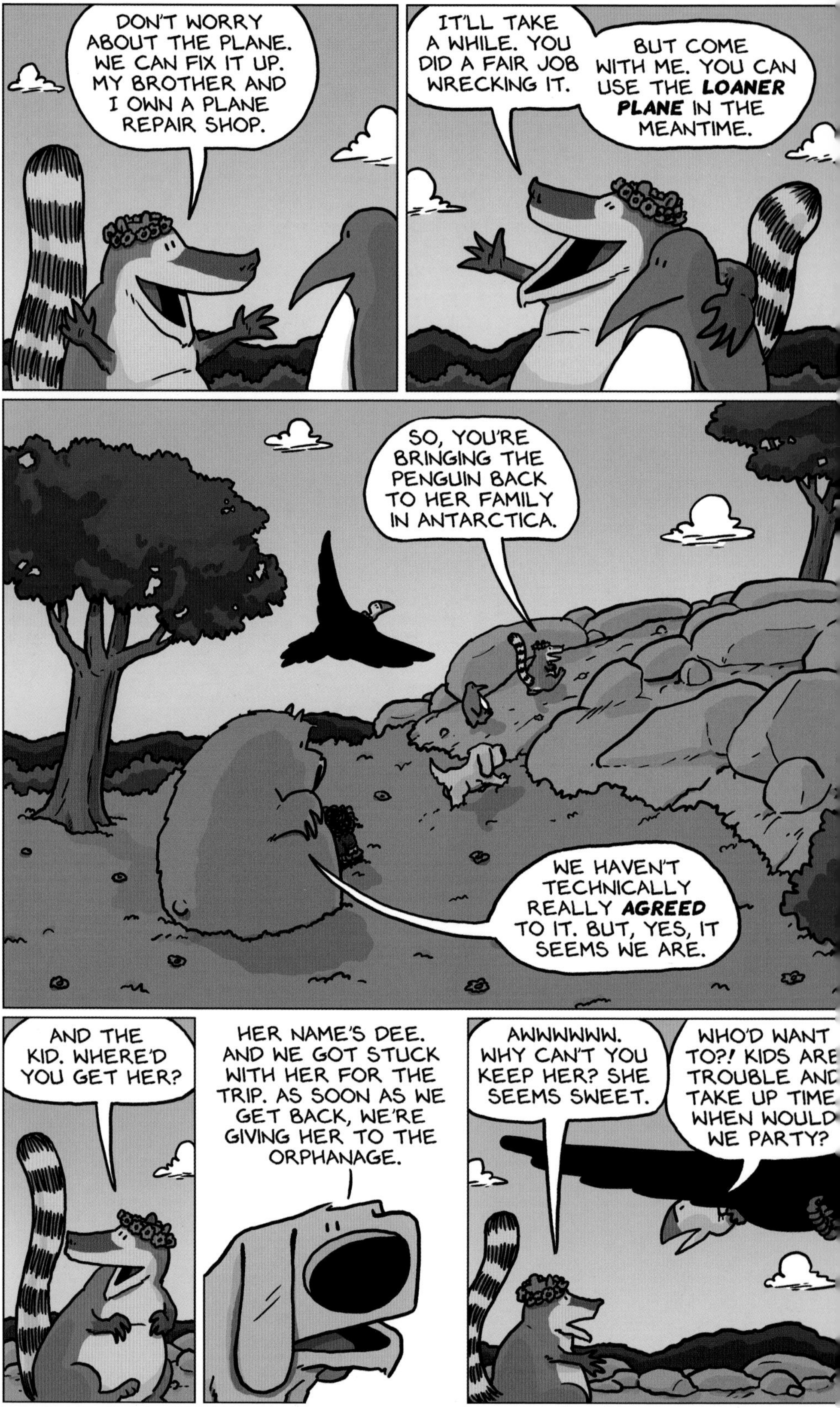
DON'T WORRY ABOUT THE PLANE. WE CAN FIX IT UP. MY BROTHER AND I OWN A PLANE REPAIR SHOP.
IT'LL TAKE A WHILE. YOU DID A FAIR JOB WRECKING IT.
BUT COME WITH ME. YOU CAN USE THE **LOANER PLANE** IN THE MEANTIME.
SO, YOU'RE BRINGING THE PENGUIN BACK TO HER FAMILY IN ANTARCTICA.
WE HAVEN'T TECHNICALLY REALLY **AGREED** TO IT. BUT, YES, IT SEEMS WE ARE.
AND THE KID. WHERE'D YOU GET HER?
HER NAME'S DEE. AND WE GOT STUCK WITH HER FOR THE TRIP. AS SOON AS WE GET BACK, WE'RE GIVING HER TO THE ORPHANAGE.
AWWWWWW. WHY CAN'T YOU KEEP HER? SHE SEEMS SWEET.
WHO'D WANT TO?! KIDS ARE TROUBLE AND TAKE UP TIME. WHEN WOULD WE PARTY?

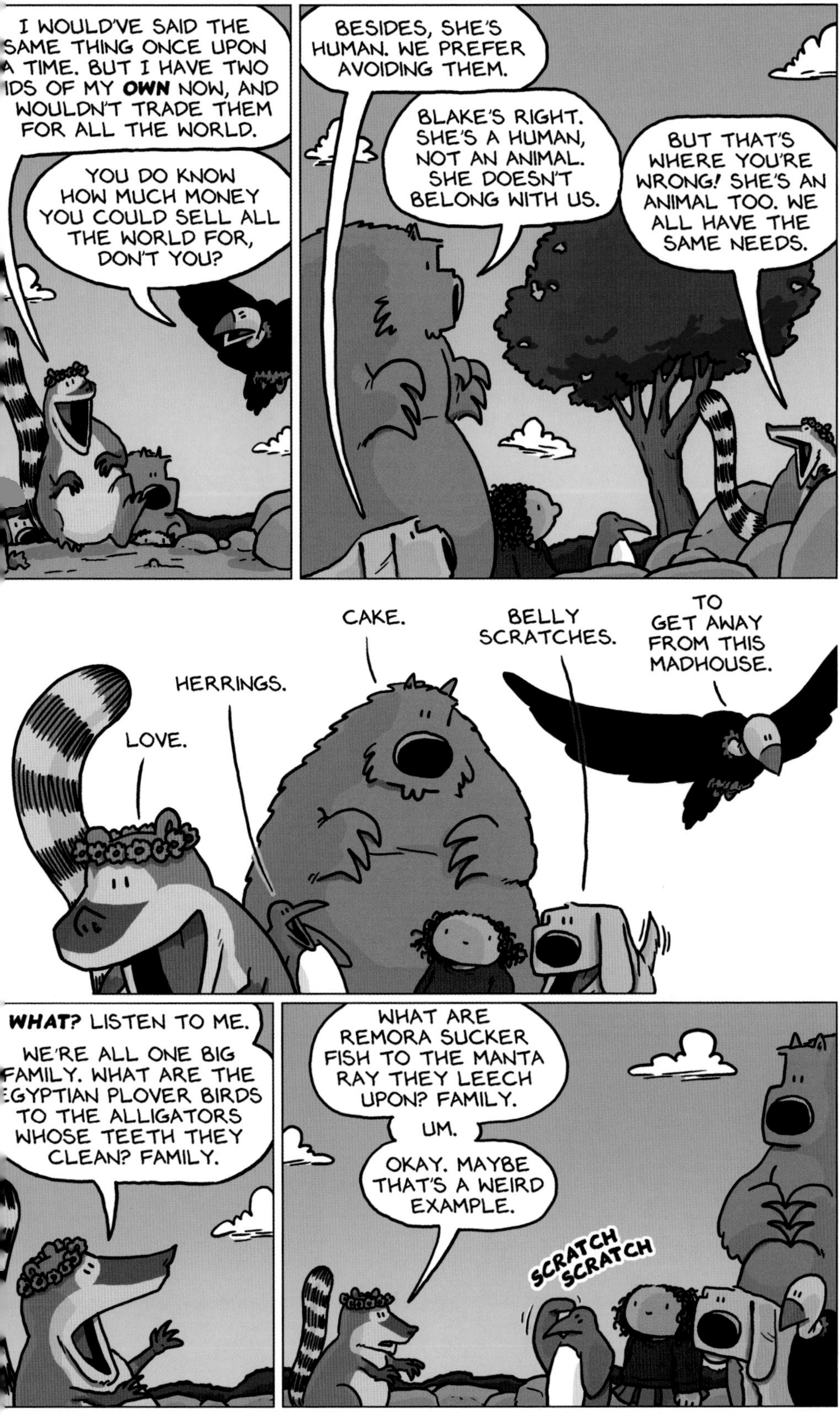

I WOULD'VE SAID THE SAME THING ONCE UPON A TIME. BUT I HAVE TWO IDS OF MY **OWN** NOW, AND WOULDN'T TRADE THEM FOR ALL THE WORLD.
YOU DO KNOW HOW MUCH MONEY YOU COULD SELL ALL THE WORLD FOR, DON'T YOU?
BESIDES, SHE'S HUMAN. WE PREFER AVOIDING THEM.
BLAKE'S RIGHT. SHE'S A HUMAN, NOT AN ANIMAL. SHE DOESN'T BELONG WITH US.
BUT THAT'S WHERE YOU'RE WRONG! SHE'S AN ANIMAL TOO. WE ALL HAVE THE SAME NEEDS.
LOVE.
HERRINGS.
CAKE.
BELLY SCRATCHES.
TO GET AWAY FROM THIS MADHOUSE.
WHAT? LISTEN TO ME.
WE'RE ALL ONE BIG FAMILY. WHAT ARE THE EGYPTIAN PLOVER BIRDS TO THE ALLIGATORS WHOSE TEETH THEY CLEAN? FAMILY.
WHAT ARE REMORA SUCKER FISH TO THE MANTA RAY THEY LEECH UPON? FAMILY.
UM.
OKAY. MAYBE THAT'S A WEIRD EXAMPLE.
SCRATCH SCRATCH

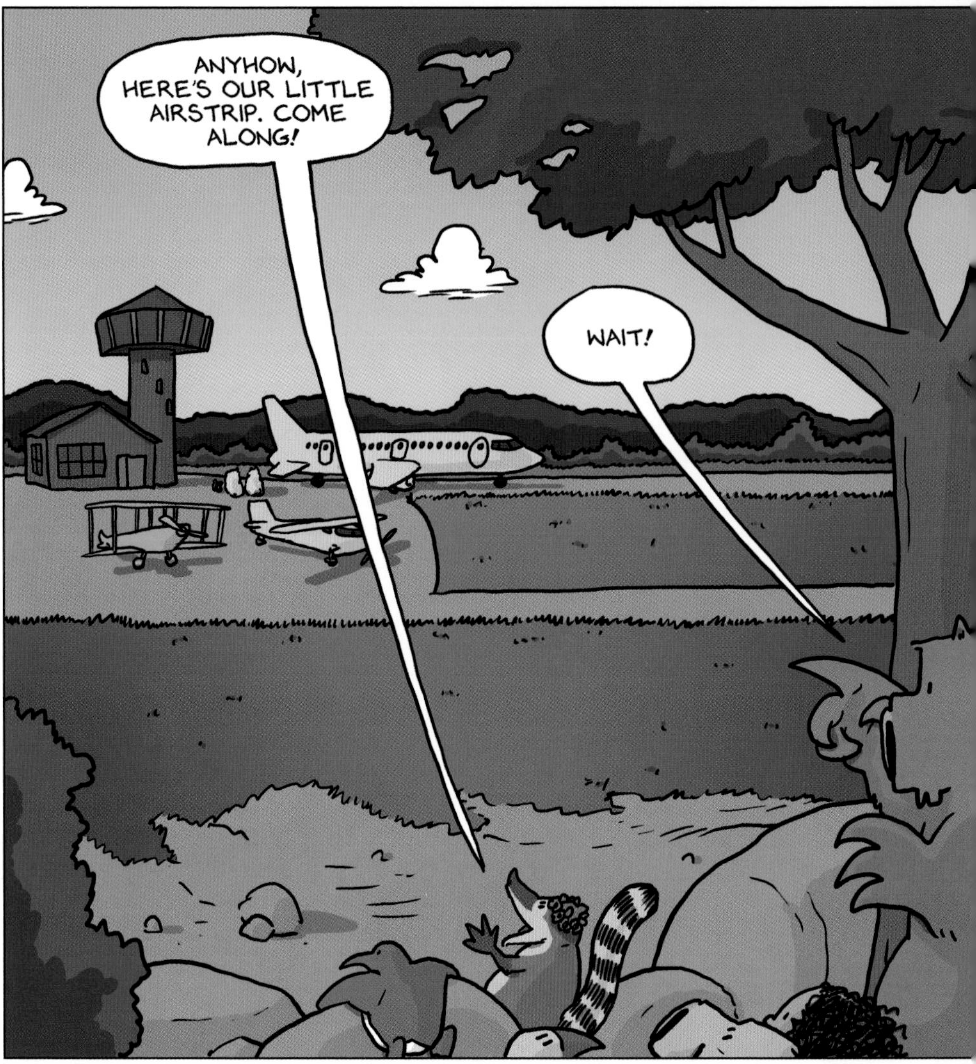
ANYHOW, HERE'S OUR LITTLE AIRSTRIP. COME ALONG!
WAIT!

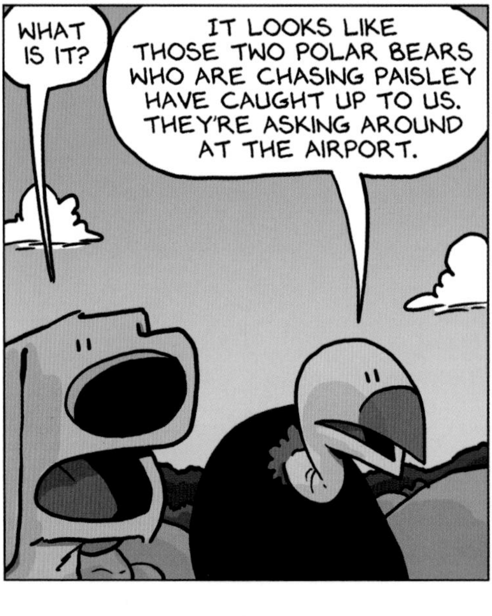
WHAT IS IT?
IT LOOKS LIKE THOSE TWO POLAR BEARS WHO ARE CHASING PAISLEY HAVE CAUGHT UP TO US. THEY'RE ASKING AROUND AT THE AIRPORT.

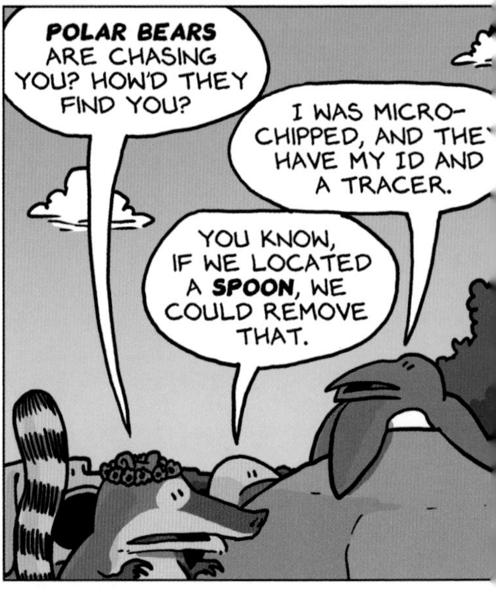
POLAR BEARS ARE CHASING YOU? HOW'D THEY FIND YOU?
I WAS MICRO-CHIPPED, AND THE HAVE MY ID AND A TRACER.
YOU KNOW, IF WE LOCATED A **SPOON**, WE COULD REMOVE THAT.

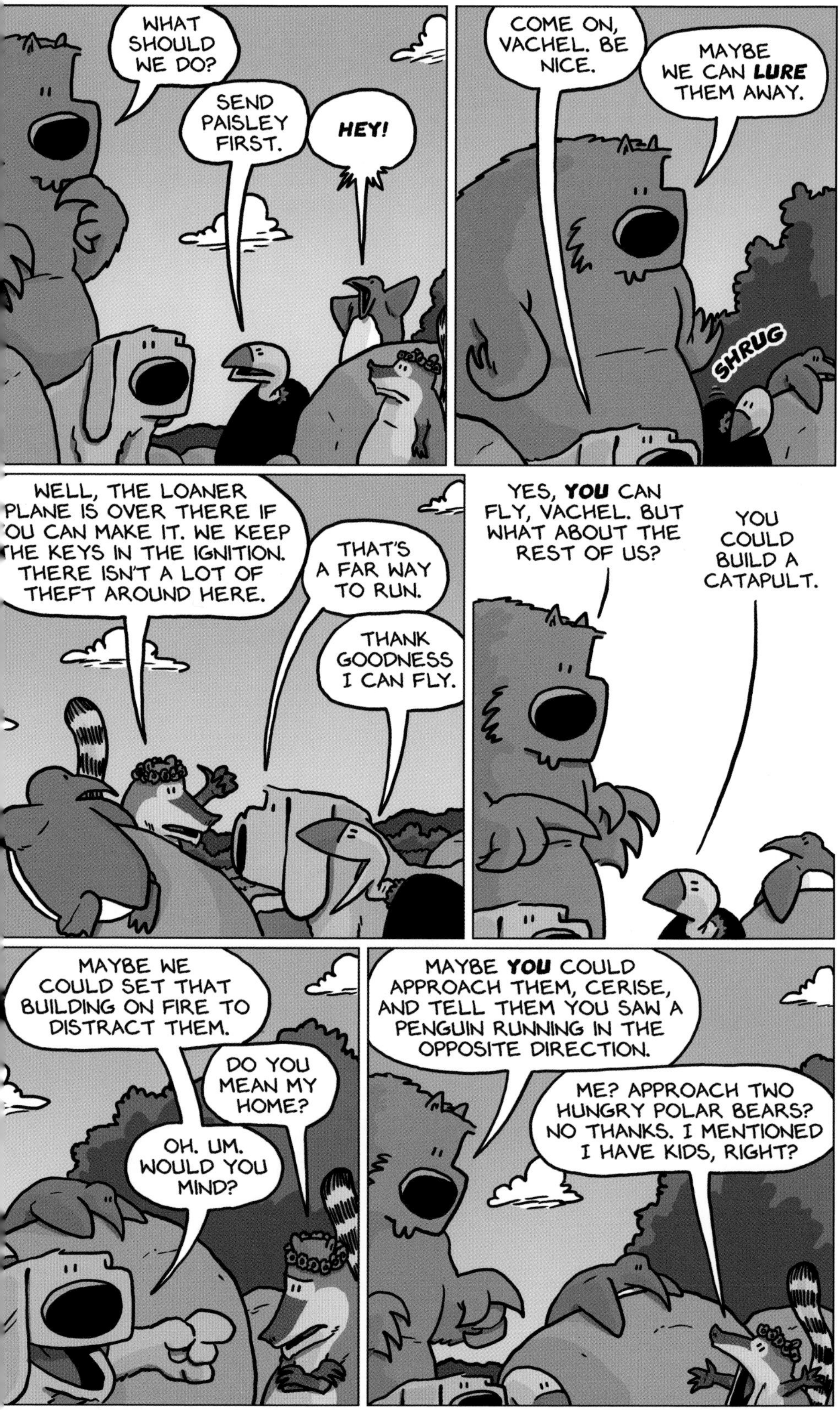

WHAT SHOULD WE DO?
SEND PAISLEY FIRST.
HEY!
COME ON, VACHEL. BE NICE.
MAYBE WE CAN LURE THEM AWAY.
SHRUG
WELL, THE LOANER PLANE IS OVER THERE IF YOU CAN MAKE IT. WE KEEP THE KEYS IN THE IGNITION. THERE ISN'T A LOT OF THEFT AROUND HERE.
THAT'S A FAR WAY TO RUN.
THANK GOODNESS I CAN FLY.
YES, YOU CAN FLY, VACHEL. BUT WHAT ABOUT THE REST OF US?
YOU COULD BUILD A CATAPULT.
MAYBE WE COULD SET THAT BUILDING ON FIRE TO DISTRACT THEM.
DO YOU MEAN MY HOME?
OH. UM. WOULD YOU MIND?
MAYBE YOU COULD APPROACH THEM, CERISE, AND TELL THEM YOU SAW A PENGUIN RUNNING IN THE OPPOSITE DIRECTION.
ME? APPROACH TWO HUNGRY POLAR BEARS? NO THANKS. I MENTIONED I HAVE KIDS, RIGHT?

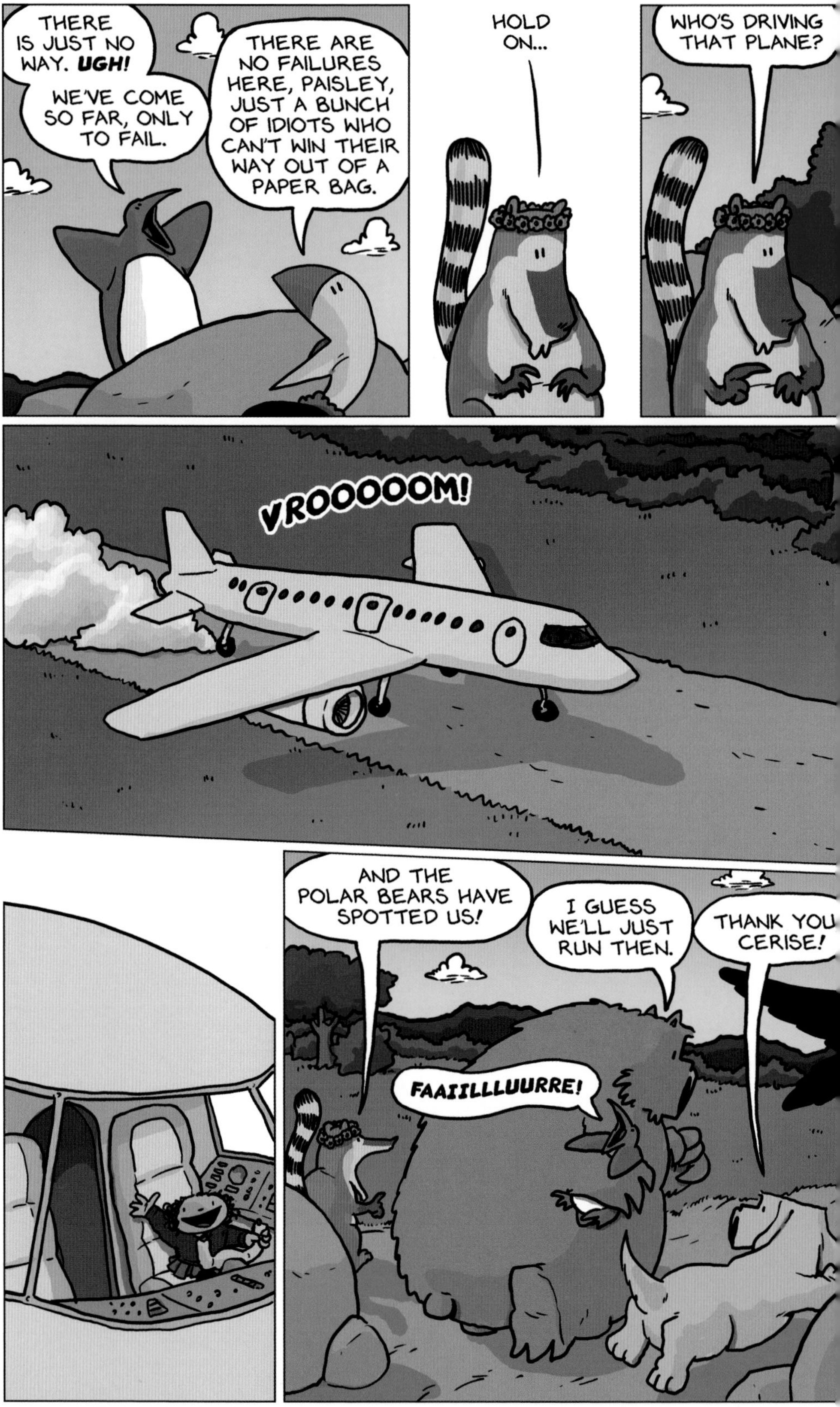
THERE IS JUST NO WAY. UGH!
WE'VE COME SO FAR, ONLY TO FAIL.
THERE ARE NO FAILURES HERE, PAISLEY, JUST A BUNCH OF IDIOTS WHO CAN'T WIN THEIR WAY OUT OF A PAPER BAG.
HOLD ON...
WHO'S DRIVING THAT PLANE?
VROOOOOM!
AND THE POLAR BEARS HAVE SPOTTED US!
I GUESS WE'LL JUST RUN THEN.
THANK YOU CERISE!
FAAIILLLUURRE!

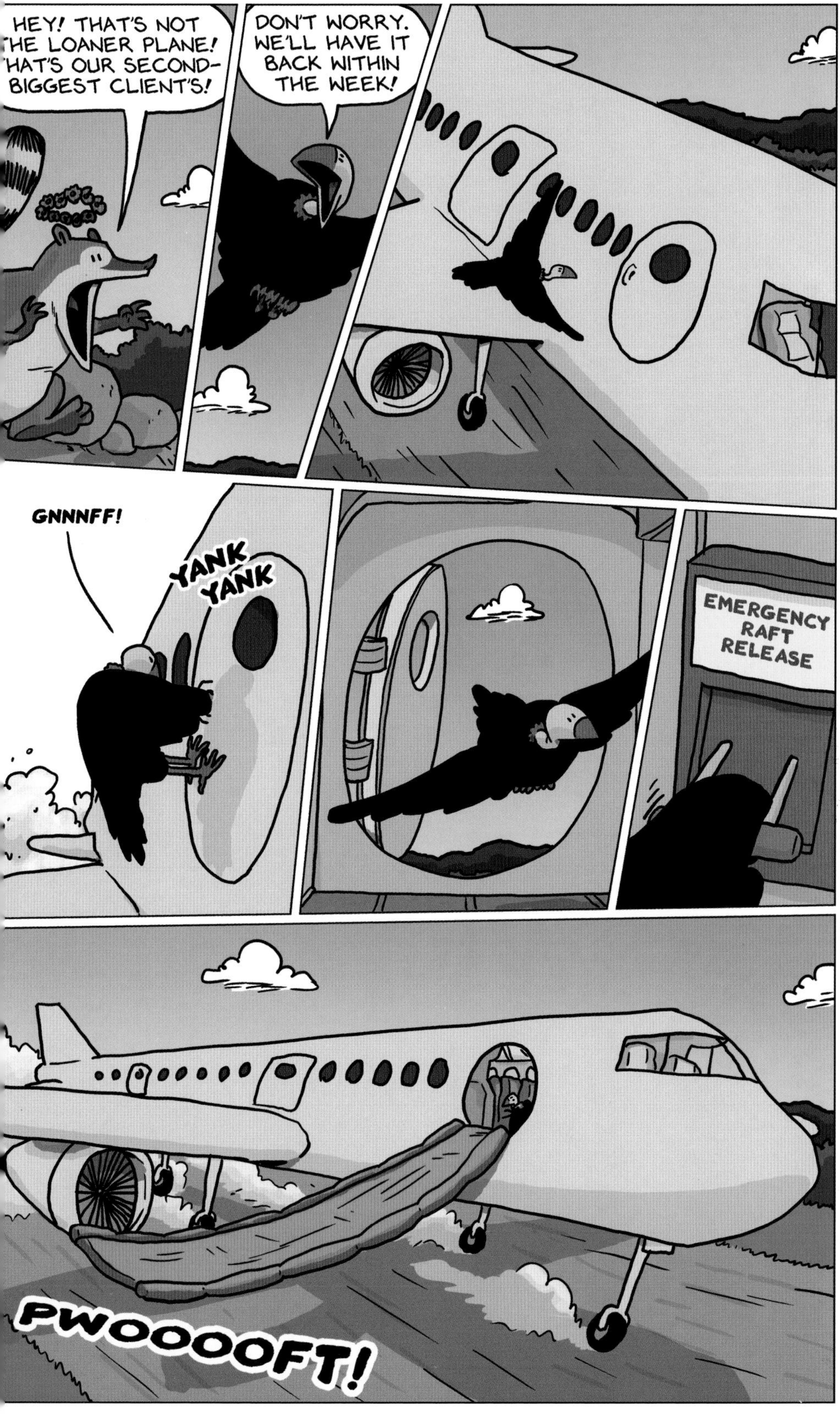

HEY! THAT'S NOT THE LOANER PLANE! THAT'S OUR SECOND-BIGGEST CLIENT'S!
DON'T WORRY. WE'LL HAVE IT BACK WITHIN THE WEEK!
GNNNFF!
YANK YANK
EMERGENCY RAFT RELEASE
PWOOOOOFT!

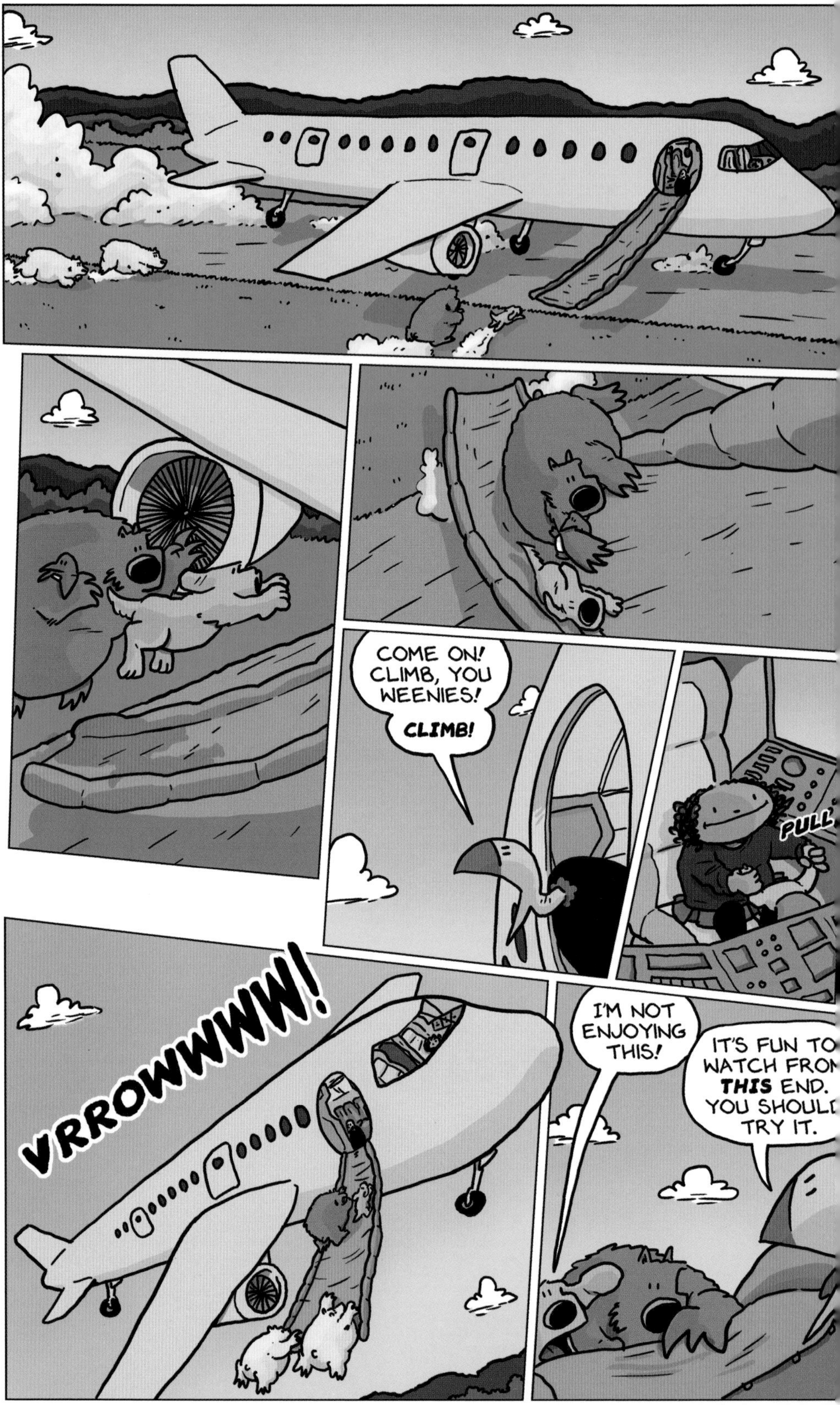
COME ON! CLIMB, YOU WEENIES!
CLIMB!
PULL
VRROWWWW!
I'M NOT ENJOYING THIS!
IT'S FUN TO WATCH FROM THIS END. YOU SHOULD TRY IT.

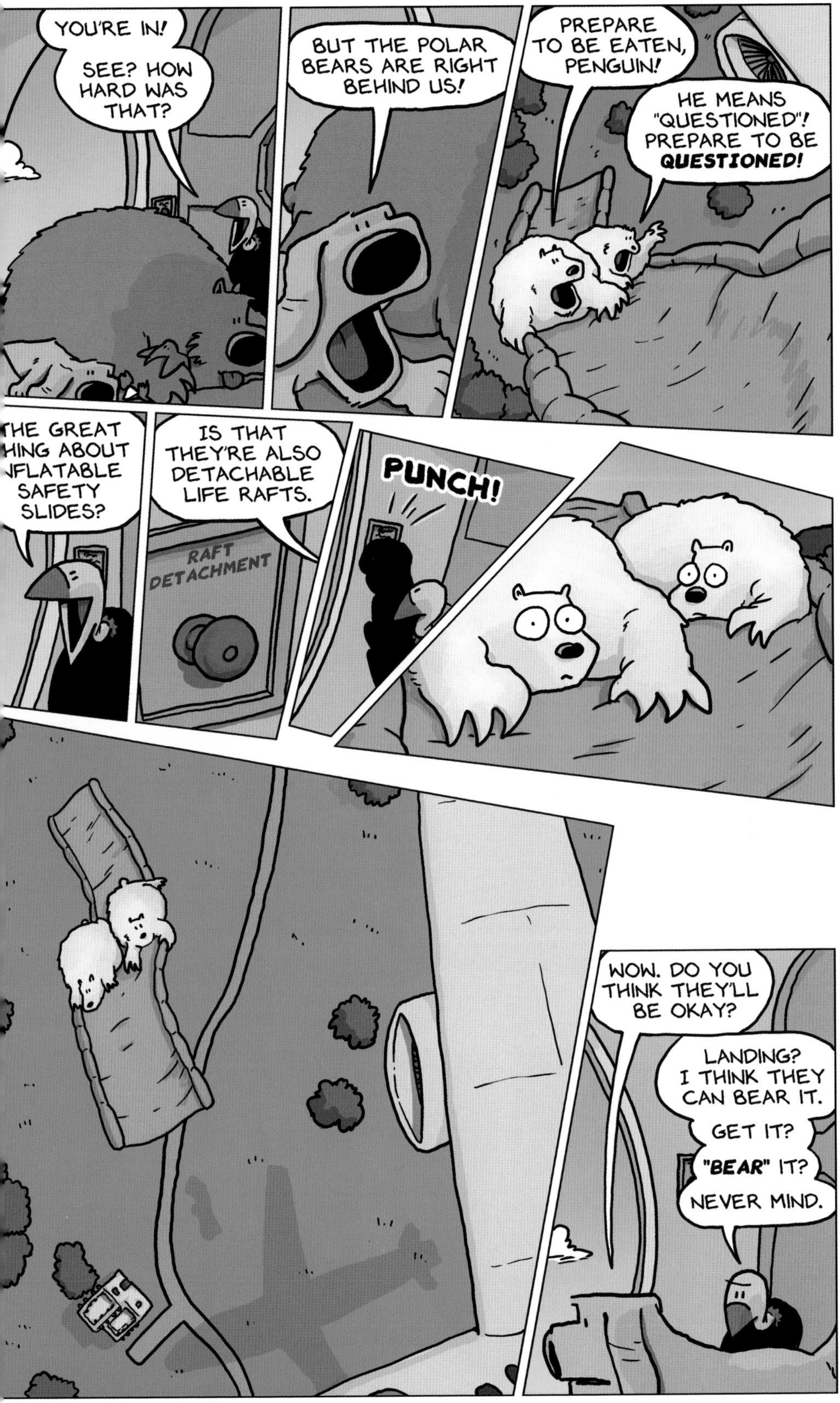

YOU'RE IN!
SEE? HOW HARD WAS THAT?
BUT THE POLAR BEARS ARE RIGHT BEHIND US!
PREPARE TO BE EATEN, PENGUIN!
HE MEANS "QUESTIONED"! PREPARE TO BE **QUESTIONED!**
THE GREAT HING ABOUT NFLATABLE SAFETY SLIDES?
IS THAT THEY'RE ALSO DETACHABLE LIFE RAFTS.
RAFT DETACHMENT
PUNCH!
WOW. DO YOU THINK THEY'LL BE OKAY?
LANDING? I THINK THEY CAN BEAR IT.
GET IT?
"BEAR" IT?
NEVER MIND.

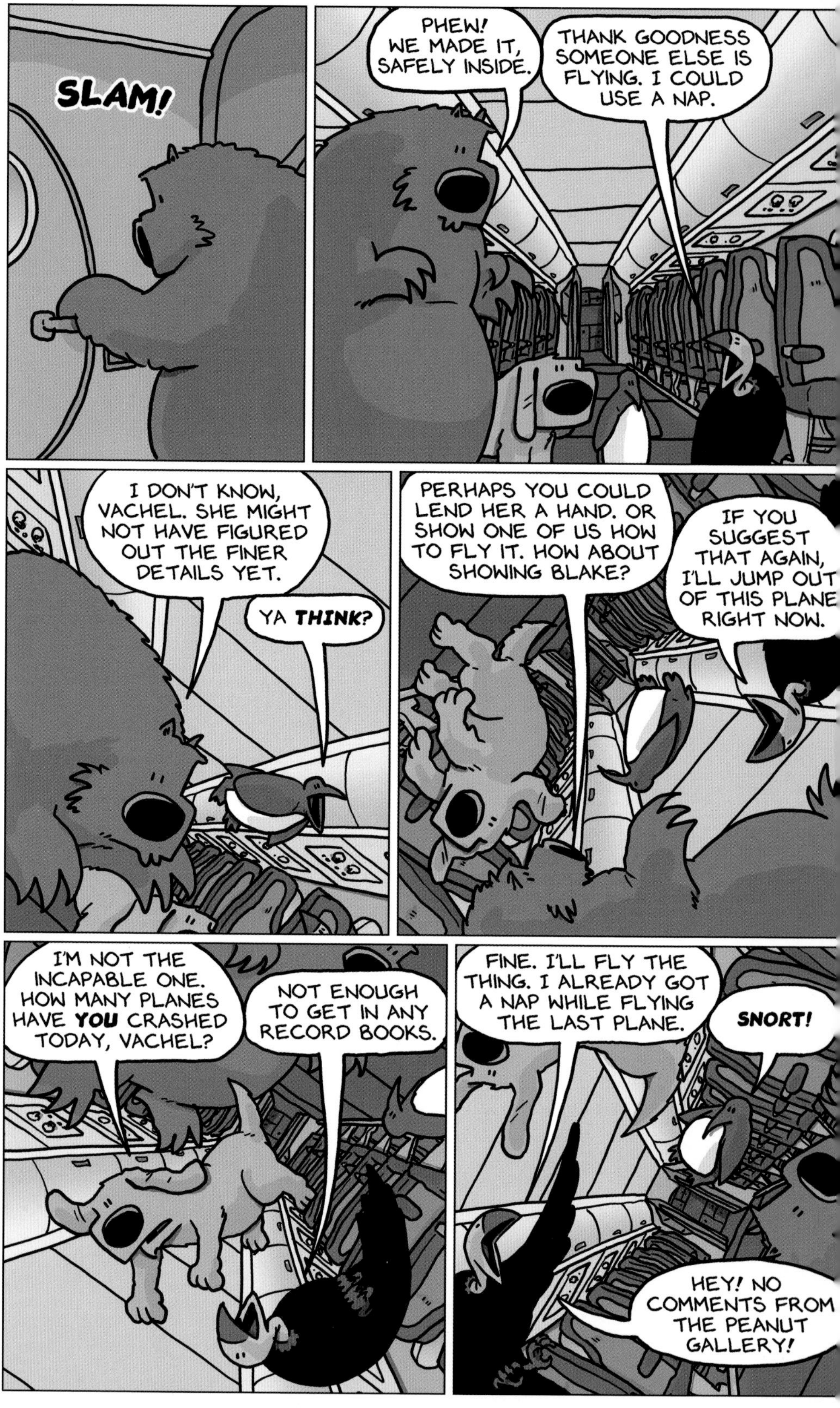
SLAM!
PHEW! WE MADE IT, SAFELY INSIDE.
THANK GOODNESS SOMEONE ELSE IS FLYING. I COULD USE A NAP.
I DON'T KNOW, VACHEL. SHE MIGHT NOT HAVE FIGURED OUT THE FINER DETAILS YET.
YA THINK?
PERHAPS YOU COULD LEND HER A HAND. OR SHOW ONE OF US HOW TO FLY IT. HOW ABOUT SHOWING BLAKE?
IF YOU SUGGEST THAT AGAIN, I'LL JUMP OUT OF THIS PLANE RIGHT NOW.
I'M NOT THE INCAPABLE ONE. HOW MANY PLANES HAVE YOU CRASHED TODAY, VACHEL?
NOT ENOUGH TO GET IN ANY RECORD BOOKS.
FINE. I'LL FLY THE THING. I ALREADY GOT A NAP WHILE FLYING THE LAST PLANE.
SNORT!
HEY! NO COMMENTS FROM THE PEANUT GALLERY!

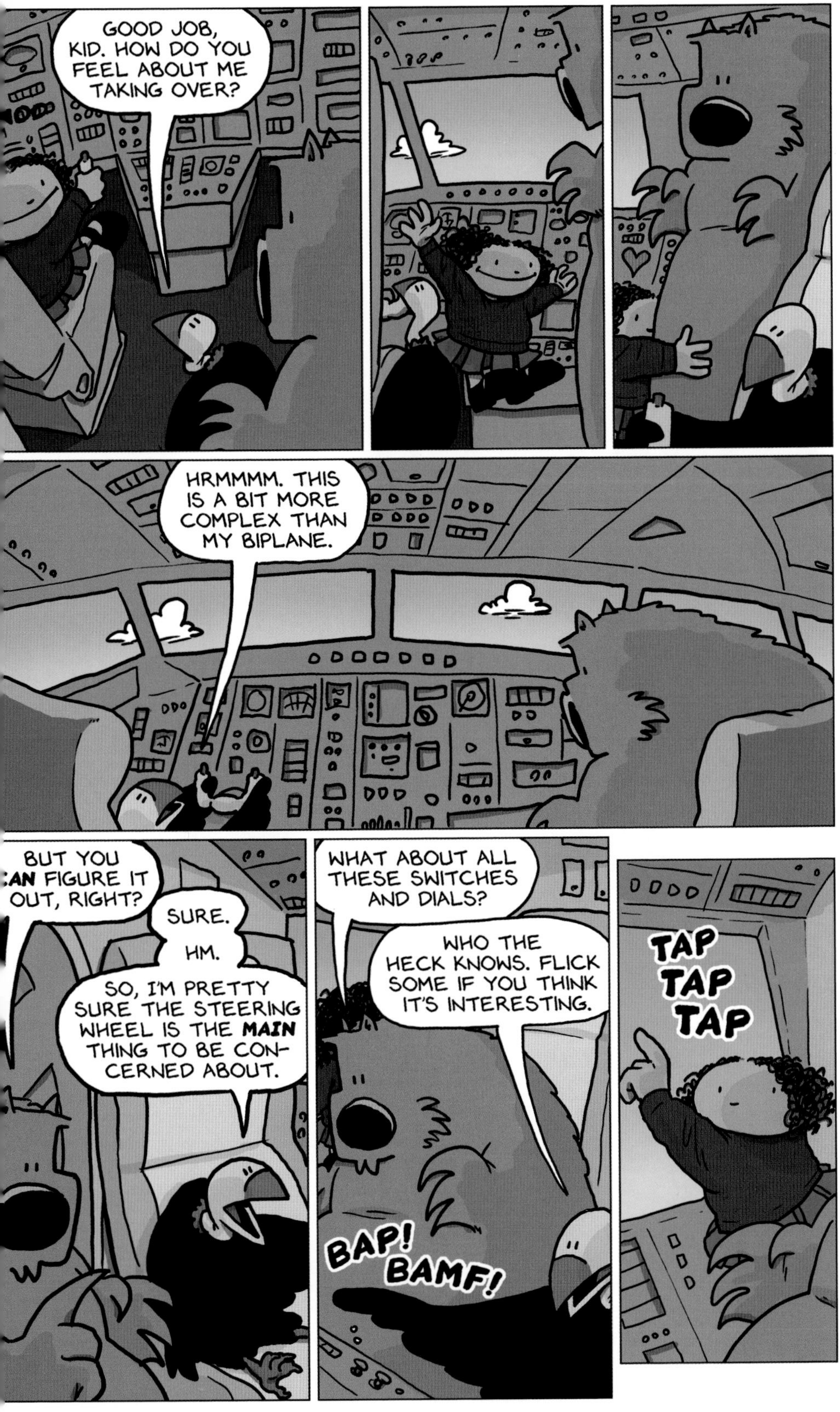

GOOD JOB, KID. HOW DO YOU FEEL ABOUT ME TAKING OVER?
HRMMMM. THIS IS A BIT MORE COMPLEX THAN MY BIPLANE.
BUT YOU CAN FIGURE IT OUT, RIGHT?
SURE.
HM.
SO, I'M PRETTY SURE THE STEERING WHEEL IS THE MAIN THING TO BE CONCERNED ABOUT.
WHAT ABOUT ALL THESE SWITCHES AND DIALS?
WHO THE HECK KNOWS. FLICK SOME IF YOU THINK IT'S INTERESTING.
BAP! BAMF!
TAP TAP TAP

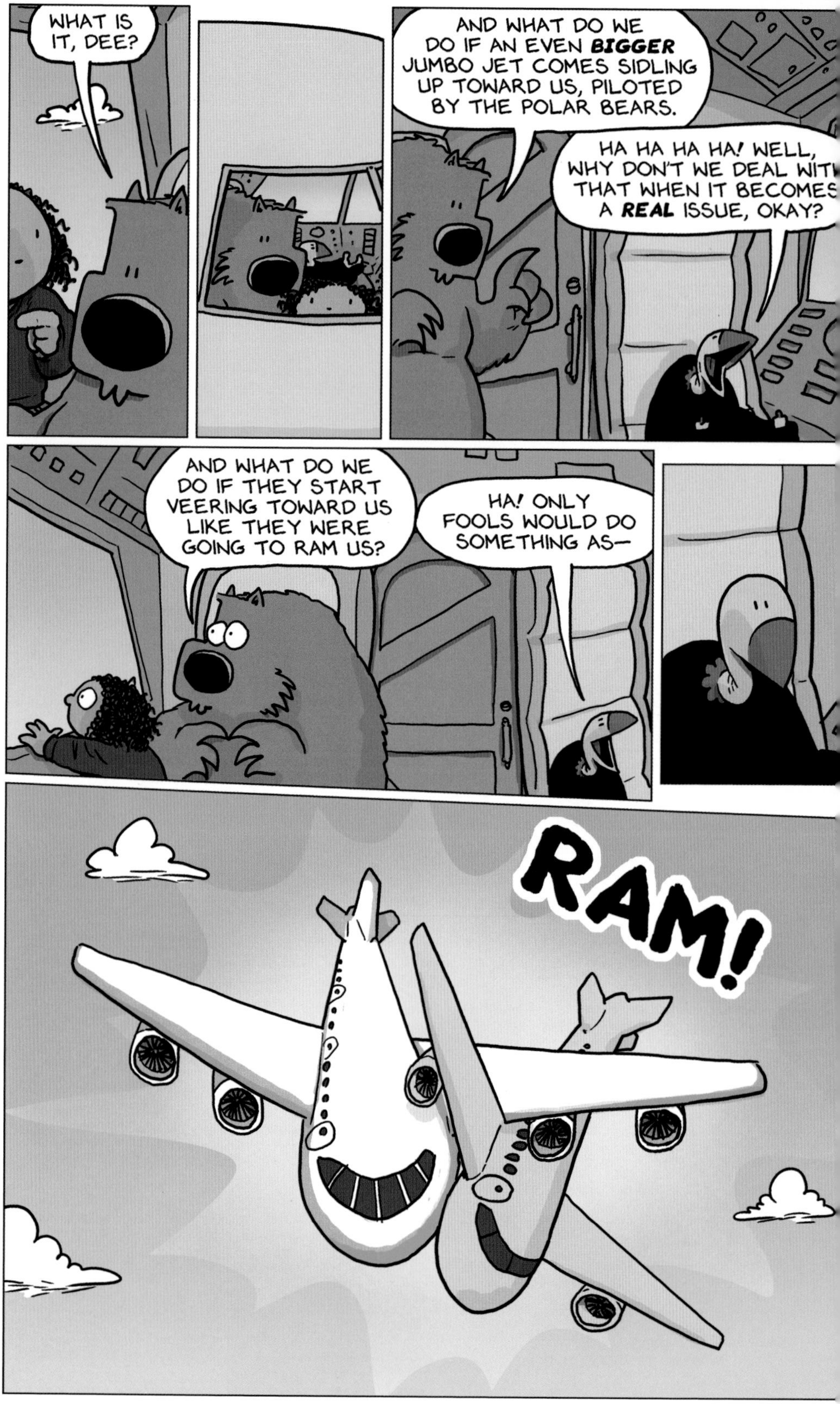
WHAT IS IT, DEE?
AND WHAT DO WE DO IF AN EVEN **BIGGER** JUMBO JET COMES SIDLING UP TOWARD US, PILOTED BY THE POLAR BEARS.
HA HA HA HA! WELL, WHY DON'T WE DEAL WIT THAT WHEN IT BECOMES A **REAL** ISSUE, OKAY?
AND WHAT DO WE DO IF THEY START VEERING TOWARD US LIKE THEY WERE GOING TO RAM US?
HA! ONLY FOOLS WOULD DO SOMETHING AS—
RAM!

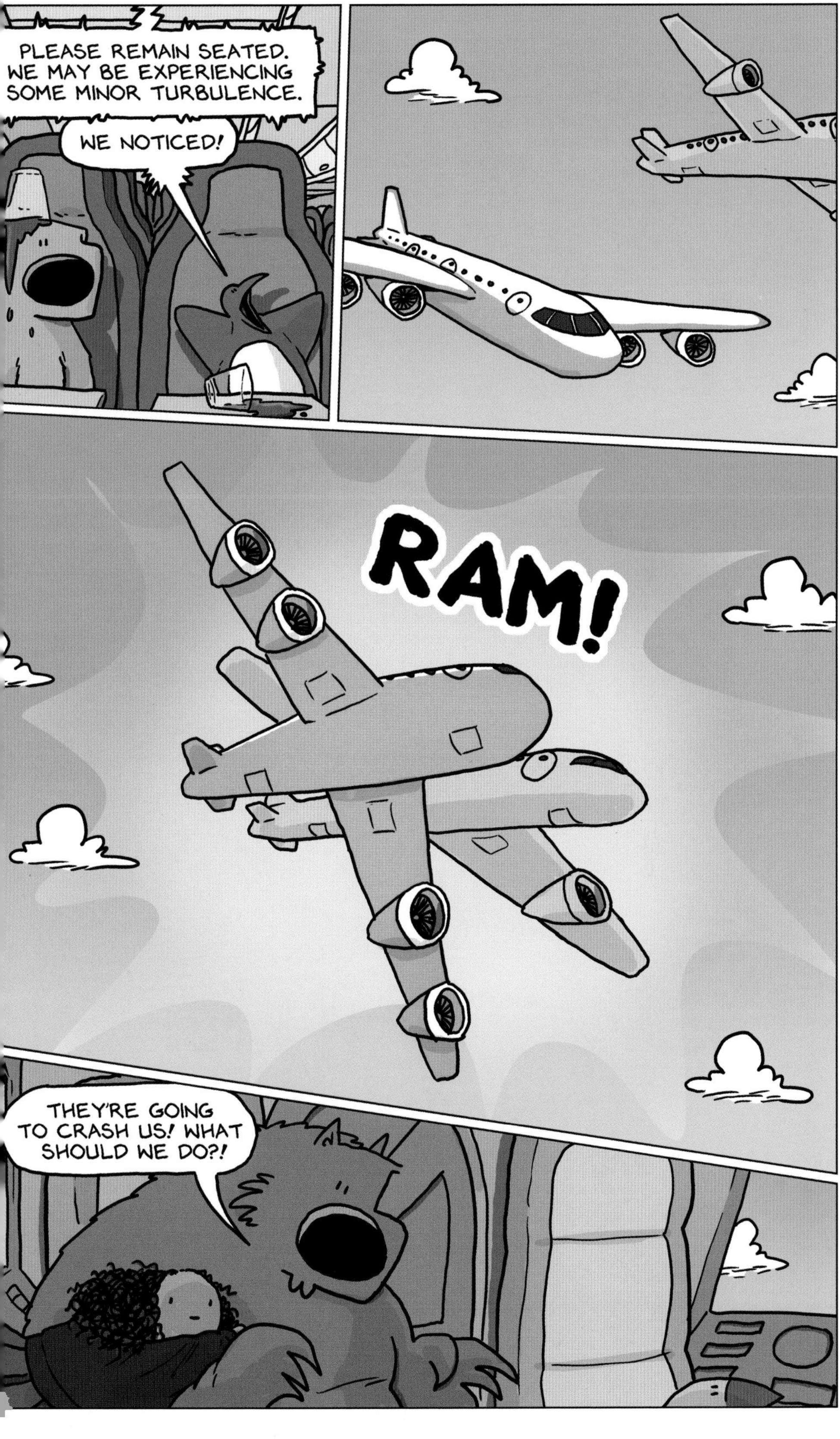
PLEASE REMAIN SEATED. WE MAY BE EXPERIENCING SOME MINOR TURBULENCE.
WE NOTICED!
RAM!
THEY'RE GOING TO CRASH US! WHAT SHOULD WE DO?!

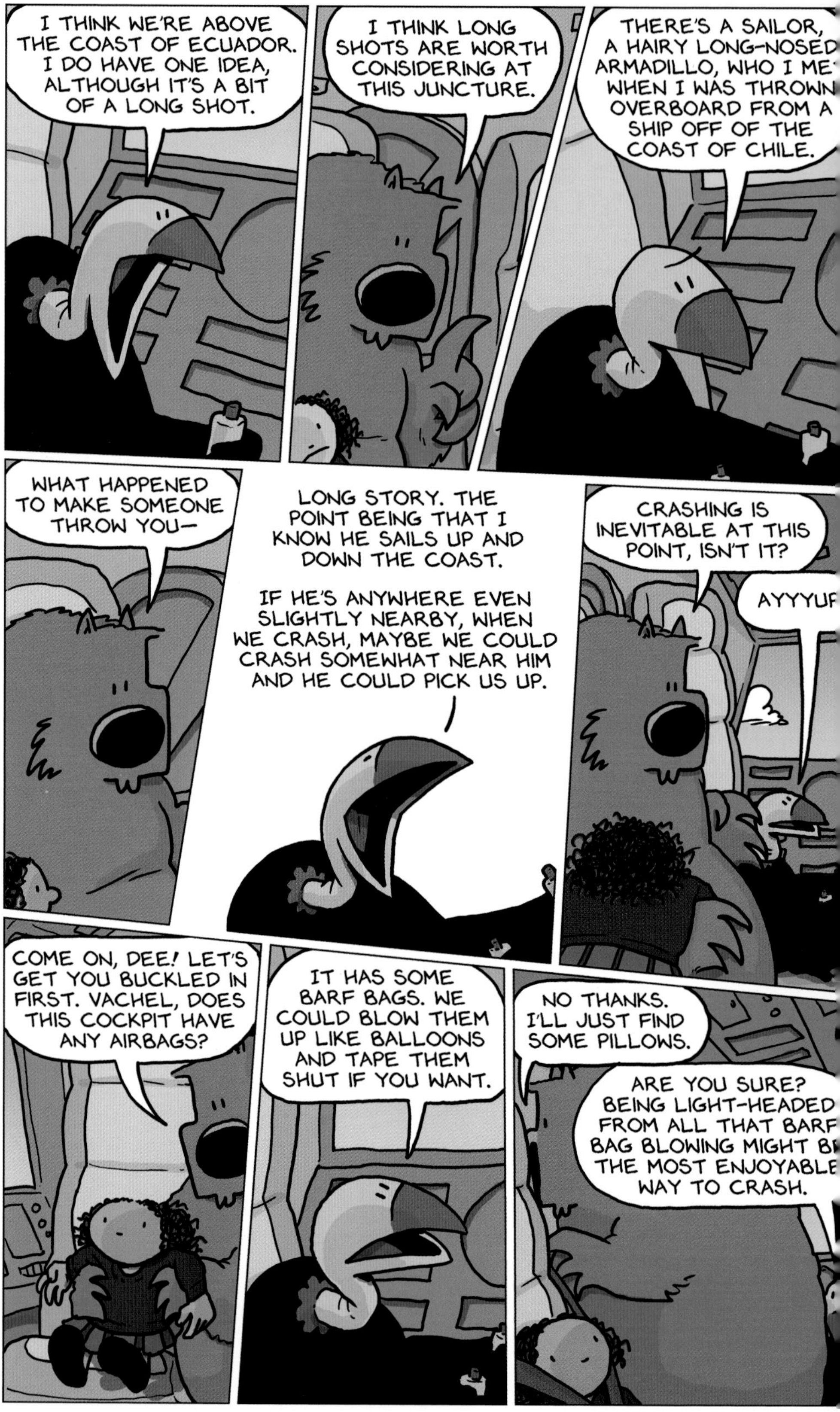
I THINK WE'RE ABOVE THE COAST OF ECUADOR. I DO HAVE ONE IDEA, ALTHOUGH IT'S A BIT OF A LONG SHOT.
I THINK LONG SHOTS ARE WORTH CONSIDERING AT THIS JUNCTURE.
THERE'S A SAILOR, A HAIRY LONG-NOSED ARMADILLO, WHO I MET WHEN I WAS THROWN OVERBOARD FROM A SHIP OFF OF THE COAST OF CHILE.
WHAT HAPPENED TO MAKE SOMEONE THROW YOU—
LONG STORY. THE POINT BEING THAT I KNOW HE SAILS UP AND DOWN THE COAST.
IF HE'S ANYWHERE EVEN SLIGHTLY NEARBY, WHEN WE CRASH, MAYBE WE COULD CRASH SOMEWHAT NEAR HIM AND HE COULD PICK US UP.
CRASHING IS INEVITABLE AT THIS POINT, ISN'T IT?
AYYYUP
COME ON, DEE! LET'S GET YOU BUCKLED IN FIRST. VACHEL, DOES THIS COCKPIT HAVE ANY AIRBAGS?
IT HAS SOME BARF BAGS. WE COULD BLOW THEM UP LIKE BALLOONS AND TAPE THEM SHUT IF YOU WANT.
NO THANKS. I'LL JUST FIND SOME PILLOWS.
ARE YOU SURE? BEING LIGHT-HEADED FROM ALL THAT BARF BAG BLOWING MIGHT BE THE MOST ENJOYABLE WAY TO CRASH.

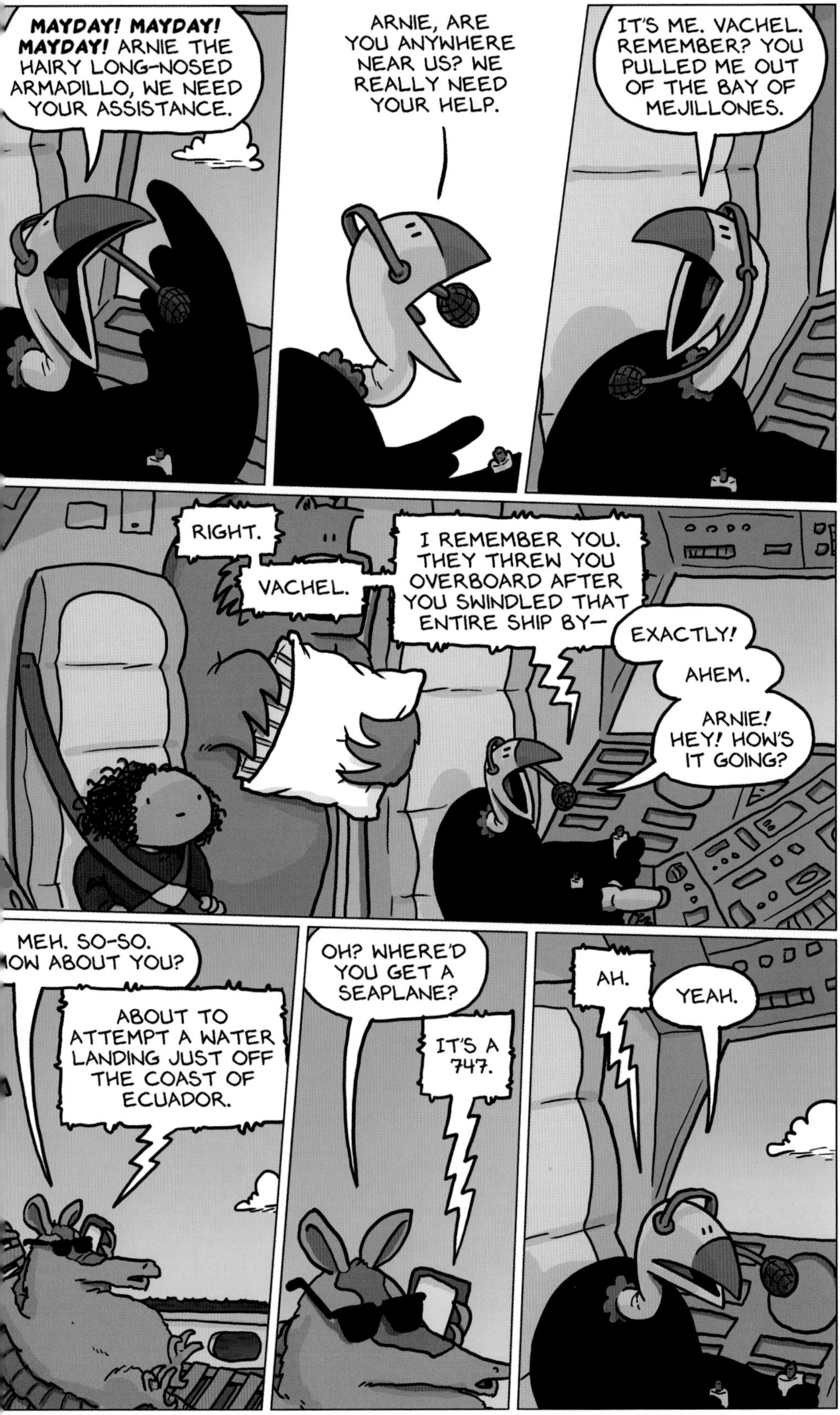
MAYDAY! MAYDAY! MAYDAY! ARNIE THE HAIRY LONG-NOSED ARMADILLO, WE NEED YOUR ASSISTANCE.
ARNIE, ARE YOU ANYWHERE NEAR US? WE REALLY NEED YOUR HELP.
IT'S ME. VACHEL. REMEMBER? YOU PULLED ME OUT OF THE BAY OF MEJILLONES.
RIGHT.
VACHEL.
I REMEMBER YOU. THEY THREW YOU OVERBOARD AFTER YOU SWINDLED THAT ENTIRE SHIP BY—
EXACTLY!
AHEM.
ARNIE! HEY! HOW'S IT GOING?
MEH. SO-SO. OW ABOUT YOU?
ABOUT TO ATTEMPT A WATER LANDING JUST OFF THE COAST OF ECUADOR.
OH? WHERE'D YOU GET A SEAPLANE?
IT'S A 747.
AH.
YEAH.

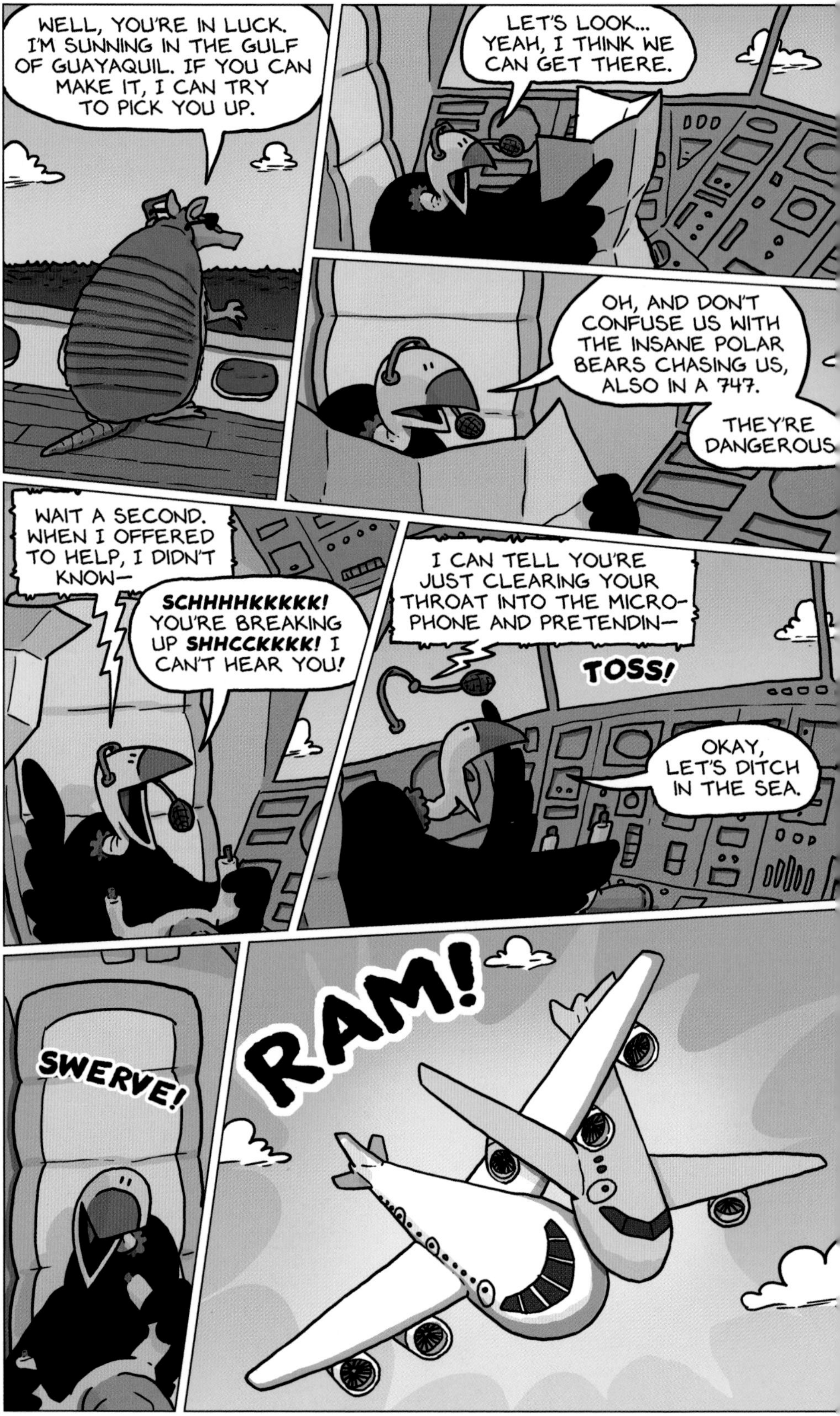
WELL, YOU'RE IN LUCK. I'M SUNNING IN THE GULF OF GUAYAQUIL. IF YOU CAN MAKE IT, I CAN TRY TO PICK YOU UP.
LET'S LOOK... YEAH, I THINK WE CAN GET THERE.
OH, AND DON'T CONFUSE US WITH THE INSANE POLAR BEARS CHASING US, ALSO IN A 747.
THEY'RE DANGEROUS
WAIT A SECOND. WHEN I OFFERED TO HELP, I DIDN'T KNOW—
SCHHHHKKKKK! YOU'RE BREAKING UP SHHCCKKKK! I CAN'T HEAR YOU!
I CAN TELL YOU'RE JUST CLEARING YOUR THROAT INTO THE MICRO-PHONE AND PRETENDIN—
TOSS!
OKAY, LET'S DITCH IN THE SEA.
SWERVE!
RAM!

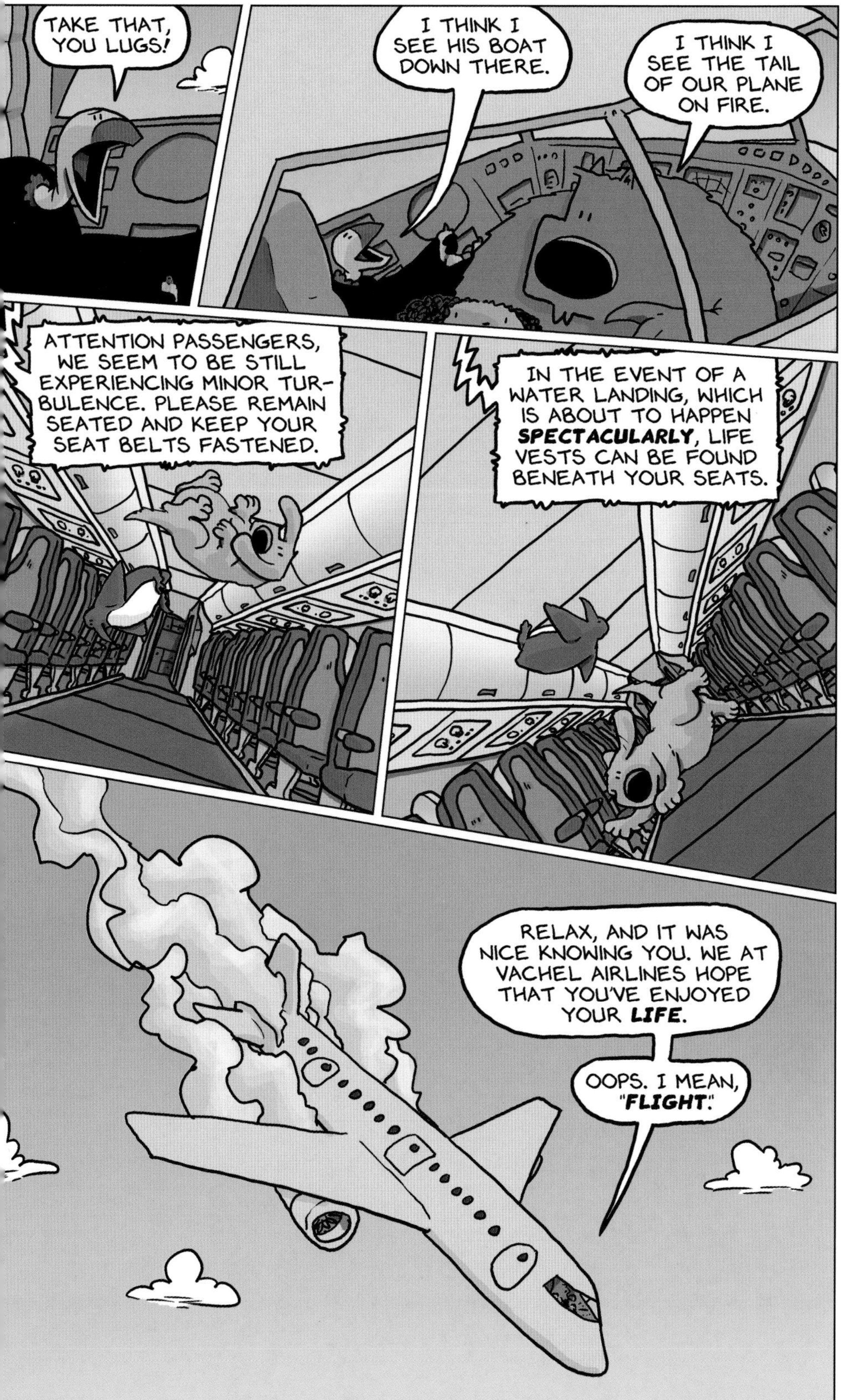
TAKE THAT, YOU LUGS!
I THINK I SEE HIS BOAT DOWN THERE.
I THINK I SEE THE TAIL OF OUR PLANE ON FIRE.
ATTENTION PASSENGERS, WE SEEM TO BE STILL EXPERIENCING MINOR TURBULENCE. PLEASE REMAIN SEATED AND KEEP YOUR SEAT BELTS FASTENED.
IN THE EVENT OF A WATER LANDING, WHICH IS ABOUT TO HAPPEN SPECTACULARLY, LIFE VESTS CAN BE FOUND BENEATH YOUR SEATS.
RELAX, AND IT WAS NICE KNOWING YOU. WE AT VACHEL AIRLINES HOPE THAT YOU'VE ENJOYED YOUR LIFE.
OOPS. I MEAN, "FLIGHT."

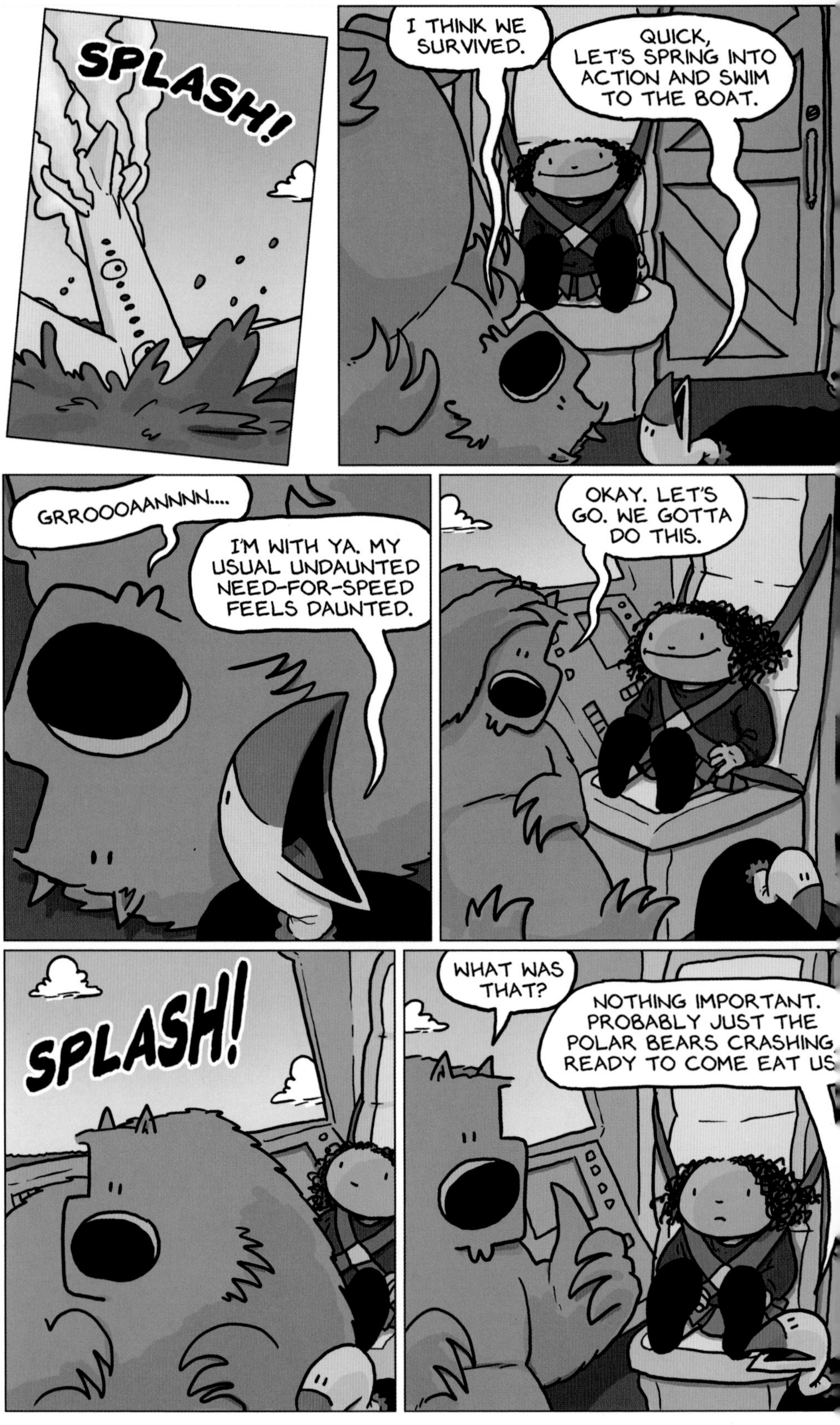
SPLASH!
I THINK WE SURVIVED.
QUICK, LET'S SPRING INTO ACTION AND SWIM TO THE BOAT.
GRROOOAANNNN....
I'M WITH YA. MY USUAL UNDAUNTED NEED-FOR-SPEED FEELS DAUNTED.
OKAY. LET'S GO. WE GOTTA DO THIS.
SPLASH!
WHAT WAS THAT?
NOTHING IMPORTANT. PROBABLY JUST THE POLAR BEARS CRASHING READY TO COME EAT US

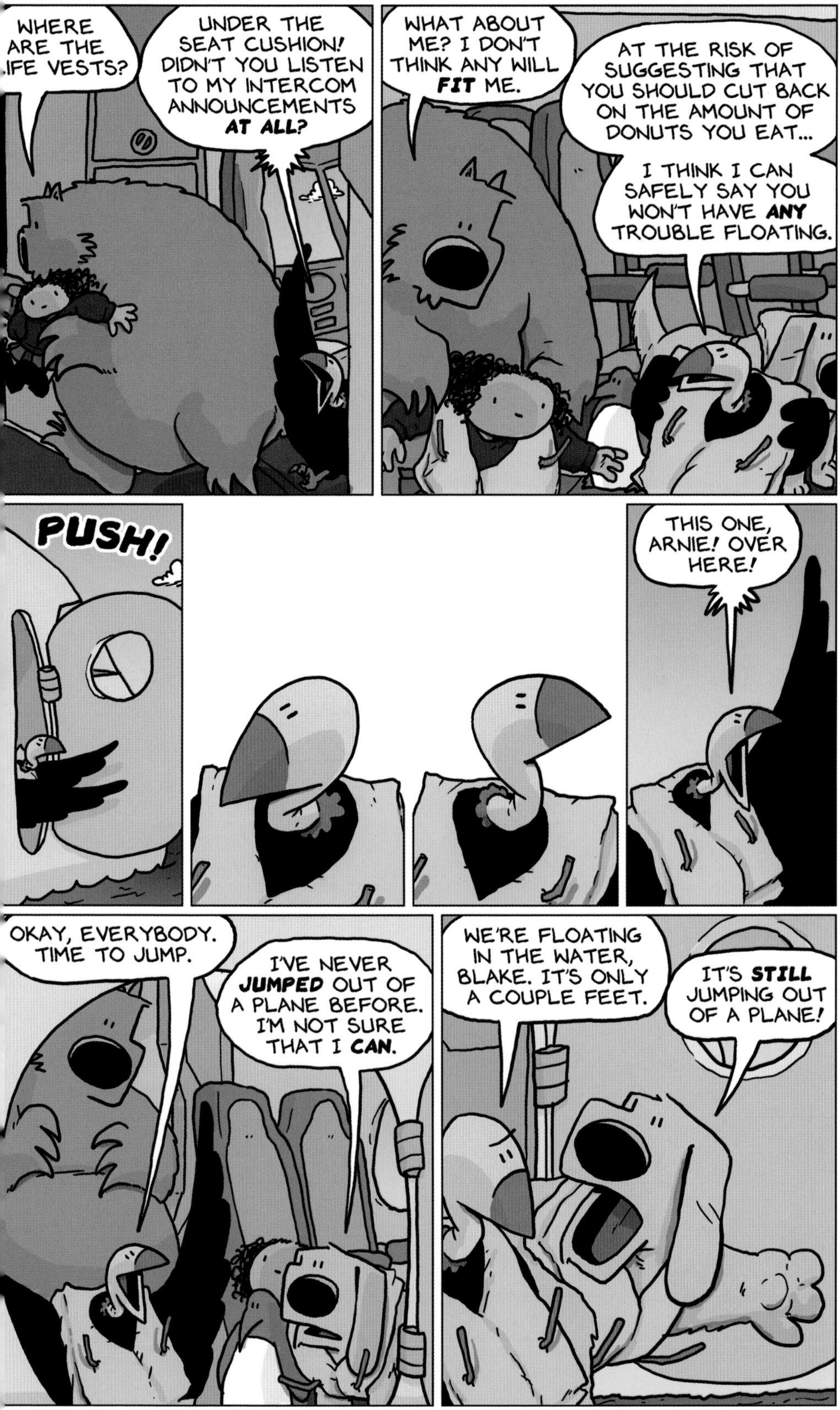

WHERE ARE THE LIFE VESTS?
UNDER THE SEAT CUSHION! DIDN'T YOU LISTEN TO MY INTERCOM ANNOUNCEMENTS **AT ALL?**
WHAT ABOUT ME? I DON'T THINK ANY WILL **FIT** ME.
AT THE RISK OF SUGGESTING THAT YOU SHOULD CUT BACK ON THE AMOUNT OF DONUTS YOU EAT...
I THINK I CAN SAFELY SAY YOU WON'T HAVE **ANY** TROUBLE FLOATING.
PUSH!
THIS ONE, ARNIE! OVER HERE!
OKAY, EVERYBODY. TIME TO JUMP.
I'VE NEVER **JUMPED** OUT OF A PLANE BEFORE. I'M NOT SURE THAT I **CAN**.
WE'RE FLOATING IN THE WATER, BLAKE. IT'S ONLY A COUPLE FEET.
IT'S **STILL** JUMPING OUT OF A PLANE!

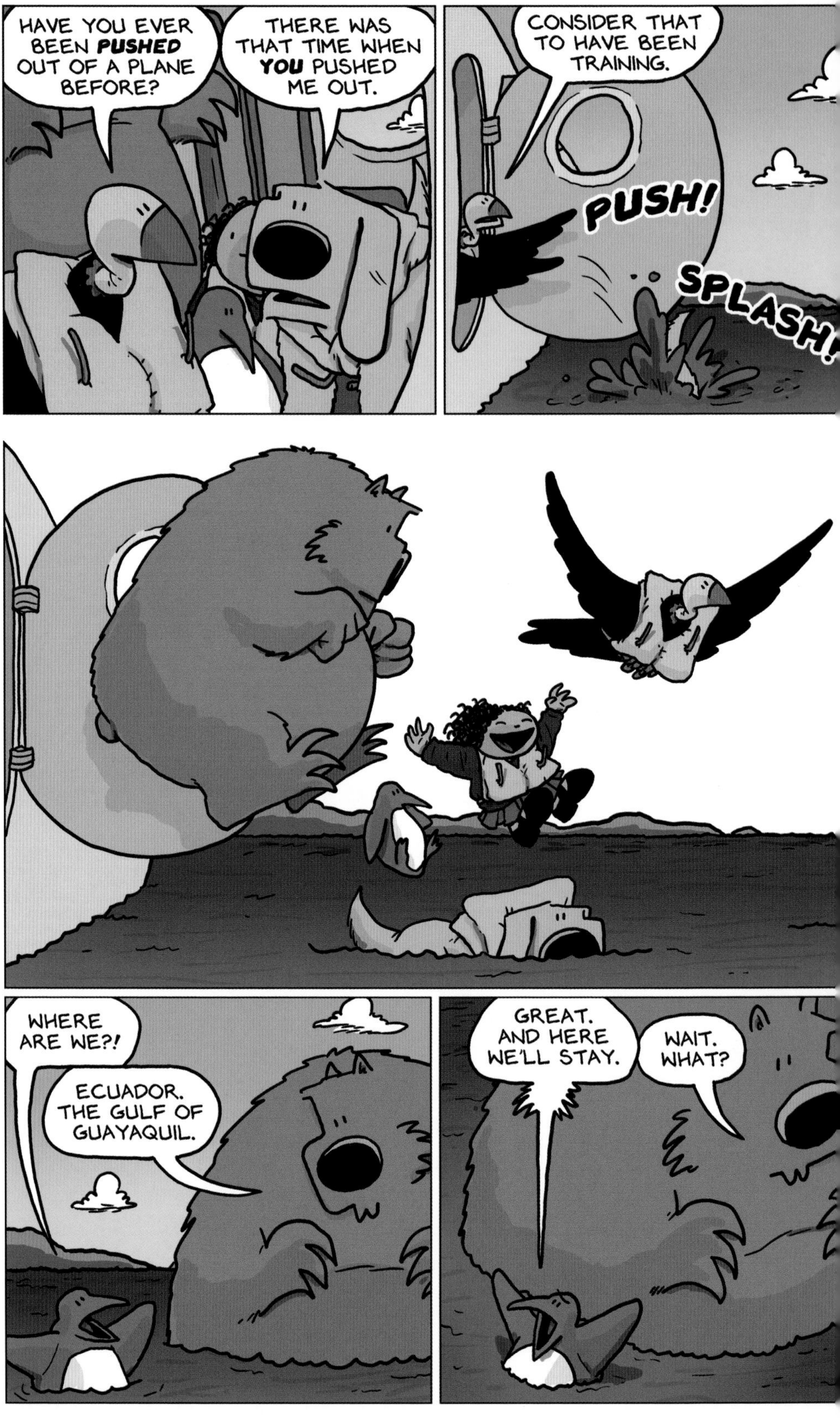
HAVE YOU EVER BEEN **PUSHED** OUT OF A PLANE BEFORE?
THERE WAS THAT TIME WHEN **YOU** PUSHED ME OUT.
CONSIDER THAT TO HAVE BEEN TRAINING.
PUSH!
SPLASH!
WHERE ARE WE?!
ECUADOR. THE GULF OF GUAYAQUIL.
GREAT. AND HERE WE'LL STAY.
WAIT. WHAT?

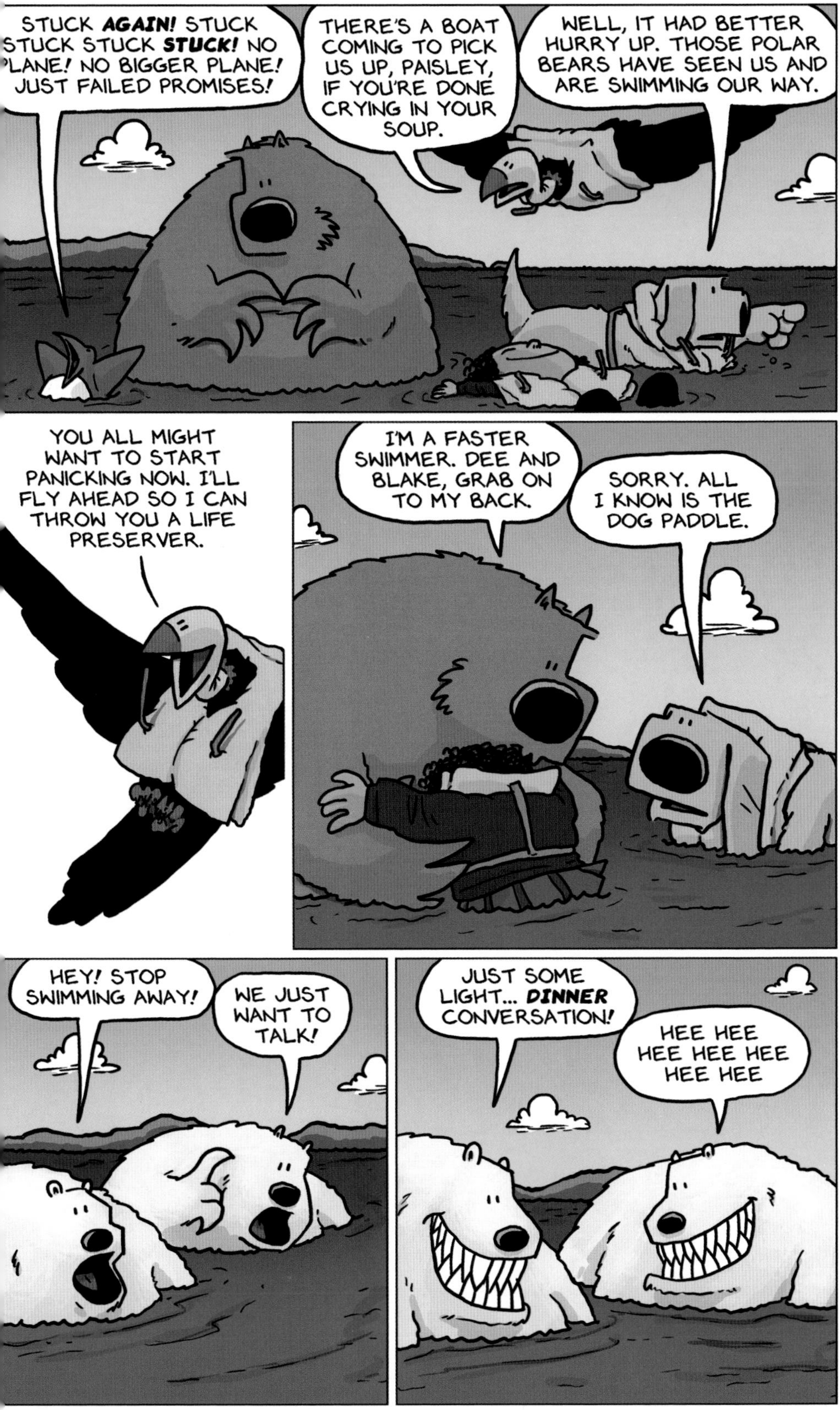
STUCK AGAIN! STUCK STUCK STUCK STUCK! NO PLANE! NO BIGGER PLANE! JUST FAILED PROMISES!
THERE'S A BOAT COMING TO PICK US UP, PAISLEY, IF YOU'RE DONE CRYING IN YOUR SOUP.
WELL, IT HAD BETTER HURRY UP. THOSE POLAR BEARS HAVE SEEN US AND ARE SWIMMING OUR WAY.
YOU ALL MIGHT WANT TO START PANICKING NOW. I'LL FLY AHEAD SO I CAN THROW YOU A LIFE PRESERVER.
I'M A FASTER SWIMMER. DEE AND BLAKE, GRAB ON TO MY BACK.
SORRY. ALL I KNOW IS THE DOG PADDLE.
HEY! STOP SWIMMING AWAY!
WE JUST WANT TO TALK!
JUST SOME LIGHT... DINNER CONVERSATION!
HEE HEE HEE HEE HEE HEE HEE

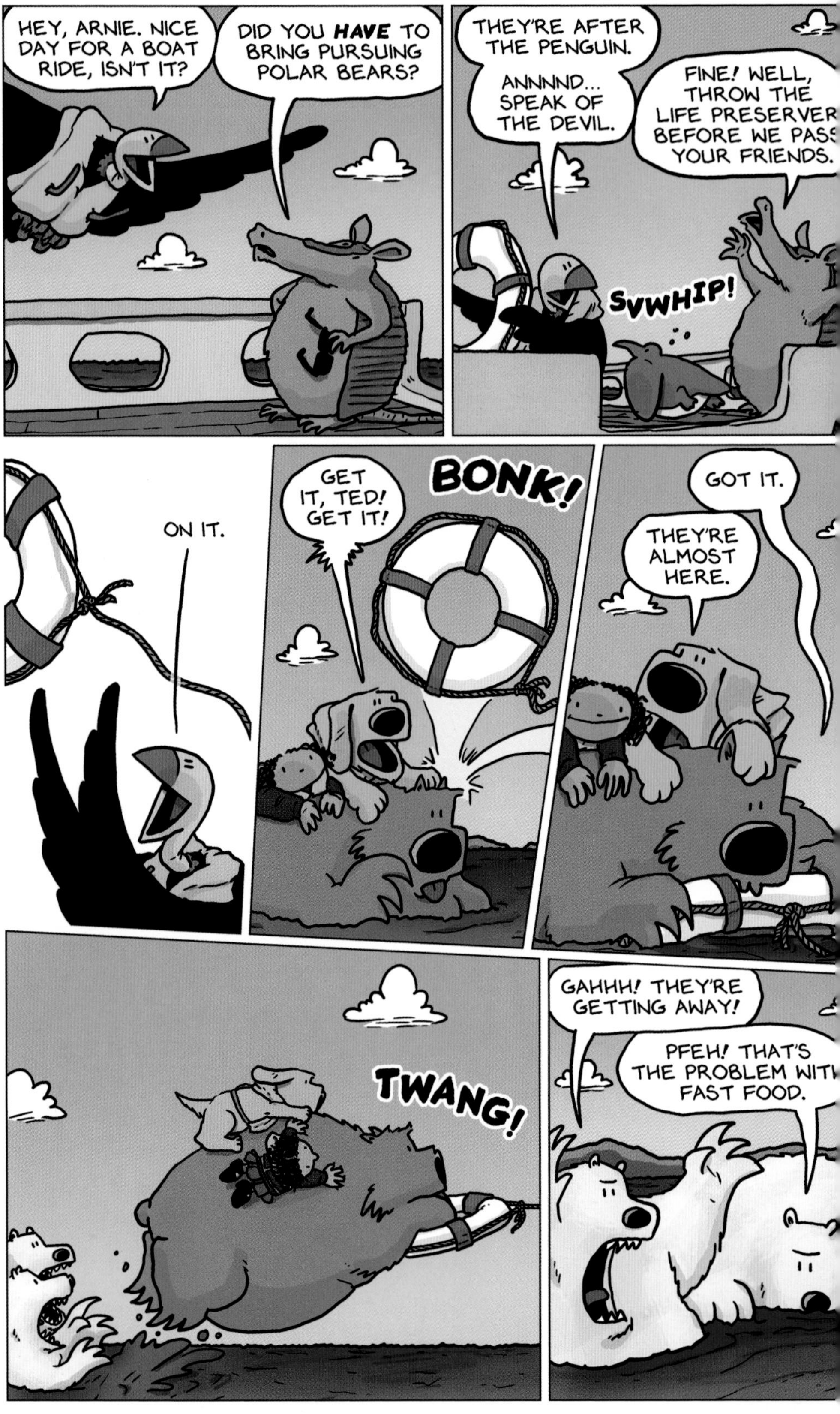
HEY, ARNIE. NICE DAY FOR A BOAT RIDE, ISN'T IT?
DID YOU **HAVE** TO BRING PURSUING POLAR BEARS?
THEY'RE AFTER THE PENGUIN.
ANNNND... SPEAK OF THE DEVIL.
FINE! WELL, THROW THE LIFE PRESERVER BEFORE WE PASS YOUR FRIENDS.
SVWHIP!
ON IT.
GET IT, TED! GET IT!
BONK!
GOT IT.
THEY'RE ALMOST HERE.
TWANG!
GAHHH! THEY'RE GETTING AWAY!
PFEH! THAT'S THE PROBLEM WITH FAST FOOD.

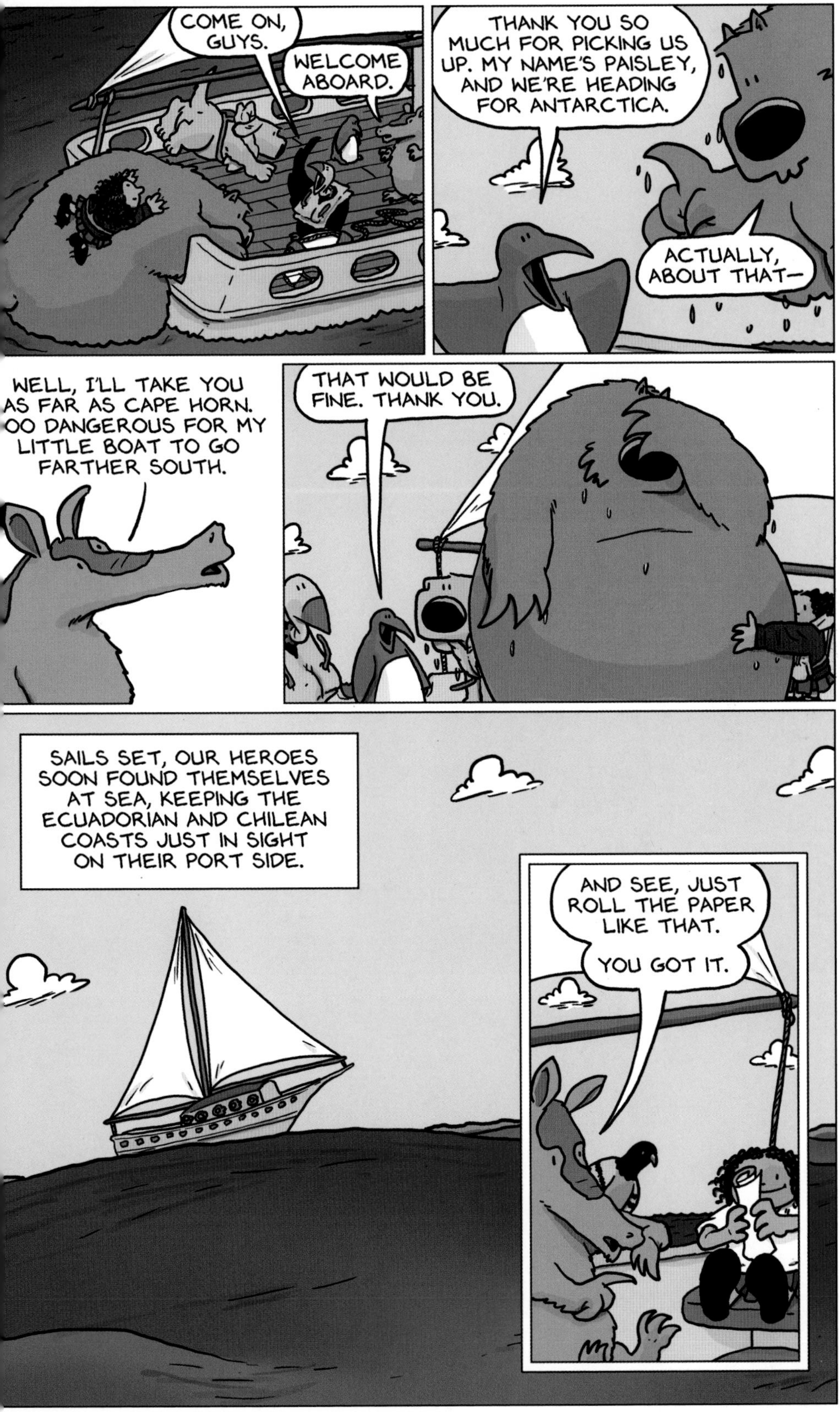
COME ON, GUYS.
WELCOME ABOARD.
THANK YOU SO MUCH FOR PICKING US UP. MY NAME'S PAISLEY, AND WE'RE HEADING FOR ANTARCTICA.
ACTUALLY, ABOUT THAT—
WELL, I'LL TAKE YOU AS FAR AS CAPE HORN. OO DANGEROUS FOR MY LITTLE BOAT TO GO FARTHER SOUTH.
THAT WOULD BE FINE. THANK YOU.
SAILS SET, OUR HEROES SOON FOUND THEMSELVES AT SEA, KEEPING THE ECUADORIAN AND CHILEAN COASTS JUST IN SIGHT ON THEIR PORT SIDE.
AND SEE, JUST ROLL THE PAPER LIKE THAT.
YOU GOT IT.

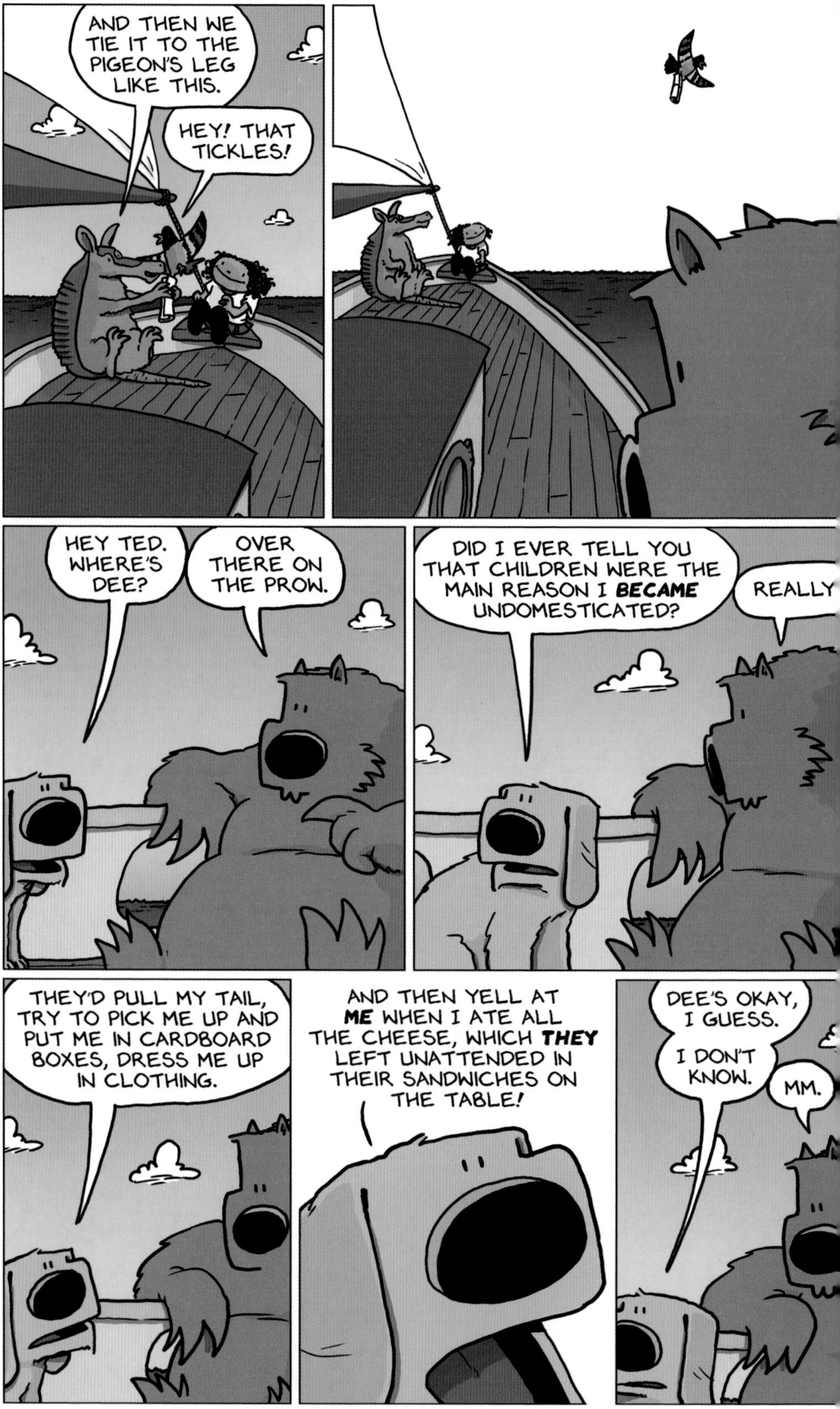

AND THEN WE TIE IT TO THE PIGEON'S LEG LIKE THIS.
HEY! THAT TICKLES!
HEY TED. WHERE'S DEE?
OVER THERE ON THE PROW.
DID I EVER TELL YOU THAT CHILDREN WERE THE MAIN REASON I **BECAME** UNDOMESTICATED?
REALLY
THEY'D PULL MY TAIL, TRY TO PICK ME UP AND PUT ME IN CARDBOARD BOXES, DRESS ME UP IN CLOTHING.
AND THEN YELL AT **ME** WHEN I ATE ALL THE CHEESE, WHICH **THEY** LEFT UNATTENDED IN THEIR SANDWICHES ON THE TABLE!
DEE'S OKAY, I GUESS.
I DON'T KNOW.
MM.

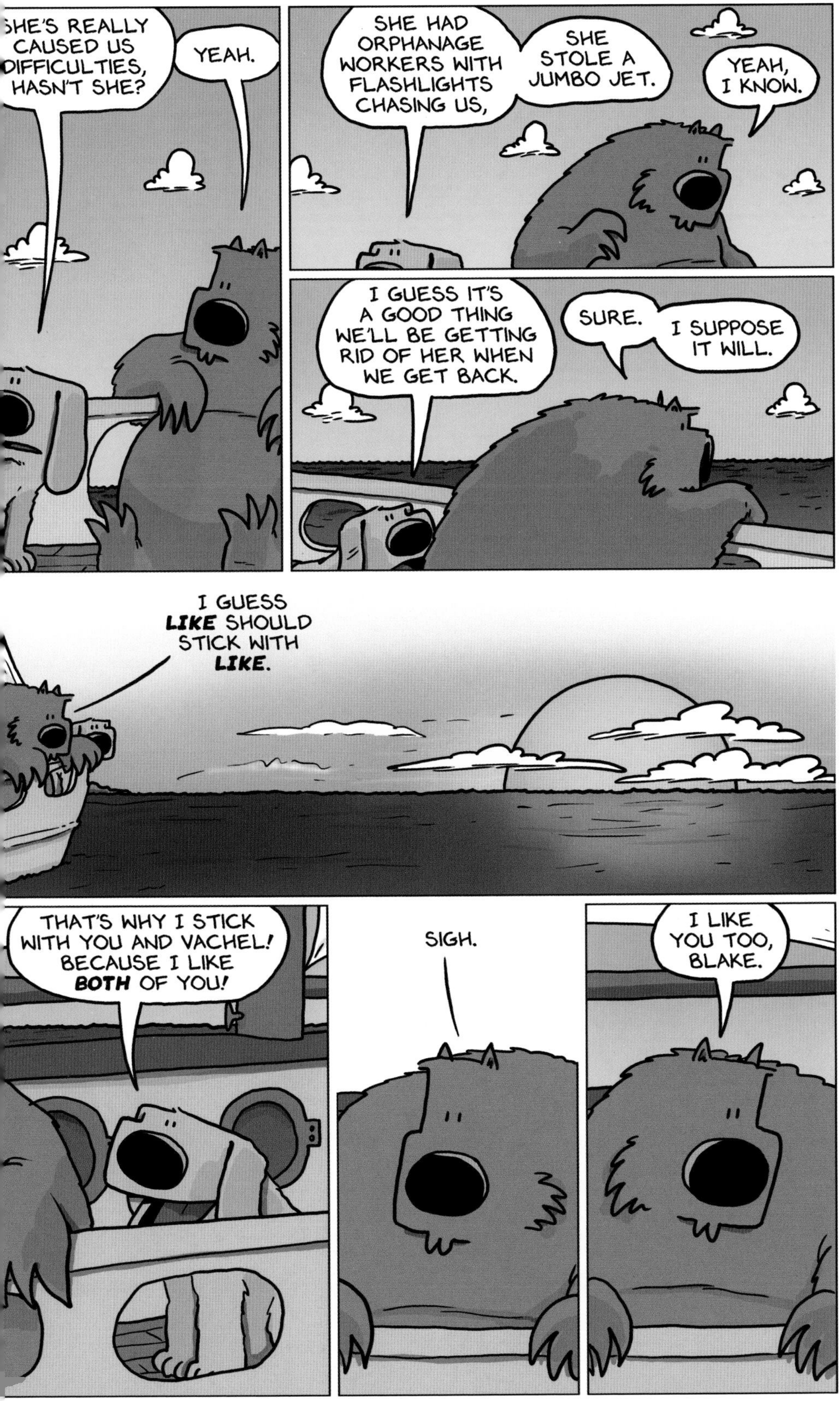
SHE'S REALLY CAUSED US DIFFICULTIES, HASN'T SHE?
YEAH.
SHE HAD ORPHANAGE WORKERS WITH FLASHLIGHTS CHASING US,
SHE STOLE A JUMBO JET.
YEAH, I KNOW.
I GUESS IT'S A GOOD THING WE'LL BE GETTING RID OF HER WHEN WE GET BACK.
SURE.
I SUPPOSE IT WILL.
I GUESS **LIKE** SHOULD STICK WITH **LIKE**.
THAT'S WHY I STICK WITH YOU AND VACHEL! BECAUSE I LIKE **BOTH** OF YOU!
SIGH.
I LIKE YOU TOO, BLAKE.

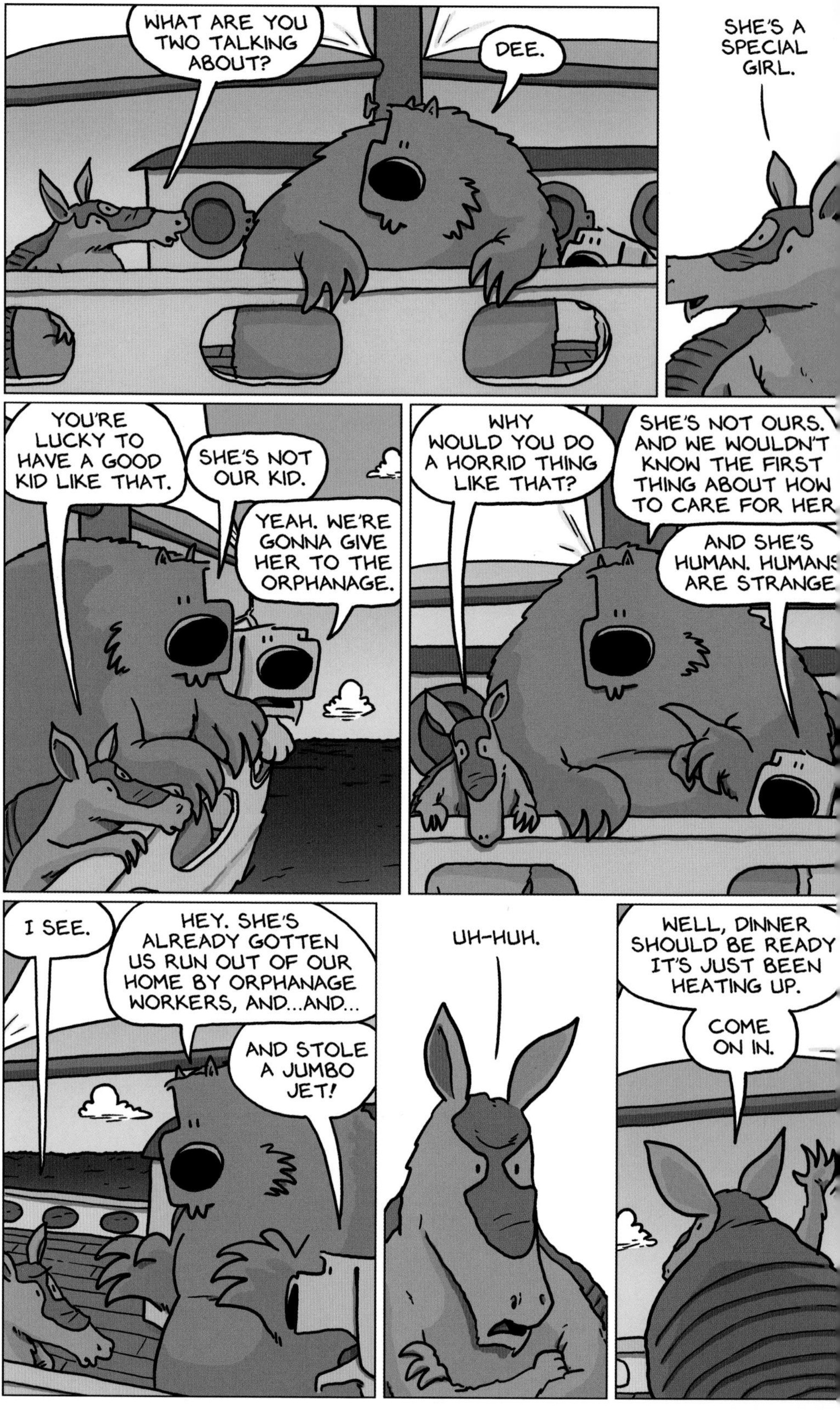
WHAT ARE YOU TWO TALKING ABOUT?
DEE.
SHE'S A SPECIAL GIRL.
YOU'RE LUCKY TO HAVE A GOOD KID LIKE THAT.
SHE'S NOT OUR KID.
YEAH. WE'RE GONNA GIVE HER TO THE ORPHANAGE.
WHY WOULD YOU DO A HORRID THING LIKE THAT?
SHE'S NOT OURS. AND WE WOULDN'T KNOW THE FIRST THING ABOUT HOW TO CARE FOR HER
AND SHE'S HUMAN. HUMANS ARE STRANGE
I SEE.
HEY. SHE'S ALREADY GOTTEN US RUN OUT OF OUR HOME BY ORPHANAGE WORKERS, AND...AND...
AND STOLE A JUMBO JET!
UH-HUH.
WELL, DINNER SHOULD BE READY IT'S JUST BEEN HEATING UP.
COME ON IN.

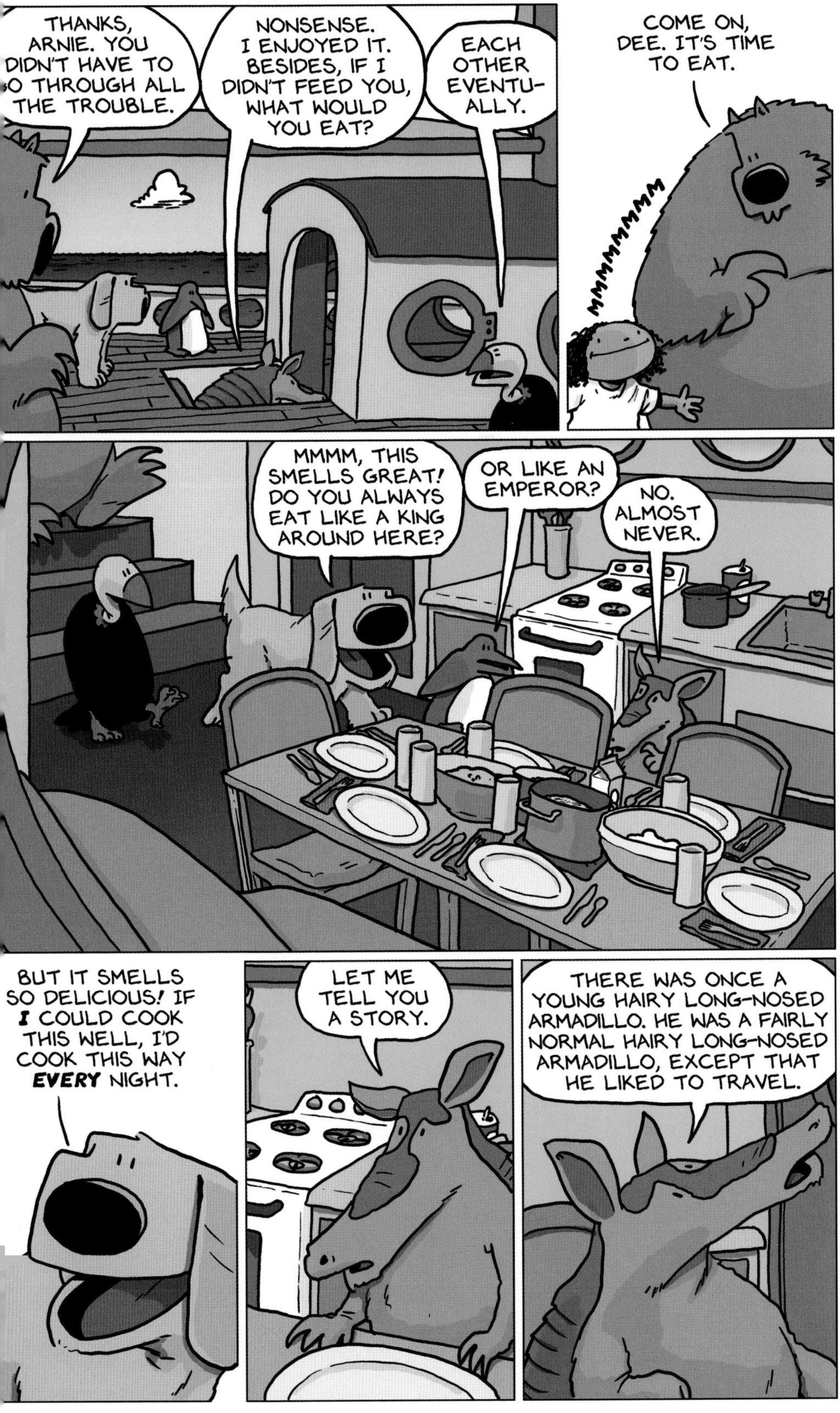
THANKS, ARNIE. YOU DIDN'T HAVE TO GO THROUGH ALL THE TROUBLE.
NONSENSE. I ENJOYED IT. BESIDES, IF I DIDN'T FEED YOU, WHAT WOULD YOU EAT?
EACH OTHER EVENTU-ALLY.
COME ON, DEE. IT'S TIME TO EAT.
MMMMMMMMM
MMMM, THIS SMELLS GREAT! DO YOU ALWAYS EAT LIKE A KING AROUND HERE?
OR LIKE AN EMPEROR?
NO. ALMOST NEVER.
BUT IT SMELLS SO DELICIOUS! IF *I* COULD COOK THIS WELL, I'D COOK THIS WAY ***EVERY*** NIGHT.
LET ME TELL YOU A STORY.
THERE WAS ONCE A YOUNG HAIRY LONG-NOSED ARMADILLO. HE WAS A FAIRLY NORMAL HAIRY LONG-NOSED ARMADILLO, EXCEPT THAT HE LIKED TO TRAVEL.

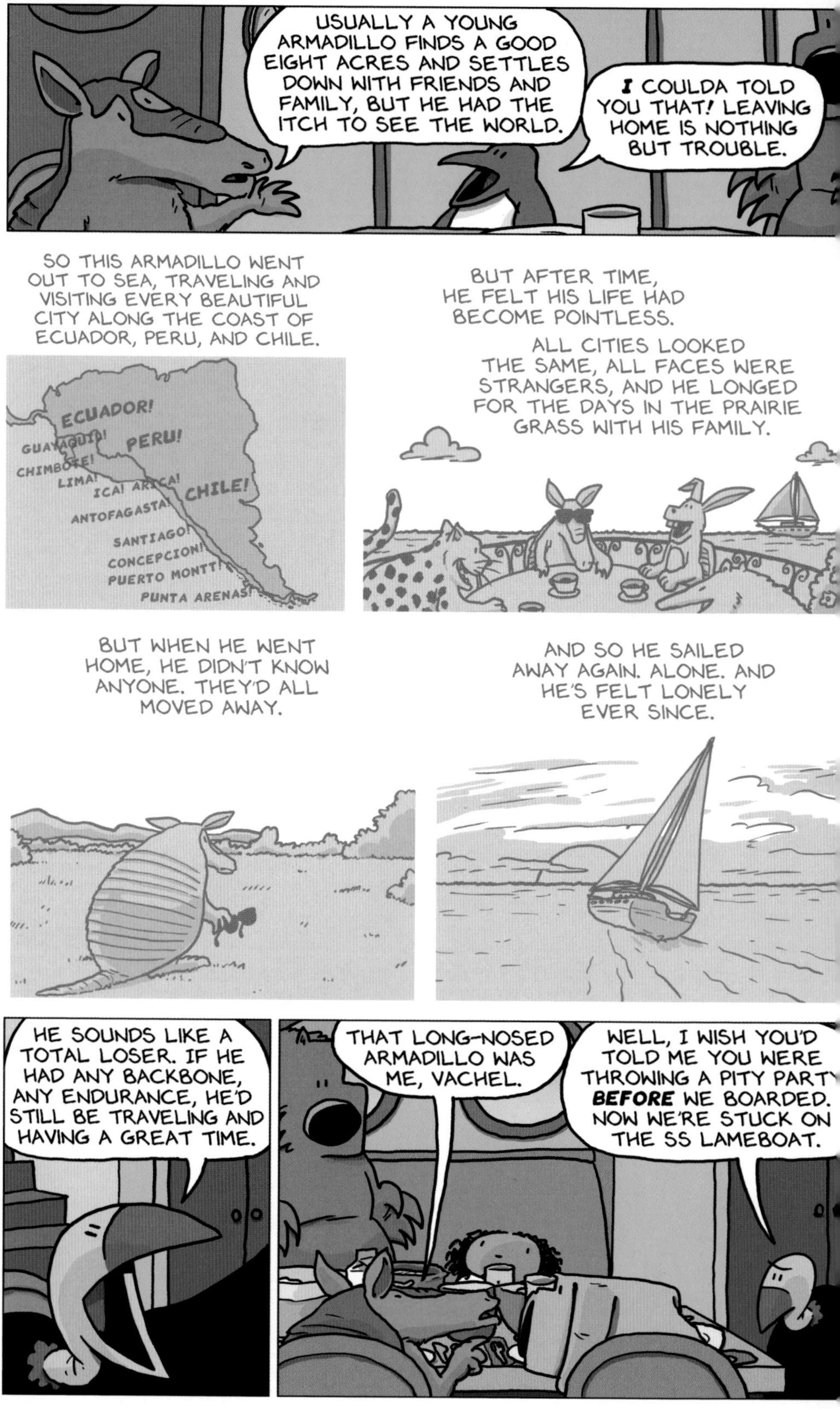

USUALLY A YOUNG ARMADILLO FINDS A GOOD EIGHT ACRES AND SETTLES DOWN WITH FRIENDS AND FAMILY, BUT HE HAD THE ITCH TO SEE THE WORLD.
I COULDA TOLD YOU THAT! LEAVING HOME IS NOTHING BUT TROUBLE.
SO THIS ARMADILLO WENT OUT TO SEA, TRAVELING AND VISITING EVERY BEAUTIFUL CITY ALONG THE COAST OF ECUADOR, PERU, AND CHILE.
ECUADOR!
PERU!
GUAYAQUIL!
CHIMBOTE!
LIMA!
ICA! ARICA!
CHILE!
ANTOFAGASTA!
SANTIAGO!
CONCEPCION!
PUERTO MONTT!
PUNTA ARENAS!
BUT AFTER TIME, HE FELT HIS LIFE HAD BECOME POINTLESS.
ALL CITIES LOOKED THE SAME, ALL FACES WERE STRANGERS, AND HE LONGED FOR THE DAYS IN THE PRAIRIE GRASS WITH HIS FAMILY.
BUT WHEN HE WENT HOME, HE DIDN'T KNOW ANYONE. THEY'D ALL MOVED AWAY.
AND SO HE SAILED AWAY AGAIN. ALONE. AND HE'S FELT LONELY EVER SINCE.
HE SOUNDS LIKE A TOTAL LOSER. IF HE HAD ANY BACKBONE, ANY ENDURANCE, HE'D STILL BE TRAVELING AND HAVING A GREAT TIME.
THAT LONG-NOSED ARMADILLO WAS ME, VACHEL.
WELL, I WISH YOU'D TOLD ME YOU WERE THROWING A PITY PARTY BEFORE WE BOARDED. NOW WE'RE STUCK ON THE SS LAMEBOAT.

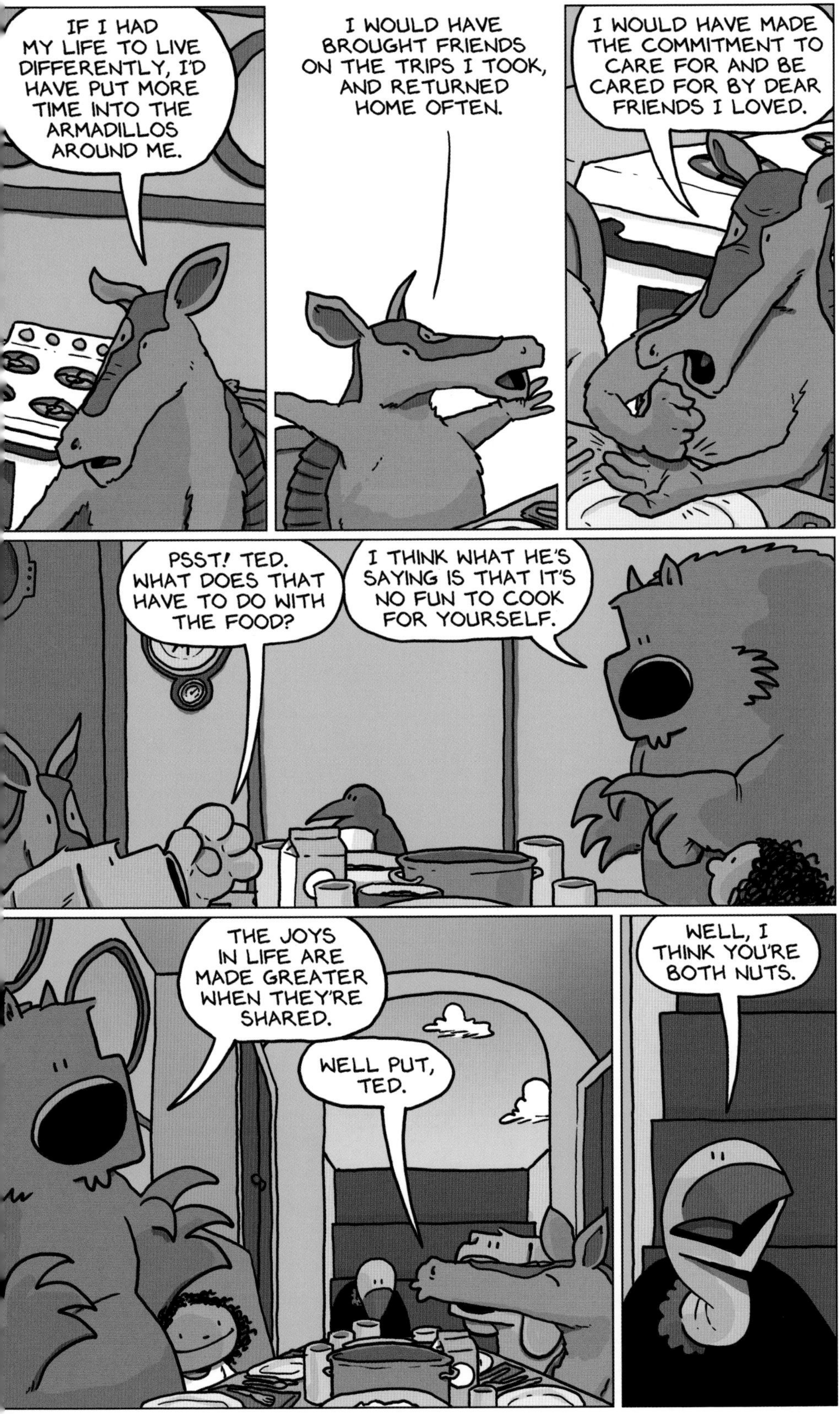
IF I HAD MY LIFE TO LIVE DIFFERENTLY, I'D HAVE PUT MORE TIME INTO THE ARMADILLOS AROUND ME.
I WOULD HAVE BROUGHT FRIENDS ON THE TRIPS I TOOK, AND RETURNED HOME OFTEN.
I WOULD HAVE MADE THE COMMITMENT TO CARE FOR AND BE CARED FOR BY DEAR FRIENDS I LOVED.
PSST! TED. WHAT DOES THAT HAVE TO DO WITH THE FOOD?
I THINK WHAT HE'S SAYING IS THAT IT'S NO FUN TO COOK FOR YOURSELF.
THE JOYS IN LIFE ARE MADE GREATER WHEN THEY'RE SHARED.
WELL PUT, TED.
WELL, I THINK YOU'RE BOTH NUTS.

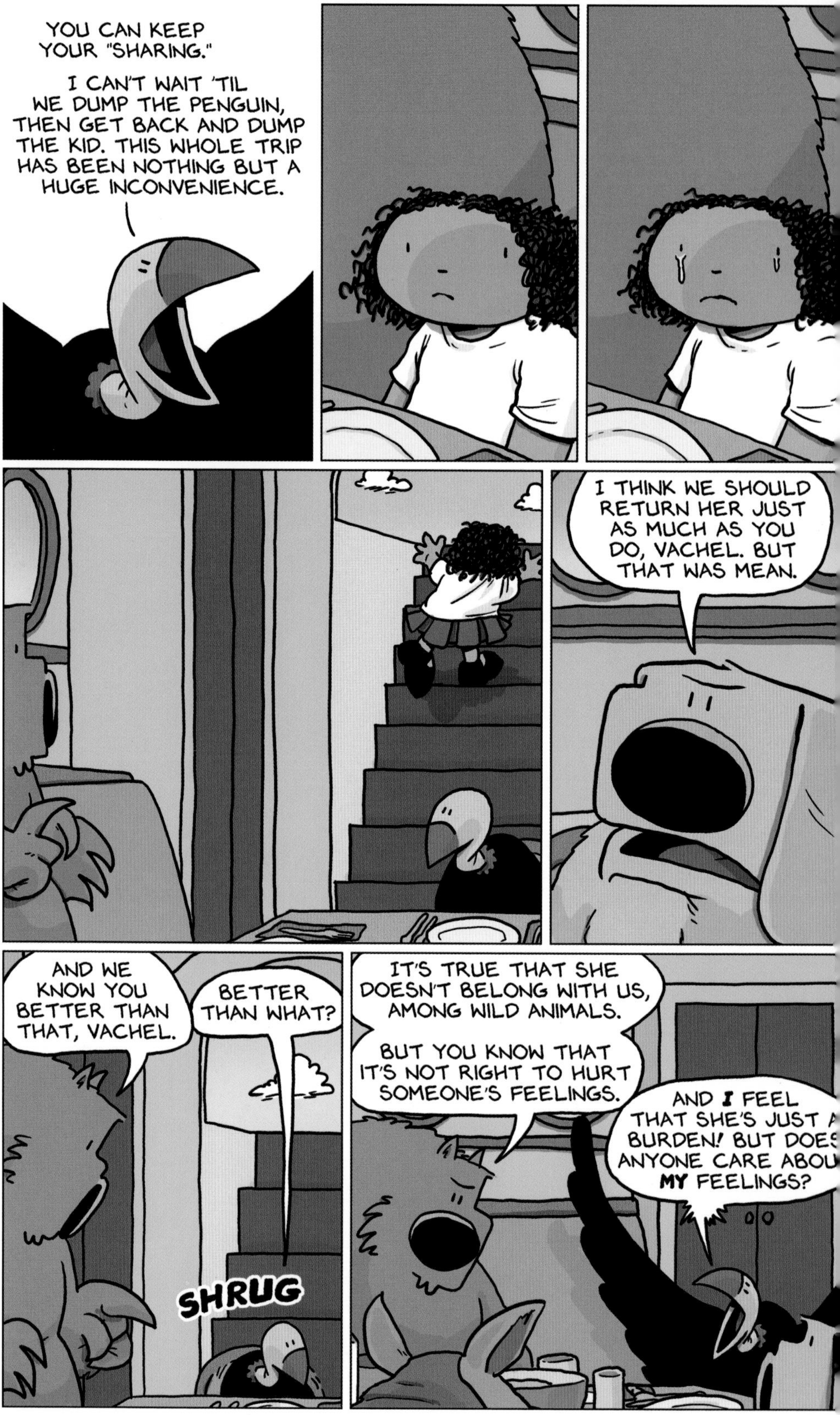

YOU CAN KEEP YOUR "SHARING."
I CAN'T WAIT 'TIL WE DUMP THE PENGUIN, THEN GET BACK AND DUMP THE KID. THIS WHOLE TRIP HAS BEEN NOTHING BUT A HUGE INCONVENIENCE.
I THINK WE SHOULD RETURN HER JUST AS MUCH AS YOU DO, VACHEL. BUT THAT WAS MEAN.
AND WE KNOW YOU BETTER THAN THAT, VACHEL.
BETTER THAN WHAT?
SHRUG
IT'S TRUE THAT SHE DOESN'T BELONG WITH US, AMONG WILD ANIMALS.
BUT YOU KNOW THAT IT'S NOT RIGHT TO HURT SOMEONE'S FEELINGS.
AND I FEEL THAT SHE'S JUST A BURDEN! BUT DOES ANYONE CARE ABOUT MY FEELINGS?

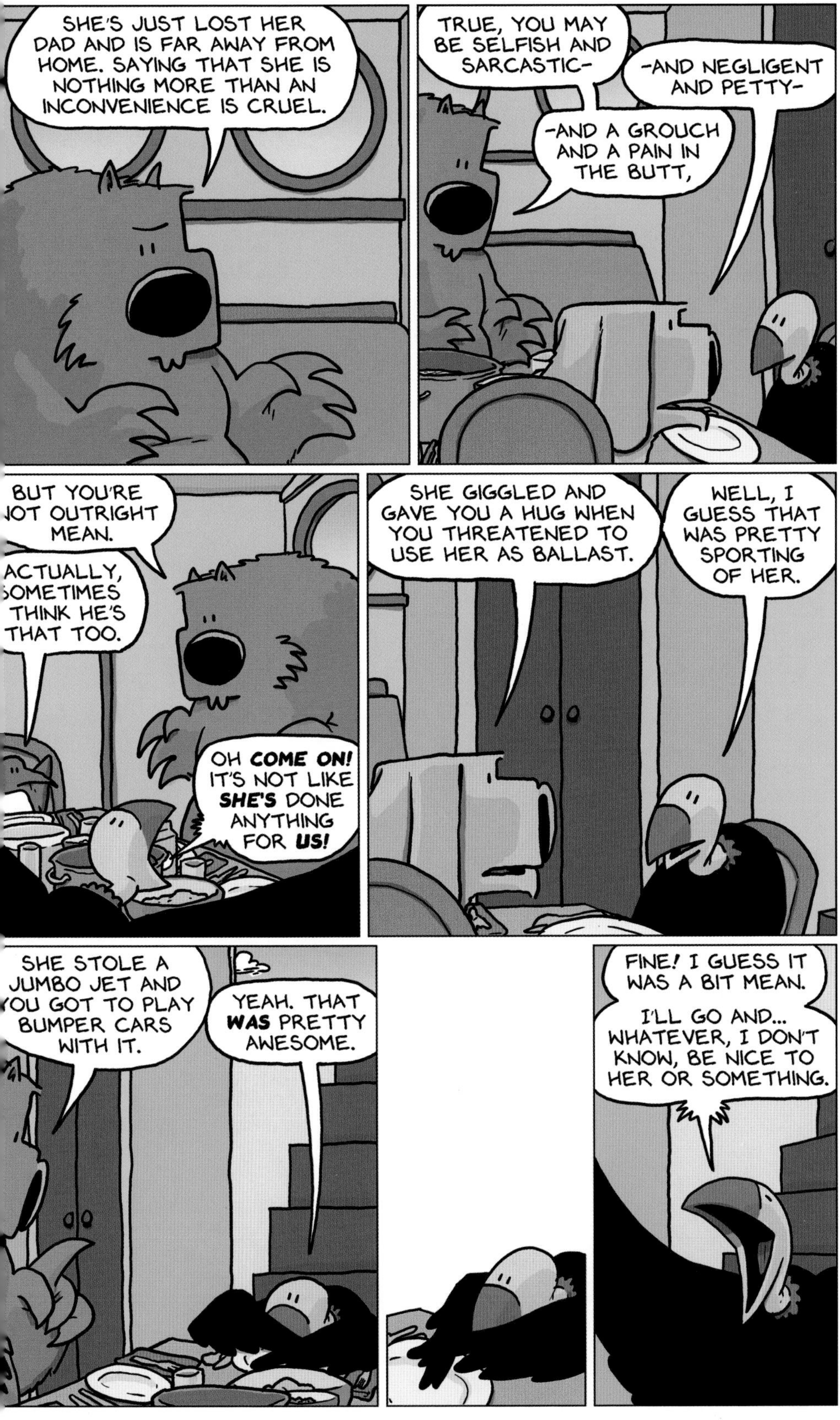
SHE'S JUST LOST HER DAD AND IS FAR AWAY FROM HOME. SAYING THAT SHE IS NOTHING MORE THAN AN INCONVENIENCE IS CRUEL.
TRUE, YOU MAY BE SELFISH AND SARCASTIC-
-AND NEGLIGENT AND PETTY-
-AND A GROUCH AND A PAIN IN THE BUTT,
BUT YOU'RE NOT OUTRIGHT MEAN.
ACTUALLY, SOMETIMES THINK HE'S THAT TOO.
OH **COME ON!** IT'S NOT LIKE **SHE'S** DONE ANYTHING FOR **US!**
SHE GIGGLED AND GAVE YOU A HUG WHEN YOU THREATENED TO USE HER AS BALLAST.
WELL, I GUESS THAT WAS PRETTY SPORTING OF HER.
SHE STOLE A JUMBO JET AND YOU GOT TO PLAY BUMPER CARS WITH IT.
YEAH. THAT **WAS** PRETTY AWESOME.
FINE! I GUESS IT WAS A BIT MEAN.
I'LL GO AND... WHATEVER, I DON'T KNOW, BE NICE TO HER OR SOMETHING.

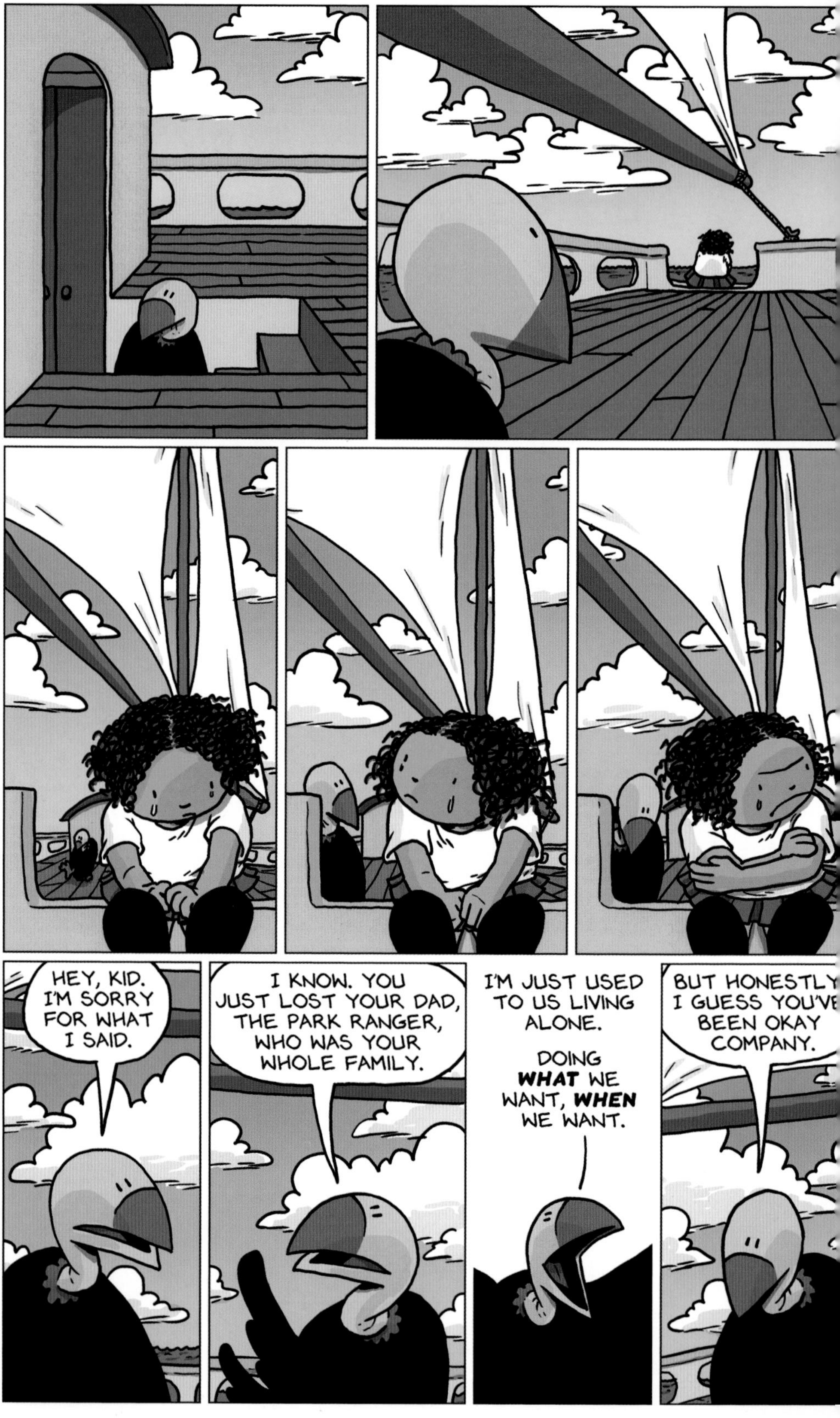
HEY, KID. I'M SORRY FOR WHAT I SAID.
I KNOW. YOU JUST LOST YOUR DAD, THE PARK RANGER, WHO WAS YOUR WHOLE FAMILY.
I'M JUST USED TO US LIVING ALONE.
DOING **WHAT** WE WANT, **WHEN** WE WANT.
BUT HONESTLY I GUESS YOU'VE BEEN OKAY COMPANY.

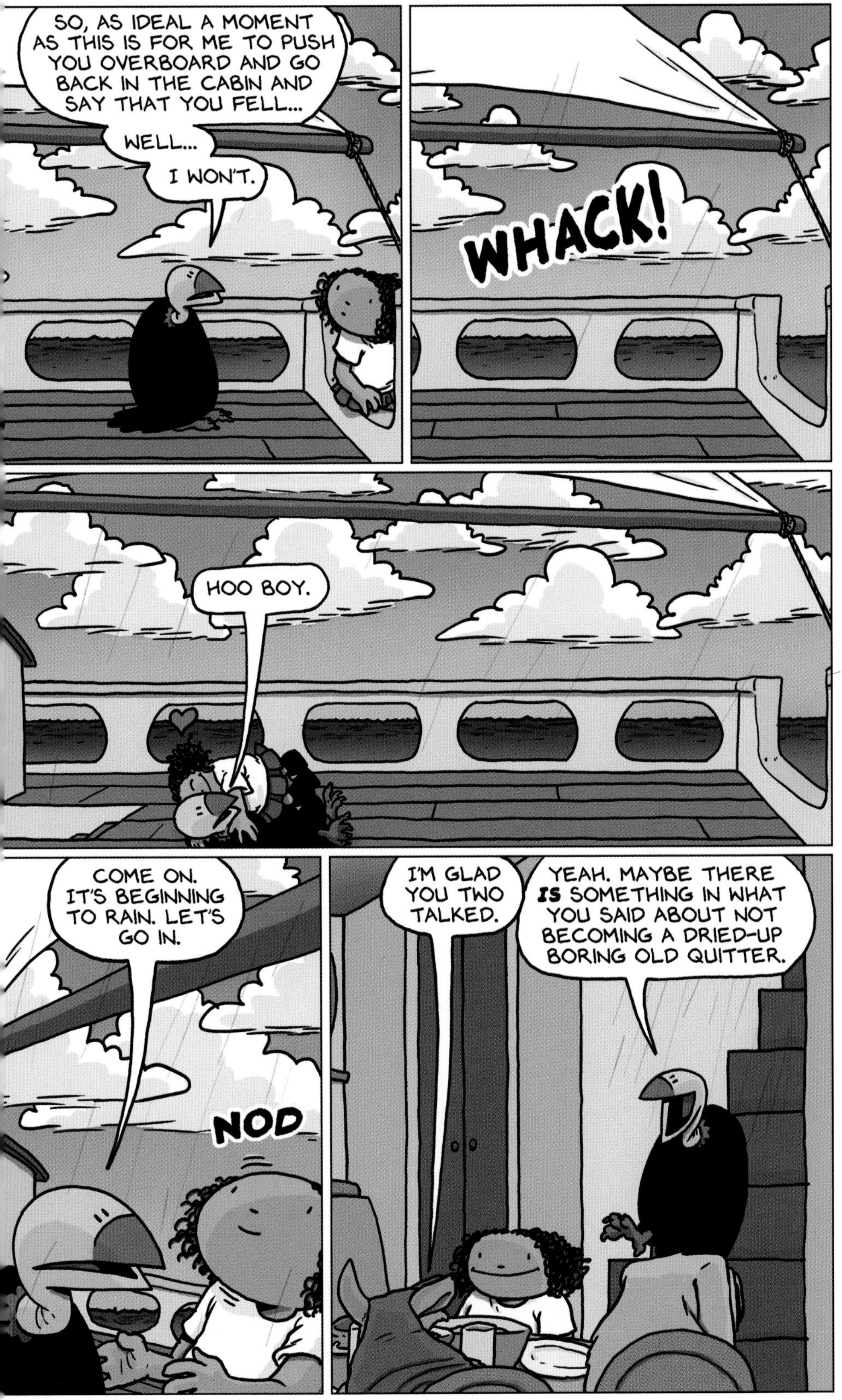
SO, AS IDEAL A MOMENT AS THIS IS FOR ME TO PUSH YOU OVERBOARD AND GO BACK IN THE CABIN AND SAY THAT YOU FELL...
WELL...
I WON'T.
WHACK!
HOO BOY.
COME ON. IT'S BEGINNING TO RAIN. LET'S GO IN.
NOD
I'M GLAD YOU TWO TALKED.
YEAH. MAYBE THERE IS SOMETHING IN WHAT YOU SAID ABOUT NOT BECOMING A DRIED-UP BORING OLD QUITTER.

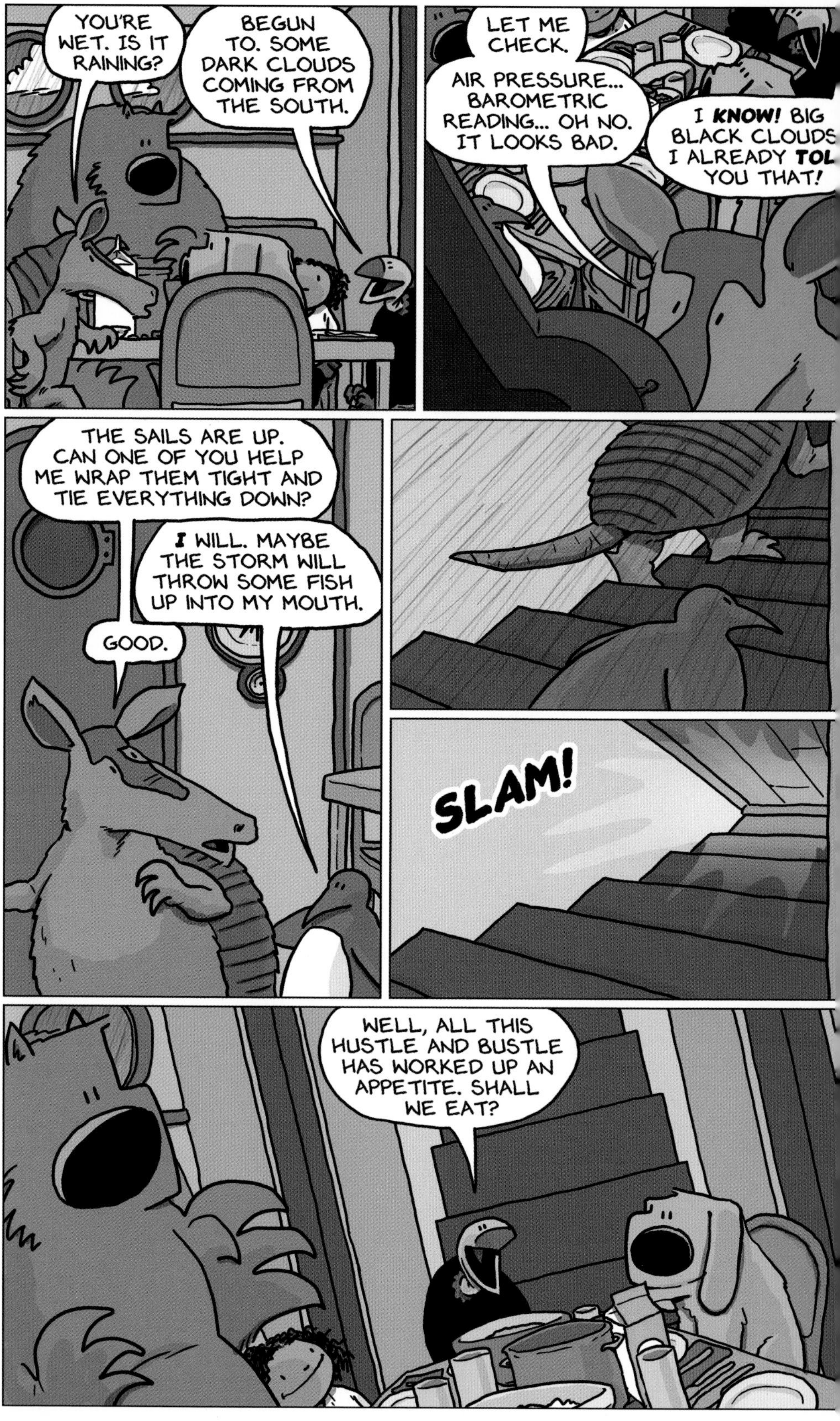
YOU'RE WET. IS IT RAINING?
BEGUN TO. SOME DARK CLOUDS COMING FROM THE SOUTH.
LET ME CHECK.
AIR PRESSURE... BAROMETRIC READING... OH NO. IT LOOKS BAD.
I **KNOW!** BIG BLACK CLOUDS I ALREADY **TOL** YOU THAT!
THE SAILS ARE UP. CAN ONE OF YOU HELP ME WRAP THEM TIGHT AND TIE EVERYTHING DOWN?
I WILL. MAYBE THE STORM WILL THROW SOME FISH UP INTO MY MOUTH.
GOOD.
SLAM!
WELL, ALL THIS HUSTLE AND BUSTLE HAS WORKED UP AN APPETITE. SHALL WE EAT?

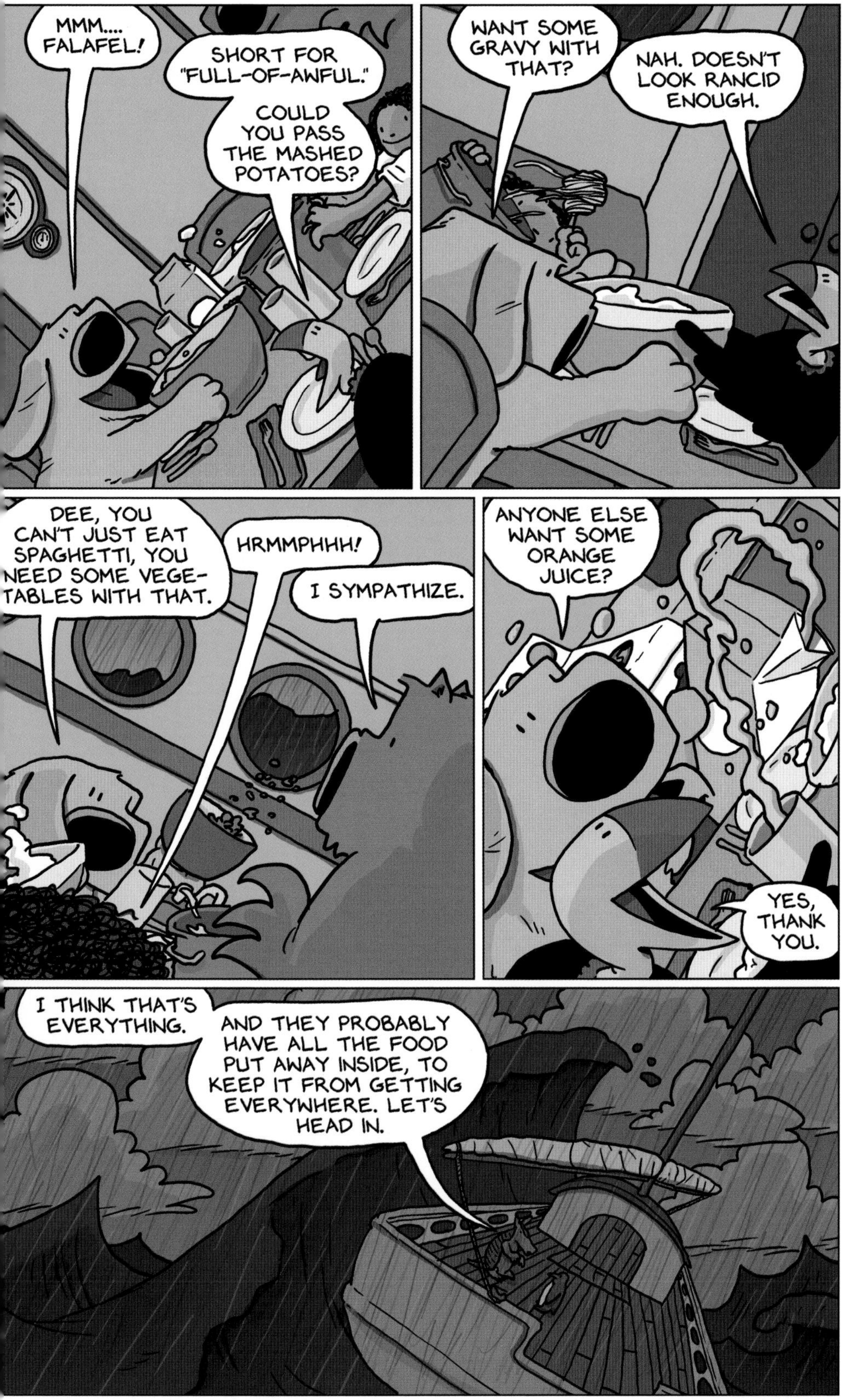
MMM.... FALAFEL!
SHORT FOR "FULL-OF-AWFUL."
COULD YOU PASS THE MASHED POTATOES?
WANT SOME GRAVY WITH THAT?
NAH. DOESN'T LOOK RANCID ENOUGH.
DEE, YOU CAN'T JUST EAT SPAGHETTI, YOU NEED SOME VEGE-TABLES WITH THAT.
HRMMPHHH!
I SYMPATHIZE.
ANYONE ELSE WANT SOME ORANGE JUICE?
YES, THANK YOU.
I THINK THAT'S EVERYTHING.
AND THEY PROBABLY HAVE ALL THE FOOD PUT AWAY INSIDE, TO KEEP IT FROM GETTING EVERYWHERE. LET'S HEAD IN.

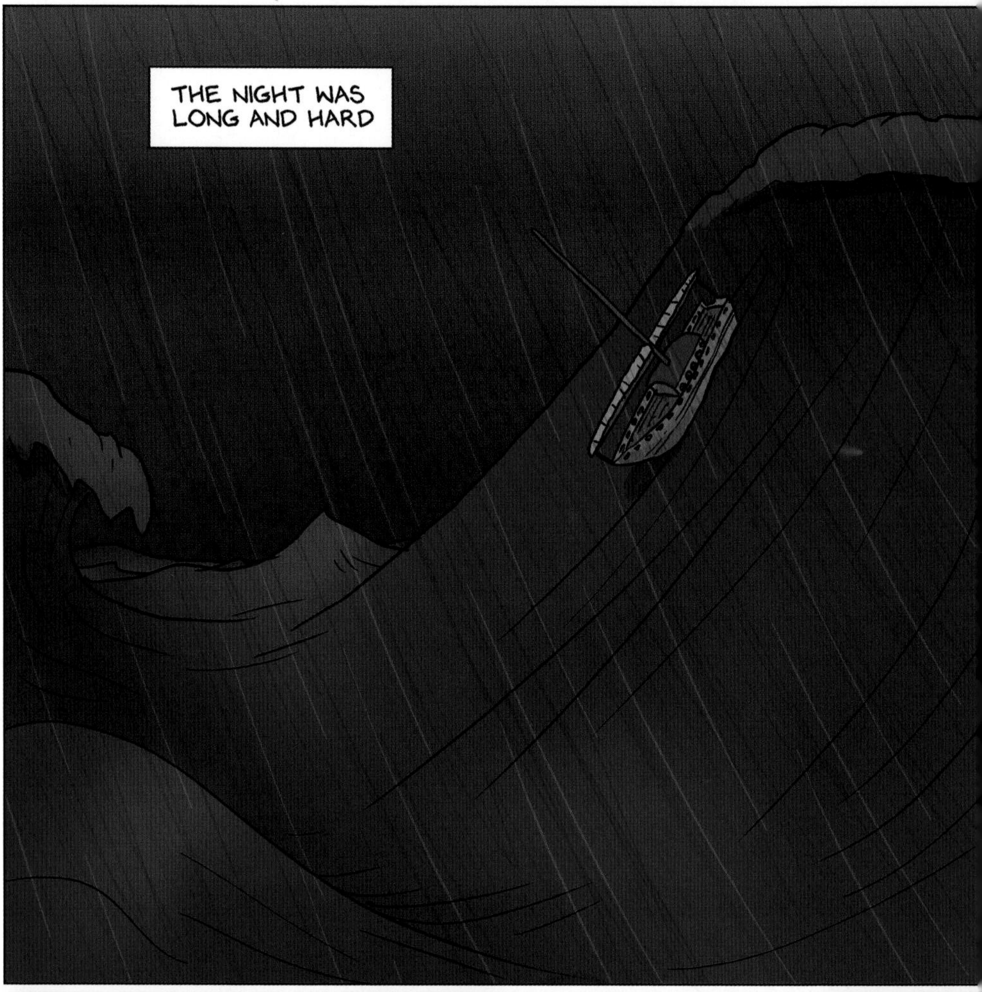
THE NIGHT WAS LONG AND HARD

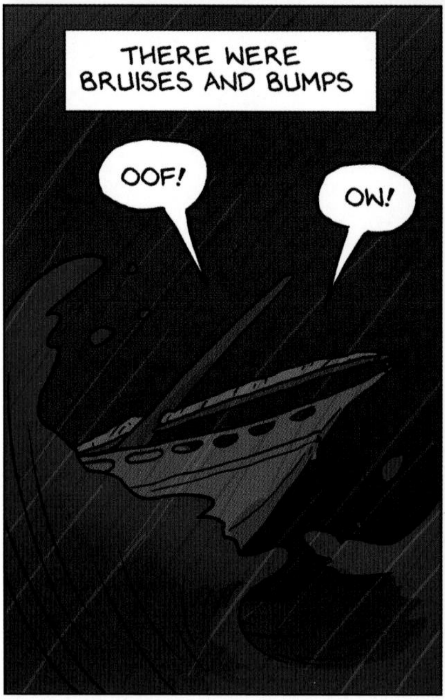
THERE WERE BRUISES AND BUMPS
OOF!
OW!

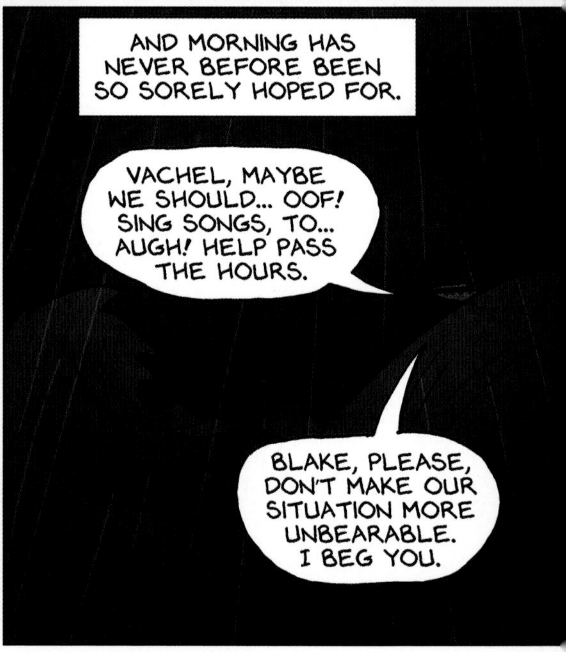
AND MORNING HAS NEVER BEFORE BEEN SO SORELY HOPED FOR.
VACHEL, MAYBE WE SHOULD... OOF! SING SONGS, TO... AUGH! HELP PASS THE HOURS.
BLAKE, PLEASE, DON'T MAKE OUR SITUATION MORE UNBEARABLE. I BEG YOU.

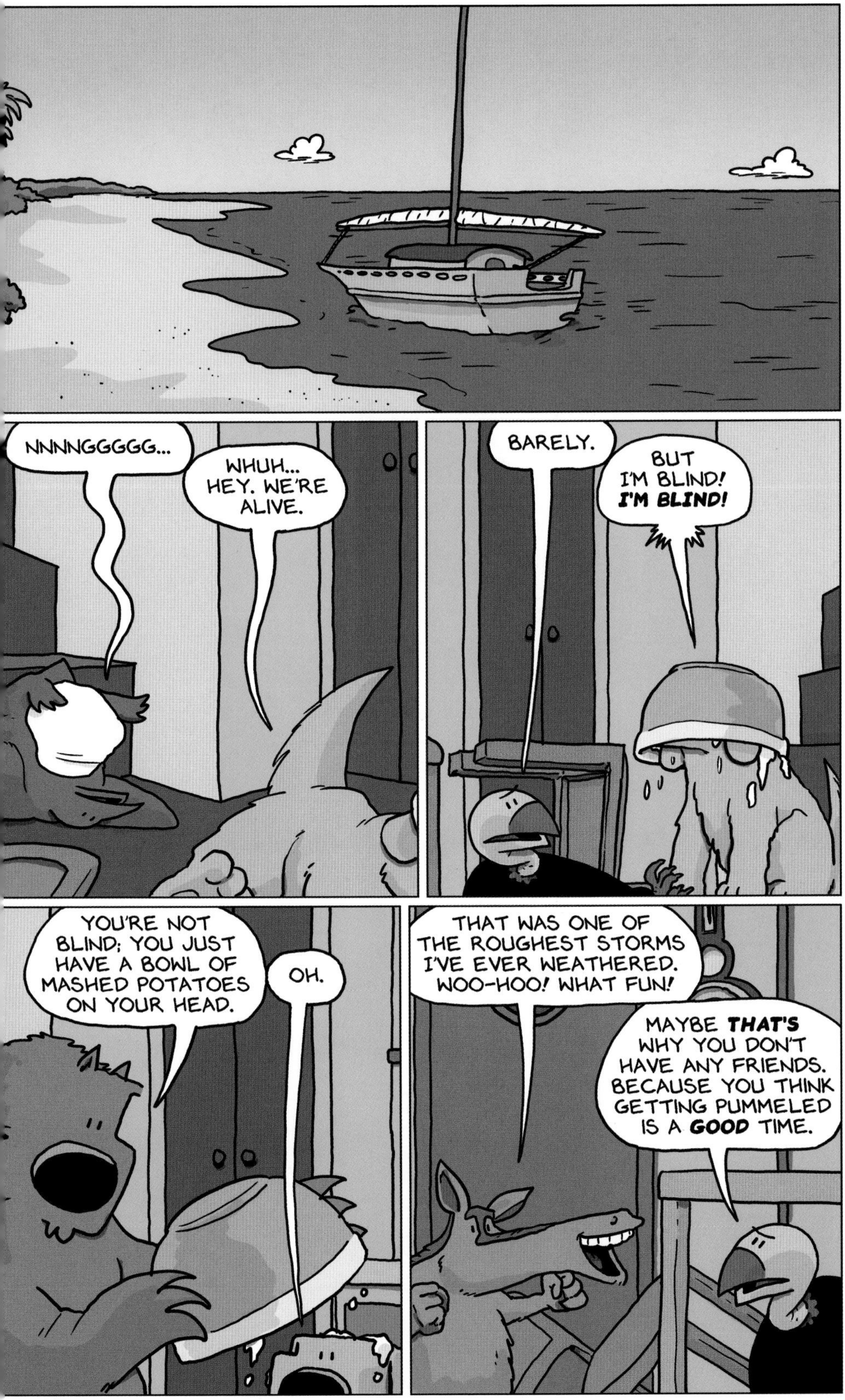
NNNNGGGGG...
WHUH... HEY. WE'RE ALIVE.
BARELY.
BUT I'M BLIND! **I'M BLIND!**
YOU'RE NOT BLIND; YOU JUST HAVE A BOWL OF MASHED POTATOES ON YOUR HEAD.
OH.
THAT WAS ONE OF THE ROUGHEST STORMS I'VE EVER WEATHERED. WOO-HOO! WHAT FUN!
MAYBE **THAT'S** WHY YOU DON'T HAVE ANY FRIENDS. BECAUSE YOU THINK GETTING PUMMELED IS A **GOOD** TIME.

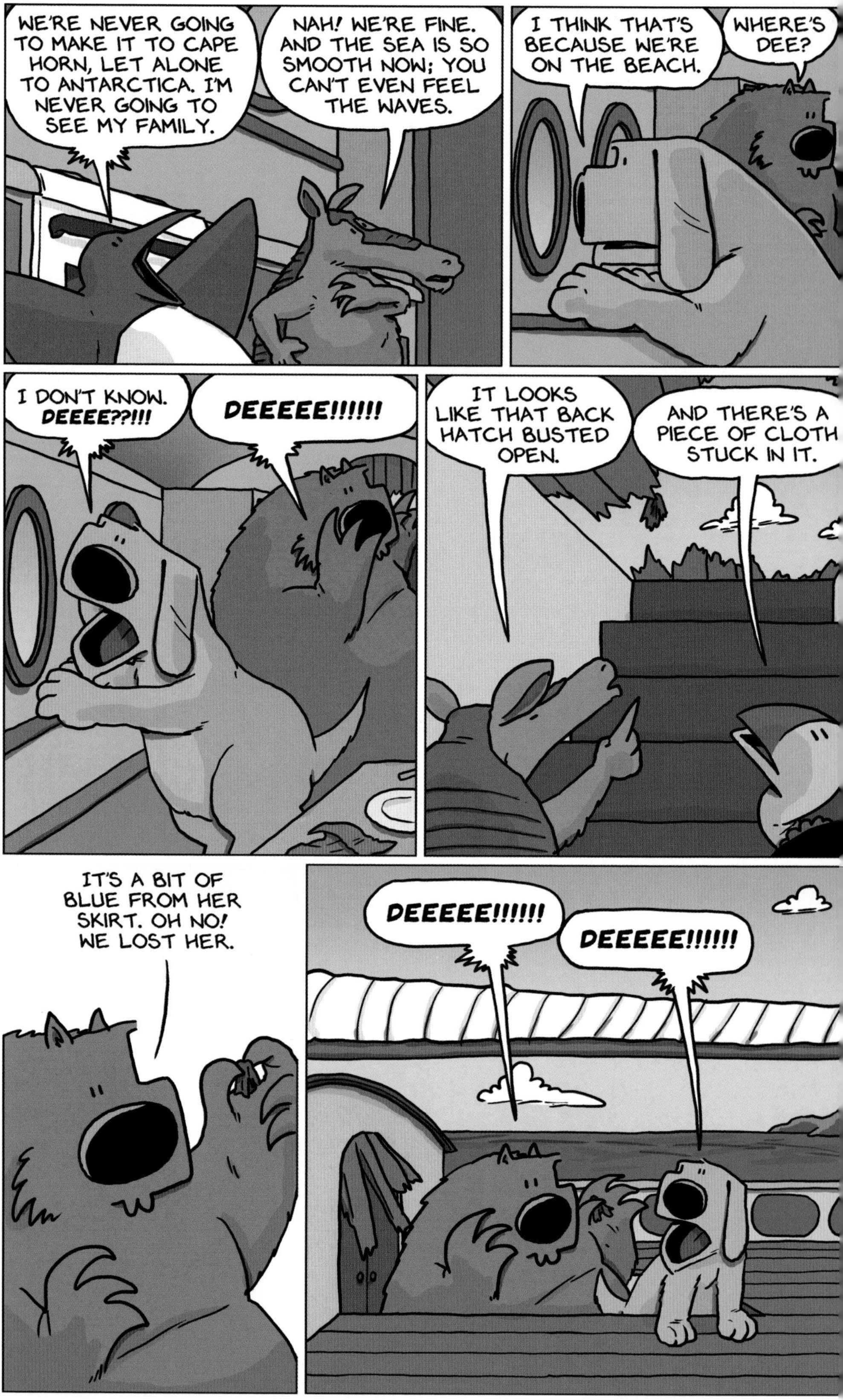
WE'RE NEVER GOING TO MAKE IT TO CAPE HORN, LET ALONE TO ANTARCTICA. I'M NEVER GOING TO SEE MY FAMILY.
NAH! WE'RE FINE. AND THE SEA IS SO SMOOTH NOW; YOU CAN'T EVEN FEEL THE WAVES.
I THINK THAT'S BECAUSE WE'RE ON THE BEACH.
WHERE'S DEE?
I DON'T KNOW. DEEEE??!!!
DEEEEE!!!!!!
IT LOOKS LIKE THAT BACK HATCH BUSTED OPEN.
AND THERE'S A PIECE OF CLOTH STUCK IN IT.
IT'S A BIT OF BLUE FROM HER SKIRT. OH NO! WE LOST HER.
DEEEEE!!!!!!
DEEEEE!!!!!!

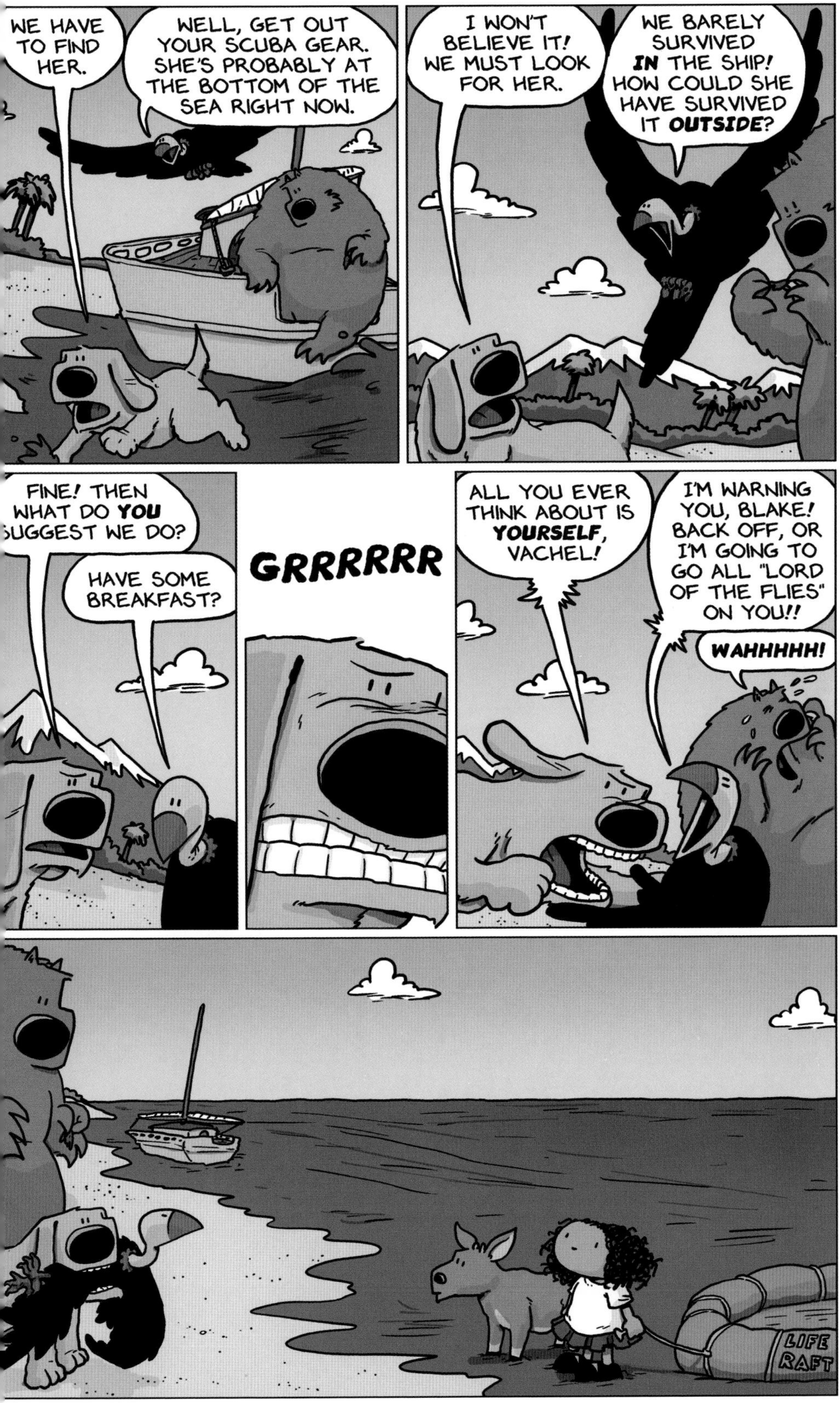

WE HAVE TO FIND HER.
WELL, GET OUT YOUR SCUBA GEAR. SHE'S PROBABLY AT THE BOTTOM OF THE SEA RIGHT NOW.
I WON'T BELIEVE IT! WE MUST LOOK FOR HER.
WE BARELY SURVIVED **IN** THE SHIP! HOW COULD SHE HAVE SURVIVED IT **OUTSIDE**?
FINE! THEN WHAT DO **YOU** SUGGEST WE DO?
HAVE SOME BREAKFAST?
GRRRRRR
ALL YOU EVER THINK ABOUT IS **YOURSELF**, VACHEL!
I'M WARNING YOU, BLAKE! BACK OFF, OR I'M GOING TO GO ALL "LORD OF THE FLIES" ON YOU!!
WAHHHHH!
LIFE RAFT

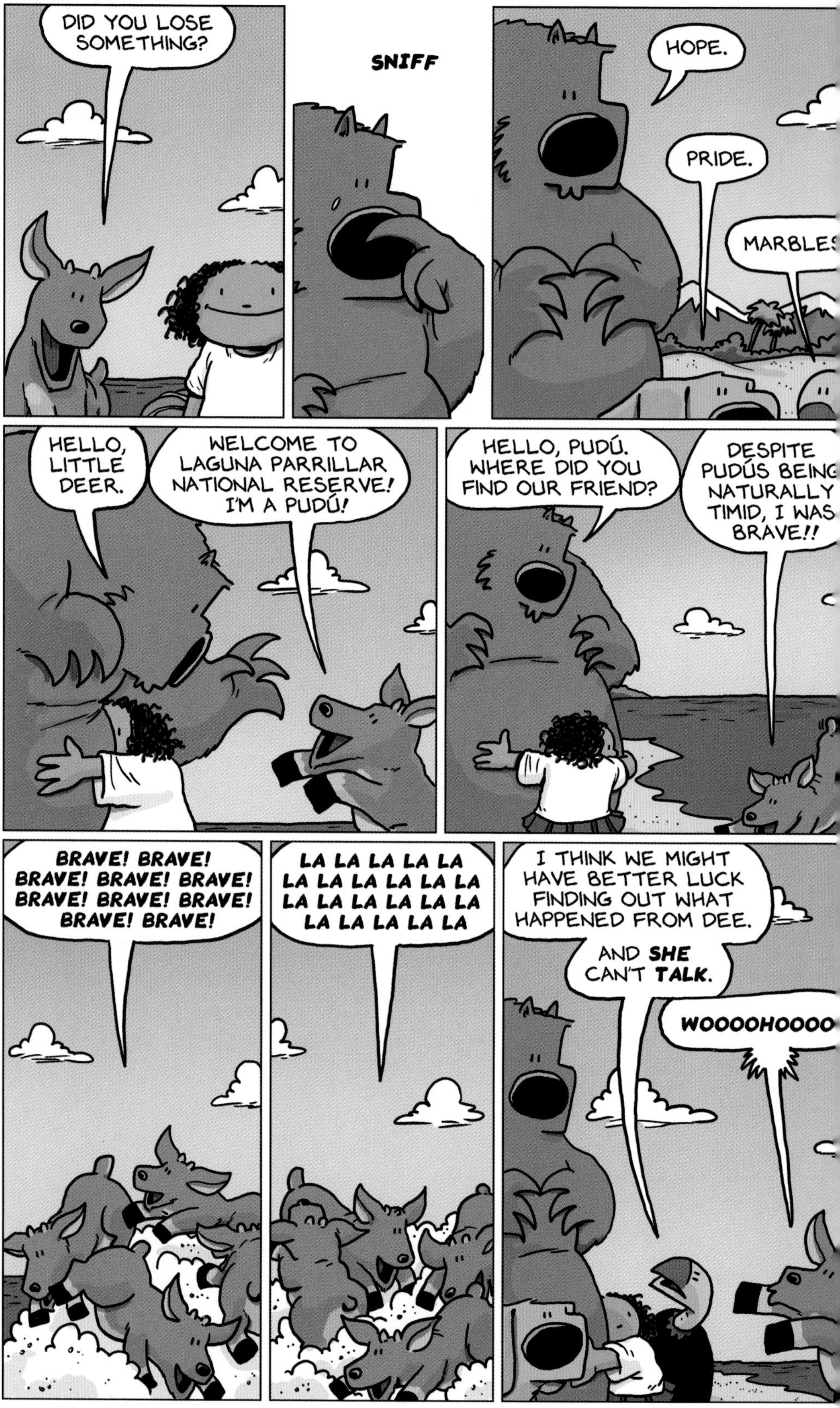
DID YOU LOSE SOMETHING?
SNIFF
HOPE.
PRIDE.
MARBLES
HELLO, LITTLE DEER.
WELCOME TO LAGUNA PARRILLAR NATIONAL RESERVE! I'M A PUDÚ!
HELLO, PUDÚ. WHERE DID YOU FIND OUR FRIEND?
DESPITE PUDÚS BEING NATURALLY TIMID, I WAS BRAVE!!
BRAVE! BRAVE! BRAVE! BRAVE! BRAVE! BRAVE! BRAVE! BRAVE! BRAVE! BRAVE!
LA LA LA LA LA LA LA LA LA LA LA LA LA LA LA LA LA LA LA LA LA LA
I THINK WE MIGHT HAVE BETTER LUCK FINDING OUT WHAT HAPPENED FROM DEE.
AND SHE CAN'T TALK.
WOOOOHOOOO

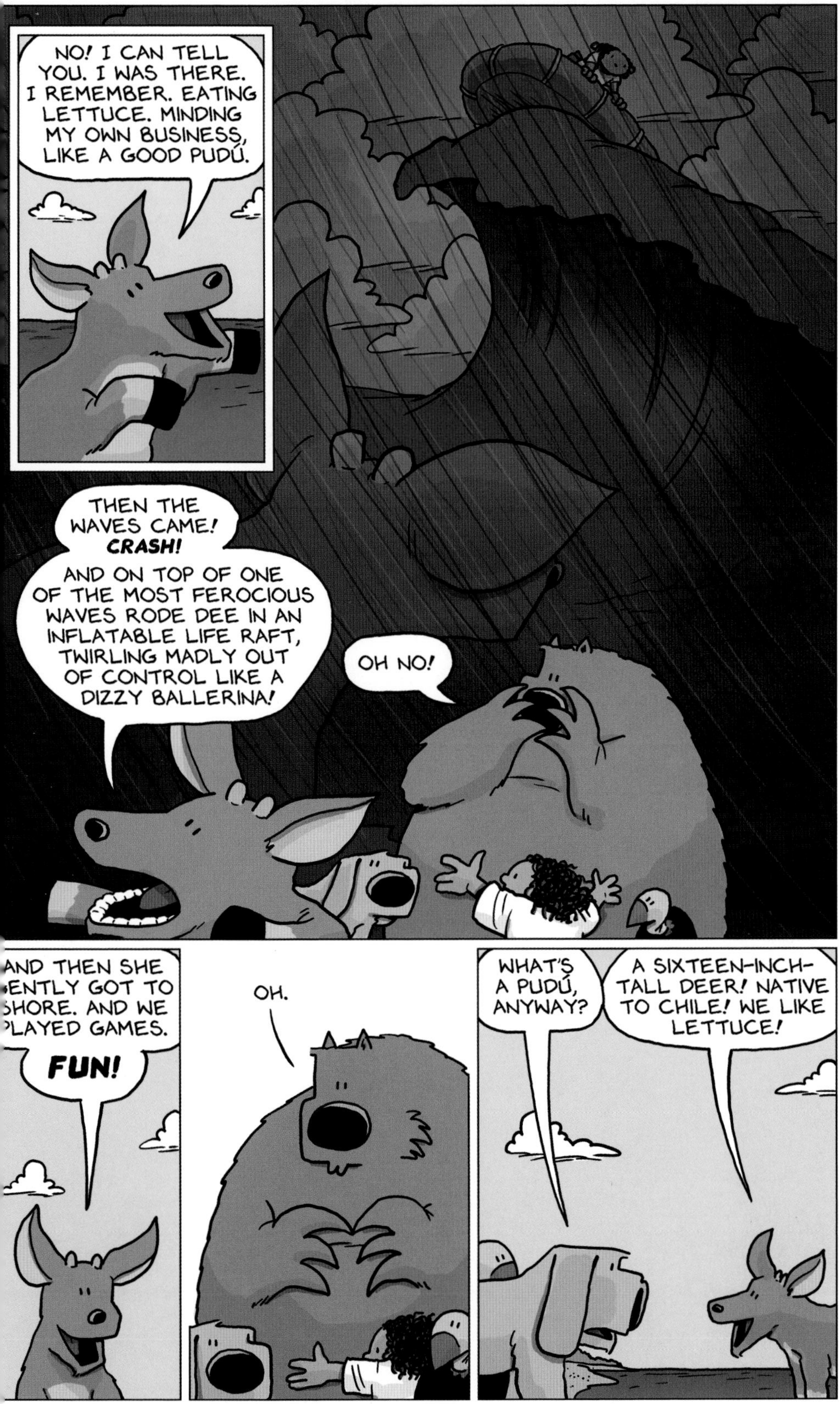
NO! I CAN TELL YOU. I WAS THERE. I REMEMBER. EATING LETTUCE. MINDING MY OWN BUSINESS, LIKE A GOOD PUDÚ.
THEN THE WAVES CAME! CRASH!
AND ON TOP OF ONE OF THE MOST FEROCIOUS WAVES RODE DEE IN AN INFLATABLE LIFE RAFT, TWIRLING MADLY OUT OF CONTROL LIKE A DIZZY BALLERINA!
OH NO!
AND THEN SHE ENTLY GOT TO SHORE. AND WE PLAYED GAMES.
FUN!
OH.
WHAT'S A PUDÚ, ANYWAY?
A SIXTEEN-INCH-TALL DEER! NATIVE TO CHILE! WE LIKE LETTUCE!

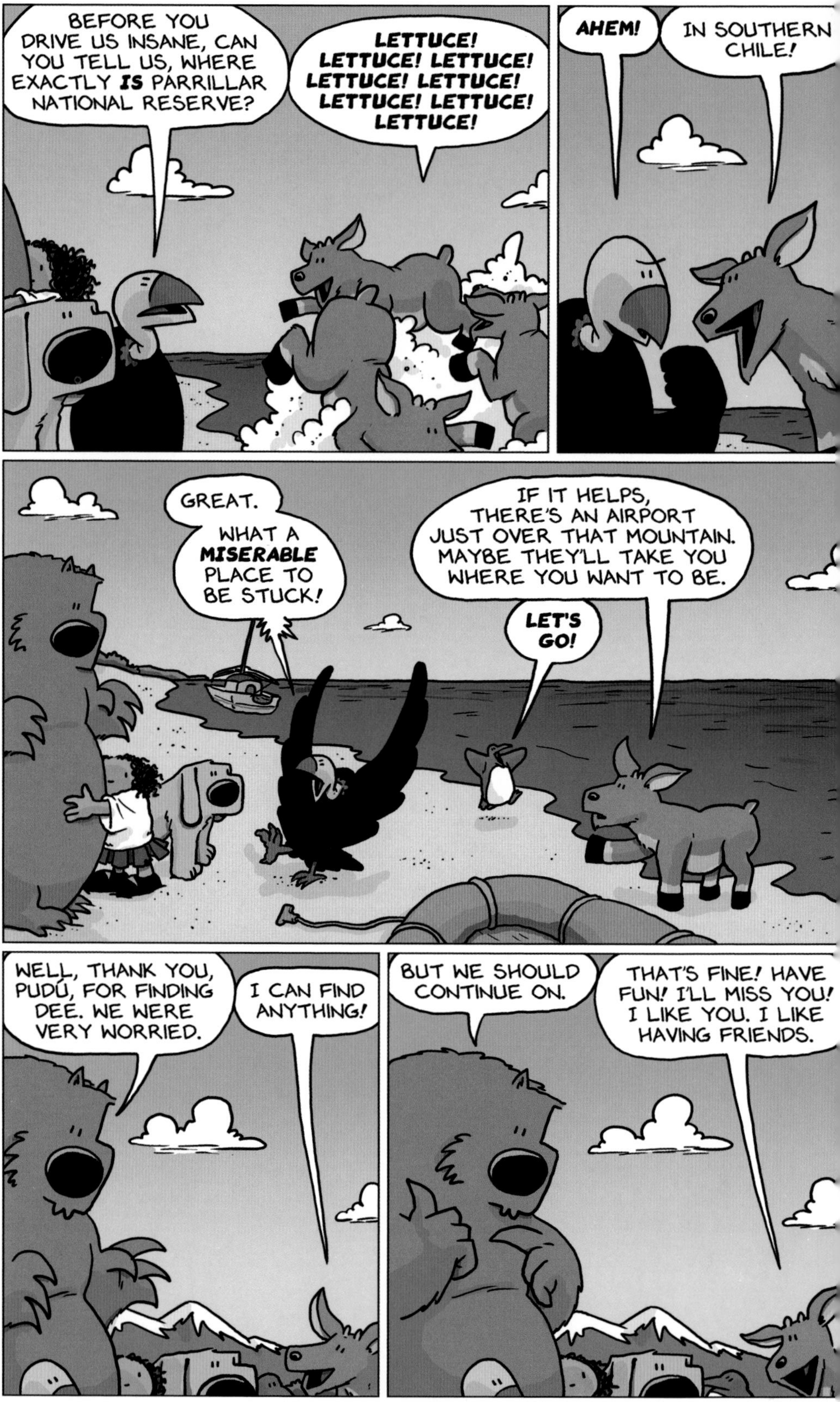
BEFORE YOU DRIVE US INSANE, CAN YOU TELL US, WHERE EXACTLY **IS** PARRILLAR NATIONAL RESERVE?
LETTUCE! LETTUCE! LETTUCE! LETTUCE! LETTUCE! LETTUCE! LETTUCE! LETTUCE!
AHEM!
IN SOUTHERN CHILE!
GREAT.
WHAT A **MISERABLE** PLACE TO BE STUCK!
IF IT HELPS, THERE'S AN AIRPORT JUST OVER THAT MOUNTAIN. MAYBE THEY'LL TAKE YOU WHERE YOU WANT TO BE.
LET'S GO!
WELL, THANK YOU, PUDÚ, FOR FINDING DEE. WE WERE VERY WORRIED.
I CAN FIND ANYTHING!
BUT WE SHOULD CONTINUE ON.
THAT'S FINE! HAVE FUN! I'LL MISS YOU! I LIKE YOU. I LIKE HAVING FRIENDS.

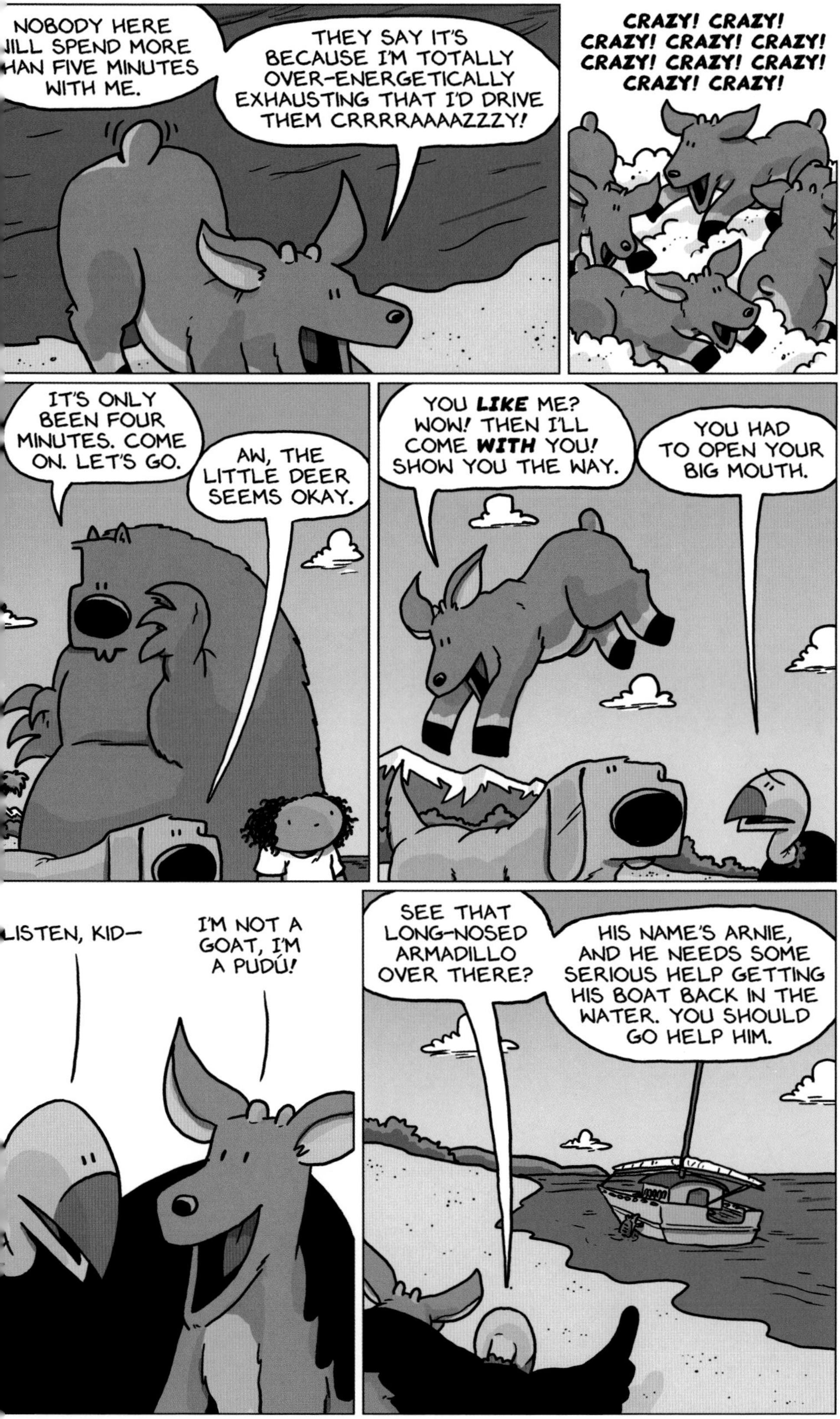
NOBODY HERE
[W]ILL SPEND MORE
[T]HAN FIVE MINUTES
WITH ME.
THEY SAY IT'S BECAUSE I'M TOTALLY OVER-ENERGETICALLY EXHAUSTING THAT I'D DRIVE THEM CRRRRAAAAZZZY!
CRAZY! CRAZY! CRAZY! CRAZY! CRAZY! CRAZY! CRAZY! CRAZY! CRAZY! CRAZY!
IT'S ONLY BEEN FOUR MINUTES. COME ON. LET'S GO.
AW, THE LITTLE DEER SEEMS OKAY.
YOU **LIKE** ME? WOW! THEN I'LL COME **WITH** YOU! SHOW YOU THE WAY.
YOU HAD TO OPEN YOUR BIG MOUTH.
LISTEN, KID—
I'M NOT A GOAT, I'M A PUDÚ!
SEE THAT LONG-NOSED ARMADILLO OVER THERE?
HIS NAME'S ARNIE, AND HE NEEDS SOME SERIOUS HELP GETTING HIS BOAT BACK IN THE WATER. YOU SHOULD GO HELP HIM.

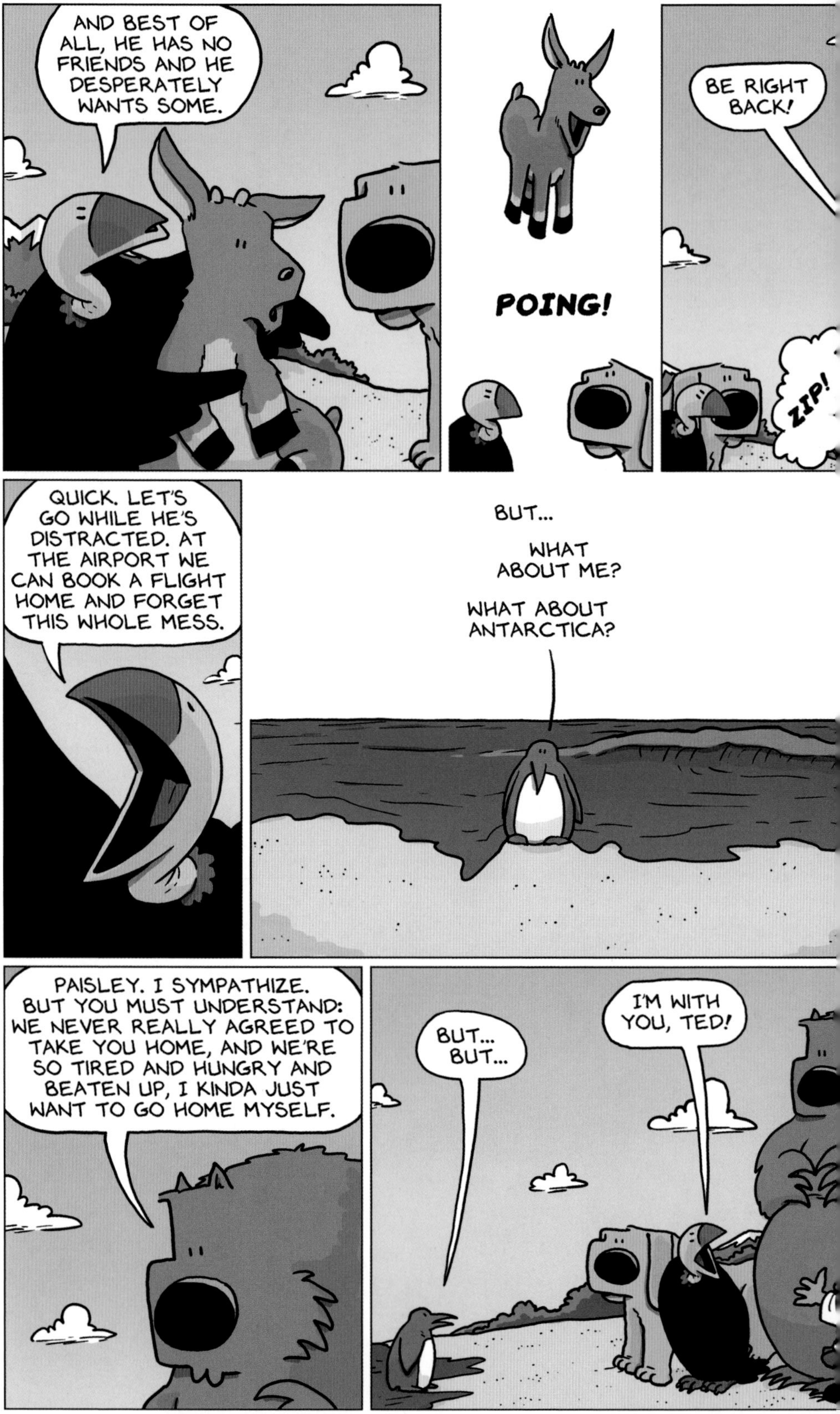
AND BEST OF ALL, HE HAS NO FRIENDS AND HE DESPERATELY WANTS SOME.
POING!
BE RIGHT BACK!
ZIP!
QUICK. LET'S GO WHILE HE'S DISTRACTED. AT THE AIRPORT WE CAN BOOK A FLIGHT HOME AND FORGET THIS WHOLE MESS.
BUT...
WHAT ABOUT ME?
WHAT ABOUT ANTARCTICA?
PAISLEY. I SYMPATHIZE. BUT YOU MUST UNDERSTAND: WE NEVER REALLY AGREED TO TAKE YOU HOME, AND WE'RE SO TIRED AND HUNGRY AND BEATEN UP, I KINDA JUST WANT TO GO HOME MYSELF.
BUT... BUT...
I'M WITH YOU, TED!

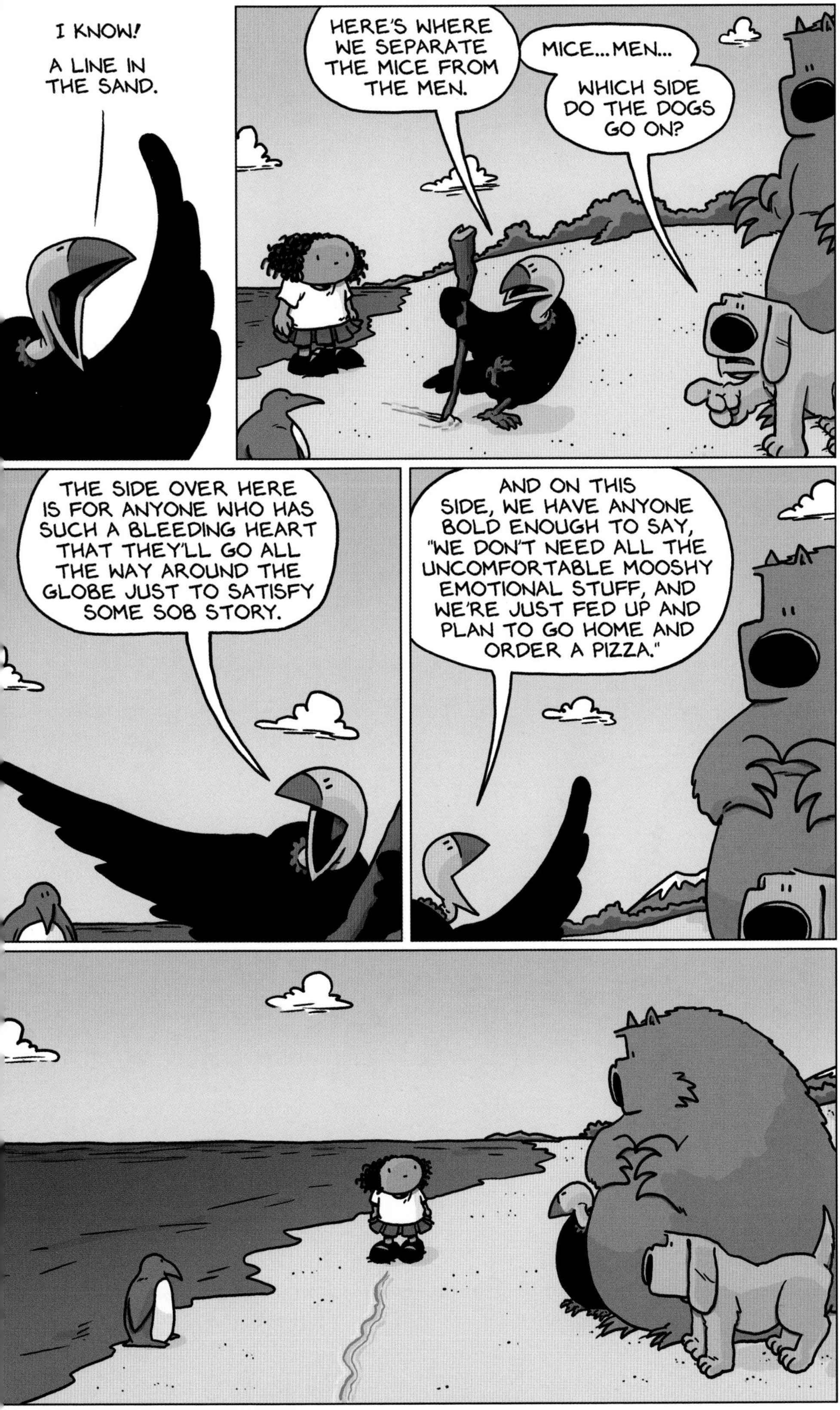

I KNOW!
A LINE IN THE SAND.
HERE'S WHERE WE SEPARATE THE MICE FROM THE MEN.
MICE...MEN...
WHICH SIDE DO THE DOGS GO ON?
THE SIDE OVER HERE IS FOR ANYONE WHO HAS SUCH A BLEEDING HEART THAT THEY'LL GO ALL THE WAY AROUND THE GLOBE JUST TO SATISFY SOME SOB STORY.
AND ON THIS SIDE, WE HAVE ANYONE BOLD ENOUGH TO SAY, "WE DON'T NEED ALL THE UNCOMFORTABLE MOOSHY EMOTIONAL STUFF, AND WE'RE JUST FED UP AND PLAN TO GO HOME AND ORDER A PIZZA."

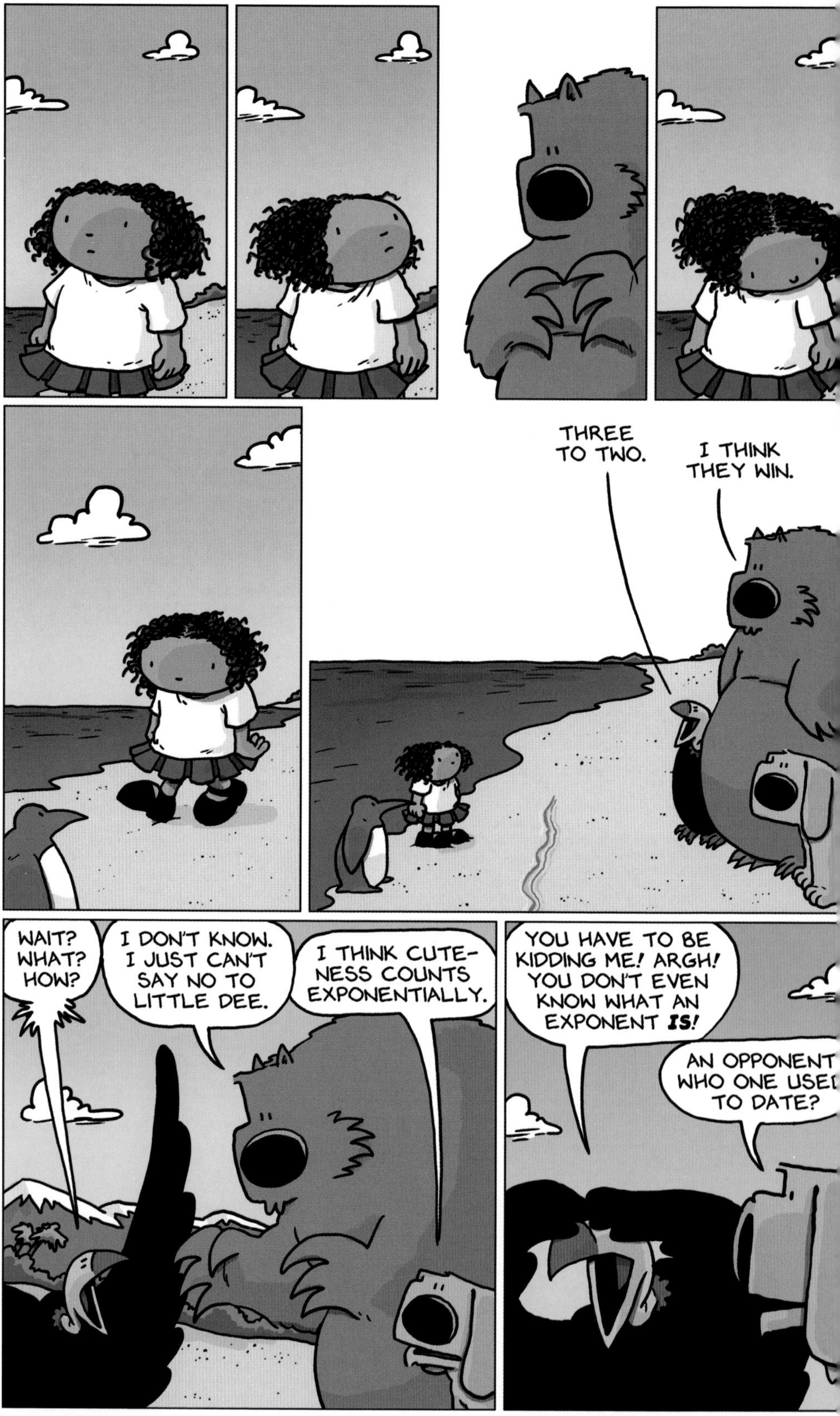
THREE TO TWO.
I THINK THEY WIN.
WAIT? WHAT? HOW?
I DON'T KNOW. I JUST CAN'T SAY NO TO LITTLE DEE.
I THINK CUTE-NESS COUNTS EXPONENTIALLY.
YOU HAVE TO BE KIDDING ME! ARGH! YOU DON'T EVEN KNOW WHAT AN EXPONENT *IS!*
AN OPPONENT WHO ONE USED TO DATE?

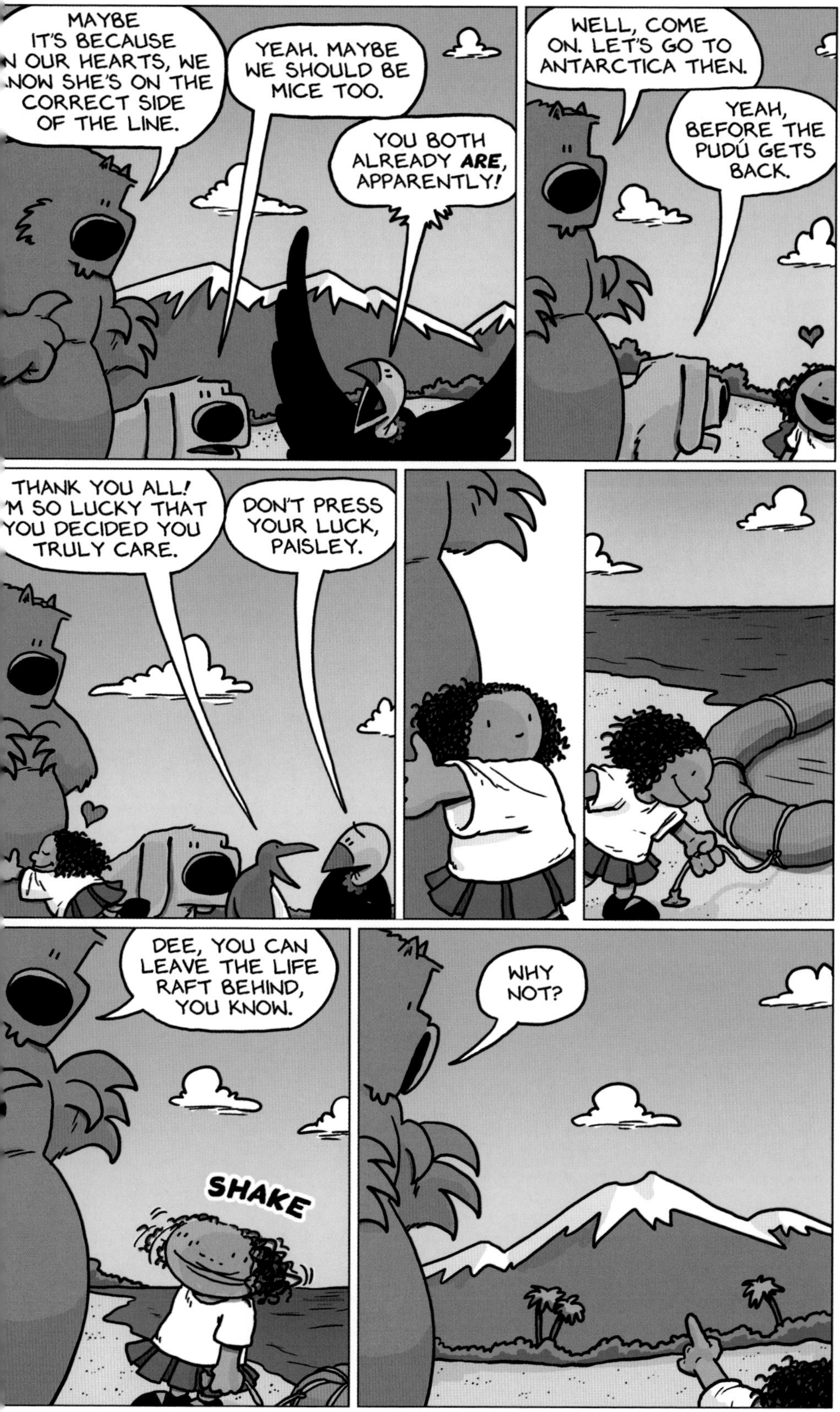
MAYBE IT'S BECAUSE N OUR HEARTS, WE NOW SHE'S ON THE CORRECT SIDE OF THE LINE.
YEAH. MAYBE WE SHOULD BE MICE TOO.
YOU BOTH ALREADY **ARE**, APPARENTLY!
WELL, COME ON. LET'S GO TO ANTARCTICA THEN.
YEAH, BEFORE THE PUDÚ GETS BACK.
THANK YOU ALL! 'M SO LUCKY THAT YOU DECIDED YOU TRULY CARE.
DON'T PRESS YOUR LUCK, PAISLEY.
DEE, YOU CAN LEAVE THE LIFE RAFT BEHIND, YOU KNOW.
SHAKE
WHY NOT?

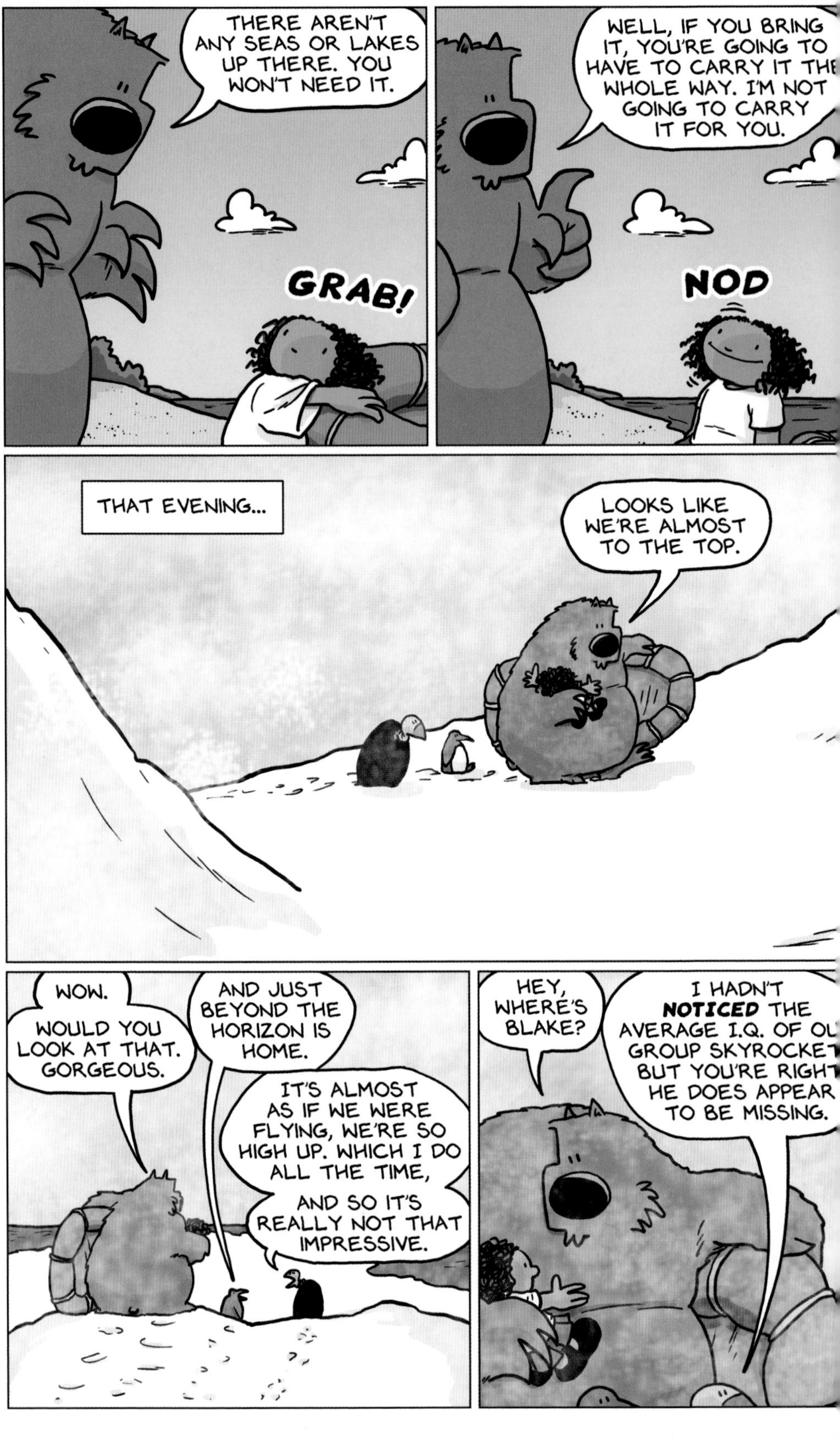
THERE AREN'T ANY SEAS OR LAKES UP THERE. YOU WON'T NEED IT.
GRAB!
WELL, IF YOU BRING IT, YOU'RE GOING TO HAVE TO CARRY IT THE WHOLE WAY. I'M NOT GOING TO CARRY IT FOR YOU.
NOD
THAT EVENING...
LOOKS LIKE WE'RE ALMOST TO THE TOP.
WOW.
WOULD YOU LOOK AT THAT. GORGEOUS.
AND JUST BEYOND THE HORIZON IS HOME.
IT'S ALMOST AS IF WE WERE FLYING, WE'RE SO HIGH UP. WHICH I DO ALL THE TIME,
AND SO IT'S REALLY NOT THAT IMPRESSIVE.
HEY, WHERE'S BLAKE?
I HADN'T NOTICED THE AVERAGE I.Q. OF OU GROUP SKYROCKET BUT YOU'RE RIGHT HE DOES APPEAR TO BE MISSING.

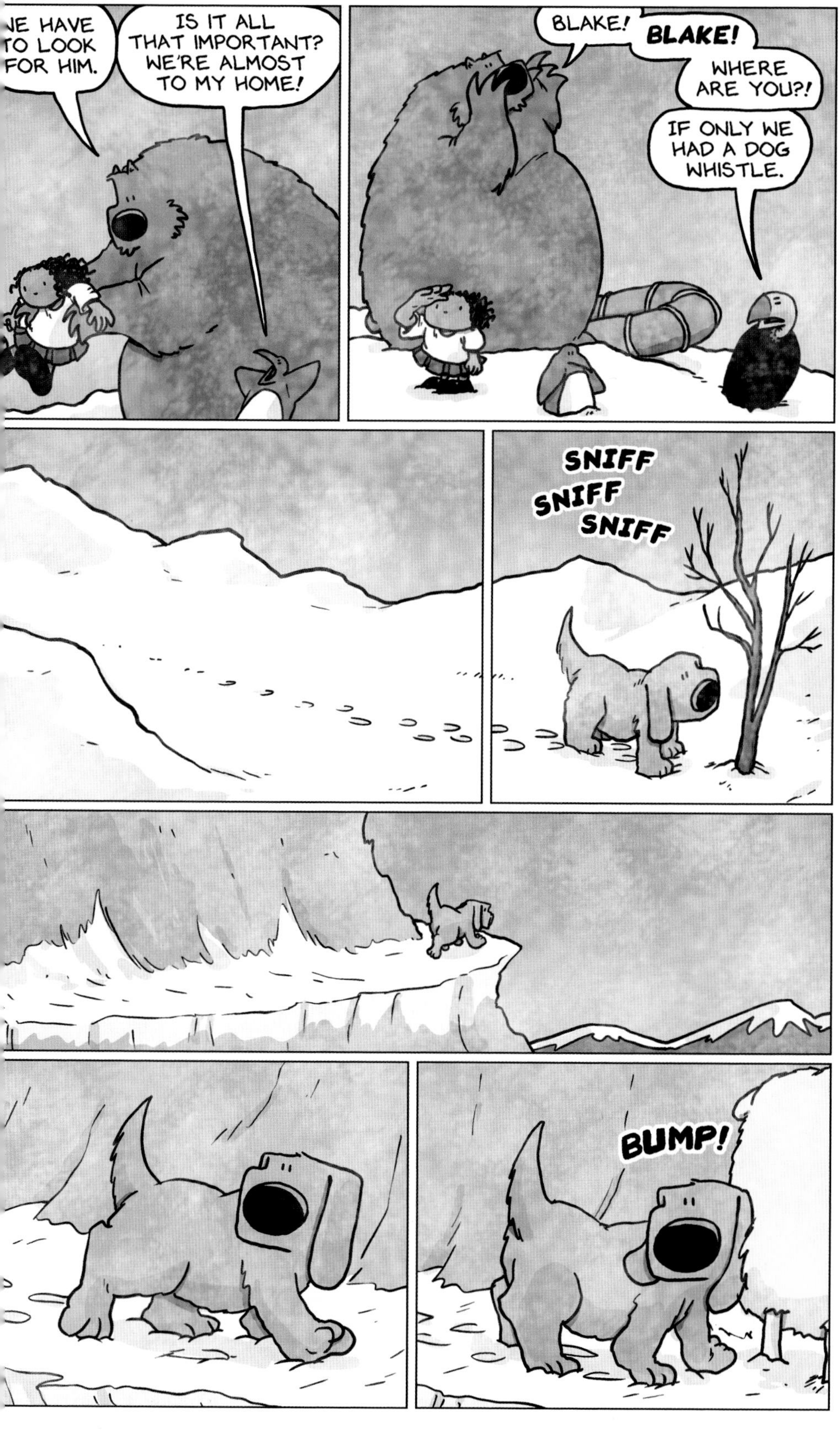

WE HAVE TO LOOK FOR HIM.
IS IT ALL THAT IMPORTANT? WE'RE ALMOST TO MY HOME!
BLAKE!
BLAKE!
WHERE ARE YOU?!
IF ONLY WE HAD A DOG WHISTLE.
SNIFF
SNIFF
SNIFF
BUMP!

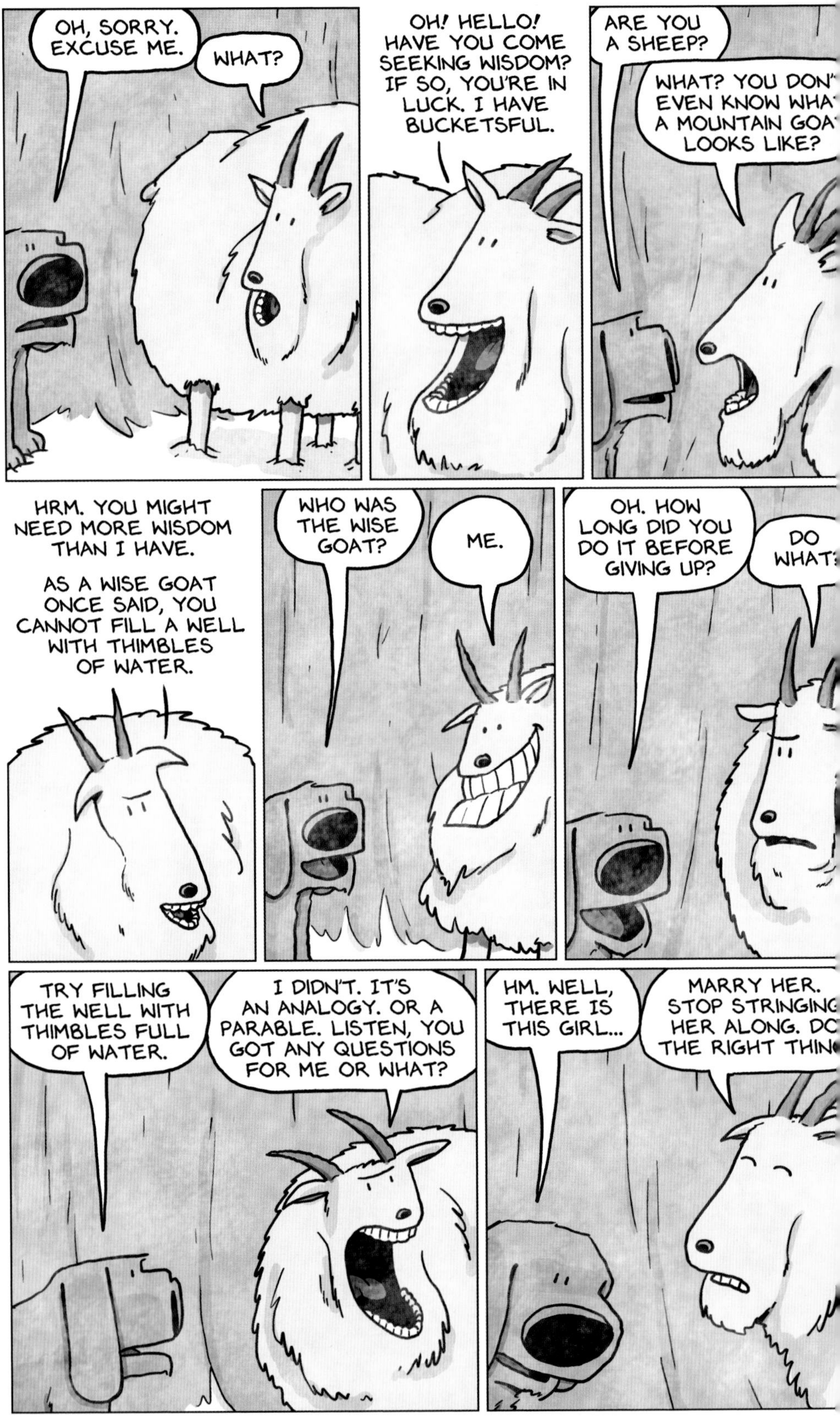
OH, SORRY. EXCUSE ME.
WHAT?
OH! HELLO! HAVE YOU COME SEEKING WISDOM? IF SO, YOU'RE IN LUCK. I HAVE BUCKETSFUL.
ARE YOU A SHEEP?
WHAT? YOU DON' EVEN KNOW WHA A MOUNTAIN GOA LOOKS LIKE?
HRM. YOU MIGHT NEED MORE WISDOM THAN I HAVE.
AS A WISE GOAT ONCE SAID, YOU CANNOT FILL A WELL WITH THIMBLES OF WATER.
WHO WAS THE WISE GOAT?
ME.
OH. HOW LONG DID YOU DO IT BEFORE GIVING UP?
DO WHAT
TRY FILLING THE WELL WITH THIMBLES FULL OF WATER.
I DIDN'T. IT'S AN ANALOGY. OR A PARABLE. LISTEN, YOU GOT ANY QUESTIONS FOR ME OR WHAT?
HM. WELL, THERE IS THIS GIRL...
MARRY HER. STOP STRINGIN HER ALONG. DO THE RIGHT THIN

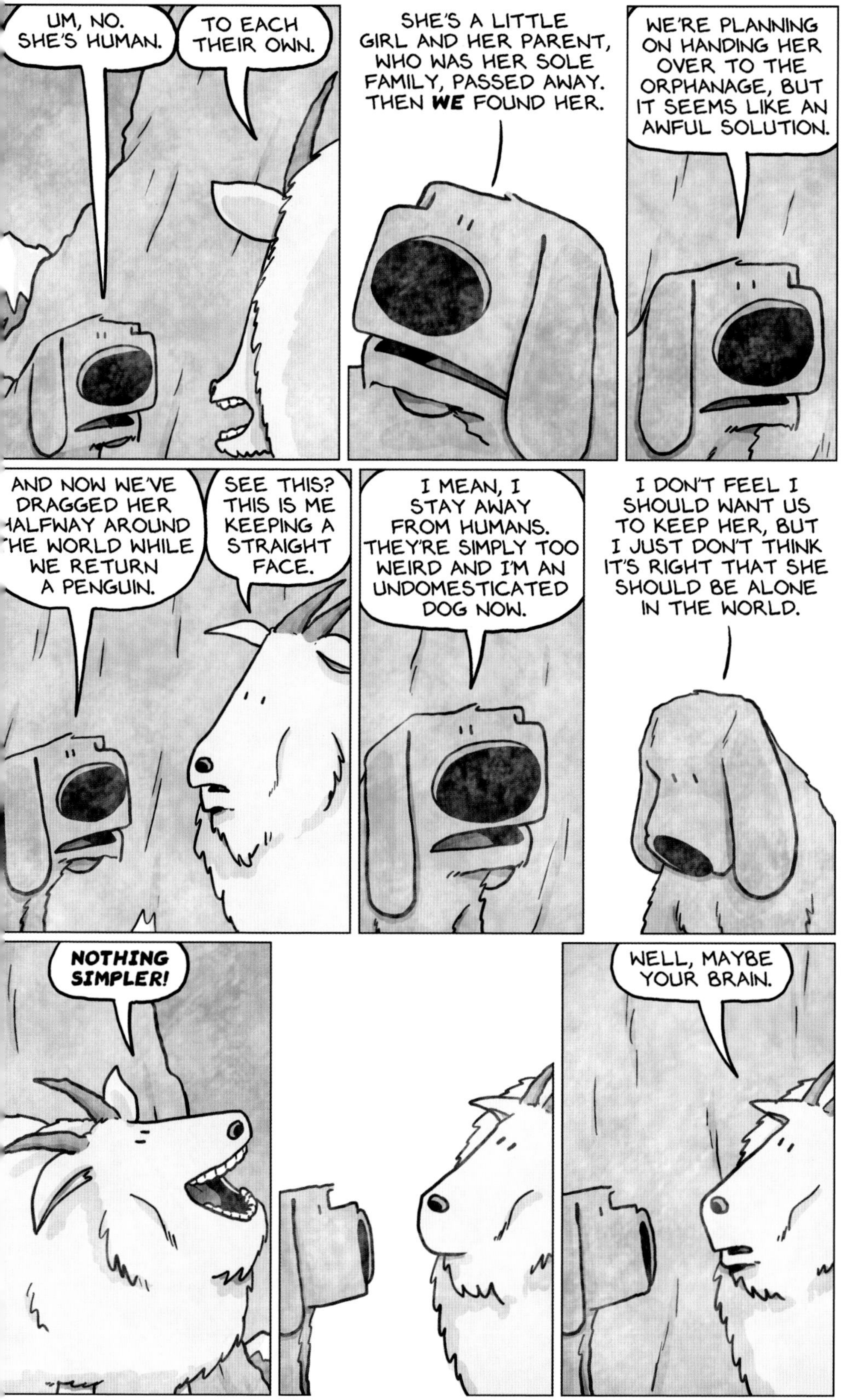
UM, NO. SHE'S HUMAN.
TO EACH THEIR OWN.
SHE'S A LITTLE GIRL AND HER PARENT, WHO WAS HER SOLE FAMILY, PASSED AWAY. THEN **WE** FOUND HER.
WE'RE PLANNING ON HANDING HER OVER TO THE ORPHANAGE, BUT IT SEEMS LIKE AN AWFUL SOLUTION.
AND NOW WE'VE DRAGGED HER HALFWAY AROUND THE WORLD WHILE WE RETURN A PENGUIN.
SEE THIS? THIS IS ME KEEPING A STRAIGHT FACE.
I MEAN, I STAY AWAY FROM HUMANS. THEY'RE SIMPLY TOO WEIRD AND I'M AN UNDOMESTICATED DOG NOW.
I DON'T FEEL I SHOULD WANT US TO KEEP HER, BUT I JUST DON'T THINK IT'S RIGHT THAT SHE SHOULD BE ALONE IN THE WORLD.
NOTHING SIMPLER!
WELL, MAYBE YOUR BRAIN.

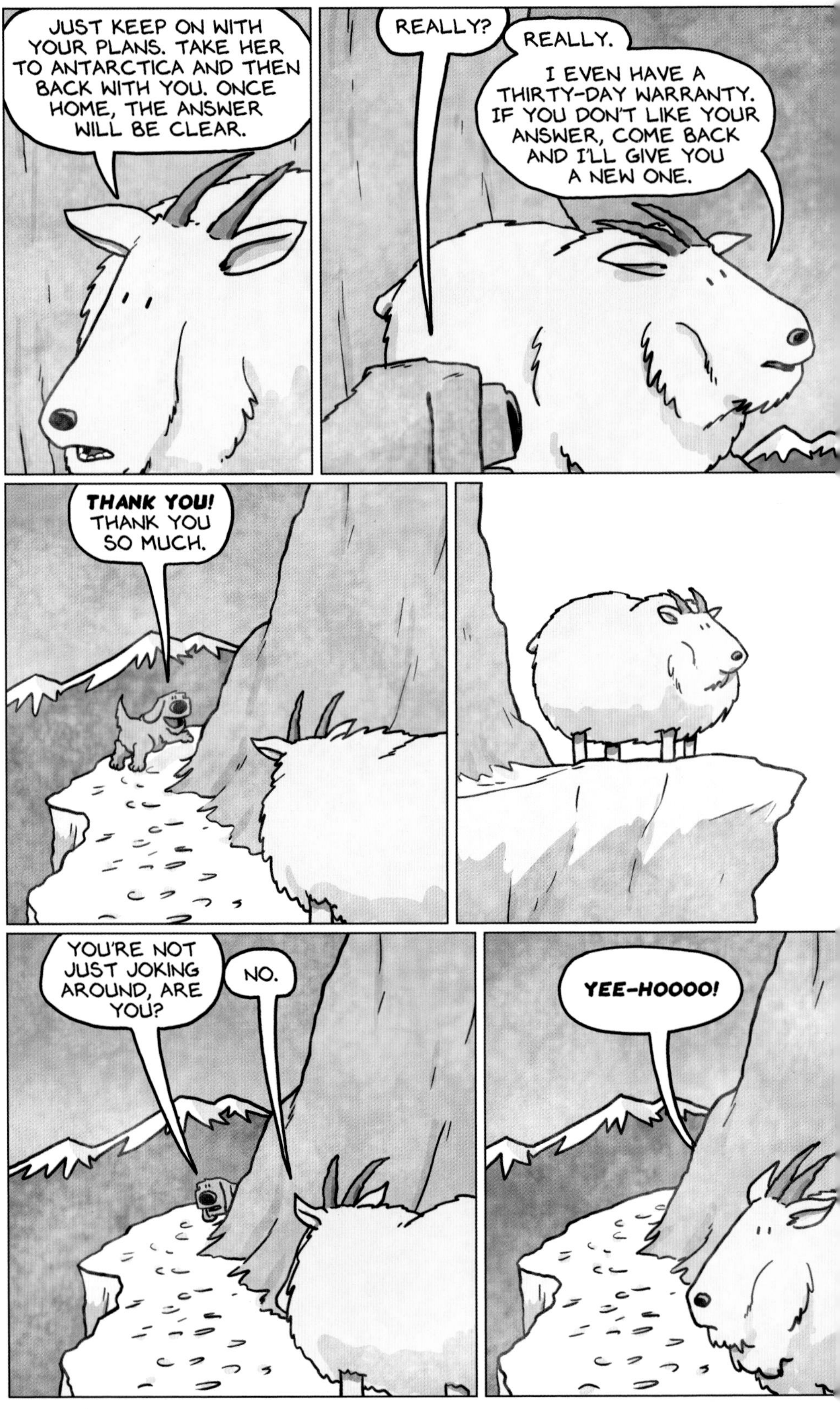
JUST KEEP ON WITH YOUR PLANS. TAKE HER TO ANTARCTICA AND THEN BACK WITH YOU. ONCE HOME, THE ANSWER WILL BE CLEAR.
REALLY?
REALLY.
I EVEN HAVE A THIRTY-DAY WARRANTY. IF YOU DON'T LIKE YOUR ANSWER, COME BACK AND I'LL GIVE YOU A NEW ONE.
THANK YOU! THANK YOU SO MUCH.
YOU'RE NOT JUST JOKING AROUND, ARE YOU?
NO.
YEE-HOOOO!

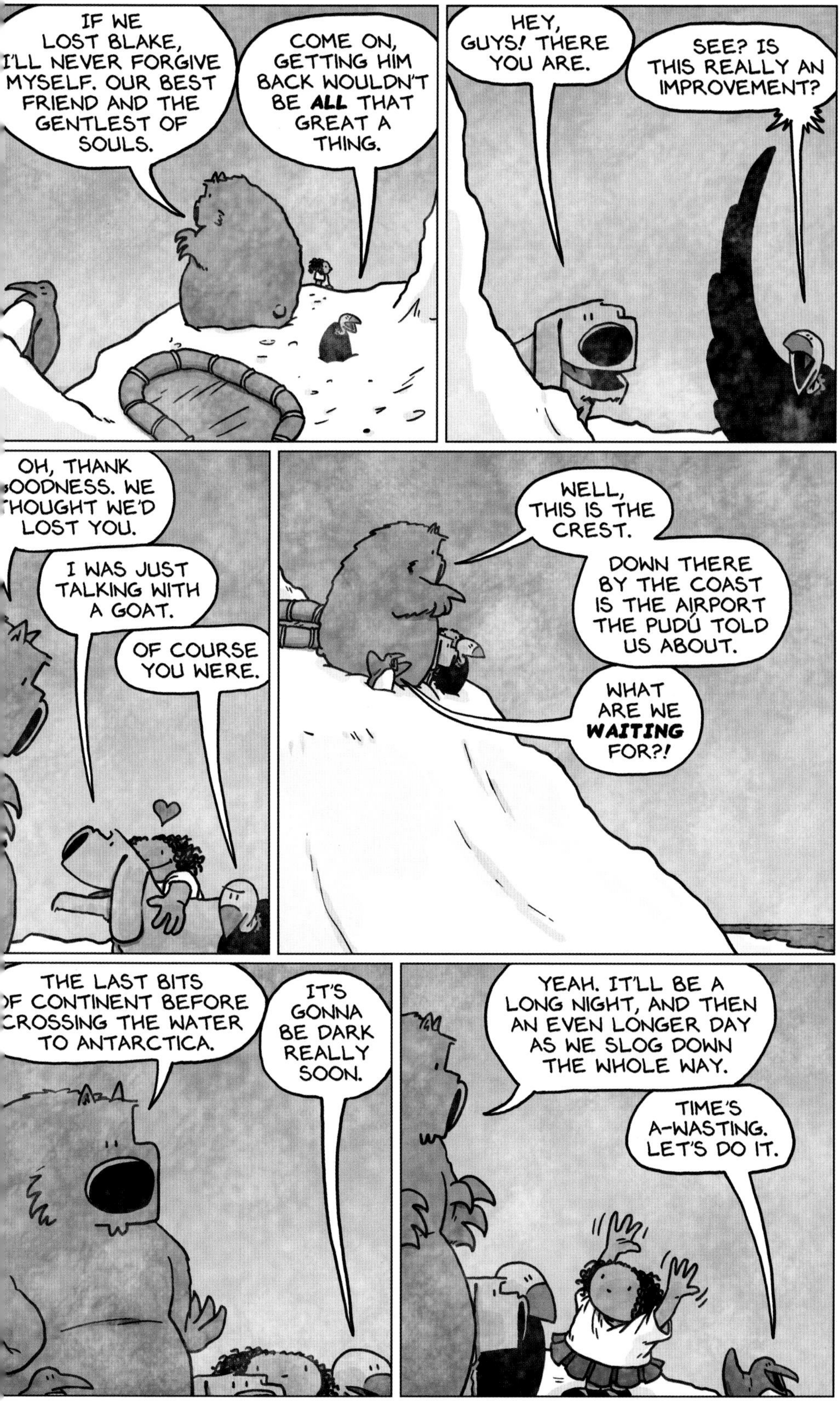
IF WE LOST BLAKE, I'LL NEVER FORGIVE MYSELF. OUR BEST FRIEND AND THE GENTLEST OF SOULS.
COME ON, GETTING HIM BACK WOULDN'T BE **ALL** THAT GREAT A THING.
HEY, GUYS! THERE YOU ARE.
SEE? IS THIS REALLY AN IMPROVEMENT?
OH, THANK GOODNESS. WE THOUGHT WE'D LOST YOU.
I WAS JUST TALKING WITH A GOAT.
OF COURSE YOU WERE.
WELL, THIS IS THE CREST.
DOWN THERE BY THE COAST IS THE AIRPORT THE PUDÚ TOLD US ABOUT.
WHAT ARE WE **WAITING** FOR?!
THE LAST BITS OF CONTINENT BEFORE CROSSING THE WATER TO ANTARCTICA.
IT'S GONNA BE DARK REALLY SOON.
YEAH. IT'LL BE A LONG NIGHT, AND THEN AN EVEN LONGER DAY AS WE SLOG DOWN THE WHOLE WAY.
TIME'S A-WASTING. LET'S DO IT.

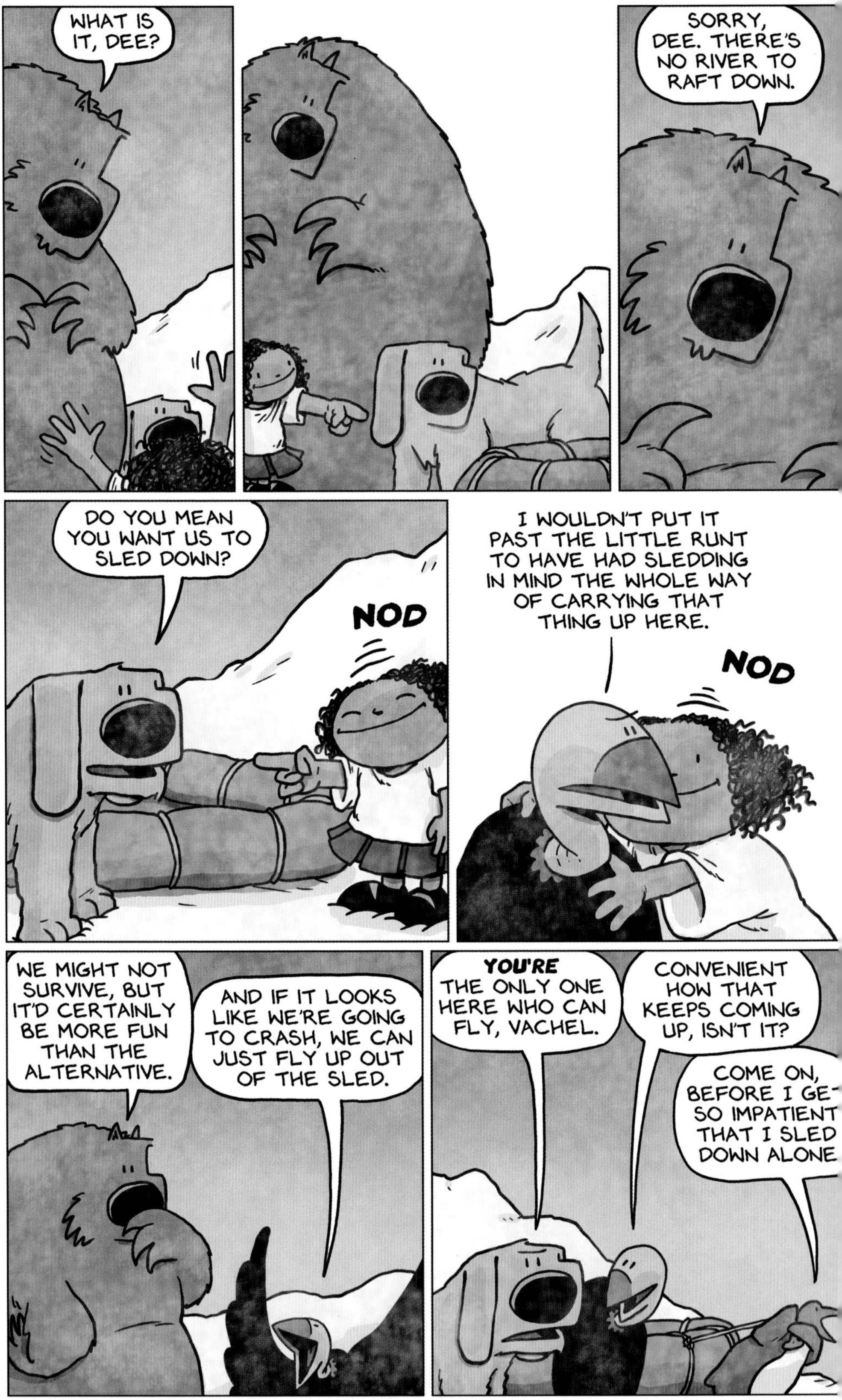
WHAT IS IT, DEE?
SORRY, DEE. THERE'S NO RIVER TO RAFT DOWN.
DO YOU MEAN YOU WANT US TO SLED DOWN?
NOD
I WOULDN'T PUT IT PAST THE LITTLE RUNT TO HAVE HAD SLEDDING IN MIND THE WHOLE WAY OF CARRYING THAT THING UP HERE.
NOD
WE MIGHT NOT SURVIVE, BUT IT'D CERTAINLY BE MORE FUN THAN THE ALTERNATIVE.
AND IF IT LOOKS LIKE WE'RE GOING TO CRASH, WE CAN JUST FLY UP OUT OF THE SLED.
YOU'RE THE ONLY ONE HERE WHO CAN FLY, VACHEL.
CONVENIENT HOW THAT KEEPS COMING UP, ISN'T IT?
COME ON, BEFORE I GE SO IMPATIENT THAT I SLED DOWN ALONE

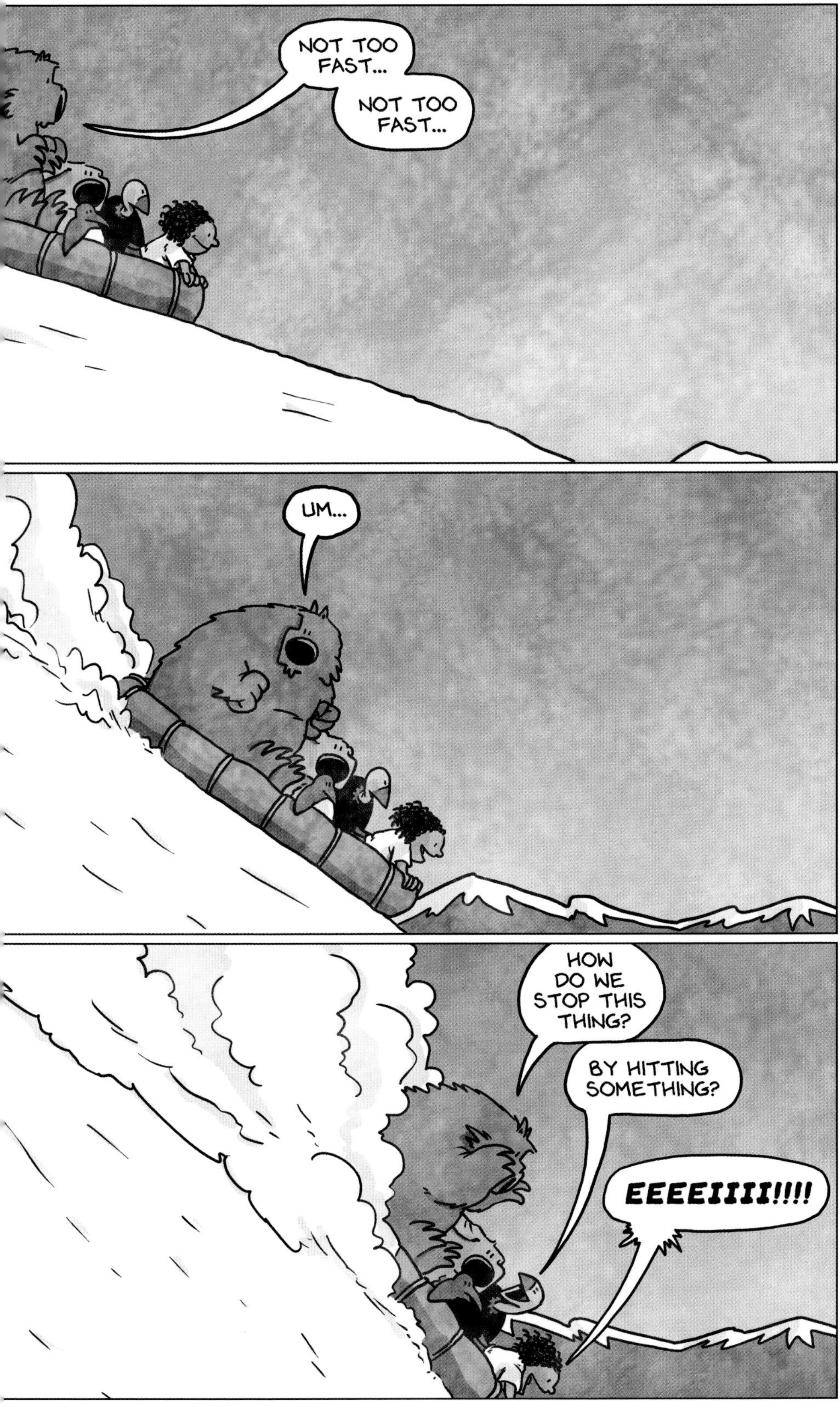
NOT TOO FAST...
NOT TOO FAST...
UM...
HOW DO WE STOP THIS THING?
BY HITTING SOMETHING?
EEEEIIII!!!!

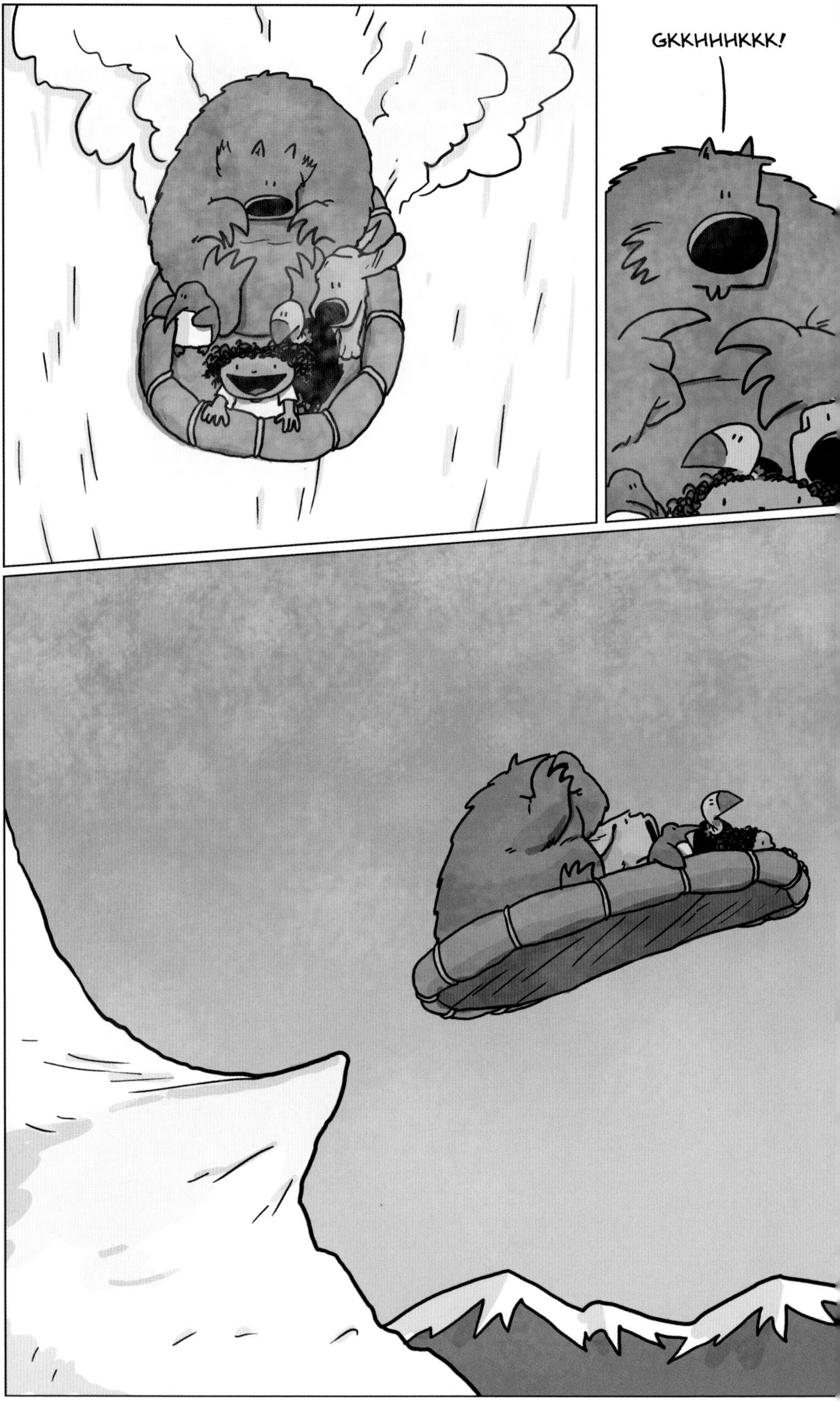
GKKHHHKKK!

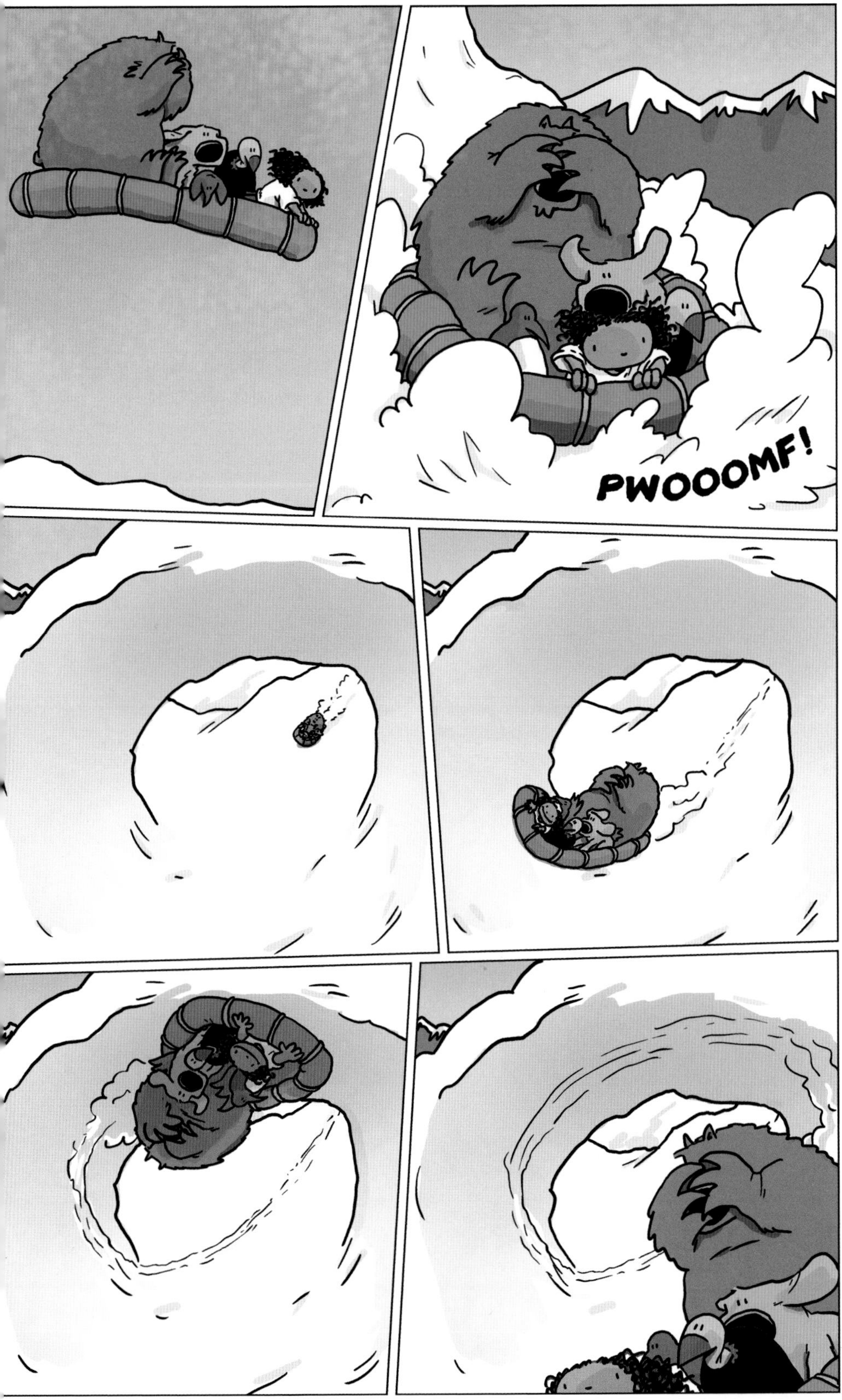
PWOOOMF!

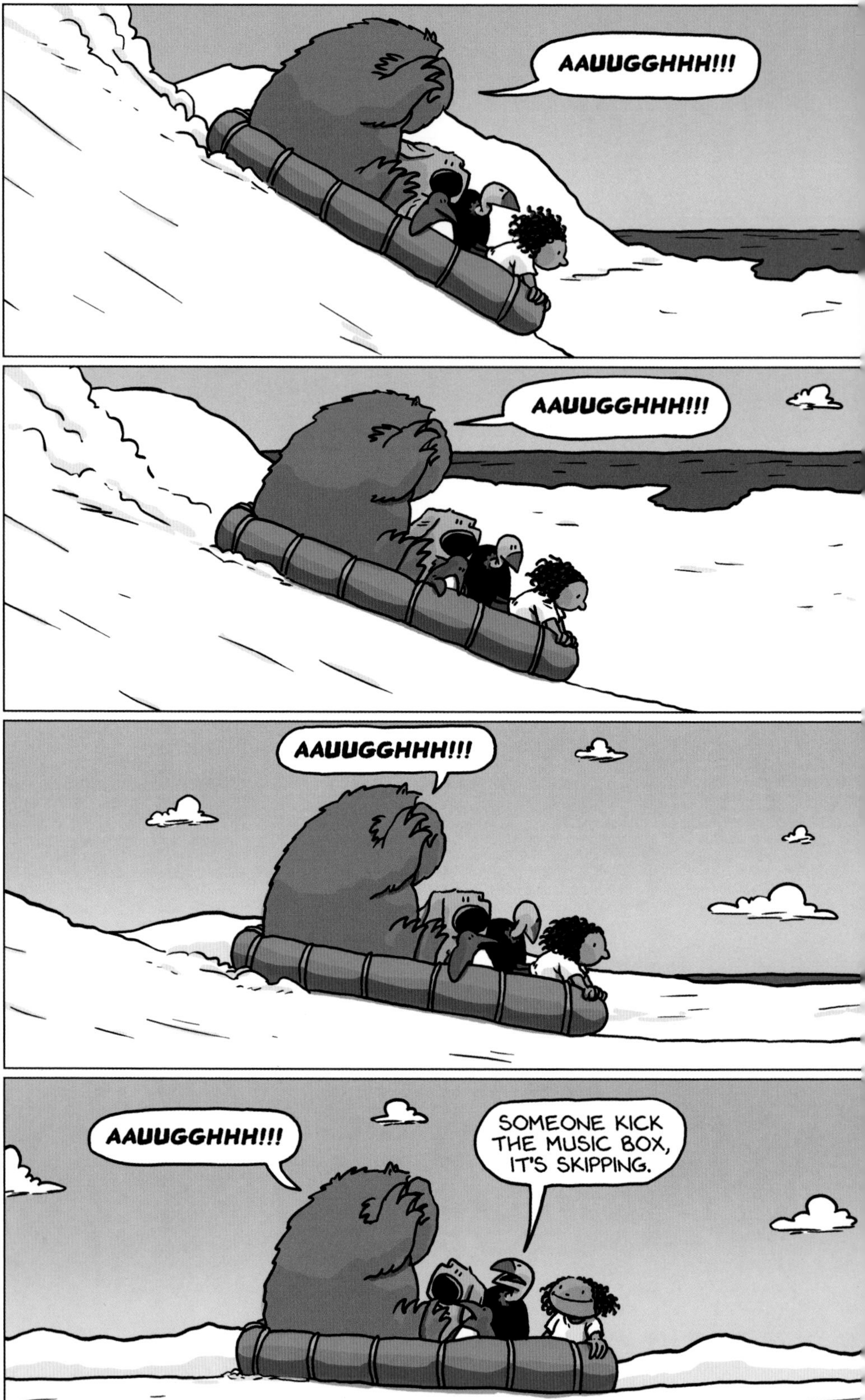
AAUUGGHHH!!!
AAUUGGHHH!!!
AAUUGGHHH!!!
AAUUGGHHH!!!
SOMEONE KICK THE MUSIC BOX, IT'S SKIPPING.

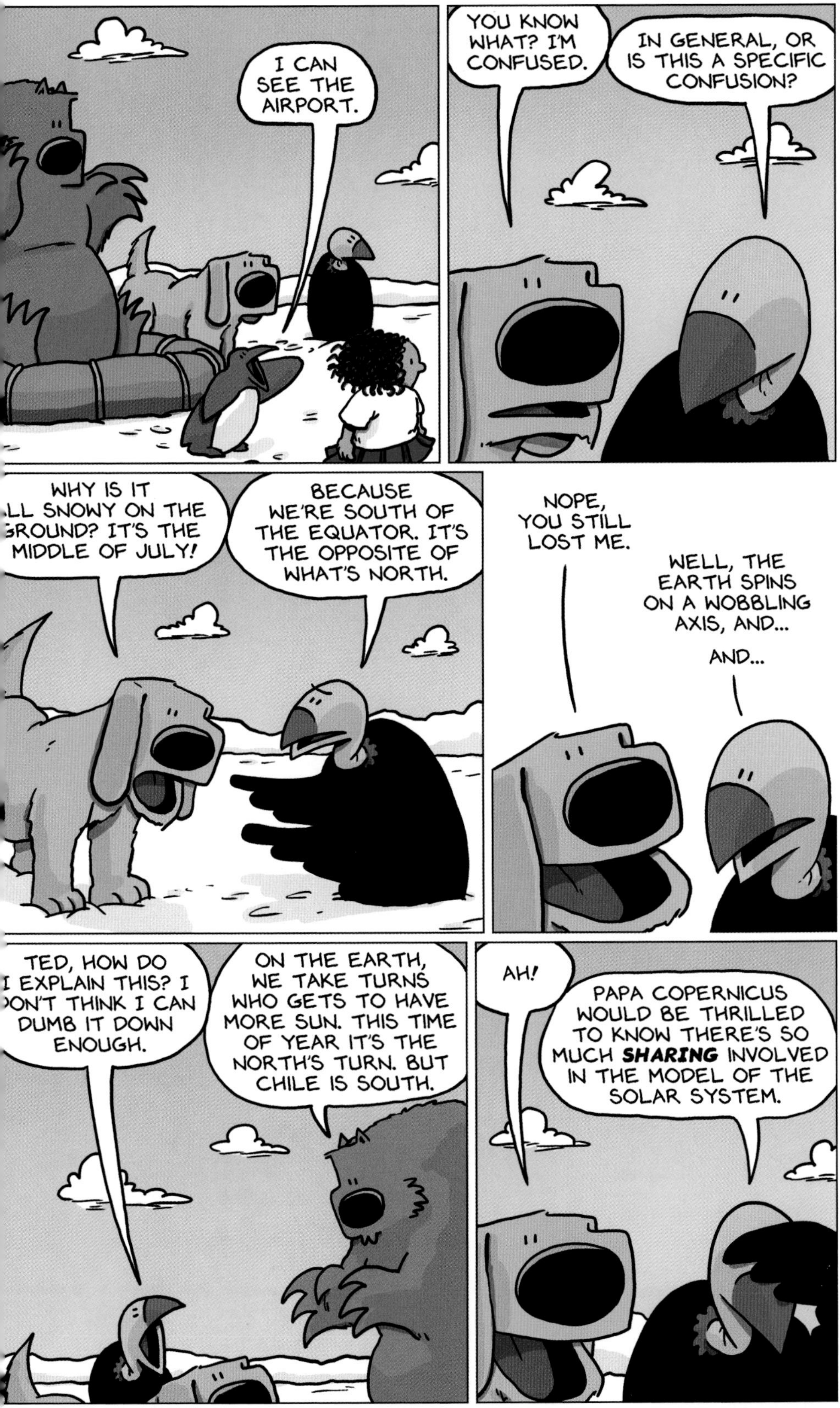
I CAN SEE THE AIRPORT.
YOU KNOW WHAT? I'M CONFUSED.
IN GENERAL, OR IS THIS A SPECIFIC CONFUSION?
WHY IS IT LL SNOWY ON THE ROUND? IT'S THE MIDDLE OF JULY!
BECAUSE WE'RE SOUTH OF THE EQUATOR. IT'S THE OPPOSITE OF WHAT'S NORTH.
NOPE, YOU STILL LOST ME.
WELL, THE EARTH SPINS ON A WOBBLING AXIS, AND...
AND...
TED, HOW DO I EXPLAIN THIS? I ON'T THINK I CAN DUMB IT DOWN ENOUGH.
ON THE EARTH, WE TAKE TURNS WHO GETS TO HAVE MORE SUN. THIS TIME OF YEAR IT'S THE NORTH'S TURN. BUT CHILE IS SOUTH.
AH!
PAPA COPERNICUS WOULD BE THRILLED TO KNOW THERE'S SO MUCH **SHARING** INVOLVED IN THE MODEL OF THE SOLAR SYSTEM.

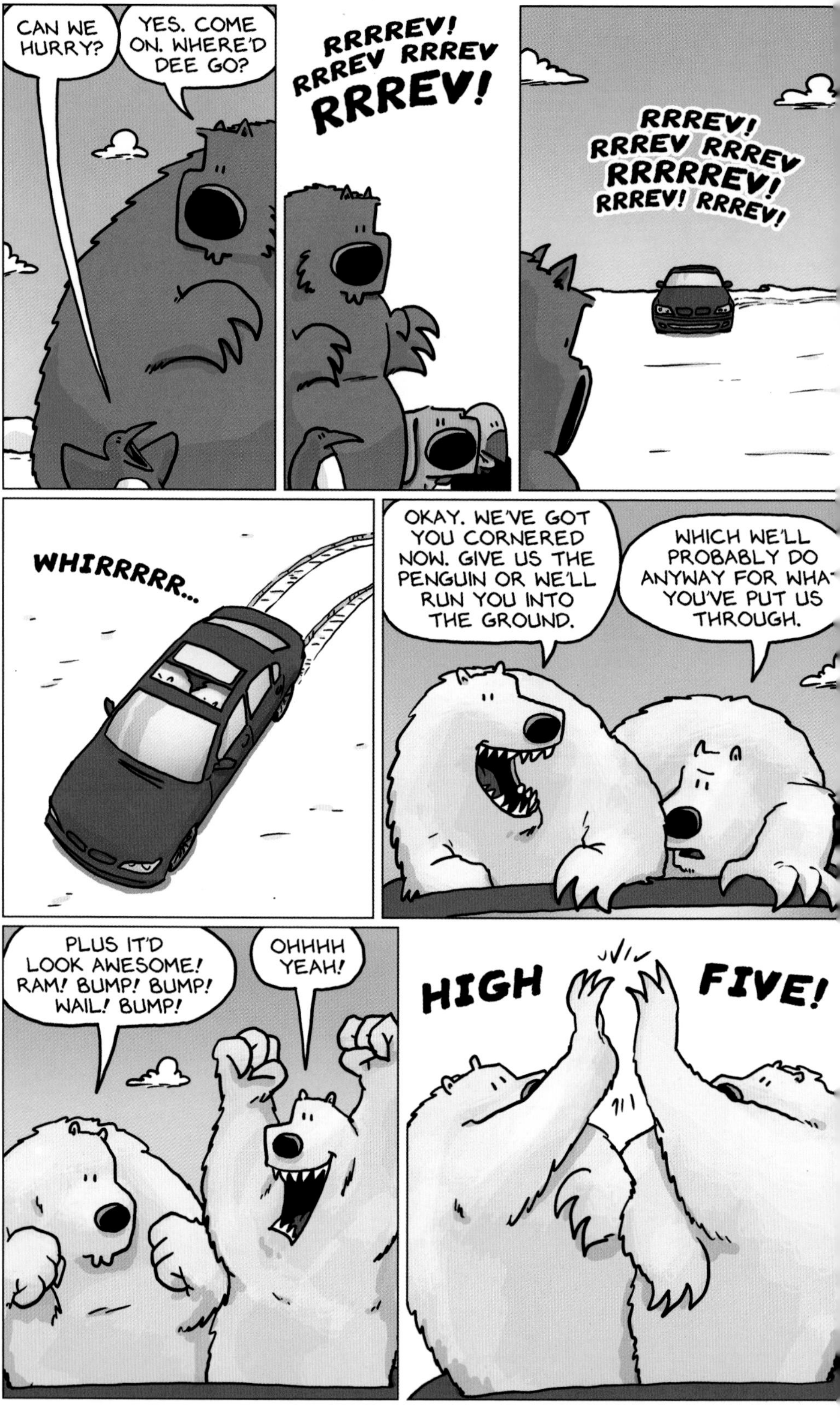
CAN WE HURRY?
YES. COME ON. WHERE'D DEE GO?
RRRREV! RRREV RRREV RRREV!
RRREV! RRREV RRREV RRRRREV! RRREV! RRREV!
WHIRRRRR...
OKAY. WE'VE GOT YOU CORNERED NOW. GIVE US THE PENGUIN OR WE'LL RUN YOU INTO THE GROUND.
WHICH WE'LL PROBABLY DO ANYWAY FOR WHA YOU'VE PUT US THROUGH.
PLUS IT'D LOOK AWESOME! RAM! BUMP! BUMP! WAIL! BUMP!
OHHHH YEAH!
HIGH FIVE!

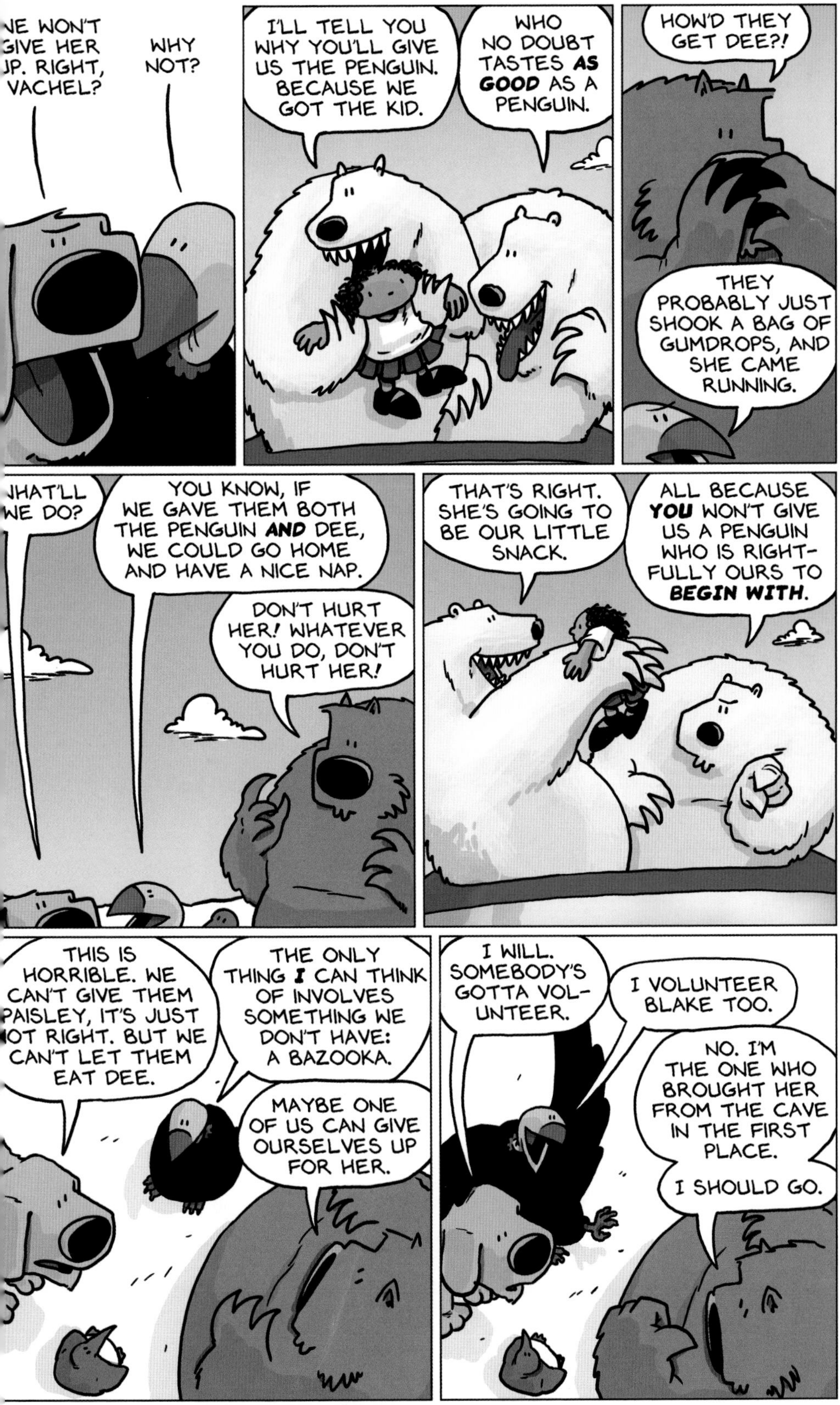
NE WON'T GIVE HER JP. RIGHT, VACHEL?
WHY NOT?
I'LL TELL YOU WHY YOU'LL GIVE US THE PENGUIN. BECAUSE WE GOT THE KID.
WHO NO DOUBT TASTES **AS GOOD** AS A PENGUIN.
HOW'D THEY GET DEE?!
THEY PROBABLY JUST SHOOK A BAG OF GUMDROPS, AND SHE CAME RUNNING.
HAT'LL WE DO?
YOU KNOW, IF WE GAVE THEM BOTH THE PENGUIN **AND** DEE, WE COULD GO HOME AND HAVE A NICE NAP.
DON'T HURT HER! WHATEVER YOU DO, DON'T HURT HER!
THAT'S RIGHT. SHE'S GOING TO BE OUR LITTLE SNACK.
ALL BECAUSE **YOU** WON'T GIVE US A PENGUIN WHO IS RIGHTFULLY OURS TO **BEGIN WITH**.
THIS IS HORRIBLE. WE CAN'T GIVE THEM PAISLEY, IT'S JUST OT RIGHT. BUT WE CAN'T LET THEM EAT DEE.
THE ONLY THING **I** CAN THINK OF INVOLVES SOMETHING WE DON'T HAVE: A BAZOOKA.
MAYBE ONE OF US CAN GIVE OURSELVES UP FOR HER.
I WILL. SOMEBODY'S GOTTA VOLUNTEER.
I VOLUNTEER BLAKE TOO.
NO. I'M THE ONE WHO BROUGHT HER FROM THE CAVE IN THE FIRST PLACE.
I SHOULD GO.

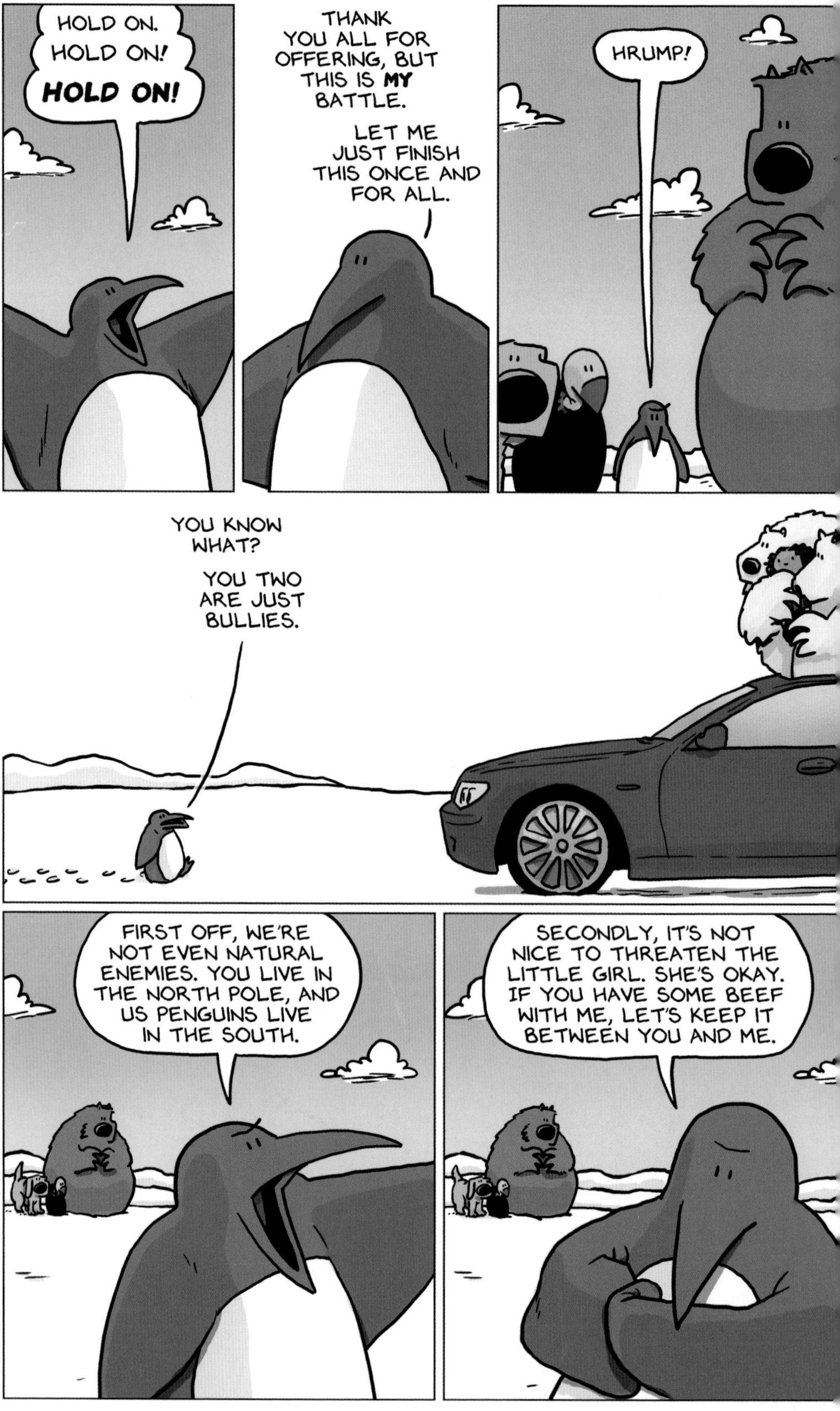
HOLD ON.
HOLD ON!
HOLD ON!
THANK YOU ALL FOR OFFERING, BUT THIS IS **MY** BATTLE.
LET ME JUST FINISH THIS ONCE AND FOR ALL.
HRUMP!
YOU KNOW WHAT?
YOU TWO ARE JUST BULLIES.
FIRST OFF, WE'RE NOT EVEN NATURAL ENEMIES. YOU LIVE IN THE NORTH POLE, AND US PENGUINS LIVE IN THE SOUTH.
SECONDLY, IT'S NOT NICE TO THREATEN THE LITTLE GIRL. SHE'S OKAY. IF YOU HAVE SOME BEEF WITH ME, LET'S KEEP IT BETWEEN YOU AND ME.

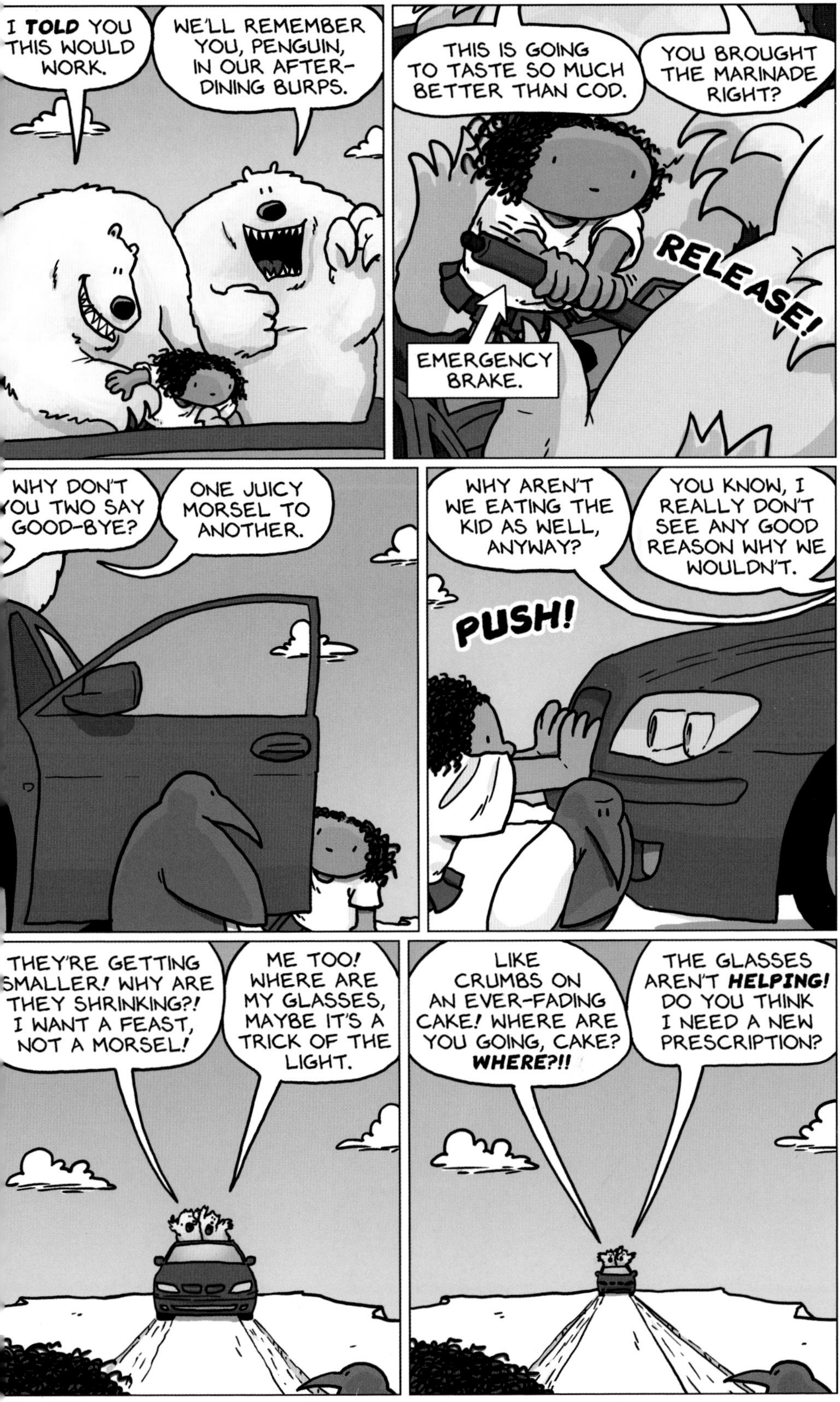
I TOLD YOU THIS WOULD WORK.
WE'LL REMEMBER YOU, PENGUIN, IN OUR AFTER-DINING BURPS.
THIS IS GOING TO TASTE SO MUCH BETTER THAN COD.
YOU BROUGHT THE MARINADE RIGHT?
RELEASE!
EMERGENCY BRAKE.
WHY DON'T YOU TWO SAY GOOD-BYE?
ONE JUICY MORSEL TO ANOTHER.
WHY AREN'T WE EATING THE KID AS WELL, ANYWAY?
YOU KNOW, I REALLY DON'T SEE ANY GOOD REASON WHY WE WOULDN'T.
PUSH!
THEY'RE GETTING SMALLER! WHY ARE THEY SHRINKING?! I WANT A FEAST, NOT A MORSEL!
ME TOO! WHERE ARE MY GLASSES, MAYBE IT'S A TRICK OF THE LIGHT.
LIKE CRUMBS ON AN EVER-FADING CAKE! WHERE ARE YOU GOING, CAKE? WHERE?!!
THE GLASSES AREN'T HELPING! DO YOU THINK I NEED A NEW PRESCRIPTION?

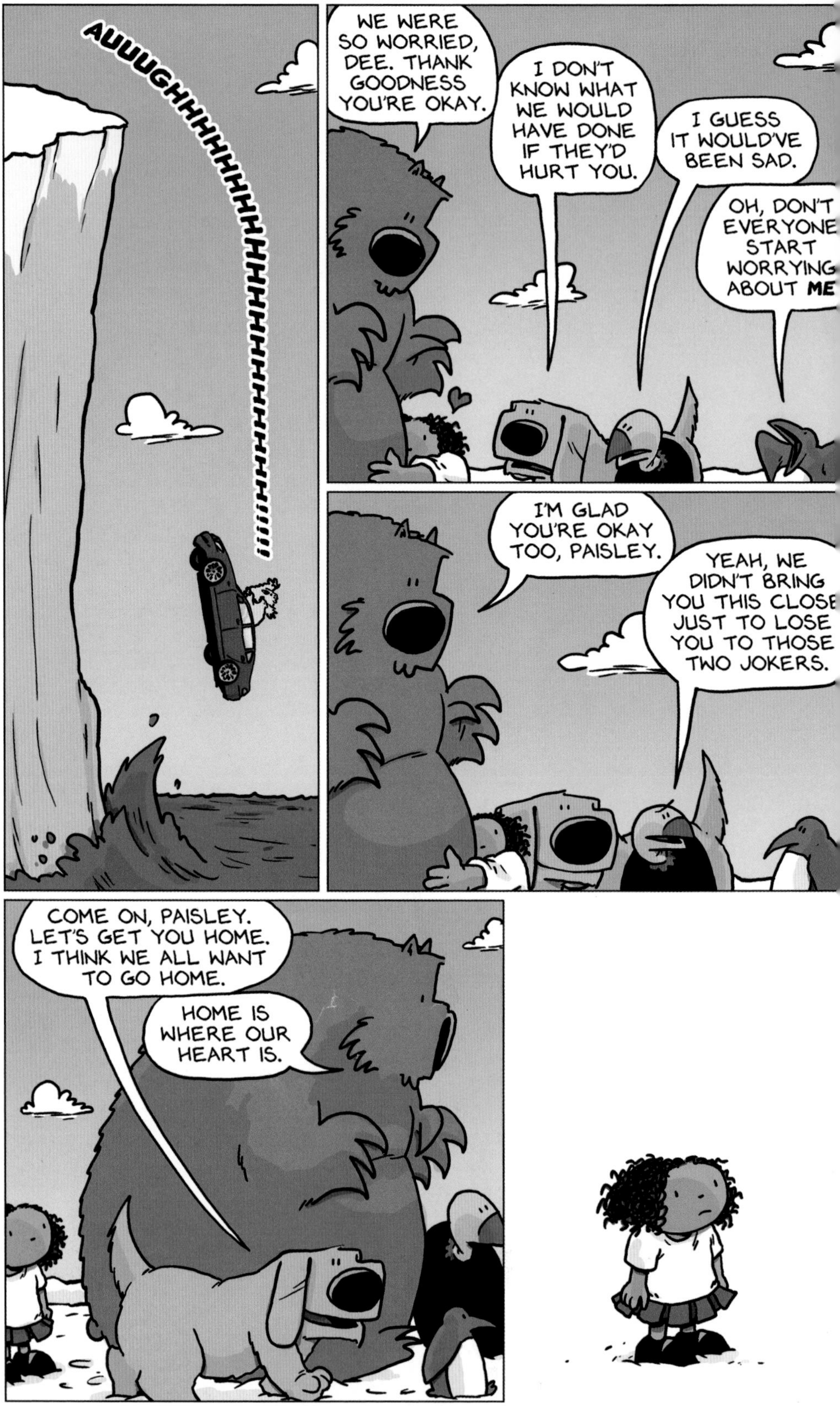
AUUUGHHHHHHHHHHHHHHHHHHHH!!!!!!
WE WERE SO WORRIED, DEE. THANK GOODNESS YOU'RE OKAY.
I DON'T KNOW WHAT WE WOULD HAVE DONE IF THEY'D HURT YOU.
I GUESS IT WOULD'VE BEEN SAD.
OH, DON'T EVERYONE START WORRYING ABOUT **ME**
I'M GLAD YOU'RE OKAY TOO, PAISLEY.
YEAH, WE DIDN'T BRING YOU THIS CLOSE JUST TO LOSE YOU TO THOSE TWO JOKERS.
COME ON, PAISLEY. LET'S GET YOU HOME. I THINK WE ALL WANT TO GO HOME.
HOME IS WHERE OUR HEART IS.

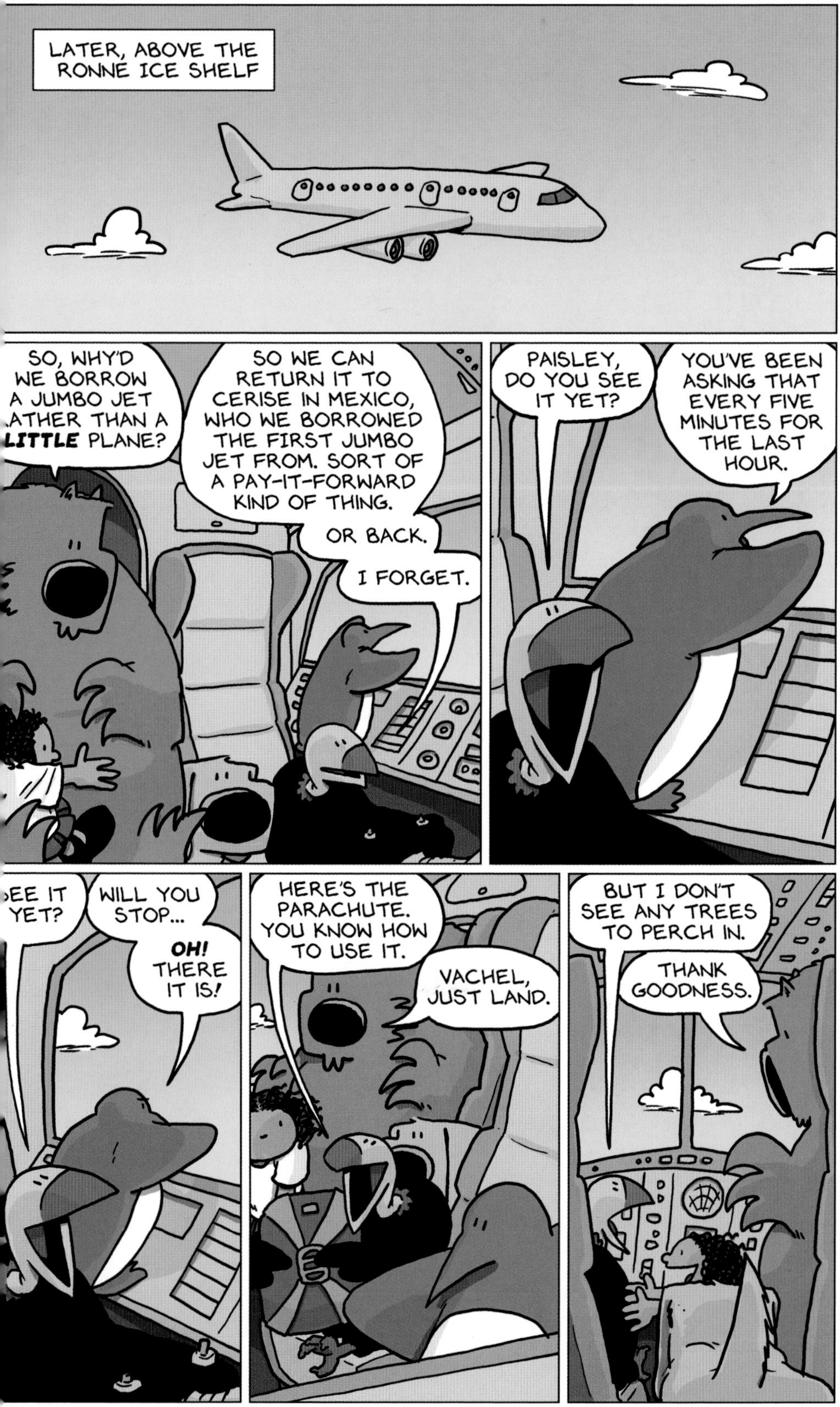
LATER, ABOVE THE RONNE ICE SHELF
SO, WHY'D WE BORROW A JUMBO JET RATHER THAN A **LITTLE** PLANE?
SO WE CAN RETURN IT TO CERISE IN MEXICO, WHO WE BORROWED THE FIRST JUMBO JET FROM. SORT OF A PAY-IT-FORWARD KIND OF THING.
OR BACK.
I FORGET.
PAISLEY, DO YOU SEE IT YET?
YOU'VE BEEN ASKING THAT EVERY FIVE MINUTES FOR THE LAST HOUR.
SEE IT YET?
WILL YOU STOP...
OH! THERE IT IS!
HERE'S THE PARACHUTE. YOU KNOW HOW TO USE IT.
VACHEL, JUST LAND.
BUT I DON'T SEE ANY TREES TO PERCH IN.
THANK GOODNESS.

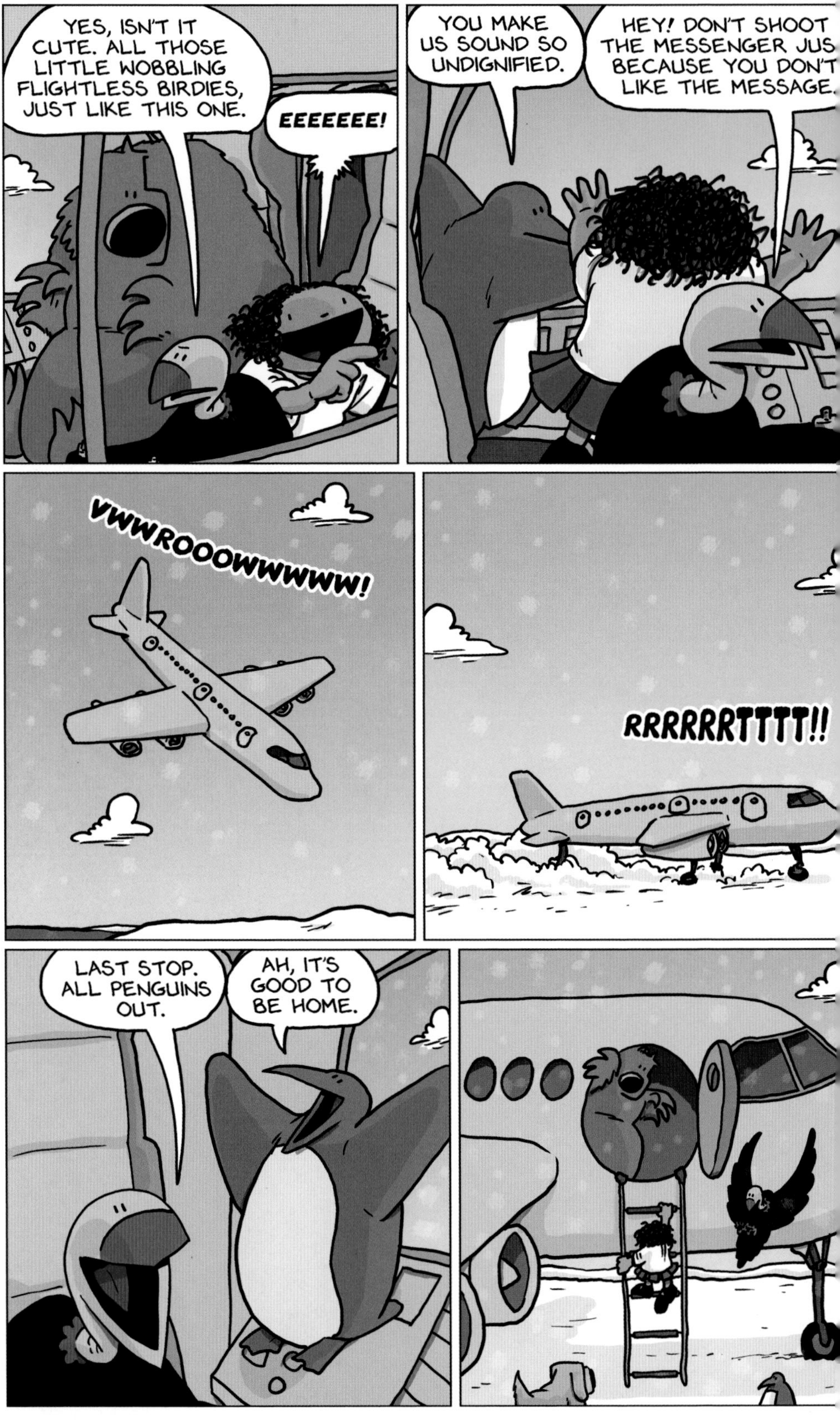
YES, ISN'T IT CUTE. ALL THOSE LITTLE WOBBLING FLIGHTLESS BIRDIES, JUST LIKE THIS ONE.
EEEEEEE!
YOU MAKE US SOUND SO UNDIGNIFIED.
HEY! DON'T SHOOT THE MESSENGER JUS BECAUSE YOU DON'T LIKE THE MESSAGE.
VWWROOOWWWWW!
RRRRRRTTTT!!
LAST STOP. ALL PENGUINS OUT.
AH, IT'S GOOD TO BE HOME.

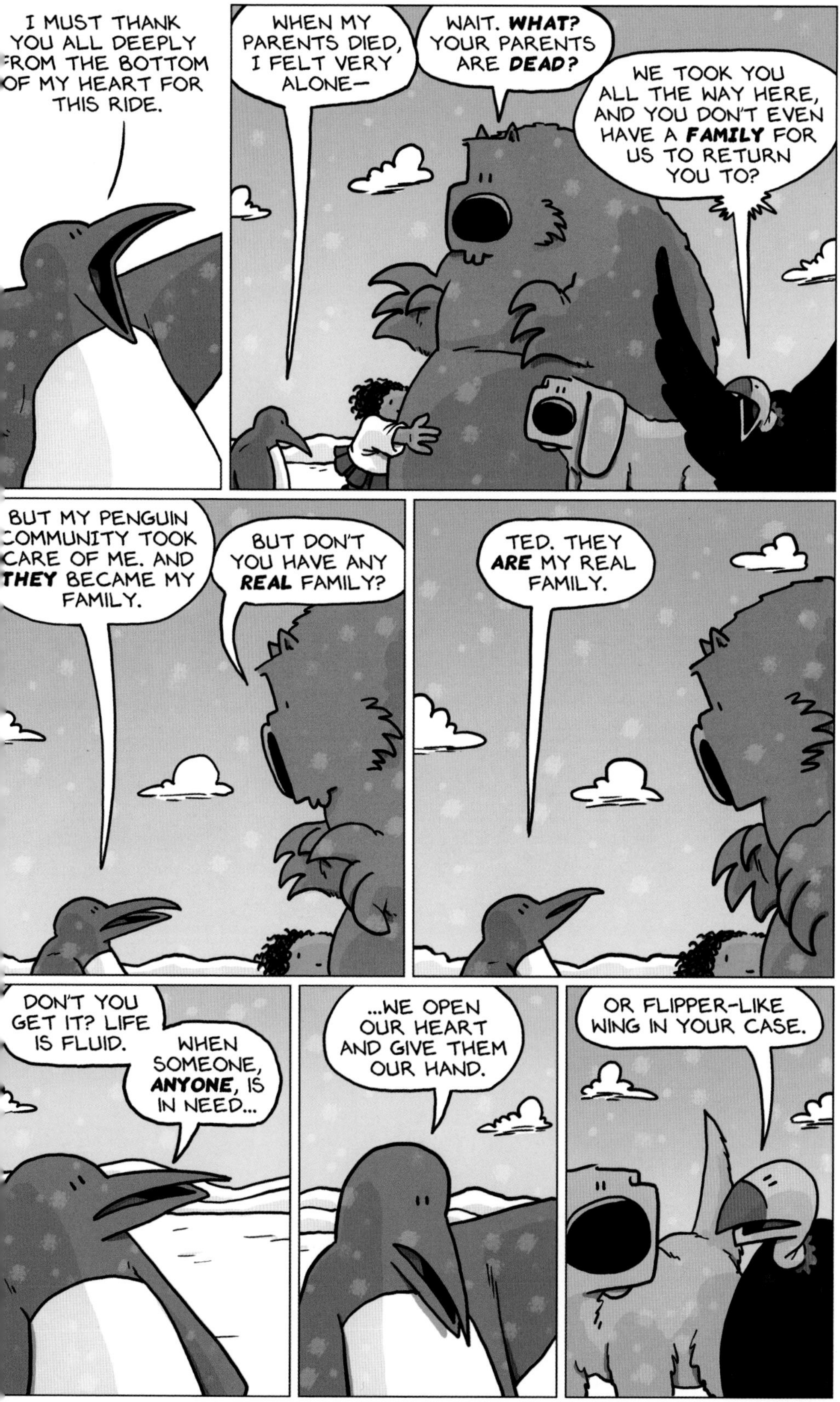
I MUST THANK YOU ALL DEEPLY FROM THE BOTTOM OF MY HEART FOR THIS RIDE.
WHEN MY PARENTS DIED, I FELT VERY ALONE—
WAIT. **WHAT?** YOUR PARENTS ARE ***DEAD?***
WE TOOK YOU ALL THE WAY HERE, AND YOU DON'T EVEN HAVE A **FAMILY** FOR US TO RETURN YOU TO?
BUT MY PENGUIN COMMUNITY TOOK CARE OF ME. AND **THEY** BECAME MY FAMILY.
BUT DON'T YOU HAVE ANY ***REAL*** FAMILY?
TED. THEY **ARE** MY REAL FAMILY.
DON'T YOU GET IT? LIFE IS FLUID.
WHEN SOMEONE, ***ANYONE***, IS IN NEED...
...WE OPEN OUR HEART AND GIVE THEM OUR HAND.
OR FLIPPER-LIKE WING IN YOUR CASE.

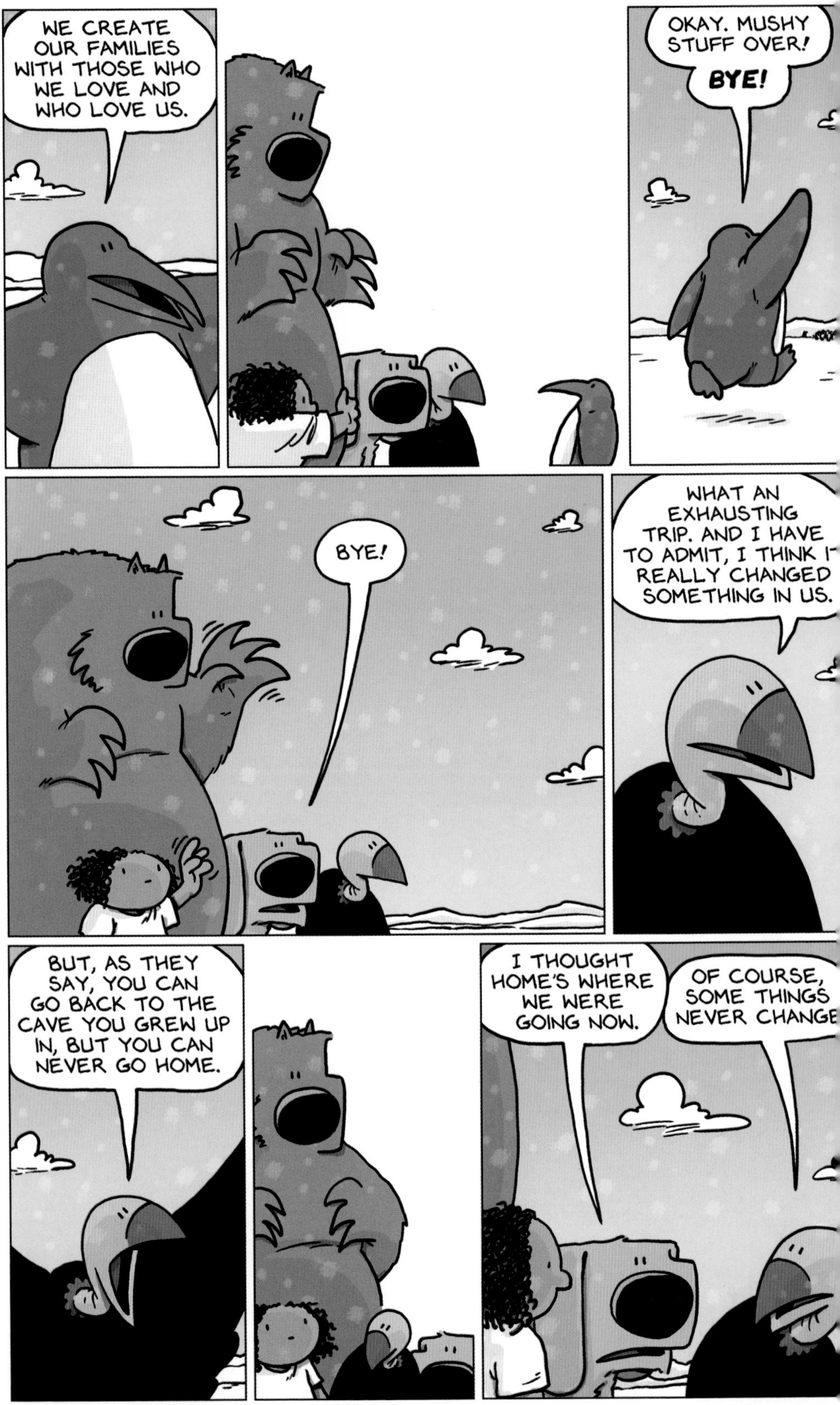
WE CREATE OUR FAMILIES WITH THOSE WHO WE LOVE AND WHO LOVE US.
OKAY. MUSHY STUFF OVER!
BYE!
BYE!
WHAT AN EXHAUSTING TRIP. AND I HAVE TO ADMIT, I THINK IT REALLY CHANGED SOMETHING IN US.
BUT, AS THEY SAY, YOU CAN GO BACK TO THE CAVE YOU GREW UP IN, BUT YOU CAN NEVER GO HOME.
I THOUGHT HOME'S WHERE WE WERE GOING NOW.
OF COURSE, SOME THINGS NEVER CHANGE

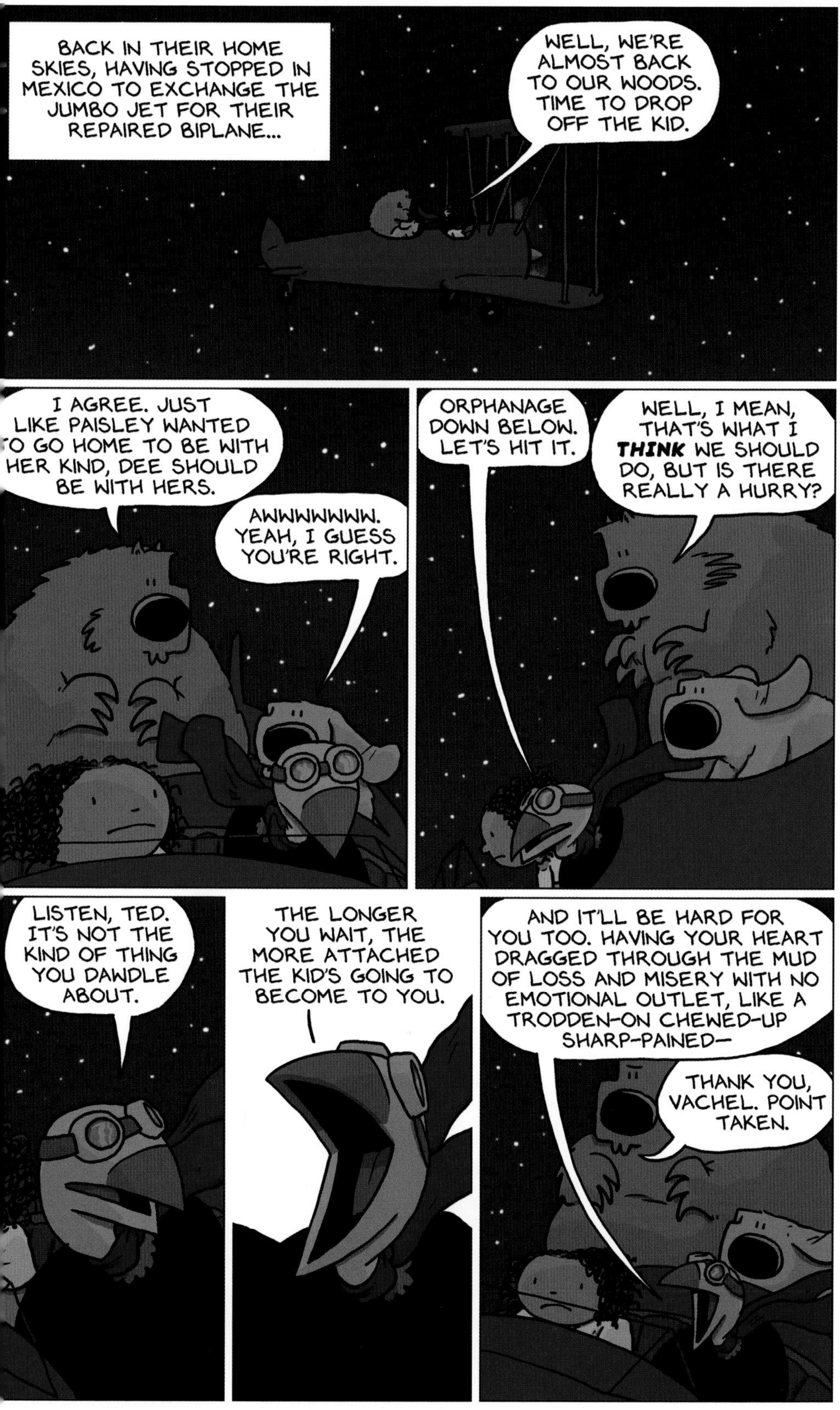
BACK IN THEIR HOME SKIES, HAVING STOPPED IN MEXICO TO EXCHANGE THE JUMBO JET FOR THEIR REPAIRED BIPLANE...
WELL, WE'RE ALMOST BACK TO OUR WOODS. TIME TO DROP OFF THE KID.
I AGREE. JUST LIKE PAISLEY WANTED TO GO HOME TO BE WITH HER KIND, DEE SHOULD BE WITH HERS.
AWWWWWWW. YEAH, I GUESS YOU'RE RIGHT.
ORPHANAGE DOWN BELOW. LET'S HIT IT.
WELL, I MEAN, THAT'S WHAT I **THINK** WE SHOULD DO, BUT IS THERE REALLY A HURRY?
LISTEN, TED. IT'S NOT THE KIND OF THING YOU DAWDLE ABOUT.
THE LONGER YOU WAIT, THE MORE ATTACHED THE KID'S GOING TO BECOME TO YOU.
AND IT'LL BE HARD FOR YOU TOO. HAVING YOUR HEART DRAGGED THROUGH THE MUD OF LOSS AND MISERY WITH NO EMOTIONAL OUTLET, LIKE A TRODDEN-ON CHEWED-UP SHARP-PAINED—
THANK YOU, VACHEL. POINT TAKEN.

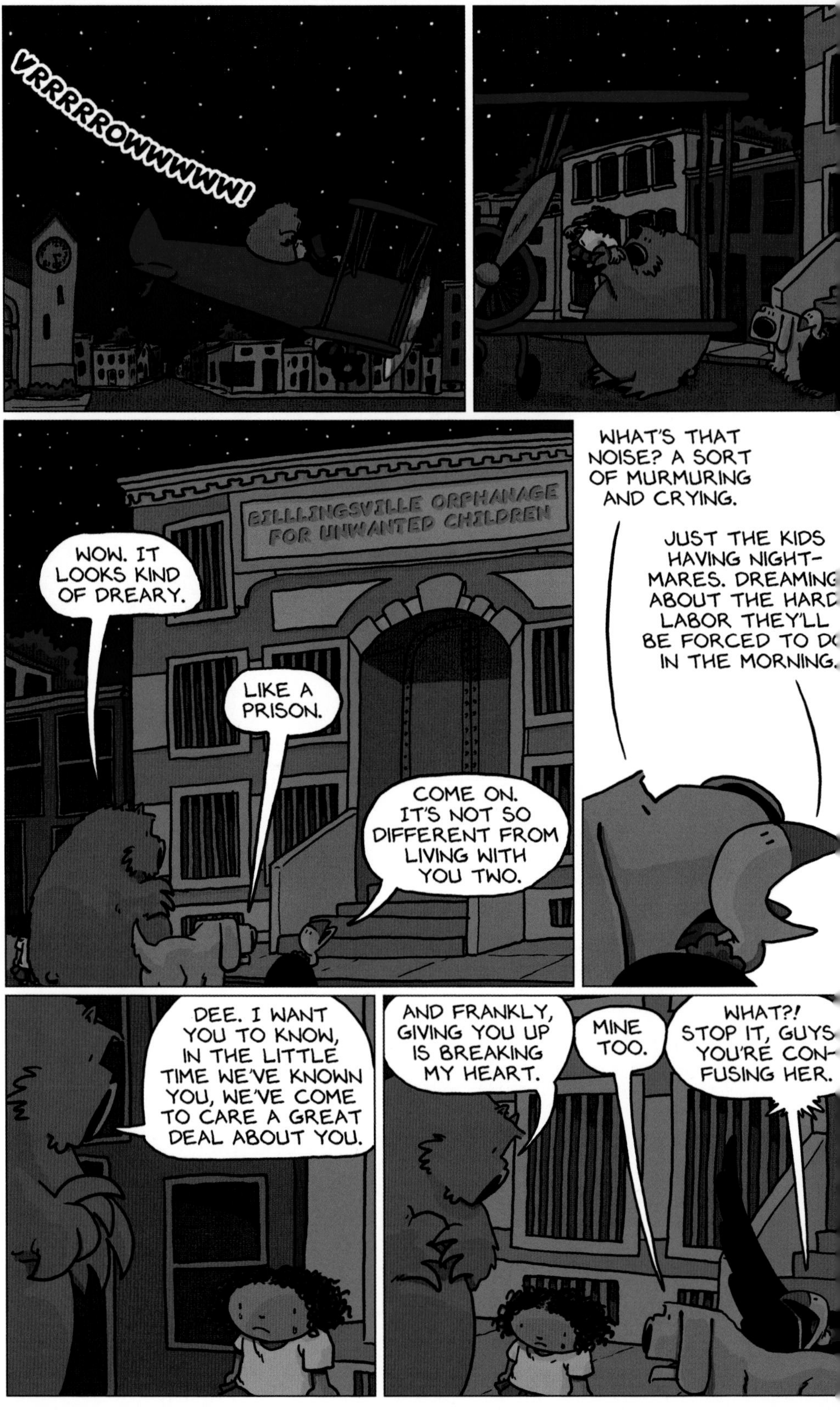
VRRRRROWWWWWW!
BILLINGSVILLE ORPHANAGE FOR UNWANTED CHILDREN
WOW. IT LOOKS KIND OF DREARY.
LIKE A PRISON.
COME ON. IT'S NOT SO DIFFERENT FROM LIVING WITH YOU TWO.
WHAT'S THAT NOISE? A SORT OF MURMURING AND CRYING.
JUST THE KIDS HAVING NIGHT-MARES. DREAMING ABOUT THE HARD LABOR THEY'LL BE FORCED TO DO IN THE MORNING.
DEE. I WANT YOU TO KNOW, IN THE LITTLE TIME WE'VE KNOWN YOU, WE'VE COME TO CARE A GREAT DEAL ABOUT YOU.
AND FRANKLY, GIVING YOU UP IS BREAKING MY HEART.
MINE TOO.
WHAT?! STOP IT, GUYS. YOU'RE CON-FUSING HER.

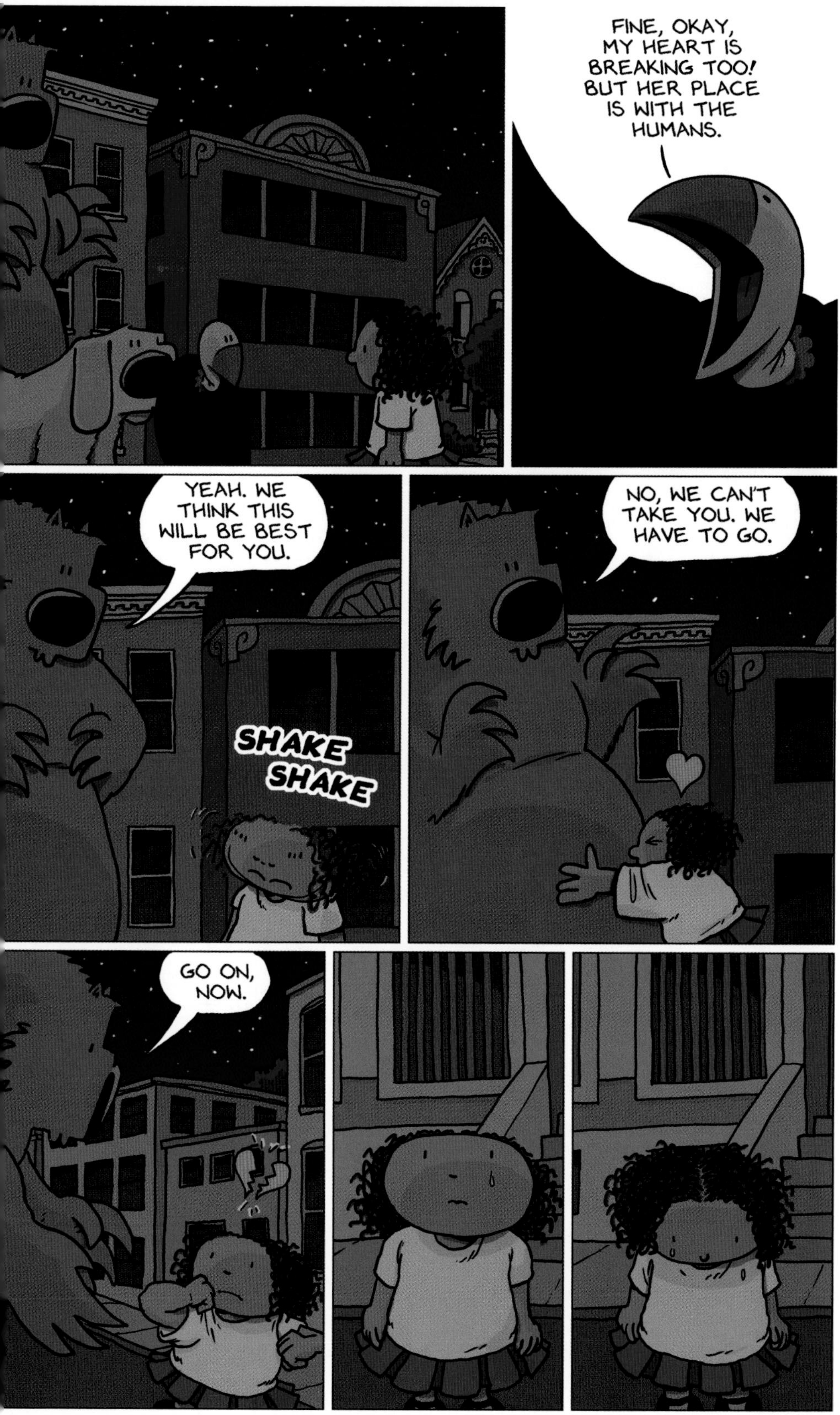

FINE, OKAY, MY HEART IS BREAKING TOO! BUT HER PLACE IS WITH THE HUMANS.
YEAH. WE THINK THIS WILL BE BEST FOR YOU.
SHAKE SHAKE
NO, WE CAN'T TAKE YOU. WE HAVE TO GO.
GO ON, NOW.

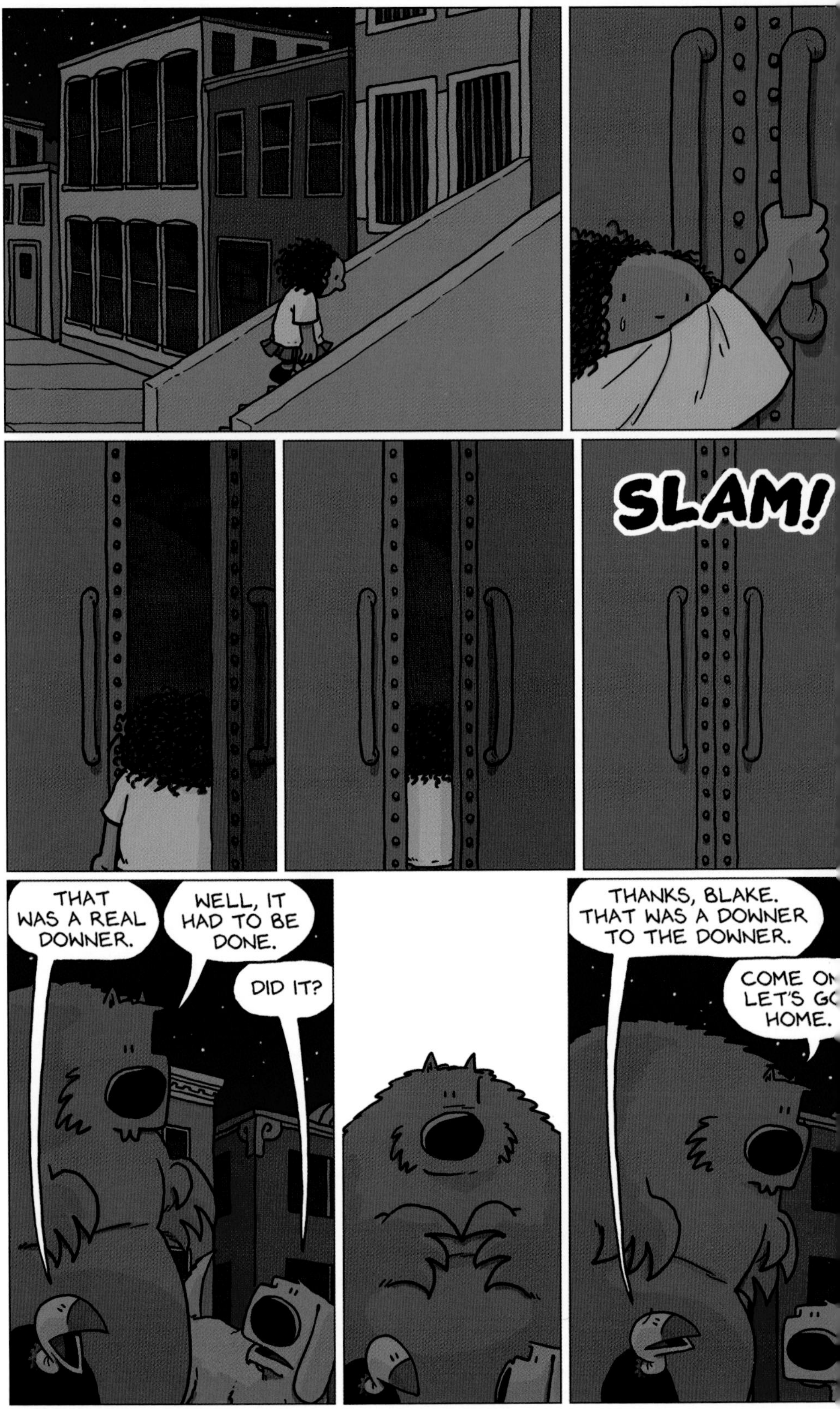
SLAM!
THAT WAS A REAL DOWNER.
WELL, IT HAD TO BE DONE.
DID IT?
THANKS, BLAKE. THAT WAS A DOWNER TO THE DOWNER.
COME ON LET'S GO HOME.

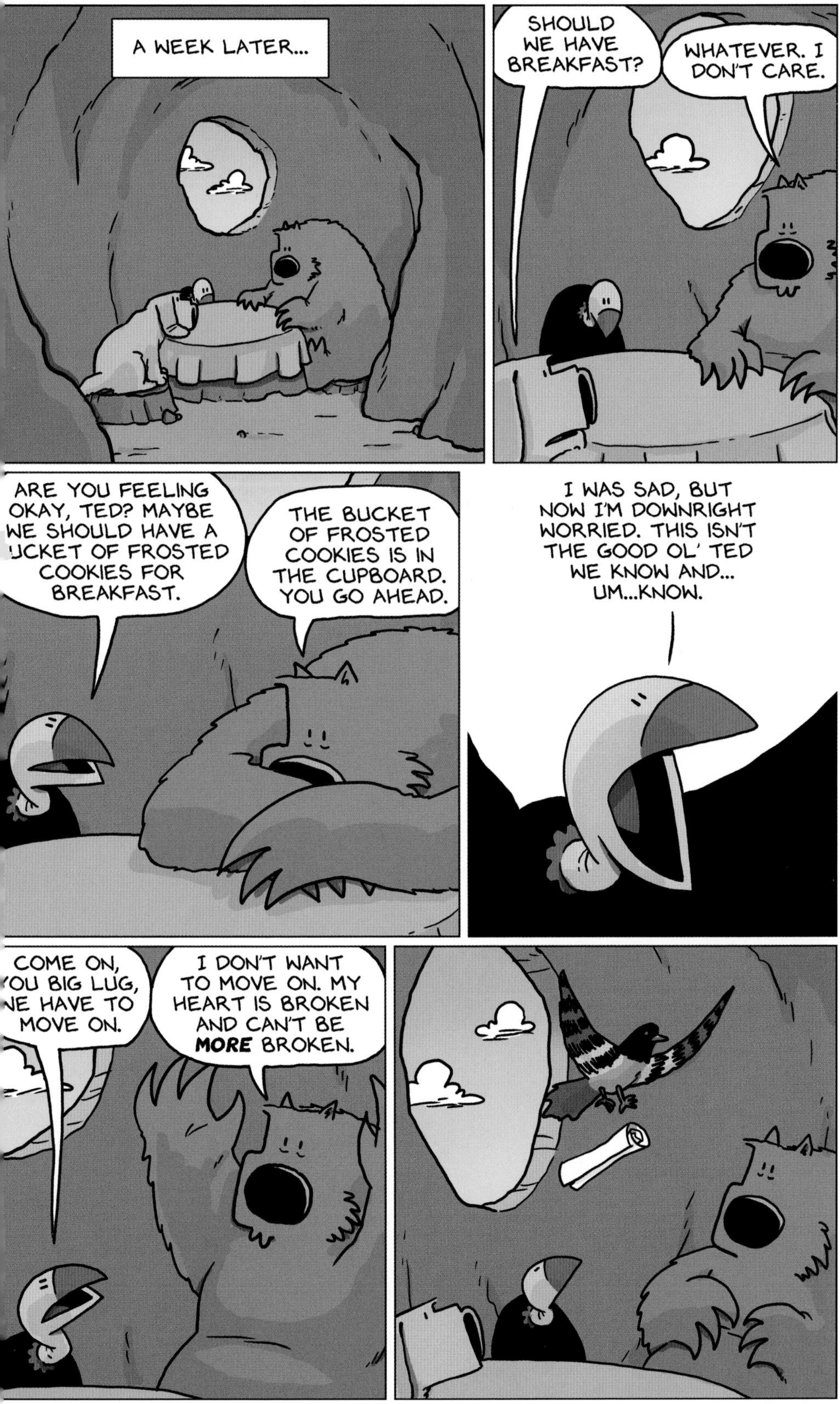
A WEEK LATER...
SHOULD WE HAVE BREAKFAST?
WHATEVER. I DON'T CARE.
ARE YOU FEELING OKAY, TED? MAYBE WE SHOULD HAVE A UCKET OF FROSTED COOKIES FOR BREAKFAST.
THE BUCKET OF FROSTED COOKIES IS IN THE CUPBOARD. YOU GO AHEAD.
I WAS SAD, BUT NOW I'M DOWNRIGHT WORRIED. THIS ISN'T THE GOOD OL' TED WE KNOW AND... UM...KNOW.
COME ON, OU BIG LUG, E HAVE TO MOVE ON.
I DON'T WANT TO MOVE ON. MY HEART IS BROKEN AND CAN'T BE MORE BROKEN.

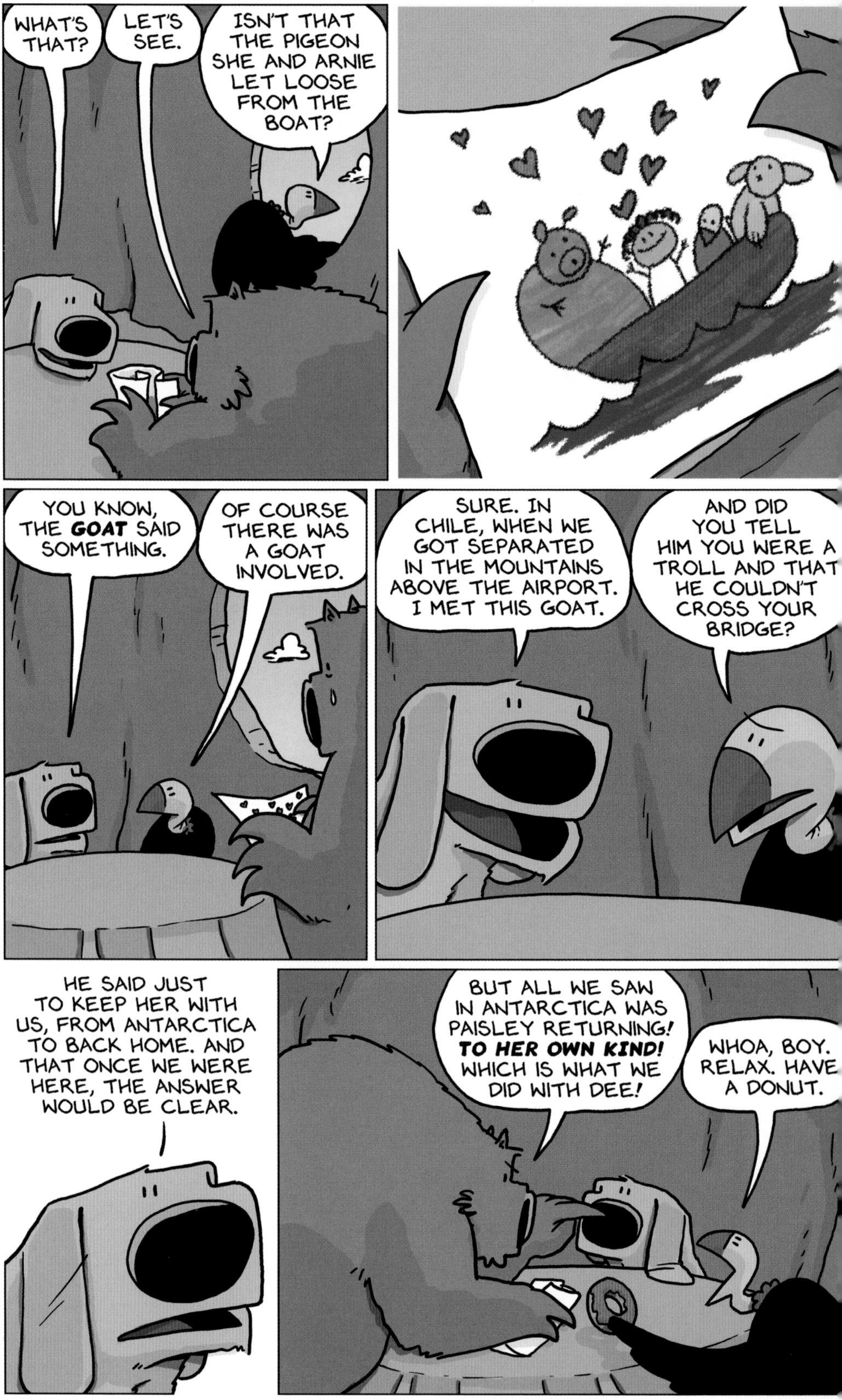
WHAT'S THAT?
LET'S SEE.
ISN'T THAT THE PIGEON SHE AND ARNIE LET LOOSE FROM THE BOAT?
YOU KNOW, THE **GOAT** SAID SOMETHING.
OF COURSE THERE WAS A GOAT INVOLVED.
SURE. IN CHILE, WHEN WE GOT SEPARATED IN THE MOUNTAINS ABOVE THE AIRPORT. I MET THIS GOAT.
AND DID YOU TELL HIM YOU WERE A TROLL AND THAT HE COULDN'T CROSS YOUR BRIDGE?
HE SAID JUST TO KEEP HER WITH US, FROM ANTARCTICA TO BACK HOME. AND THAT ONCE WE WERE HERE, THE ANSWER WOULD BE CLEAR.
BUT ALL WE SAW IN ANTARCTICA WAS PAISLEY RETURNING! ***TO HER OWN KIND!*** WHICH IS WHAT WE DID WITH DEE!
WHOA, BOY. RELAX. HAVE A DONUT.

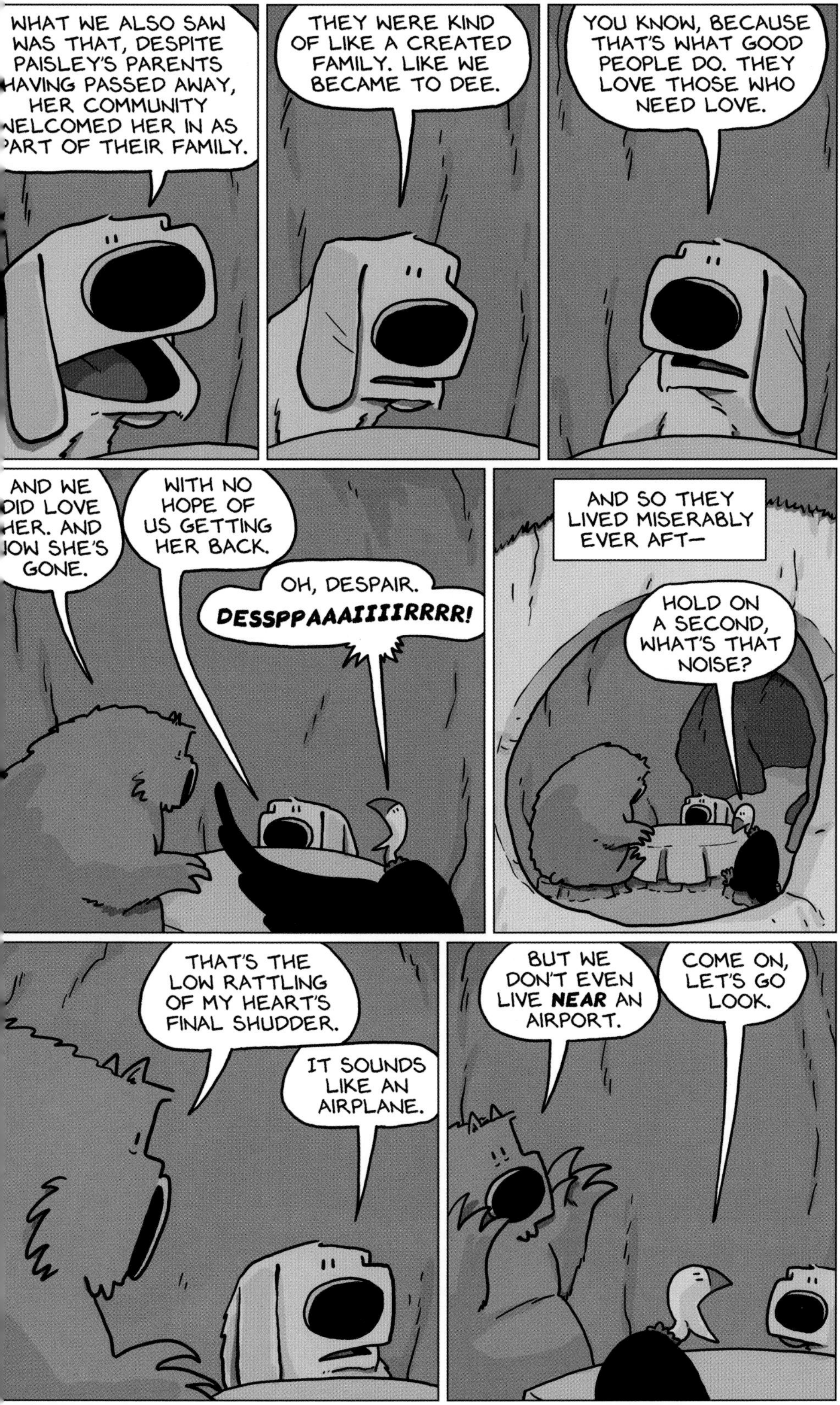

WHAT WE ALSO SAW WAS THAT, DESPITE PAISLEY'S PARENTS HAVING PASSED AWAY, HER COMMUNITY WELCOMED HER IN AS PART OF THEIR FAMILY.
THEY WERE KIND OF LIKE A CREATED FAMILY. LIKE WE BECAME TO DEE.
YOU KNOW, BECAUSE THAT'S WHAT GOOD PEOPLE DO. THEY LOVE THOSE WHO NEED LOVE.
AND WE DID LOVE HER. AND NOW SHE'S GONE.
WITH NO HOPE OF US GETTING HER BACK.
OH, DESPAIR.
DESSPPAAAIIIIRRRR!
AND SO THEY LIVED MISERABLY EVER AFT—
HOLD ON A SECOND, WHAT'S THAT NOISE?
THAT'S THE LOW RATTLING OF MY HEART'S FINAL SHUDDER.
IT SOUNDS LIKE AN AIRPLANE.
BUT WE DON'T EVEN LIVE **NEAR** AN AIRPORT.
COME ON, LET'S GO LOOK.

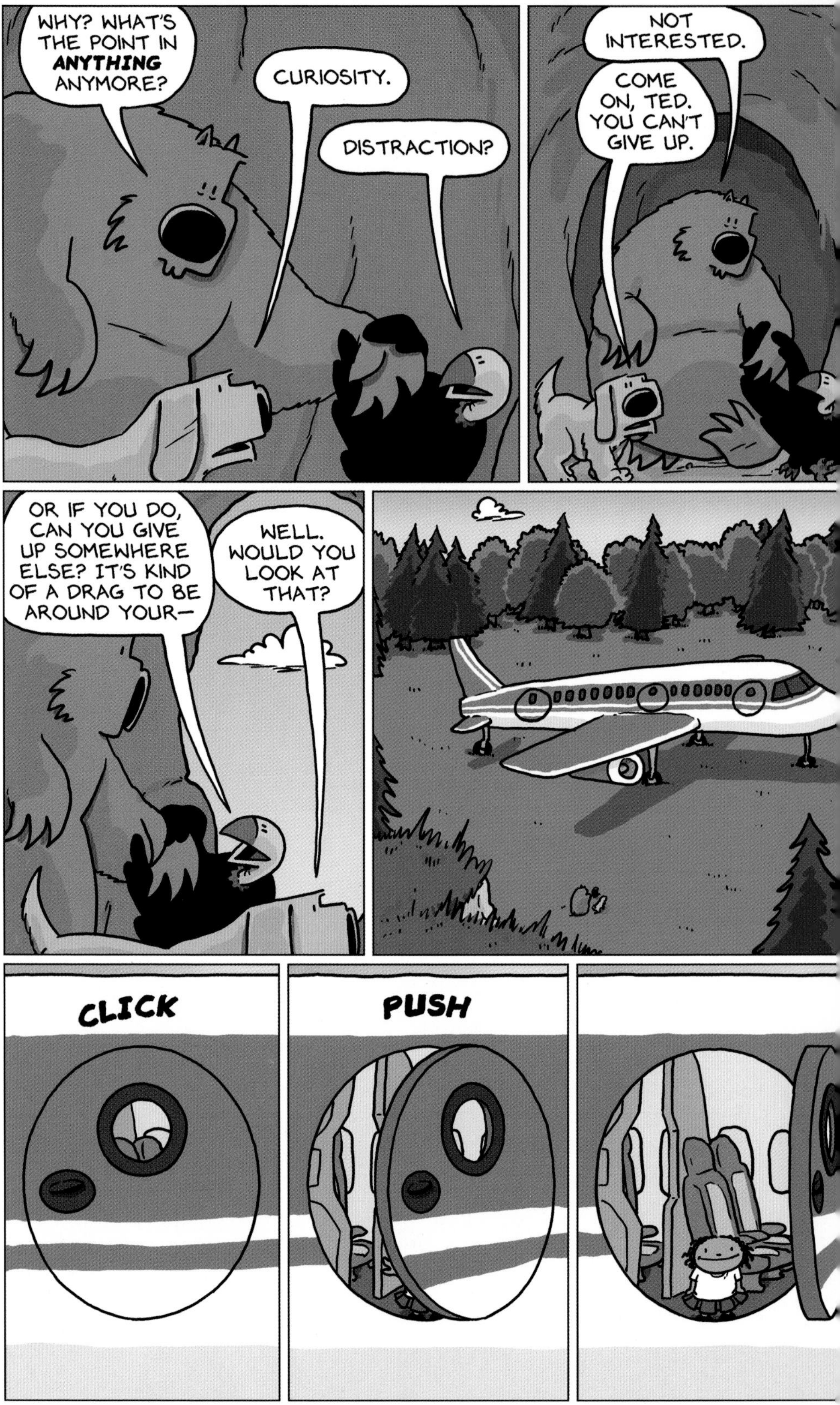
WHY? WHAT'S THE POINT IN ANYTHING ANYMORE?
CURIOSITY.
DISTRACTION?
NOT INTERESTED.
COME ON, TED. YOU CAN'T GIVE UP.
OR IF YOU DO, CAN YOU GIVE UP SOMEWHERE ELSE? IT'S KIND OF A DRAG TO BE AROUND YOUR—
WELL. WOULD YOU LOOK AT THAT?
CLICK
PUSH

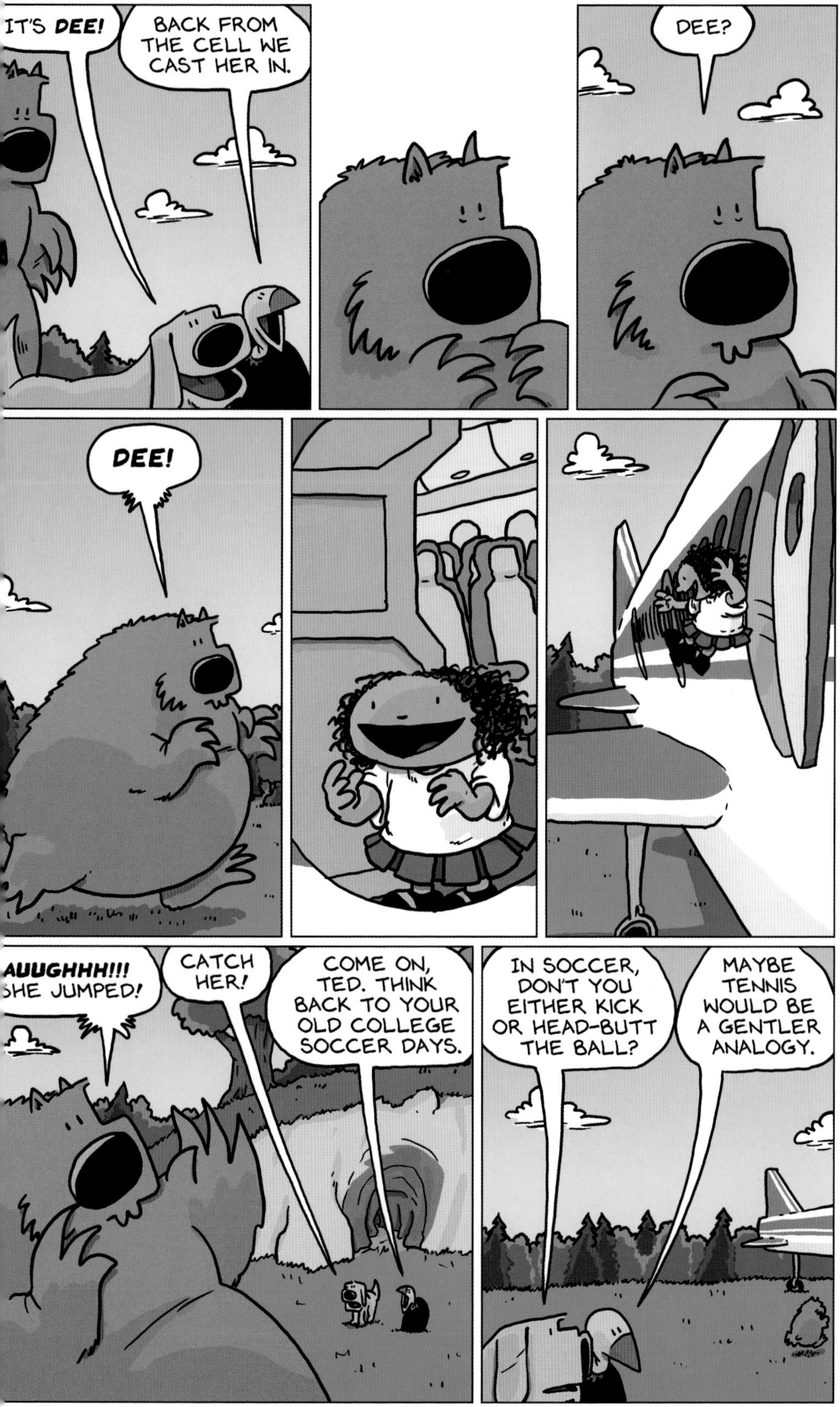
IT'S **DEE!**
BACK FROM THE CELL WE CAST HER IN.
DEE?
DEE!
AUUGHHH!!! SHE JUMPED!
CATCH HER!
COME ON, TED. THINK BACK TO YOUR OLD COLLEGE SOCCER DAYS.
IN SOCCER, DON'T YOU EITHER KICK OR HEAD-BUTT THE BALL?
MAYBE TENNIS WOULD BE A GENTLER ANALOGY.

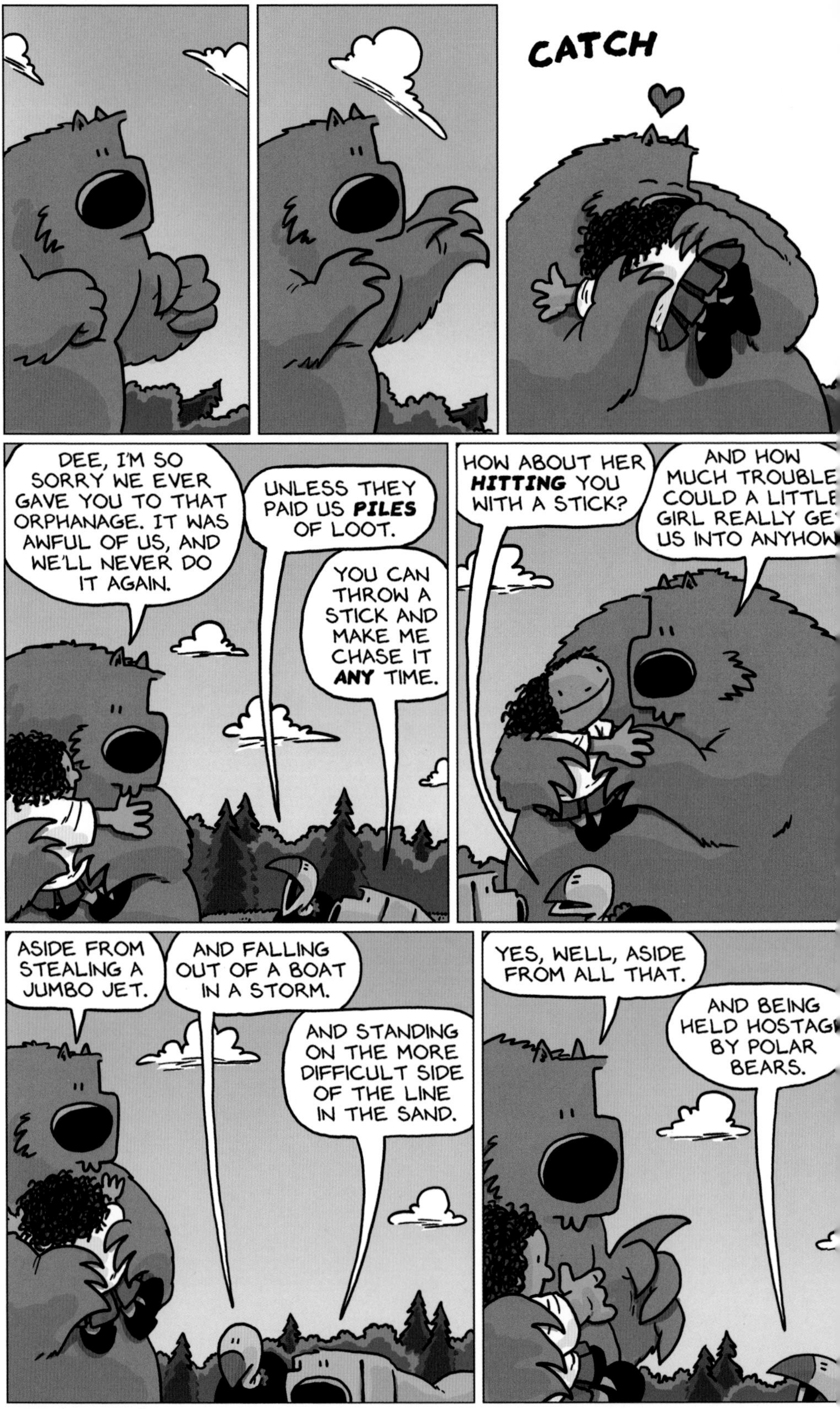
CATCH
DEE, I'M SO SORRY WE EVER GAVE YOU TO THAT ORPHANAGE. IT WAS AWFUL OF US, AND WE'LL NEVER DO IT AGAIN.
UNLESS THEY PAID US **PILES** OF LOOT.
YOU CAN THROW A STICK AND MAKE ME CHASE IT **ANY** TIME.
HOW ABOUT HER **HITTING** YOU WITH A STICK?
AND HOW MUCH TROUBLE COULD A LITTLE GIRL REALLY GE US INTO ANYHOW
ASIDE FROM STEALING A JUMBO JET.
AND FALLING OUT OF A BOAT IN A STORM.
AND STANDING ON THE MORE DIFFICULT SIDE OF THE LINE IN THE SAND.
YES, WELL, ASIDE FROM ALL THAT.
AND BEING HELD HOSTAG BY POLAR BEARS.

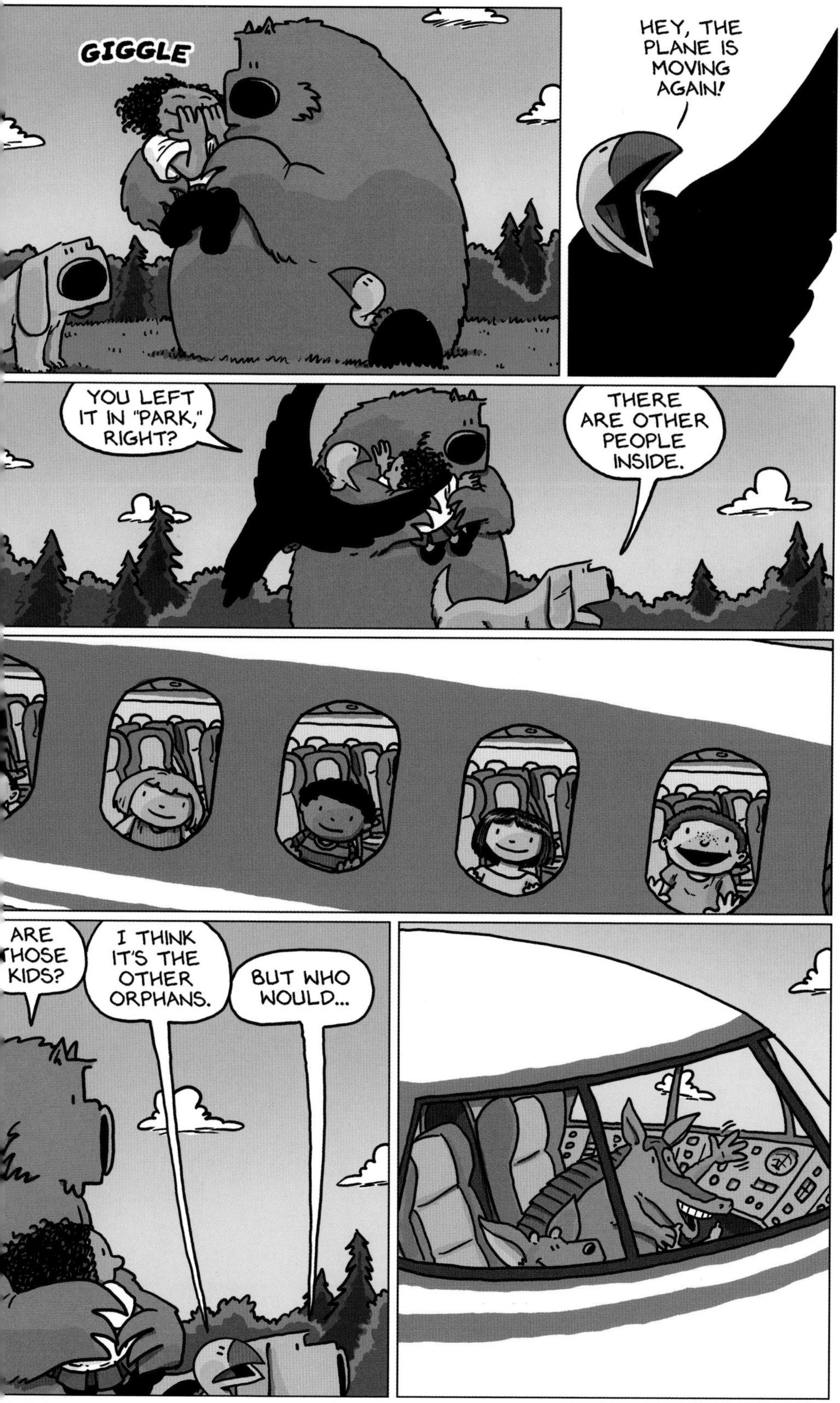
GIGGLE
HEY, THE PLANE IS MOVING AGAIN!
YOU LEFT IT IN "PARK," RIGHT?
THERE ARE OTHER PEOPLE INSIDE.
ARE THOSE KIDS?
I THINK IT'S THE OTHER ORPHANS.
BUT WHO WOULD...

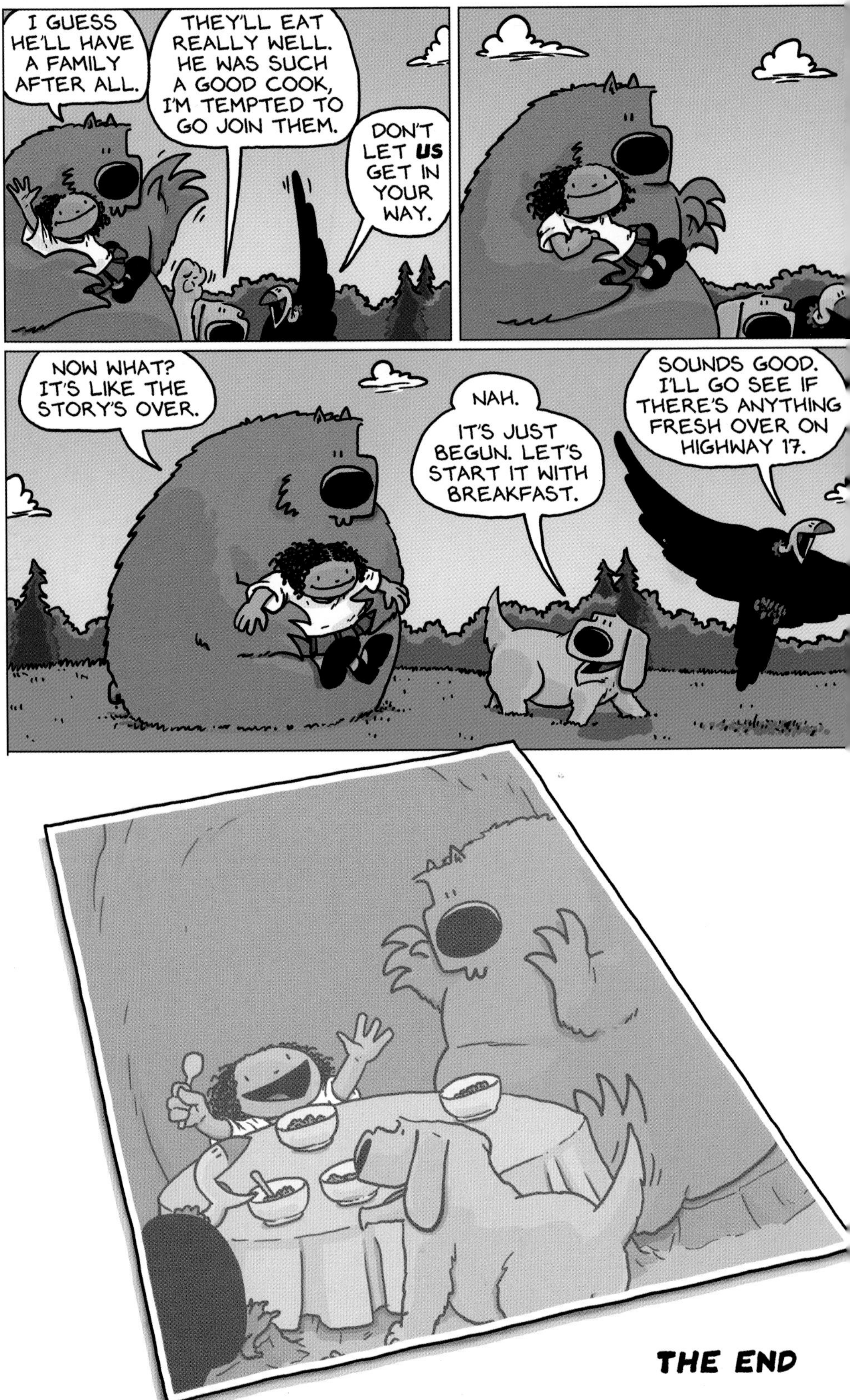
I GUESS HE'LL HAVE A FAMILY AFTER ALL.
THEY'LL EAT REALLY WELL. HE WAS SUCH A GOOD COOK, I'M TEMPTED TO GO JOIN THEM.
DON'T LET US GET IN YOUR WAY.
NOW WHAT? IT'S LIKE THE STORY'S OVER.
NAH.
IT'S JUST BEGUN. LET'S START IT WITH BREAKFAST.
SOUNDS GOOD. I'LL GO SEE IF THERE'S ANYTHING FRESH OVER ON HIGHWAY 17.
THE END